YEAR
OF
CHANGE

YEAR
OF
CHANGE:

More About *The New Yorker* & Me

E. J. Kahn, Jr.

VIKING

VIKING

Published by the Penguin Group
Viking Penguin Inc., 40 West 23rd Street,
New York, New York 10010, U.S.A.
Penguin Books Ltd, 27 Wrights Lane,
London W8 5TZ, England
Penguin Books Australia Ltd, Ringwood,
Victoria, Australia
Penguin Books Canada Ltd, 2801 John Street,
Markham, Ontario, Canada L3R 1B4
Penguin Books (N.Z.) Ltd, 182-190 Wairau Road,
Auckland 10, New Zealand

Penguin Books Ltd, Registered Offices:
Harmondsworth, Middlesex, England

First published in 1988 by Viking Penguin Inc.
Published simultaneously in Canada

Copyright © E.J. Kahn, Jr., 1988
All rights reserved

Library of Congress Cataloging-in-Publication Data

Kahn, E. J. (Ely Jacques), 1916–
    Year of change : more about the New Yorker & me / by E.J. Kahn,
    Jr.
        p.   cm.
    Includes index.
    ISBN 0-670-82411-9
    1. Kahn, E. J. (Ely Jacques), 1916–   . 2. New Yorker (New York,
1925–   ) 3. Journalists—United States—Biography.   I. Title.
PN4874.K25A3 1988b
070'.92'4—dc19
[B]   88-5658
                                                                      CIP

Printed in the United States of America by Haddon Craftsmen, Inc.
Set in Janson Roman and Italic by Crane Typesetting Services, Inc.
Produced by Unicorn Production Services, Inc.

For Jaime, Ian, Ely, Matthew,
Jacquelene, Curtis, and, I hope, more TK.

"Up, and to the office,
where busy getting before hand
with my business as fast as I
can. Busy till night, pleasing
myself mightily to see what a
deal of business goes off of
a man's hands when he stays by it."
—*The Diary of Samuel Pepys*, 14 January 1667.

31 December 1986

Sitting in my cluttered corner eighteenth-floor office at 25 West Forty-third Street a while ago (our printed *New Yorker* letterhead is so tricky to decipher that respondents to our inquiries often address us at 23 West, but the 10036 post office people down on the lobby floor know who and where we are), I got to reflecting that the year immediately ahead was going to be a pivotal one for me. I was in the process of celebrating three birthdays I deem consequential—Harvard University's 350th, Horace Mann-Barnard School's 100th, and my own comparatively modest 70th—and over the next few months a couple of more milestones would come and go: my fiftieth college-class reunion and my fiftieth year of writing for *The New Yorker*. So I thought that for the first time in a decade I'd keep a daily journal.

A lot of things can happen in ten years, and did. I have gone from two grandchildren to six. I am far deeper into my second marriage, which in a curious way makes me more appreciative of my first, in which Jinny showed me how to raise children. My discovery of, introduction to, and friendship with a brother, in 1976, whom I never knew I had, has made me more understanding, I like to think, of my father than I ever was before. As one gets older, too, one's professional life undergoes change. I still like to travel, but the three- or four-month reportorial journeys that I once took away from home would now strike me as anathema. And I hope that after nearly a half century of nonstop writing of books and articles—the most of these for *The New Yorker*—I have become somewhat more reflective. I like to think that, for better or worse, there are resemblances in my life to those bugs who skitter across the top of the water, never visibly engaged in total immersion, but always getting around; and, in my case, always trying to be closely involved with my immediate family and what I sometimes think of, perhaps with hubris, as my extended family—the outside world.

1 January 1987

The *Times*'s obit page, where I naturally turn first, says a longtime friend is dead. Age sixty-five, of lung cancer. I seem to recall that he was a heavy smoker. It's amazing how few people one knows smoke any more. At the end-of-year cocktail party that sisters Joan and Olivia habitually give, Joan dressed down her best and oldest friend for not yet having quit. (That was while I was telling Cecille Shawn, who I don't think quite believed me, that I finally had a brother.) I guess it was not quite two years ago that I finally kicked the habit myself. I had just finished my annual physical at Dr. Gorham's, and as I was leaving he asked if there was anything special on my mind.

"No—oh yes," I said. "My wife told me to tell you to tell me to stop smoking."

"Stop," he said.

Now look what Ellie had gone and done! It was at exactly 4:37 that afternoon that I finished the last of the long-beloved Salems in my pocket. True, over the next few weeks my renunciation was made more tolerable by Dr. Gorham's having bestowed on me prescriptions for some nicotine-enhanced chewing gum and some deterrent pills; but even so I was surprised how relatively easy it was to jettison a half-century's joyful indulgence.

I only wavered once. I was out in Decatur, Illinois, heavily engaged in soybean research, and lodged at one of those motels I know so well, the ambience of which is conducive to making one feel sorry for one's self. It was cold and it was raining. Not as troubling, to be sure, as my previous trip to Decatur (soybeans take a lot of learning), when the pilot of our small plane revealed over the intercom, as we cruised through a starless night, that he had no way of ascertaining whether his landing gear was up or down. To get rid of fuel, we circled for what seemed like, and may have been, hours, the chap across the aisle from me staring rigidly ahead, his lips moving nonstop in what I assumed was, and hoped would be duly heeded, prayer. We finally landed, with foam on the ground, floodlights blazing, and ambulances standing by. But there was no further sweat; our wheels were down after all.

Where was I? Oh yes, smoking. Well, I backslid that evening, sidled up to the motel's newsstand, and, not even glancing at *Penthouse*, asked in a hushed voice for Salems, regular. I took three puffs before I got myself under control, marched back to my chamber, and held the pack with the remaining nineteen temptations in it under the tap of my bathroom sink.

But the old formula seems to apply: less smoking, more weight. I have to switch suits before going to the Henry Hydes' for lunch today, because I can't zip up the pants of my first choice. (Henry—Uncle Henry, as he has long fancied being known to Ellie's sons David and Lexy—says I look slimmer, for which charming fib I am grateful— just about as pleased as I was last month when Joe Anthony told me at Truro, in I think dead seriousness, how much he admired my nonexistent face-lift.) After lunch, and dog-walking, and changing pants again because it is raining and cabs are scarce this holiday afternoon, the phone rings. I tell Ellie as I head toward it that it is Shawn's ring. I know by now. I was right. Bill wants to let me know he likes the "Profile" I've turned in on Helen Suzman. He calls it a "beauty." That's a novel word of praise from him, in my experience, and it rings sweetly in the ear. I urge him to run it soon, because P. W. Botha has called for South African elections, probably in mid-March, and who knows what may happen, though Helen's seat in Parliament is probably invulnerable. Bill says he is awfully tightly scheduled up to then, but he will do whatever he can. He has been the editorial tsar at the magazine for more than thirty-five years, of course, and he and I both know that he can do whatever he wills.

I'm especially glad the Suzman piece worked out, because I've been wanting to do her ever since we met and became friends in Johannesburg back in 1966. I could have done a better reportorial job this time, obviously, had the South Africans given me a visa, but they turned me down again, and I guess I'm on a permanent shit list. But I did get one break. It turned out that Betsy Landis, who lives downstairs (our very same elevator bank) at 1095 Park, has in her apartment a nearly complete set of the South African Hansard—their counterpart of the *Congressional Record*. First time I've ever been able to use our freight elevator for in-depth, cogent research.

To cocktails at the Hamburgers'. Phil says gloomily that most of the people he knows are dead. Not at all, for among those trooping in animatedly are the Gerry Holtons, the Brendan Gills, the Paul Resikas, Connie Breuer, Jon Schueler, Sheila McGrath, and Joe Mitchell. And who should arrive just as we are on the point of leaving but the Shawns! Bill wonders if he can draw me aside to—second time in a single day!—discuss business. Sure. Would it be all right with me if he ran my postal-inspection piece very suddenly? I am flabbergasted. That isn't even one I was sulking about. I thought it had long since been killed. If he really wants to use it after all this time—I think first-class postage was still in the teens when I wrote it —you bet it's all right. But where on earth, if the checkers want them, as they no doubt will, are my notes?

2 January

It's a Friday, office closed because of the holiday weekend, and inasmuch as I am staying at home, that gives me an opportunity, on different networks, to watch "Wheel of Fortune" twice. No, I am no more smitten with Vanna White than I was, in her heady heyday, by Toby Wing. In keeping with one variation of the Kahn rule for nonsalaried writers like me—"Always have something to do next"—I aim to do a "Profile" on Pat Sajak, its master of ceremonies. I admire his informality—genuine or studied. (I heard him say not long ago, for instance, while sandwiched between White and another blonde dazzler, "What a lucky guy I am! It's a tough job, but someone's got to do it, America." Over the years, by and large, the people I've liked best are those who don't take themselves too seriously.) Joe Wapner was happy about the piece I wrote on him and his "People's Court" last year, and I am thinking of getting the judge to put me in touch with Sajak.

Hey, know what? Being seventy has its points! In the mail today, got my very first Social Security check.

Jerry Cohen, our good friend and neighbor in both New York and Truro, is trying to raise $3 million for a Peking University law library, and I call on him for a "Talk of the Town" piece about that laudable pursuit, at the brand-new Avenue-of-the-Americas digs of Paul, Weiss, Rifkin, Wharton & Garrison. Three hundred and fifty lawyers, 900 employees, twelve floors of offices for that one firm. My parents' friend Billy Weiss, one of the founding partners, I believe, would have been amazed at its growth. He had multiple sclerosis, or some such handicap, and he practiced his law from his apartment, in a wheelchair near a window. When he had something to mail, he'd toss it out the window, rightly confident from trial and no error that someone would pick it up and put it in a letter box. That was half a century ago. Times have changed, and trust in people, too.

I observe that Jerome Alan Cohen, who is probably the leading American expert on the Chinese legal system and who spends about half his time now working out of other offices in Beijing and Hong Kong, has on his Manhattan coffee table a copy of the coffee-table book on China that he wrote with wife Joan. The last time I spotted it was, aside from our own coffee table, in a royal palace, at Fez, Morocco. Ellie and I had been granted a private audience there with King Hassan, who didn't ordinarily receive women. But we were late, and our host and escort, United States Ambassador Joseph Verner Reed, pushed Ellie to the fore as we rushed down a corridor where we could see His Majesty tapping his foot, and Hassan was too much of a gentleman to spurn a lady's advances. The purpose of that particular trip to Africa, my fifth to that ever-beckoning continent, where by now I've been lucky enough at least to set foot in sixteen countries, was to write a *New Yorker* piece about the King and his subjects; and Joseph had been kind enough to offer us his prodigious hospitality. For much of the time we were bedded down *chez lui*, another houseguest was General Vernon Walters. We got to spend a good deal of time with him, and after he became Reagan's ambassador to the United Nations (Joseph Reed by then one of his ranking deputies), I decided to try a "Profile" on Walters for the magazine. I thought everything was moving along smoothly. Then one day I got a phone call from the former television announcer Richard Hottelet, who'd become the General's press attaché. Could we have lunch? Certainly; I figured he wanted to set up specific arrangements for my sessions with Walters. At the Century? Fine, I said, and after we'd agreed on a time, I added, "Meet you at the members' bar."

There was a pause. "Are *you* a member?" I had never before heard haughtiness and condescension so devastatingly blended.

Maybe Hottelet didn't like to have to associate with his peers. In any event, the message he had for me at lunch, which his phone call could have conveyed in the first place, was that the General had decided he didn't want his "Profile" done after all.

An at-home evening, watching a British spy film on our VCR and then Penn State beating Miami at football. During halftime, Ronald Reagan comes on, live, blathering away about his sportscasting days and running over, it turns out, into playing time. He is followed by an announcer who says, "Some linebackers have the hands of a sixty-five-year-old man." What does this announcer's own blather mean? I must ask Hottelet next time I bump into him at our club.

Some of our friends who know we have a VCR in our bedroom make snide cracks about the kinds of films we look at. Let them mind their own business, and we will keep all our X's in our own basket.

3 January

It is Saturday, and along with today's *Times* we find outside our door the innards—book review, magazine, et al.—of tomorrow's. That means I get to do the Sunday crosswords and other puzzles a day ahead of myself. I'm not sure I like this new order of things, but if you're an addict you have to grab the substances you crave whenever and wherever they come to hand.

In the evening, E. joins me, though she is admittedly not much of a sports buff, to watch a cassette I got for my birthday last month, a handsomely crafted documentary on the 1984 Olympics at Los Angeles. My sixth Summer Games, they were, dating back to Tokyo in 1964. I certainly hope the magazine will send me to Seoul in 1988. (I've covered the last few Winter Games, too, but they tend to leave me, if you'll forgive the word, cold.) I won't be any older in Korea—which has been a quondam stamping ground since I was a war correspondent there in 1951—than Red Smith was when we hung around Montreal together in the summer of 1976.

4 January

One of David's friends, female newspaper reporter from Connecticut, seems to be asleep, when the dog and I arise for her morning walkaround, on the living-room couch. Young people are to be thus expected at holiday times; we've even had nephew Keith Prufer in from Hawaii, where, he tells us, he has a Chinese girlfriend and a plantation harboring fifty thousand orchids. He has brought his Aunt Ellie some Hawaiian coffee. Keith's sister Diana comes by to dine *en famille* and says she is leaving her steady publishing-house job in favor of "temping"—a verb unknown to me until this evening. The other day, somebody ascribed to somebody else the verb "ascripting." Who says you can't learn new things at my age? Diana is also mildly complaining that although she held the job she's relinquishing for almost a whole year, she is entitled to a mere two-weeks' paid vacation. I manage to refrain from retorting that after almost a whole half century in one byway of the publishing industry I have never had a single day's such perk, if perk is a word.

To the Whitney Museum, last day of big John Singer Sargent show. He died in 1925, when I was nine. My God, a contemporary!

5 January

My first day at the office in 1987. It looks just about the same as when I left it in 1986.

This could be a special day. At Jeannette Rohatyn's cocktail party last week, I was introduced to the senior editor of Little, Brown's publishing operations in New York. After a couple of drinks, I was emboldened to lay on him some of my difficulties with his house, which has brought out my two most-recent books. (Just for instance, when it became clear that Little, Brown was going to do nothing to mark the advent of one of them, Ellie gave me a splashy pub-day party; but the fellow who was supposed to be my editor never even bothered to show up.) My new friend professed to be appalled by my litany of woe and to make amends proposed a lunch date for today. I have a forgiving nature, and I accepted. Le Perigord. Twelve-thirty sharp. I know the restaurant—on Fifty-second Street between Second and First. It was convenient enough when I was doing a "Profile" on Josh Logan, who lives at River House, and for interviewing Helen Suzman, who while in New York usually stays down the block with a friend. But it's a longish haul from West Forty-third Street, even on a day of atonement.

I get there on time, ask for the Little, Brown guy, and am escorted to a table. At twelve-forty-five, I decide he has been held up—some big deal with an agent no doubt—and order myself a drink. At twelve-fifty-five, the maître d' comes over. He is puzzled. My lunch date is always prompt, and what's more, he always phones for a table, which today he didn't do. I wait fifteen more minutes, leave $4 on the table for my drink and tip (I hadn't touched the rolls or butter), and depart with as much dignity as I can muster. Total outlay so far, for taxis and drink: $13. I go to the Harvard Club, steaming, for a sandwich, let myself get inveigled into a backgammon chouette, and disburse 110 more. I wonder how much of my total outlay can be ascripted, when income-tax time rolls around, to a business expense under the general rubric of not having lunch with one's publisher.

Afterward, once I have dashed off a note to Mr. Little, Brown, wondering what went wrong, it is time I start in on a piece I promised to write for *Yankee* magazine about Harvard. It has long been my sensible practice never to read anything I've written once it's in print (what changes, after all, can one make?), but now, to avoid possible repetitiousness, I look over a "Talk" piece I did for *The New Yorker* at the time of the university's 350th anniversary. I am horrified. I shudder at how the last line was mangled. I had written, "How much of what we learn at school we all too soon forget!" I thought that had a beautiful cadence, a rhythm, a lilt. It was damn near poetry, though Howard Moss might have demurred. But before we went to press, and without consulting me, somebody had excised the crucial "all," giving what was left about as much lilt as a lump of coal.

A piece I wrote for the *Harvard Crimson* at the time of the 350th attracted some attention; it disclosed how I'd never made that newspaper's staff because, as its managing editor explained to me in the spring of 1934, its Jewish quota for that year was filled. Joe Thorndike, who was the president of the *Crimson* at that time and moved on like a rocket to edit *Life* and *American Heritage*, phoned me last fall to express his dismay and consternation and indeed unawareness, forty-two years afterward, that such a quota had ever existed. (What a blow Joe's perennial sidekick James Parton suffered not long ago! Jim's written a biography of General Ira Eaker, one of the Second World War's celebrated big brass, and *Publishers Weekly*'s preview of it, composed I suppose by someone unaware of the existence of that war, refers to the subject throughout as Ira Baker.) Anyway, Professor Harry Levin told me, anent my *Crimson* revelation, that at about the same time John Kenneth Galbraith tried to get Theodore H. White into a Harvard house with which Ken had a tutorial affiliation. The housemaster said no, because Teddy was Jewish, and that housemaster from then on was unique in Harvard faculty annals: he never once got invited to even a second- or third-level Galbraith soirée.

The Galbraiths gave a cocktail party, unarguably top level, while the 350th was being observed, and the Justin Kaplans said it would be OK for

7

me to let Professor G. know that Ellie and I were going to be around. So we got invited. David Rockefeller made the grade, too, and he told me he had finally decided— no hard feelings—that he did not want me to undertake his biography. You win some, you lose some. I'd thought I'd have been a good choice because we were longtime acquaintances and I'd done a "Profile" on him for *The New Yorker* way back when there'd still been a chance to interview Brother Nelson et al., and maybe I could find *those* notes.

It was not, all things considered, my most propitious year for Davids. David Durk, the intellectual New York cop who made something of a name for himself in 1970 by trying to recruit police on college campuses, and about whom I'd also written a "Profile" (one of those that Shawn bought, never ran, and held too long for it to be peddled elsewhere), called me about *his* biography. We had lunch, my treat, at the Harvard Club. I was supposed to hear afterward from his putative publisher but never did. Perhaps just as well; I gathered from our conspiratorial dialogue at a corner table that David D. wanted to proclaim, or wanted me to, that just about everybody connected with any aspect of New York City law enforcement was a crook.

6 January

I am reading a book by J. R. Ackerley, *My Dog Tulip*. He seems obsessed by dogs—possibly because there's no mention of any wife or children— and how and where in London they move their bowels. When I accompany our dog, Hopi, to the street for her matutinal voiding today, the Dalton School kids are beginning to arrive next door in their stretch limos. (I prefer those who come by cab, because in bad weather if you're spry enough you can grab one as they yield it up.) I haven't yet noticed student reactions, if there are any, to some terribly obscene holiday graffiti—they allude to how young Dalton ladies allegedly spend extracurricular hours—that have been painted on a wall of our building abutting theirs and which our faithful superintendent, Ernest Martinez, has been valiantly but vainly trying to scrub off since Boxing Day. There's something basically wrong with a society in which a conscientious citizen, after stooping to pick up his dog's shit, has on straightening up to find such scurrility looming over his shoulder.

Before we brought our puppy to New York, we availed ourselves on Cape Cod, at no little cost, of the instructional services of a professional dog trainer. This guy appeared to operate on the premise that while you can always teach a new dog old tricks, dog owners are a different breed. He said at the outset that it was not so much the dog who had to be trained as Ellie and me. Of course he was right, and we have flunked his course. Ellie, at no cost save corkage, did once, however, devise her own method of quieting Hopi when she got rambunctious; E. dipped a finger into a wine glass, and the dog licked her finger and settled down. But Hopi, part husky and resembling one, also a gray wolf, is hyperactive. I sometimes have the impression, when she is straining at her leash, that she takes me for a sled.

Last night was Daphne Hellman Shih's annual bash at the Village Gate. Mailer was there, so I guess he must have the film he's been shooting on the Outer Cape pretty much in the can. (On our way home from dinner in Provincetown last month, Ellie and I stopped by a Truro cemetery, ablaze with lights at 9:45 P.M., where his movie crew proved to be on location. Just as we arrived, somebody shouted, "OK, everybody—lunch break." *Lunch* break! I *am* getting old.) The usual huge crowd has turned out, and I wonder, as always, why some of these people elect to seat themselves at a table early on and seemingly never thereafter to budge. I should have sat down more myself. I am getting the gout. Dancing with the gout (till the tune ends) is aggravating.

In the lobby of our block-through office building, a sad parting notice pinned to the locked door of the little store over which the Ben Feldmans, kindly jeweler *et ux.*, have so long presided: "44 years on 44th St." If I had a better memory, I could probably recall their grand-opening sale.

Eugene Kinkead, whose eightieth birthday I was privileged to help celebrate not long ago, tells me in the men's room that our mutual good friend George Woodward—who Gene estimates was seventy-six—is gone. George was the original man in the gray flannel suit—in the 1930s, some of us surmised, his only suit. After all sorts of bizarre wartime adventures, he ended up running a *New Yorker* business department's office in London. Some bars—the Harvard Club's for one—have little brass plaques embedded in the mahogany where an especially loyal patron's elbows had been habitually bent. I hope that George will in some such fashion be immortalized for his long and assiduous patronage of the Connaught Hotel.

Professor Rotberg is on the phone from MIT. Bob's involvement with South Africa figured in my Suzman "Profile," and he got me interested then in doing a piece about his daughter, who had a singular brush with death during a tumble down a Wyoming mountainside. He says Nicola has gone to California. If I need to interview her, that would give me a nice excuse for going West, too.

This being Tuesday, it is Shaplen's day, I know, to come into the city from Princeton. Bob seems to become privy to more office gossip out there than I do in the proverbial swim of things. Today, Shaplen rattles off that Andy Logan has told him that Shawn thinks Harold Brodkey—who has lately written a couple of "Notes and Comment" items that I find incomprehensible—is the world's greatest novelist; that Ved Mehta, who once told me that he feared that *The New Yorker* had surely run as much about his childhood in India and elsewhere as it was ever likely to, has another hundred thousand or so words in type about his education, which should take him about through grade school; and that Chip McGrath is moving into Tony Gibbs's old office and is the current betting favorite to succeed Shawn. We have all been indulging in speculation about *that* for more than ten years. Well, at least Chip and I have one thing in common: we have both taught writing courses at Columbia's Graduate School of the Arts. I must ask him someday if he finds it as disturbing as I do that many graduate students are such atrocious spellers that they are flirting with illiteracy.

7 *January*

Nancy Franklin, who is handling my postal-inspection piece but has never edited me before, is kind enough to bring page proofs down to my office, which she has apparently never visited, and she wonders what's the meaning of the nameplate, souvenir of my Second-World-War desk-job combat, that reads "CWO Kahn." I try to tell her what manner of critter a chief warrant officer is, or at any rate was when I was one. I suspect she thinks my explanation could stand some editing.

When she leaves, I should be going over the pages she delivered, but instead I start looking around the room. If you can tell something about a person by what he has on his office walls, I wonder, what do mine tell me about myself? Not that I am necessarily a fair test. John O'Brien, one of whose important jurisdictions at the magazine is walls, has forbidden me to try to affix anything to any of mine unless he is present; he seems to be under the impression that I could huff and puff and blow something down. I can't for the life of me understand why he is all that fussy. My eastern-exposure wall is so ravaged by wet weather that it may collapse and bury me any day now. But then that jibes with the overall ambience of our institution. A few years ago, Jonathan Schell got a package in the mails that for some reason or another he thought might contain a bomb. His office was roped off, and the police were called. The first two cops on the scene, as they were being ushered along one of our eighteenth-floor corridors, asked their guide what sort of premises they'd been sent to reconnoiter. A weekly magazine. And what was its name? *The New Yorker.* One of the cops broke stride. "*The New Yorker?*" he said. "But that's supposed to be a high-class magazine, and this place is"—out of politeness he hesitated—"a *dump.*"

Aside from the fact that my couch has been so littered with papers for the last seven or eight years that it is unnappable, I rather like the looks of my hideaway. (Draped over the back of the couch is a zebra skin, or the half of the one we brought back from Tanzania that was left after our dear departed dog Rainbow, whom we never submitted to the rigors of training, ate the other half.) There is not much more wall space to work with, I reflect, and, if O'Brien consents, I may decide to take down a couple of venerable exhibits about which I've harbored doubts all along:

an autographed photo of Harpo Marx, whom to the best of my knowledge I never met, and a framed letter in Thai, which for all I know of that language may say no more than that a Bangkok hotel reservation is confirmed. Here, also, as my glance strays, are, among yet other relics, a frame embracing the original February 21, 1925, *New Yorker*, a valued gift from my valued friend Palmer Williams, who all but invented television; a no-less original Cat in the Hat, in full color, from Dr. Seuss, aka Ted Geisel, thanking me for writing his "Profile"; the original of Whitney Darrow's handsome cover for my book, *Who, Me?*; autographed cartoons by Edmund Duffy and Bill Mauldin; photographs of grandparents, parents, children, grandchildren, and my most memorable army general Forrest Harding; a Literary-Lion medallion from the New York Public Library draped around a toy cloth lion that Ellie gave me to wear it; citations for the Legion of Merit and the Sidney Hillman Award and the Horace Mann Distinguished Alumnus Award and an honorary degree from Marlboro College; and a sculptured head by Sidney Simon, not my head, with a big "70" on it. One of the nicest exhibits is a color photograph taken of me and my five sons (three sons and two stepsons, to be technical), which I was delighted to receive on the actual septuagarian birth date last December, when we all convened at the Concord, Massachusetts, home of Jean and Mike Curtis, the long-lost brother I finally found—C. Michael Curtis, as he more formally appears high on the editorial rigging of the *Atlantic*'s masthead. Lexy, setting his camera and then leaping back in range, took the photo of the sextet. Lexy stopped by my office yesterday, as it happened. He is twenty-three and—*o tempora!*—had never heard of Bill Mauldin.

There is a bulletin board facing me as I sit shirking work at my desk. I have pinned to it various press credentials accumulated over the years and other special keepsakes, like the stub of a ticket to the 1980 Olympic hockey game at Lake Placid, when the Yanks beat the Russkies; and if I'd thought to hang on to a stub from the 1968 Ivy-League game when the Harvards made up sixteen points in forty-two seconds to tie the Yales, 29–29, I'd have that up there, too. The top of my desk is usually a mess, covered with all sorts of loose odds and ends, including work in progress, and also a stack of red routing slips. "For use only with rush messages or material," they say, dominated by a big black encircled "T" for "Timely." I also have some very special routing slips there—they are gray—that I must have taken from the stockroom down the hall twenty or thirty years ago. They have printed on them—the name never appears in the magazine itself—"RUSH—The attached manuscript is to go to Mr. Shawn immediately." I have never heard of one being used and have never had the temerity to use one myself. But there is still plenty of time. Though Bill turned seventy-nine last August, he remains firmly, if not formidably, in charge, and the on-flowing talk of succession, which has surged so much in recent years, now appears to be at ebb tide.

8 January

My gout feels a little better this morning. Ellie, who often takes a different tack ("The dishwasher's broken," "The dog has cancer"), very considerately says it may never have been the gout at all but merely my adjusting to the new shoes she bought me.

Ran into Betsy Landis on the front elevator. She had given me a list of South African detainees. Their names can't be published over there but can, with me as an intermediary, in "Notes and Comment." Betsy would like six copies of the magazine to send to South Africa. I wonder if they'll get through. She says Oliver Tambo is going to speak at the Riverside Church on the twenty-first. The Landises aren't going to Florida till the twenty-third, because, winter weather being what it is around here, the twenty-second has been designated Tambo's snow day. How many times can the African National Congress have had to cope with one of these?

It is hard to take when Lexington Avenue bus drivers no longer demand proof that I am a senior citizen and can thus ride for fifty cents instead of a dollar. If only one would challenge me!

My postal-inspection piece is going to press today. So it is perhaps perverse of me to send Shawn a memo this morning complaining that my other half dozen accepted pieces haven't even been scheduled. (Should I use one of those gray slips, finally? No, after a spirited debate with myself, I make it a "Dear Bill" communication on my personal letterhead.) The squeaking wheel does after all get greased. Within an hour, John Bennet tells me he's going to be putting the Suzman piece into type; and fifteen minutes after that Shawn is on the phone. May he come down to see me? He may, and does, and says he is sorry, the pieces will indeed run, Suzman leading the pack. But the big news he wishes to impart, behind a closed door, is that Chip McGrath is now Deputy Editor of the magazine. I am henceforth to send to Chip everything that I'd customarily have sent to Bill, although Shawn will—"for the time being"—retain final authority. So we may be approaching the end of an era, or at least a bend in the road. Before Shawn leaves—I suppose I should have waited and discussed this with McGrath —I bring up a couple of African pieces I'd like to do this year and get his approval. So now I have the framework of an agenda.

Dinner at Rita Gam's. She's distressed because her book about other actresses isn't being as widely publicized as she'd hoped. Welcome to the club. I wrote a blurb for that book, and next thing I knew it was printed on the invitations sent out for a pub-day party (we were on the Cape and couldn't make it) with *"The New Yorker"* appended to my name. Made my endorsement look like a quote from a review in the magazine. I decided not to raise a stink about it, since the book wasn't getting much attention anyway. I stand in great admiration of the writing of Nadine Gordimer, and when

I was asked once to compose a blurb for one of her novels, I was happy to oblige, though so pressed for time I didn't read it first. Somewhat to my surprise, when the book came out, there I was cited on the back of the dust jacket. I made haste to peruse it and was relieved to find that my unstinting praise was thoroughly warranted.

9 January

I decided to work at home today. It will give E. a chance not to have to walk the dog quite as often. Moreover, after yesterday's session with Shawn, I don't feel as pressured about work. It is still my chore to handle Hopi's dawn patrol. Curiously, no matter when she was taken out the night before, she nudges me awake within a minute or two of the grandfather's clock striking seven. I would almost rather walk her then, come to think of it, than at eight, when Dalton opens. Of course, nine, with all the school kids tucked indoors, would be even preferable.

Gerry Holton has sent us an *American Scholar* piece by Jeremy Bernstein, "Breaking in at *The New Yorker*," part of a memoir. Jeremy seems to have broken in much in the fashion of our hotshot young reporter Bill McKibben—via an out-of-the-blue phone call from Shawn. (In McKibben's case, he was a Harvard junior, working for the *Crimson*, and the first time a guy called and said he was William Shawn of *The New Yorker*, Bill McK., who knew a *Lampoon* prank when he heard one, hung up.) Jeremy goes on to say that now, after twenty-five years of contributing to the magazine, he spends about five minutes a year actually conversing with Shawn. I didn't clock yesterday's visit (I do not include Bill's travel time to and from my office), but it cannot have been longer than four minutes, and would have been seconds shorter had I not detained him, after he rose, to inquire about Nigeria. My most vivid memory of Jeremy, an unregenerate bachelor, goes back to what must have been the beginning of his association with *The New Yorker*. We chanced to be vacationing concurrently at Montego Bay, and I saw him there, three nights running, escorting each evening a beauty-contest-type date more dazzling than the one before—a white, a black, an Oriental. It was an achievement any male *New Yorker* contributor would have envied.

10 January

Jon Schueler has an opening, on Madison Avenue. His big cloud paintings are the pièces de résistance, inevitably, but he also has some smaller watercolors on display. We walk home. E., exercising a woman's prerogative to change her mind, says it'll be good for my gout. We stop off at a bookstore, looking for Jerry Weidman's autobiography (he was the editor of my very first book when he worked for Simon and Schuster during the war) and for Mona Simpson's new novel (she was my student at Columbia), which we know, this being Saturday, is being reviewed in tomorrow's *Times*. (I also know, from outraged experience, that there is a mistake in the Sunday Double-Crostic.) What does my roving eye espy, not entirely by chance, but a copy, high on a shelf, of my very own *The Problem Solvers*! I mention this to Ellie, and the proprietor hears me, and he pulls it down and asks me to autograph it. Gladly. He is also aware that I have written other books. See—there are nice people involved in book publishing after all.

11 January

Son Joey phones. He is going to leave the staff of *Inc.*, probably in July, and go on contract-writer status there and also with *New England Monthly*. Maybe I should try to get him a deal with *The New Yorker*, too. Family ties are not uncommon at the magazine. Jonathan Schell was Shawn's son Wallace's Harvard roommate. Dick Harris has had two *New Yorker* wives. Jim Lardner, Ring's grandson and John's nephew and David's brother and Susan's cousin, has an office a few feet from mine. Perhaps I'll find a way to mention Joey to Chip McGrath.

To dinner at the David Shainbergs' new lower-Fifth-Avenue loft. Lots of space, including a huge painting studio, but Ellie thinks maybe not the ideal location to live with a new baby, so distant from most friends. Small-world department: When Catherine talks about childbirth and thresholds of pain (she used no drugs), I am reminded of Tony's birth. Jinny had cesareans, and Tony, our third, was born with a dent in his head. Question was: will it pop out on its own, or do we resort to surgery before the skull hardens? We had, happily, let nature take its course, I told the Shainbergs, on the advice of the pediatrician to whom we'd ever since been grateful—Rusty McIntosh. David is elated to be able to chime in: when he was a medical student, Rusty McIntosh was his preceptor in pediatrics.

In bed last night, Ellie chided me for not having been more severely critical of an introduction she wrote for a Nancy Hale biography about Mary Cassatt, which she sent off by express mail yesterday.

12 January

I want to leave for the office early this morning, but E. asks me to wait so I can read the new version she's going to express today. So I didn't reach the office until 12:15. I had planned to write McGrath a congratulatory note, in view of Shawn's chat Thursday. Bill happened to arrive at the ground-floor lobby just as I did, though, and he drew me aside to say that what he'd told me was now in abeyance and also that the order of scheduling of my pieces had been changed and that indeed one of them—a "Profile" on Oxfam America—had been killed. He had reread it and changed his mind about it. I'm not heartbroken. I'd started working on that one mainly to write about Oxfam's efforts in Ethiopia during the famine there and had agreed (as had Ellie) to be a paying participant—*The New Yorker* frowns on freeloading—on an Oxfam-sponsored press trip to Ethiopia. But everything had got screwed up, in large part because the Boston-based organization's "minority" employees had demanded in an affirmative-action action that the press people include at least one black. To mollify its staff, Oxfam had ended up by giving a black reporter from California a sort of scholarship, but by that time it had been too late for most of us to obtain Ethiopian visas, and we'd ended up by visiting only Mali and, for a couple of sybaritic days, the Côte d'Ivoire. I had at least managed to salvage a piece about Timbuktu from the frustrating episode.

Today went along calmly enough until 5:15, when Sheila McGrath came into my office, ashen. Had I heard the news? Yes, I said, Shawn had spoken to me Thursday and again this morning. Her "No! No!" was a drawn-out shriek. S. I. Newhouse had called on Shawn, and a memo to the staff was going to be released tomorrow, to the effect that Shawn was going to retire the first of March and that Robert Gottlieb, of Alfred A. Knopf, would be taking over as editor. Apparently the press had got the word from owner Newhouse as soon as Shawn had. Sheila and I speculate whether Bill suspected anything. Now I remember some badinage at noon, in the elevator going up. I'd put on one of my gaudiest Turnbull & Assers today, and Lillian Ross, who'd happened to be riding with Bill and me, had said to him lightheartedly, "Why don't you get a shirt like that?" and all three of us, knowing that Bill would rather step down from *The New Yorker* than step into a yellow-and-red-striped shirt like that, had laughed at the absurd notion. Shawn certainly hadn't struck me then as a man burdened with thoughts of impending gloom, or doom.

Should I go to Cambridge tomorrow, as I'd arranged, for preliminary research on the depredations in East African lakes of the Nile perch? In case I do and anybody is going to vote on anything, I give Sheila my proxy.

I am supposed to meet Ellie at my sisters'. I am still in a daze when I get there. Olivia says she talked to Cecille Shawn at about four o'clock, and nothing seemed out of the way. The *Washington Post* has tracked me down to her place, and I call back. (Later, at home, it is the AP on the phone; everybody wants Reactions.) I phone Shaplen at Princeton. He has already heard the news from Bill Knapp, in Connecticut. Bad news travels fast.

Ellie says we have met Bob Gottlieb. He came to a book party Nora Sayre gave at our apartment. And we certainly know his writer father-in-law, Niccolo Tucci. There was a time when, a *New Yorker* contributor himself, Niccolo would spend an occasional night on an office couch. These days, I occasionally espy him strolling up or down a midtown avenue, hands clasped behind back, abstracted, contemplative, as if conceptualizing an epic. But I don't remember Gottlieb stopping by our apartment. I hope he had a good time.

13 January

I decide to go ahead with my Cambridge trip, because it had taken some doing to set up an appointment with Melanie Stiassny, an ichthyologist at the Museum of Comparative Zoology. As soon as I am airborne on the shuttle, though, I wish I hadn't and resolve to get to the office later in the day.

The *Times* says Mr. Shawn will have no comment. The story says that among Gottlieb's authors at Knopf are Renata Adler and Jonathan Schell, but a rather strong anti-Gottlieb quote is attributed to Jonathan. The Newhouses own Random House, which owns Knopf, of course; could they have ordered Gottlieb to switch? He is credited with loving the ballet, never having affairs, never going out to lunch, never wearing a tie. (I look him up later in the Century yearbook. He is not a member, so no awkward dress-code problems there.)

A South African expert I was supposed to have lunch with can't make it. By noon, I have examined as many Nile perches in formaldehyde as I feel I need to, so I invite Ms. Stiassny to join me for lunch before I head toward the airport. I pick the Wursthaus; at Harvard Square I can catch the T for Logan and also buy the *Washington Post*. It costs a dollar. I am going to put that on my expense account, because I am the only *New Yorker* writer quoted by name in it. I don't have anything to say that I'm especially proud of, or ashamed of, but is this minor notoriety good or bad? How will Gottlieb react to it? Maybe he never reads newspapers, either.

The Wursthaus may not have been a tactful choice. My lunch date turns out to be a vegetarian. She makes do, uncomplainingly, with sauerkraut and potato skins. Ms. Stiassny knows the ichthyologist I went to London to see four or five years ago, as I recall; looking for a drawing of a rare fish, he had stumbled upon some Mozart manuscripts. That "Profile" never ran, either. (Later, I look at the date on the galley proofs, 1978—it was nine years.) I am fairly sure this one is dead. If it isn't, maybe it's Gottlieb's sort of thing.

When I get to the office, threeish, there is a sign outside the eighteenth-floor entrance door: go to nineteenth. I don't need a receptionist to buzz me in anyway; I have a key. (Will Gottlieb let me keep it, or change locks? Uncertainty can make the imagination reel.) Shawn is standing on the interior steps that connect my eighteenth and his nineteenth, with several dozen staff people clustered around him. He looks calmer than he did when the magazine changed ownership. There is going to be a letter, copy to S. I. Newhouse, asking Gottlieb to reconsider and step down. Anyone who wants to may sign it—in alphabetical order. Roger Angell, one of a hastily designated committee to draft it, apologizes that his name will perforce come first. Not everybody is going to sign. Lee Lorenz, for one. He thinks it is a lousy idea—pointless and maybe harmful.

We are to meet again, and listen to the text of our group entreaty, at five. There are numerous rump gatherings in the interim—not unlike some I remember that bleak December day in 1951 when we learned that Harold Ross was dead. One share-owning writer, whom I could name but won't, was chiefly concerned with how the loss of our founding editor might affect the price of *New Yorker* stock. With the Newhouses owning everything, at least nobody can indulge such egregiously poor taste today. Some people are manning telephones, trying to reach individuals not on the scene—Salinger, Updike, the like—who might want their names on the letter. Word comes that the *Times* and other journals have staked out the street-level lobby. When we reconvene at five, somebody asks Shawn, "You feel all right?" and when he does there is thunderous applause, which clearly moves him, and impels him to say sotto voce, if I heard him aright, "We may save the magazine yet."

Down in the lobby, I am propositioned—well, approached—by a young woman from *USA Today*, who says she has been hanging around for hours and is cold and hasn't learned a thing, and what can I tell her? I am a model of forbearance.

14 January

I get to the office at ten. Bill McKibben wonders if it makes any sense for him to go out on a "Talk" piece he had in mind. He and I both dreamt last night of a padlocked office with security people outside, barring entry. Bill says Shawn had a meeting with Newhouse at the Algonquin yesterday evening and returned to the office at nine, shaken. The eighteenth-floor corridors, so often comatose, are astir. Rumor is that Gottlieb, who got the letter all right some time last night, may take over as early as next week. Lis Harris says she was told at a party yesterday that Gottlieb is a kitsch collector and owns one hundred ladies' plastic handbags from the 1950s. Hey, McKibben—here's a "Talk" personality piece for you: head of big publishing house and his plastic handbags! Sheila says 160 people—yes, they got through to Jerry Salinger—signed The Letter. The *Times* doesn't have the text—yet. The press is hungry: *Time, Newsweek*, maybe even tout *Le Monde*. Jim Lardner is featured in today's *Washington Post*. Chip McGrath thinks Shawn and Gottlieb are having lunch at the Algonquin. What will Gottlieb eat or wear? I once invited a black playwright whom I was writing about to lunch at the Algonquin, and when he arrived coatless and tieless there was a good deal of confusion and embarrassment all around.

After lunch, while I am mailing my income-tax payment due tomorrow (why does everything have to happen at once?), Jeremy Bernstein wanders by. He was at the Algonquin and saw Shawn and Gottlieb together, and they looked friendly enough. I forgot to ask how they were sheathed. There is a lively corridor colloquium. Schell thinks there is still a possibility Gottlieb might bow out. Mark Singer says that's nonsense, his takeover is inevitable, and that, incidentally, the papers have already got hold of our letter. It is Fred Shapiro's opinion that we have already peaked as a news story and are on the downgrade. Well, maybe; I am summoned to the phone, and Edwin McDowell, calling from the *Times*, ties me up a whole half hour for a feature piece he's putting together. While we're talking, he says somebody has just slipped a note under his door: there are paparazzi hovering outside the Algonquin.

3:45 PM. Shawn is back from lunch and is supposed to be huddling with McKibben and I don't know who all else. The word is that Gottlieb had ice cream.

4:30. Stop the presses! Andy Logan says it was vanilla ice cream.

4:45. The *USA Today* woman phones. Can I tell her anything now? Sorry, lady, and I am busy later.

4:50. Natasha Turi thinks there's a meeting in progress on the twentieth floor, where fiction editors hang out. I climb up there. People are just milling about. Suddenly Shawn appears, smiling tentatively: "Is this another meeting?" He hasn't lost his sense of humor. The gathering at once becomes a meeting, during which he informs us that the changeover is definite but that our petition has demonstrated to Mr. Newhouse and Mr. Gottlieb that they cannot do just anything and expect to get away with it.

I ask Bill about the paparazzi. Yes, he says, he tried to sneak out the hotel's back door (in a sixty-year alliance with the Algonquin, I've never known it had one), but they were waiting for him there, too, and he now regrets that he threw his hands up across his face. He also wants me to know, in an aside, that when he talked to me about Chip last week he had no idea what was in the offing.

I toddle on homeward and without much verve go to a book party for Mona Simpson at the Arthur Allens'. Not everybody there seems to regard the *New Yorker*'s crisis as earthshaking and all-consuming, except probably for Pete Spelman, the Business Department's onetime liaison man with the outside world. Pete does tell me something interesting about copper bracelets, like the one I'm wearing that Ellie gave me for Christmas: they are supposed to ward off arthritis.

Ellie suggests that now that Gottlieb is in despite everything, perhaps we should all write him another, conciliatory letter. I begin framing mine.

15 January

A day that commences with a visit to the dentist can go nowhere but up. Dr. Magnani wants to sell me several thousand dollars' worth of false teeth. His nurse, sounding like a shoe salesman, says—I think it is supposed to be complimentary—that I have a wide arch.

The *Times* has another McDowell story but not the feature he was interviewing me for. In the *News*, Liz Smith berates us as a bunch of fuddy-duddies living in the past and says the magazine is "almost an anachronism." Sons Terry and Tony both phone: the *Boston Globe* has had stories two days' running. Somebody says there's a piece in *USA Today*, and *Newsday* has a big spread—with, on its front page, alas, a shot of Shawn shielding his face.

At the office, Tom Whiteside says that he's heard that Newhouse said to someone who wondered how an outsider could ever discover what makes *The New Yorker* tick, "He'll learn everything he needs to know in a week." (I have a hunch that Shawn would say that after fifty-four years he's still learning.) Whiteside's scenario: Newhouse will move the magazine to other premises, cut way back on rental space, and tell office-holding writers like Tom and me that, inasmuch as we work at home much of the time anyway, we can jolly well do that all the time, so please pack up our things.

I take Sheila and Natasha to lunch. I wonder what Gottlieb will do about all the long-fact pieces on Shawn's bank. They tell me that there is a bank, physically, on a wall of the collating room. The what? I didn't even know we had a collating room. And he is supposed to learn everything in a week!

Chip McGrath had dinner with Gottlieb last night. That was why, Chip tells me, he had to miss the do for Mona Simpson, who was his fiction student at Columbia when I was trying to teach her nonfiction. Her novel is attracting a lot of deserved attention, so I guess he won that round.

16 January

Yet another *New Yorker* story in the *Times*—illustrated with a posed photo of Shawn in his office, hands sensibly at his side, but with no accompanying comment. I am quoted again, also some people, Barbara Tuchman among them, who think our protest was silly, as in widening retrospect it may well have been. But I don't have time to dwell too much on this, having to drive out to Long Island. Some years ago, mailing a tax return to the

IRS at Holtsville, N.Y. 00501, I got to wondering just what and where this Holtsville was, and Shawn agreed a visit might result in a "Talk" piece. I have an ulterior motive: to see if I can't get somebody out there to correct their computers' spelling of my wife's name as "Eleanuor." I am hospitably enough received, and all hands know what publication I represent, but if any of them have been following Gottliebgate nobody mentions it. The IRS woman I have lunch with is an admirable public servant; she will not let me pay for her hero and Coke and put it on my expense account. That makes me feel guilty, because she could have bought her combo more cheaply at her federal cafeteria than at the restaurant I drag her to so I can buy myself a drink. She has some complaints about her own taxes— but only the Long Island real-estate sort. She says small single-family homes on tiny lots out this way are going for two hundred thousand. And we're an hour-and-a-half's drive from the city in wintertime. Come summer, the trip must be brutal.

The IRS has two thousand employees at Holtsville who process 9 million returns. The town's Postmaster, when I pay him a courtesy call, apologizes for the relatively puny size of his local operations. He has only thirty-five hundred resident customers—families, that is. To arrive at a head count, he multiplies by 2.9. An associate has been listening in and interrupts: "We don't think about people, we think about deliveries." Then, realizing that might sound unfeeling, he puts this input, as far as *The New Yorker* is concerned, off the record.

I am advised that there is no way anybody anywhere in Holtsville can, without recourse to mysterious forces far away and much higher up, contrive to delete that "u" from "Eleanuor."

To the Palmer Williamses for dinner. Lots of Truro people: Dick Millers, Sidney Simons, David-and-Bess, Leo Salzmans up from Washington. Amazing how many of our crowd still smoke; four or five, at least, out of twelve. They are all cognizant of *The New Yorker*'s turmoil, and question me about it at length, but not one of them mentions having seen, in the issue that came out yesterday, my "Talk" piece about their Truro buddy Jerry Cohen. Can it be that our magazine has become more bandied about than read?

Most astonishing incident of the evening: Somebody refers to a fairly well-known American who's lately been to Moscow, and I say casually that I once dated his present wife. Palmer chirps up that he did, too. He and I have been pals for over thirty years, and never before was I aware of this common interest. Barbara Williams says *she* never was, either. I figure Palmer probably saw Madame X between marriages but am too gentlemanly to attempt to pin him chronologically down.

Ellie and I share a cab uptown with the Salzmans. Even though Leo is a psychiatrist, they are worried about their daughter, also a doctor, because she is working with Mother Teresa's AIDS patients.

17 January

In the *Times*'s regular Saturday quiz about the week's events: "Cartoon-
ists, editors and writers, including the reclusive J. D. Salinger, wrote a
brief letter of protest. To whom was it addressed and what did the letter
protest?"

Shaplen phones. He has it at secondhand that on "All Things Considered,"
last evening, some gravelly voiced *New Yorker* writer spoke up—he suspects
(wrongly) that it was I—who complained about the week's goings-on and
was followed by Gottlieb himself, saying he wanted pieces that were shorter,
timelier, and funnier. I can subscribe to all that. But Shaplen's informant
said Gottlieb also indicated that henceforth the magazine would pay more
attention to the wishes of its advertisers. I hope he was misquoted or mis-
understood.

We have champagne and caviar at the Cohens', before Jerry takes off on
one of his simpler journeys: Zurich-Helsinki-Hong Kong, I think he says.
He liked the piece about the Chinese law library, and once that campaign
gets rolling he is going to dig in and, for Ed Koch's sake, try to borrow
some giant pandas for the Bronx Zoo. Sounds like another possible "Talk"
piece if he can pull it off.

Jerry says some of his law partners are distressed because I described
their firm as "mammoth," inasmuch as the mammoth is extinct. He also
reveals that the ninety-odd partners tend to arrive late for most meetings.
However, for their semi-annual mass get-together—there was one today—
they practically knock each other down in transit, because they receive
twenty dollars in cash apiece for being on time. I inquire whether this is
taxable income, and after a moment's contemplation—I hope I don't get
charged for his time at his usual rates—he gives it as his measured opinion
that in his best judgment, offhand, of course, he can have someone look it
up, in most circumstances, all things considered, he could be wrong, it
probably is.

Cozy in bed, we watch *Klute* on the VCR. I sit up with a start when Jane
Fonda, playing a sweet young call girl, explains, with reference to the odd
behavior of a client who pays for her time but never lays a hand or anything
else on her, that, after all, he is over seventy.

18 January

I search "News of the Week" for a *Times* Sunday wrap-up about Shawn-
to-Gottlieb. There is nothing. Fred Shapiro may have been right. But hold
on! Here is a "Mr. Shawn" editorial! Much of it is a quotation from Brendan's

book about *The New Yorker*, but I can swallow that by now. The editorial says there are young writers around who will never have the marvelous chance to work with Shawn, which "was like being asked to dance with Fred Astaire." All I would know about that is that when I went to Astaire's California home to interview him for my biography of his close friend Jock Whitney, his conversation was the antithesis of his footwork—hesitant, plodding, heavy. Ray Bolger died a couple of days ago. Now *there* was a dancer of all-around liveliness.

At breakfast, E. laments that I have an armchair to sit in at the dining-room table, whereas she must always make do armlessly. I propose bringing one like mine in from the living room, and do so. E. says it's the most brilliant thing that's happened in all the twenty-two years she's lived in this apartment. I feel enormously pleased. Who says seventy-year-olds have no get up and go?

19 January

Martin Luther King, Jr., Day is being celebrated this Monday. It's a holiday but not a universal one: the stock market is open, zipping along to increasingly rarefied heights, and so is *The New Yorker*. I had planned to go downtown but have a head cold. I'd like to postpone a lunch date I have tomorrow with Ted Worner, but I can't reach him because he has an unlisted phone. A press agent with an unlisted phone! That's Newcastle without coal.

Ellie is soliciting contributions to a special PEN newsletter she's editing, in which writers will reflect on other art forms. She asks me to write about dancing. Beg your pardon? She explains that my life is largely spent in or on rectangles—tennis and squash courts, backgammon boards, crossword-puzzle diagrams—and that I should write about constructing crosswords, because that's only a step away from choreographing a ballet. How can I resist such blandishment?

Annie Dillard phones. Not about PEN. She wants me to sail down the Mississippi with her for four days. Wants *us*? No, just me. With her husband? Nope, just she and I. If Annie thinks of me as a safe companion for an attractive young woman on a riverboat cruise, I am crushed. Ellie restores my flagging spirits by announcing that if anybody's going, she is going along.

Our new TV set arrives from 47th Street Photo. The delivery man is an Orthodox Jew, in full regalia. I wonder if he will accept a tip. As he is leaving, he says to me, "*Gesund*—you know what that means?" He knows a lapsed Jew when he sees one. I know what "gesundheit" means. I have been sneezing all day. I say, tentatively proffering a tip, "Sure, and *Gesund* to you." He accepts my pourboire. Ellie says later that Orthodox Jews are not supposed to look strange women in the eye, but this one did.

22

20 January

I get up late, let E. do the 7:00 A.M. dog walk. But I do the 11:00, and then repair, still feeling lousy, to the office. Almost at once, Sheila comes down to tell me the bad news that Johnny Murphy is very sick. You talk about *The New Yorker* and merely two editors over sixty-two years; well, the Make-up Department has quite a record of its own when it comes to long-running chargés d'affaires—Carmine Peppe, Frank Grisaitis, Joe Carroll, and Johnny. Only four. Some of them began as teenagers. Since the magazine does not cut for space, or let pieces be continued to some remote back-of-the-book dump site, they and their subordinates have to perform miracles every week. Gottlieb would do well to cultivate Make-up right off.

At lunch, Ted Worner, still living in Westchester so long after I abandoned the county, gives me his phone number and says (his wife is in real estate) that the Scarborough house Jinny and I sold for a comparative pittance in 1968 is probably worth a million two today and that unadorned land there—we had three acres—is now fetching a hundred and eighty-five thou an acre.

The *Wall Street Journal* has a front-page story about *The New Yorker*, which reports, inter many *alia*, that when the matter of the Newhouses' acquiring the magazine first came up, the then-stockholders were assured that the staff would be consulted before any decisions were made about editorial succession.

Re pending Dillard fling: Bill Knapp has taken the *Delta Queen* along the Mississippi and says it's a nice boat.

Can *The New Yorker* really function without Shawn? Shaplen, who is pushing seventy, has been talking about loss of memory. (During Harvard's 350th celebration in November, a classmate of mine whose name I can't remember reminded me in some detail how he and I had traveled across the Atlantic together, in 1937, on the *Normandie*, which would have been a splendid testimonial to the acuity of his memory except that I never set foot on the *Normandie*.) I can remember at least as far back as 1961, when the usually indomitable Shawn was laid low for quite a stretch—could it have been all of six months?—with some indisposition. Gardner Botsford moved—temping, it might be called now—up to the bridge of our ship and, while he was there, heaved overboard several African pieces of mine that Bill had bought. But even with Shawn hors de combat the magazine did continue to come out every week.

The current *Nation* has a mean little squib about *The New Yorker*, but then what can you expect from a magazine that has only Calvin Trillin and its crosswords to justify its existence?

21 January

We have a new early-morning routine: Ellie to go swimming at the Ninety-second Street Y, I to hang around for a 9:30 or 10:00 dog walk. Trouble is, if Hopi performs at 7:00, it is the dickens to coax a reprise out of her at 9:45. I had her outside at that time today and it took half an hour before she yielded up one pathetic little piddle.

I sent Bob Gottlieb a welcome-aboard letter and while I was communicating with book-publishing eminences sent to the Little, Brown guy a bill I received for some copies I ordered of one of my books. I had imagined I'd have heard from him by now about that lunch-hour mix-up at Le Perigord, but I guess he's had more important things on his mind.

22 January

It is snowing, first real snow of the year, and the prediction is from four to six inches before dark. Our pseudohusky pet should be ecstatic.

The *Times* has an editorial chiding the Century for its resistance to admitting women. Written by a Centurion? We are not supposed to make our private concerns public. I know that Abe Rosenthal is a member, but editorial-page editor Jack Rosenthal, I am relieved to learn when I check it out, isn't.

Liz Smith is having at us again in the *News*. We fuddy-duddies at the magazine have been promoted, or demoted, to crybabies.

At the office, Alec Wilkinson wonders what will happen to the "Talk of the Town" if, as the latest rumor has it, Bill McKibben is going to pull up stakes like Schell? Turns out that Alec has become a buddy of Steve Florio, whom the Newhouses invested with the title of publisher. They got acquainted at a sales conference put on by the magazine's business-people. I was invited to one of those one 1965 weekend and have to prove it a nonworking desk clock with a plaque on it identifying me as "TENNIS CHMPION." They need a checking department downstairs. The current *Newsweek* has Florio complaining about some editor who has purportedly claimed the "right" to spend May through September on Cape Cod. Alec, who frequently stays with his parents at Wellfleet, says this does not allude to either of us. It certainly shouldn't. We are nonsalaried noneditors, and it is Florio's nonbusiness where we choose to roost.

I had planned, on my way home, to stop by a reception for Oliver Tambo at Africa House, thinking that the African National Congress leader might give me a quote about Helen Suzman that I could throw into my piece before it runs. But the snowstorm has been getting worse all day. People are leaving work early. I deem it prudent to head straight home. After waiting half an hour for a Madison Avenue bus, I take the subway. The crazies I pass in Grand Central! But one could hardly expect them to stay outside in a blizzard. The train I catch is so crowded it could pass muster in Tokyo. By the time I get home, some ten inches have fallen, and when I take Hopi out and a guy comes by towing a kid on a sled she is almost beside herself.

Mea culpa! Some years back I raised hell with Marjorie Iseman because she had been stupid enough (in my narrow view, that was) to invite people to cocktails on Super Bowl Sunday. I assured her that no men worth her salt would come—I myself was planning to watch the spectacle with brother-in-law Patrick Smith—and I was so nasty about it that she called everybody up and changed the hour. You talk about being hoist on one's own petard! When Ellie said a while back that she was going to invite some people—including Marjorie Iseman—for dinner one forthcoming Sunday, I said, sure, fine, not realizing that she was talking about The Day and that the kickoff would probably coincide with supper time. Well, we have the new TV, and I will pretend to Marjorie we got it just so she could better watch The Game. There isn't a prayer she'll believe me. But how am I ever going to be able to hold my head up again in the company of Patrick J. Smith?

It could save people like me a lot of grief if people who print up date books and calendars would just put "Super Bowl" on them along with "Yom Kippur" and "Thanksgiving."

23 January

To Dr. Gorham's at dawn for my annual checkup. A pleasant surprise: on his admirable scales I weigh a pound and a half less than a year ago. He brings up my book *The Staffs of Life*, confesses to being a potato aficionado, and says he has one patient who raises potatoes at Easthampton, has his own brand name, and once brought the good doctor a sackful. Sounds like the old days, when physicians often got paid in almost anything but cash.

I reach the office at ten, having already walked the dog and had a thorough-going probe. It's easy to feel smug in such circumstances. Dr. Gorham pronounced me fit enough for someone my age, and he didn't seem too interested in my gout. When I see him again next year—assuming there's no need for an intervening consultation—I must remember to tell him about a really awful senescent thing that happened when I got on a bus this morning a few minutes after leaving him. A young woman offered me her seat.

Sheila wants me to amplify an expense account. It seems the IRS is demanding that if you deduct a lunch, you have to specify what you talked about. The IRS woman at Holtsville paid for her own hero, but I put my share and the tip on a voucher, and I can and do truthfully add that the purpose of that repast was to talk to the Internal Revenue Service about the Internal Revenue Service. In extenuation of my Wursthaus lunch in Cambridge, I am happy to be able—first time ever on a *New Yorker* expense account, Sheila and I surmise—to use the word "ichthyological."

This afternoon, at the honey-voiced request of one Melissa Jo Reeves, I take the subway down to the Municipal Building for a radio appearance on WNYC to discuss you know what. Turns out I've been paired, to tell all about *The New Yorker* and its throes, with Bud Trillin. No easy matter, to have to compete with a stand-up-comedian veteran of the Johnny Carson show, but I give it my earnest best and am gratified, on returning to the office, to have Tony Hiss say, "You got your licks in."

Tonight, a potluck party at the Frank Taplins' for Abby Zito, who runs the up-country lecture series that Ellie appeared in last summer. E. concocts a sumptuous paté. But the luckless guest of honor, because of the storm, never gets closer to the scene than the Burlington, Vermont, airport. Old friends Kenny and June Wilson are there, along with their well-remembered little-girl daughter Connie, who seems since I saw her last somehow to have evolved into a grown woman with grown children of her own. Time goes by fast. Frank sits at the piano, and I gravitate over, and soon we are contentedly rendering, à duo, "As Time Goes By" and "How Deep Is the Ocean" and "Say It Isn't So" and a slew of other memorable oldie classic contemporaries.

Bill McKibben is reputed to be able to turn out "Talk of the Town" stories faster than most mortals, but I am no slouch, as our duet brings suddenly to mind. I'd met Irving Berlin on and off for years and some thirty-five years ago, when we were both younger, had had a helpful interview with him while I was doing research on a biography of Herbert Bayard Swope. Berlin turned ninety in 1978, and inasmuch as he'd been a crony of the whole gang involved in launching and nurturing *The New Yorker*, I thought it might be appropriate to have a birthday chat with him for "Talk." The composer had already become somewhat reclusive, but both his daughters are friends of ours, and I was made privy to *his* unlisted phone. I called in midmorning, got an intermediary, identified myself, stated my mission, and requested an appointment.

Walking toward my office after lunch, I heard my phone ringing. I answered it standing up, overcoat still on.

"This is Irving Berlin."

How agreeable of him to call back to set up the date himself! We chatted desultorily for a couple of minutes, and then I inquired when it would be convenient for me to come by.

"Oh, I never give interviews. Nice to talk to you, young man. Good-bye."

I was still on my feet, notebook untouched, when he hung up. But I managed notwithstanding to distill a publishable "Talk" piece out of our reunion, such as it was. Take that, McKibben!

24 January

As I pick up the Saturday *Times* outside our door, an insert slides onto the floor. It is a *New Yorker* advertisement, with a quote from a "Talk" piece of mine quoting the gadabout international civil servant Maurice Strong: "One of the hardest parts of my job has been to stay in any one place long enough to get the laundry done." (My suspicions about one chap who gave as his bona fides a chumminess with Strong were confirmed when he kept calling him "Maur-*ees*," whereas those of us who are chummy with the Canadian and know how he handles his laundry know that he prefers "*Mor*-ris.") No attribution to me, naturally, in the ad (thirty-two issues for $19.97, guarantee to the new subscriber that "If ever the magazine fails to delight me, I just cancel and get a prompt refund on all copies still to go"), and I'd have been surprised had there been any; Lillian Ross is the only "Talk" writer in my experience who's actually collected and taken credit for these anonymous bits and pieces. I'm thinking of proposing to Gottlieb that "Talk" stories, as is already the case with equally unsigned "Notes and Comment" items, be pasted into the individual writers' scrapbooks over which Helen Stark vigilantly watches in our library.

I guess I've been brainwashed by all the newspaper accounts about how nobody ever addresses our editor-to-be-emeritus except as "Mr. Shawn." I referred to him that way, respectfully, on the air yesterday, but I have never in nearly half a century addressed him save as "Bill." And if he ever called me anything but "Jack" I'd be horrified.

Bud Trillin remarked yesterday that he, too, had sent a personal note to Gottlieb. I wonder how many others of us have. Bud's wife, Alice, has a piece on today's op-ed page in the *Times*, about how she got lung cancer even though she's never smoked and speculating whether her heavy-smoking parents could have been inadvertently responsible. Yesterday, Dr. Gorham said that he's been telling other patients about how I flushed cigarettes down a toilet in a midwestern motel. He had the wrong bathroom fixture, and his version could raise havoc with plumbing, but I didn't want to quibble and merely thanked him for the publicity. Oh, no, he said, he wouldn't ever use my name—doctor-patient confidentiality and all that. I am not sure how appreciative I am of this particular recourse to anonymity.

25 January

The Super Bowl got under way at six, so I was able to watch the first half, or most of it, before Marjorie and the other dinner guests arrived. The second half didn't matter too much anyway, because the Giants by then had romped away from the Broncos.

26 January

Ellie asks me at breakfast to explain to her what this Super Bowl is, and did my team win? I didn't have a team but would have bet on Denver if Patrick Smith had given me twelve points, which—the more fool he—he wouldn't. The Giants won 39–20. He could have given me eighteen and made a mint.

Still another *Times* story about *The New Yorker*. McDowell must be just about running out of notes. This time he uses an anecdote Shaplen gave him about Shawn and me: the ancient one about how when I was desperate for an idea and Shawn knew it we passed in a corridor and without either of us breaking stride he queried "Coca-Cola?" and I answered "Yes," and without another exchange of words that dialogue resulted in a four-part "Profile." Except that in the Shaplen-McDowell version it is *six* parts. No wonder people complain that our long-fact pieces are too long. And the *New Republic* in today's mail also has a *New Yorker* piece, by someone who says he was at the Algonquin the other day while Shawn was waiting for Gottlieb and that Shawn had a drink. Bill has never touched hard liquor, as far as I know, but if he did that once I wouldn't blame him.

27 January

The weather report for the Boston area is favorable, and I decide to keep a date to interview Nicola Rotberg about her fall down the mountainside. So I fly up and rent a car and drive out to Lexington. Miss Rotberg's directions are easy to follow (so, in due course, is her account of her tragic accident), except that there has been a lot of residential development in her neighborhood and she has forgotten that the road to her house is no longer first left turn but second. When we drive into Lexington for lunch and park in a municipal lot, I am made privy to one of the true bargains of our overpriced era: parking costs twenty cents.

Nicola is calm and collected. Of course, it has been months since her tumble, and she has fully recovered, aside from a few small scars. But it will not be a simple piece to write, because of the other young woman central to the story—the friend who also fell but died. Before agreeing to talk to me, Nicola sensibly asked that girl's parents if they would have any objection, and they didn't. I will certainly try to talk to them myself before anything appears in print.

I pick up a New York *Post* for homeward reading. One story has it that, according to an outfit called Accountemps, your average top business executive (vice president or higher) goes to bed at 10:47, rises at 5:49, and gets seven hours' sleep. I am not a whiz at arithmetic, but I figure that this middle-of-the-roader falls asleep two minutes after his head hits the pillow and isn't interrupted until he throws back his sheets—no bedtime reading, no bathroom calls, no avoiding being licked by a dog, no sex when it comes to that. I feel sorry for the guy.

Two sons on the phone. Joey, back from Pasadena, had a ticket to the Super Bowl but was too busy writing about the game to be able to attend it. Tony, housebound at Wellfleet, says Cape Cod had two feet of snow, probably its most ever, and that when he and older son Ian mushed downtown, everything was closed except the liquor store.

It is State-of-the-Union-speech night. Reagan's coiffure is flawless. I wonder in how many other American homes from coast to coast the major concern is not what the president has to say about the budget but whether his hair is dyed.

28 January

Lunch at the Harvard Club with Broward Craig, its president, and George Kramer. Broward is unashamedly gray. Lunch is on the club, because they want to discuss a history of the institution and who might be available and willing to write it. I name a few possibilities, principal among them Bill Knapp, who I know wants to mix in some useful writing with his regular *New Yorker* editing. Bill once wrote a handsome preface to a collection of my magazine pieces, and if the club-history project goes through and he's interested, I intend to propose that I be allowed to reciprocate.

A handwritten note from Bob Gottlieb. He appreciates my note to him.

Justin Kaplan phones. He is in town from Cambridge. He knows Bob Gottlieb well, he says, having worked with him at Simon and Schuster way back when. Why is Joe here? Well, the *Times* could hardly have one of its regulars review tonight's opening of a play by managing editor Artie Gelb's wife, Barbara, so he's been asked to do it. Would he like to join me for a drink later this afternoon? No thanks; he is trying to keep calm. Is he taking Anne to the theater with him? No, just his overcoat.

29 January

When you have insomnia, as I seem to be having these days from 4:00 A.M. on, a grandfather's clock, even one restricted to hourly peals, can be a nuisance. An hour seems to go by terribly fast when you find yourself trying to doze off before another round of chimes. I haven't yet discovered anything comparable to counting sheep. Closest I've come is to try to get from a word to its opposite, provided they have the same number of letters, by changing one letter at a time. "Came" to "went" is child's play—cane, cant, cent, went. Working on "black" to "white" at around five this morning, the best I could come up with was slack, stack, stark, stare, stale, shale, whale, while, white. There may well be a shorter progression, but I don't care, because, blessedly, I never heard the clock strike six.

Son Joey has a piece in the *Washington Post* about one Frederick Exley, a name new to me. Joe tells me he's a writer who's become something of a cult figure, used to be a drinking companion of John Cheever's, and didn't care for Susie C.'s revealing book about her father. A lot of others of us who more than once clinked glasses with John were surprised by some of what she disclosed—his bisexuality, for instance—but I thought it was rather brave of her to tell all.

30 January

I decide to work at home, to break the back, so to speak, of the Harvard piece I promised to write for *Yankee*. They suddenly want it by mid-February.

Dr. Gorham calls. He has the reports in from my various tests and says I am normal in every respect—even my cholesterol. I refrain from saying that according to my doctor friend and classmate, Peter Ahrens, who's been in cholesterol research at Rockefeller University practically forever, a person's cholesterol count is irrelevant once he has reached fifty-five.

We watch the movie version of Edwin O'Connor's *The Last Hurrah* on the VCR. Ed was one of those special people, now alas gone, whom one considers one's self fortunate to have known. Among the true stories he liked to relate was an incident that took place on the steep driveway leading up to his house in the Wellfleet woods. Bob Manning, then the editor of the *Atlantic*, was coming for lunch, and at the last minute Ed remembered he'd run out of whatever it was that Bob liked most to drink. O'Connor leapt into his car, hoping to race to the liquor store and back before his guest arrived, and went charging down the driveway, at just the same time that Manning, under the impression he was dreadfully late, came charging up it. Happily, no injuries were sustained in their head-on crash.

At the annual dinner of the Harvard Club the other night, which I felt that as a member of the Board of Management I had a responsibility to attend, I was seated next to Martina Yamin, wife of a fellow Manager. She and I got onto the subject of Toulouse-Lautrec (her letterhead, I learned afterward, says "Conservation of Drawings and Prints") and specifically on his celebrated *Divan Japonais* lithograph, showing the actress Jane Avril sitting in a theater box. When I mentioned that I had one of these at home, her eyebrows went up. Was it authentic? Original? Not one of those thousands of copies in circulation? Because if it was, I should be aware that five years ago one of the few extant fetched close to twenty thousand dollars at an auction. My eyebrows soared into space. All I know about it is that my father gave it to me in 1933, to cover some blank wall space in my freshman dormitory room in the Harvard Yard, and that I think he picked it up in 1903 in Paris, while studying architecture at the Beaux Arts. I've seen a couple of others like it (David Rockefeller has one at his office), but mine is slightly different; there is a splotch of white paint on Jane's left hand, as if someone had tried to make it look gloved. Martina said I ought to consult Herbert Schimmel, an investor who's the city's leading expert on Toulouse-Lautrec. So I've written to him. Could it be that Toulouse-Lautrec fanciers have been searching for my rarity for more than eighty years?

Before the day is out, in a burst of energy I get the Harvard piece entirely outlined and even partly written. It'd have taken me a week at the office.

31 January

This is the Saturday with which I always have a love-hate relationship. (Love, lave, have, hate.) Every four weeks the Sunday *Times* offers two diagramless crosswords, which irritatingly increases the time one has to allocate to solving. I got stuck for a while today on one of tomorrow's, because—as I was man enough to confess to Ellie when the truth dawned —I couldn't figure out whether the answer to the definition "holy state," a word that manifestly had to have an "at" in it somewhere, was "Vatican" or "Lateran"—only to discover in the end that I was supposed to be thinking of "matrimony."

In the late afternoon, we walk down to Fifty-fifth and Third to see, belatedly, *Blue Velvet*. It's not as shocking as we'd been led to believe, and along with its scariness and kinky sex there's a lot of hokum. Toward the beginning, a young man sneaks into Isabella Rosselini's apartment to open a window, presumably so he can return through it at his pleasure, for his pleasure. Much is made of that; at least twice later, we got glimpses of fluttering drapes, to indicate that the window is still open and God knows what dreadful things might not ensue. But nothing comes of it all; we have been tricked, merely to give us one more scare, as if we needed any more.

Afterward, Ellie and I have some pasta at a Third Avenue yuppie joint, teeming with the affluent younger set. It's nice to find that there's still a place in New York where you can get a simple one-course meal, with a couple of drinks, for only fifty-odd dollars.

1 February

I've been reading the second part of Jeremy Bernstein's memoir of his life as a young physicist. He mentions having been worried he might not get a security clearance at Los Alamos one time, because he had a great-aunt who subscribed to the *Daily Worker*. Could she have been acquainted with my Uncle Rudolph? My father's brother-in-law never had a job, as far as I know, and never had a home of his own. When he was eighty, he was still a permanent guest in the brownstone of his ninety-five-year-old mother-in-law. (It was one of those houses that, when they were fashionable, had a Turkish Room. It also had a live-in German couple who never seemed to smile at any of us. Maybe they were anti-Semitic.) Rudolph's wife ran a Madison Avenue shop specializing in modern European objets d'art—she had lived in Vienna and her merchandise was patterned on that of the *Wiener Werkstätte*—and catering, she never failed to let it be known, to a high-class clientele. Why, some days there were Rockefellers practically tripping over each other. Uncle Rudolph—they were childless—would accompany Aunt Rena to work, and he would be stashed in a back room, invisible to the customers, where he would sit and read the *Daily Worker*. I wonder now if he was ever actually a dues-paying Communist or, indeed, was known to any member of the party. I'd be surprised if his wife and his mother-in-law had ever let him go to a party meeting. So he probably never knew Jeremy's great-aunt. Nobody ever questioned me about Uncle Rudolph, but then I never had to be cleared for Los Alamos.

The Pro Bowl, as meaningless a football contest as there can be, is on television, and I watch part of it. It's being played in Honolulu, and a camera focuses on a girl in a T-shirt proclaiming, "My parents think I'm in college." Is that supposed to be funny, or cute, or am I getting crotchety? Why should sentiments like hers be applauded or, at any rate, aired? Timothy Leary is still working the lecture circuit, which is how Abbie Hoffman has told the *Times* he now supports *him*self. He also says that all his children have been on drugs, as if that were somehow praiseworthy. I can't help wondering how many other people's children, in or out of college, these hawkers of hallucinogens have ruined.

In a *Times* story about S. J. Perelman (a play he wrote with his brother-in-law Nathanael West has just been discovered in a collection of Sid's papers at Brown), Harold Ross is quoted as saying he would "rather work in Paris sewers than choose the life of a freelance." Hard to believe Ross said anything like that, especially when that was the arrangement he preferred for most of us contributors to his magazine. Whatever anybody else may believe, I have always thought myself a cut above a sewer rat.

At the office, Bill McKibben, who seems to have a pipeline to authority, informs me that Gottlieb is slated to arrive next week and to sit, for a week, in Shawn's office, watching and listening and learning the ropes. A "Profile" of mine about Dwayne Andreas, the soybean man, is going to press this week, but I am more concerned about when Shawn (or Gottlieb) plans to run Suzman. The South African elections are scheduled for May sixth. I send Shawn a memo saying that if possible it would be nice to have her "Profile" run in the forthcoming issue dated April twentieth, because that would be almost exactly fifty years since—on April 19, 1937—my very first appearance in the magazine.

In an eighteenth-floor corridor, I catch up with some of the rumors the weekend has engendered. (1) Shawn's personal papers are being put under guard, because someone has threatened to make off with them. (2) Shawn told somebody he still hoped Chip McGrath would succeed him. (3) There was to have been a meeting in Shawn's office, last week, with Si Newhouse, and all the writers were to have been instructed to go to the nineteenth floor and make their owner run a gauntlet on leaving while they cried "Shame!"

Two flights up, Sheila says that I cheated myself on the last expense account I turned in by forty cents. She has a higher opinion of my arithmetical skills than I do, and she has a theory that I always put in one deliberate mistake to see if Natasha and she are on their toes. She thinks I am in collusion therein with John Hersey, in her view a onetime seventy-seven-cents trickster.

Editor John Bennet stops by. He wants to go over the Andreas piece with me tomorrow. He says he has been reading over some of the stuff I wrote while I was in the army, four years before he was born. He is curious about the relationship between Ross and Shawn. (It was a special one, never alas repeated; Ross had his Shawn, but Shawn never got around to nurturing a Shawn of his own.) John is convinced that the magazine is going to undergo radical changes and that there will be attrition in the staff.

I have been waiting to see how the *National Review* would handle the *New Yorker* saga, or soap opera, or whatever it is we are living through and acting out. Bill Buckley is, after all, among his many other roles, one of our contributors. (I once spent a night at his Connecticut home, after a sybaritic cruise up the coast on his yacht. Didn't get much sleep, because Pat Buckley wanted to play gin rummy, and she and I sat up till all hours, and Bill sat up just as long, pounding a piano at the other end of their living room until we called it quits.) The February thirteenth issue of the *Review* arrives today, and it praises Bob G. for his love of work, family, and ballet—the same traits that Liz Smith, who all but has us under siege, sneers at this morning, nattering in the *News* that he'd be better off if he admitted to donning women's clothes for office parties. She says she won't read *The New Yorker*, which is a pity, because people who want to get a broad perspective about what's going on in the world should read it and also, as I do, the *National Review*, the *Nation*, and Liz Smith.

Joan and Olivia come to dinner with the Patrick Smiths, a nice blend of relatives. Joan says she is going to retire from book editing at seventy-five and is going to live until ninety, which seems genetically not implausible, considering that the average age at death of three of our four grandparents was higher. I am not entirely sure I share her aspiration to such extreme longevity, but I could be persuaded to change my mind. Are not octogenarians, as I begin to close in on them, looking more and more attractive every day? Not to mention girls in their sixties.

3 February

At the office, Shaplen says that Tom Whiteside phoned him at home yesterday and said that all writers' foreign trips were off. My whole winter and spring had been dedicated to Africa. I wonder what to do with the letter that came in today from Larry Stifel in Nigeria, saying how happy he is that I will be visiting his International Institute for Tropical Agriculture and that they'll meet my plane at Lagos.

The rough copy of this week's issue—first-run copy is the new parlance —contains a Bill Buckley confessional about his latest voyage. His route is going to include Kapingamarangi. Who ever would have thought that this remote Pacific atoll would make *The New Yorker* twice! I spent some time there—the only place on earth, in my experience, with no way of communicating with any other place—in 1964, when I was doing a series on Micronesia, and must ask Bill or his crewman Dick Clurman what the deal is there now if, say, someone is stricken with appendicitis. Bill writes of Dick's "towering incompetence on board a boat," with which I would have to concur, if testifying under oath, remembering the day when a motorboat with *Time*'s former Chief of Correspondents at the helm leapt out of a Martha's Vineyard berth, but not without first ripping off a hunk of dock.

New York, the other magazine, in its *New Yorker* piece this week calls Joe Mitchell, who came to our mag in 1938, the year after me, our "elder statesman—friend of Liebling and Perelman and link to the glory days." If I ever write a memoir about old times, I suppose now I could call it *The Missing Link*.

Shawn must be tidying up. Derek Morgan phones. He has been given my Socialist Workers' Party piece, which was set in type in 1982, for updating.

4 February

I go home early, because Herbert Schimmel, the Toulouse-Lautrec expert, is coming by for a drink and to look at our *Divan Japonais*. We remove it from the living-room wall so he can study it close up. It's the genuine article, he assures us, and if it can somehow be established that Lautrec himself painted that left hand white, worth a good deal. It was not uncommon, says this editor of Lautrec's letters and prodigious collector of his works, for that artist to touch up his own lithographs, and Schimmel points out that ours has a dab of white paint down at the bottom, too. He suggests that we take it down to Martina Yamin's place and have her remove it, gingerly, from its frame, and when it's out he wants to have another look at it, and at the back of it, where for all he knows there might be something significant.

5 February

Paula Span of the *Washington Post* phoned last night, seeking advance information for a piece she plans to write Monday, after Gottlieb turns up. (Shaplen went by Shawn's office yesterday and says it is nearly bare.) Jim Lardner wants my opinion as to whether there ought not to be some sort of staff meeting tomorrow, where people could express themselves about the magazine and its condition. I don't think that's a very good idea, but when he says Shawn has approved it I shrug. But I warn Jim that whatever happens is virtually sure to be leaked to the press and, maybe, to generate a whole new spate of stories. I had planned to work at home tomorrow, but now I guess I won't.

Terry phones. He is having lunch with George Plimpton, who's in Boston to promote a book, and my son wants to know if Plimpton and I are enemies. Why, no, whatever made him think that? I don't know George well, but I was at his house not long ago at a party he gave for his parents-in-law, the Willard Espys, whom I know better. I tell Terry that I can't think offhand of any enemies I have. How about him? He says no really important ones since that one in Provincetown who beat him up on account of that girl— the fellow, do I remember, who made those disagreeable threatening calls to E. J. Kahn III but to the number listed for E. J., Jr.? I remember extremely well; we even had our own phone tapped in the hope of catching him in the act.

At 11:45, Lardner says tomorrow's gathering will be at 4:30. Shawn is going to say a few words, and I'm welcome to, also. Whatever happens, I am not going to prepare a speech.

A few minutes later—we live in a world of ironies—our head messenger, Bruce Diones, warning "Watch the glitter!" hands me a star-spangled invitation to *The New Yorker*'s sixty-second birthday party, Grand Ballroom of the Pierre, February 26, 5:30–10:30. Which if any editor in chief will attend? If it's Gottlieb, will he wear a tie?

Sheila comes by to reassure me about travel. She cornered Whiteside, who said he'd got the word from Ved Mehta. She cornered Ved, who said he'd got it from Orville Schell, who apparently was told by Shawn or somebody that Gottlieb might not want him to go to China. Sheila is astonished to learn from cornering me about tomorrow's assembly. It seems that nobody has informed the office manager about the office meeting.

At 4:00 P.M., Lardner says the meeting is off. Apparently a few people —Roger Angell, Chip McGrath, Martin Baron among them—told Shawn they took a dim view of it. Now Jim says that Shawn was never for or against it to begin with, had merely agreed to talk if an audience convened. I am relieved. Also, now I can work at home tomorrow.

Somebody has tacked to the eighteenth-floor bulletin board a copy of the agreement between the Newhouses and *The New Yorker* in which consultation on the choice of a new editor was formally pledged.

To the Century for the monthly black-tie dinner, which I rarely attend nowadays but am happy to tonight because William Jay Smith is the speaker and has asked to have me seated at the president's table. Before dinner, there is talk of an attack, in the *New Criterion*, by some female professor named Hooker, on a Smith review of a translation of an Italian poet, and Bill seems pleased when someone refers to his adversary as "the Hooker." When and if women are admitted to our club—this is the overriding topic of conversation at the Century these days—we may have to curb that kind of talk. I'm surprised to discover that Ralph Ellison, one of my tablemates, is against the change so many of us favor. Sidney Simon, another for-men-only partisan, voices his concern about the alterations, quite apart from bathrooms, that would have to be made: What's to become of Jimmy Flexner, Sidney demands, and his long-standing habit of taking his shoes off while enjoying an after-lunch nap in the library?

I take the Madison Avenue bus home with David Prager, who solicits my views on the ongoing controversy over whether a J. D. Salinger biographer should be allowed, without the writer's permission, to use Jerry's letters or paraphrases thereof. I am ambivalent; by and large, I think the use of private correspondence should belong, at least while they're alive, to the writers of the letters. On the other hand, as a sometime biographer myself, I am generally in favor of having unlimited access to relevant material wherever it exists.

6 February

I stay at home to get my *Yankee* piece on Harvard out of the way. I have it nearly finished, early in the afternoon, when Ellie returns surprisingly quickly from walking the dog. She has slipped on the ice, from a sled-dog tug on her leash, has hurt her wrist, and appears to be in shock. I help her to the living-room couch, and when she can talk we debate whether I should take her straight to Emergency at Lenox Hill. I call Dr. Gorham. He wants us to come to his office for an X-ray. So we do. No fracture that he can detect. He sends us to a corner pharmacy, for a wrist splint. By the time we get home, Ellie seems better, but it was scary, and Hopi was worried, too, and climbed up on the couch with her and licked her pale face. E. says that all she can remember about managing to get back to the apartment after her fall was that somebody had covered the monochromatic carpet in the lobby with stars.

While she naps, I finish the piece. It seems these days that I can only write at home. My home has become my office, and my office, I suppose, considering all the intrafamily events occurring there in recent days, my home.

7 February

Betty and Patrick are going to see a French film at Third and Sixty-eighth, and we join them. Turns out to be *My Sweet Little Village*, a Czech film, but no matter. Subtitles are subtitles, and the Czechs perhaps do better than the French could have done when it comes to making a larksome comedy about a village idiot.

8 February

Ben Makihara, E.'s brother's Harvard roommate, has moved to New York to run the Mitsubishi office here and comes for dinner. Turns out he hasn't seen Don Munro in twenty-five years. We have the Japanological professor Donald Keene to meet him, also Margaret Croyden, heading toward Asia for five weeks to study Japanese theater, also Jim and Patricia Grant. Patricia is thinking of chucking her investment-banking job and going to work with Jim, who has moved to the Woolworth Building and into F. W. Woolworth's very own private office. Jim says his biweekly *Grant's Interest Rate Observer* now has a circulation of one thousand, which is not bad at $375 for a year's subscription. The Newhouses could probably use someone with a record like that.

9 February

A sort of blizzard. Ellie and Betty Smith are scheduled to take part in some kind of sororal convocation in Boston and are going to take the train instead of flying.

I get to the office at 11:45. Natasha doesn't know if Gottlieb has arrived, or if Shawn is here. He is. Judy Mellecker saw him, and he told her he had approved my suggestion of a "Profile" on Pat Sajak of "Wheel of Fortune."

At 3:20, Paula Span phones again. The *Washington Post* knows more than I do. She says Shawn arrived at 11:30 and Gottlieb at 12:15. She wonders if 11:30 is early for Shawn. No, this is Monday—going-to-press day. Span says Gottlieb was wearing corduroy pants, a parka, a cap, and sneakers. (Seems sensible enough, aside from, considering the snow, the sneakers.) She wants to know if Shawn always wears a dark suit and tie. I say I really don't know, but I suppose like many of us he has more than one suit. Ah —do the rest of us wear suits to the office? I look down. My suit coat and trousers don't match. I start to tell her about Davies and Son and my lovable old tweed jacket, but before I can even get close to my gray flannels she says—I agree, I didn't start this—that the conversational subject has been exhausted.

Bill Haskins, '37, phones from Harvard. In answer to my query, anent my *Yankee* piece, he says that at last report there were 692 still-living members of our class. Bill is working for the Harvard College Fund, and he should know. He says that people of all kinds are living so much longer that fifty-fifth reunions are now becoming major events. By our fifty-fifth, our average age should be about seventy-seven.

I call Martina Yamin. She operates from a fifth-floor walk-up and doesn't want me to have to lug my Lautrec to her aerie (not my age, *its* preciousness), so we are to meet, later this month, at a picture framer's.

I am walking homeward on Eighty-ninth Street, east from the Madison Avenue bus stop, in semidarkness, when a woman catches up with me and, even before reaching my side, greets me by name. It is Lee Seldes. She says she has recognized me, from the back, by my walk. Is my stride that distinctive? (Ellie says I slouch, but that's not unique.) Lately, to be sure, I have been limping on and off from the gout, but how can Lee, whom I don't know all that well and haven't seen for quite a while, possibly know that? After she walks on past—I watch her intently, hoping to be able to spot *her* if my chance comes—I get to thinking that maybe there is something to this business of identifying people from behind. I recall walking toward the office the other day, realizing that the person thirty or forty feet ahead of me had to be Helen Stark, but not knowing how or why, knowing only that I had never consciously studied her gait before.

10 February

I buy the *Washington Post*. A dollar-fifteen here. Cambridge was cheaper. Paula Span leads off with our editors' clothing (she fails to mention mine) and then goes into a departing statement that Jonathan Schell appears to have issued—a communiqué in a war I didn't know had been declared. He is on his way to Harvard's Institute of Politics. The *Post* adds, moreover, that Gottlieb has been meeting, over at his Knopf office, with McGrath, Bennet, Lorenz, Pat Crow, and Baron—an estimable selection—and that there's a full-page ad in the current *Variety* signed by a number of *New Yorker* people, a sentimental farewell tribute to Shawn. Most of the names on it—I was not invited to join, indeed knew nothing about it—are of what I think of as the younger set: McKibben, Singer, Lardner, Veronica Geng, George Trow, and Shawn's daughter-in-law Jamaica Kincaid, going public with her private grief. What is the ad supposed to mean, anyway? That they're the ones who love him most, or the only ones who love him at all?

I am working at home, trying to choreograph crossword puzzles, when Dr. Gorham phones. Further study of Ellie's X-rays discloses that she does after all have a nondisplaced fracture of the radius. She is to phone an orthopedist, whose secretary, Audrey, will make arrangements. An hour or so later, Gorham calls back. Audrey is gone. Now it is Goldie we should ask for. None of these women seems to have last names. For some years, ever since the women's lib movement convinced me that I was a heel for having so long been so malely chauvinistic, I have made a point, when, say, buying Christmas presents via telephone from a mail-order catalogue, of asking whomever I'm connected with, after she identifies herself as Joanna or Rosie or Kate or whatever, for her surname. I do this in what I conceive to be the spirit of the Equal Rights Amendment. Whoever heard of a man identifying himself solely as Charlie or George? The strange women I thus get involved with are rarely offended, but they are almost always astonished.

And scarcely have I hung up when the phone rings again—God, is it always like this at the apartment?—and it is somebody for Ellie from a publishing house named, if I hear her right, Shari, or Cherry. I don't want to waste the time it would take to get both of us straightened out, so I keep mum. What a relief it is when the next caller, Patty Bosworth, tells me who she is in full. She doesn't actually have to; I recognize her voice.

Today's *Post* says that Shawn has been invited to the birthday party at the Pierre. I don't believe he ever went to one in bygone days—probably out of his sensitive awareness of the risks inherent in having to fraternize with associates whose behavior is apt to be unpredictable when they've had unlimited access to free drinks. The announcement about the party is attributed to a *New Yorker* spokesman with a name I never heard of.

11 February

Emily Hahn and Renata Adler have been elected to the Institute of Arts & Letters. Maybe it can give T. J. Renata's number. He called yesterday because his university wants to invite her to make some sort of appearance but doesn't want to pay her standard fee and thus doesn't want to go through her agent. Her rates may be higher today.

Joan and Olivia had lunch with Cecille Shawn. She told them that Bill had been "ordered" to leave the office Friday—the day after tomorrow.

Because *The New Yorker* rarely prints letters (is Gottlieb likely to revive our dormant Department of Amplification, Correction, and Abuse?), its articles don't generate as much mail as they otherwise might. Here at hand, though, on an ornate letterhead, is a reaction to my postal-inspection piece from no less than the State Treasurer of West Virginia, who is taking umbrage—not unjustifiably, I am bound to admit—at my having employed the gratuitous phrase "relatively poor, relatively uneducated rural folk . . . in . . . the hills of West Virginia." One should always try to anticipate other people's sensitivities. I hope he wouldn't find my characterization of his letterhead objectionable.

Presumably because my name, ever since my *Staffs of Life* was published, has been on all sorts of mailing lists relating to foodstuffs, I am in receipt this morning of Volume 1, Number 1, of a brand-new publication, *Soya Newsletter*. Bob Gottlieb, Associate Editor. I'd have thought he'd have lasted here longer.

Sheila, who has met Newhouse's Gottlieb and has straightened him out on pronouncing her McGrath ("McGraw"), stops by and I give her the newsletter. She espies a boater I got at my twenty-fifth Harvard reunion and asks for that, too. Why not, it doesn't fit me any more, and maybe I'll get a larger one at our fiftieth. I say she can have it on one condition, though—that she wear it all the way back up to her twentieth-floor office. Two minutes later, I get a call from Natasha; Sheila obeyed orders, all right, and the first person to see her thus oddly topped was, as luck would have it, her new boss. Good; let him learn right off that when things are said around here they're taken seriously.

Ellie is back from Boston and has arranged for Hopi to spend three hours every weekday morning with a professional dog-walker. My only responsibility—nonfiduciary responsibility, that is—is to have the dog on the sidewalk outside our building at 7:00 A.M. sharp.

To dinner at the Harvard Club with Helen Vendler, who is lecturing on poetry and draws a gratifyingly large audience. One of our new editors, Alice Quinn, is sitting right behind us, and I invite her to come down from her twentieth-floor perch and see how the eighteenth floor lives.

12 February

Lincoln's Birthday—and what a break for crossword-puzzle constructors that there are the same number of letters in "abrahamlincoln" and "stephendouglas."

Yet another *New Yorker* story in the *Times*—this one to the effect that Bill McKibben is jumping ship. Even though he's still in his twenties, Bill was for a time a presumptive, if not apparent, heir to the throne. One piece of evidence was the receptacle on the outside of his office door, where mail and proofs would be deposited in his absence; for a while, unlike other writers, he'd been getting proofs not only of his own stuff but everybody's else. (I haven't yet been able to adjust to "everybody else's.") The only logical reason for this was that he was being asked to familiarize himself with the entire contents of the magazine—and perhaps to comment thereon—before it went to press.

The *Times* also says that Gottlieb is planning to use a piece about Afghanistan that Shawn had previously rejected. That's news to me; if it's not to McKibben, that would have been another straw in the wind.

At the office, Bill McK. tells me he hasn't decided to leave. He adds that he hasn't decided not to, either.

Sheila says she showed my *Soya Newsletter* to Gottlieb, and he said he was going to tack it to his bulletin board. I take that as a promising portent.

Andy Logan comes by to collect five dollars for some kind of an office party tomorrow—whether a farewell-to-Shawn or welcome-to-Gottlieb affair she does not make clear. Compared to what, in my addled state of mind, I lost at backgammon at lunch, her demand is a bagatelle.

At five o'clock, Bruce Diones distributes to all editorial hands a farewell letter from Shawn. The word he dwells on, six times, touchingly, is "love." The letter mentions Harold Ross, whom not too many of the recipients can have known (he died just over thirty-four years ago), but does not refer— no need to, probably—to future leadership.

13 February

This is Friday the thirteenth, and the moon is full, and that triple juxta-position occurs only six times a century. Well, an editor has left *The New Yorker*, as William Shawn is expected to do today (if, indeed, he didn't depart for good after the distribution of his letter yesterday), only twice in a century, and only once on a Friday the thirteenth.

Another free lunch, this time Bill Knapp joining Broward Craig, George Kramer, and me, for further discussion of the Harvard Club history. Leaving the dining room, I notice George Gianis playing backgammon. A lot of stockbrokers have just been arrested and led away in handcuffs. I am relieved to see that George looks unruffled (he is probably winning, as usual) and has both hands free. He told me yesterday that when their Long Island house caught fire Tamara and he lost a lot of expensive, uninsured art. I wonder if we should take out a special policy on our Toulouse-Lautrec.

A phone call from a writer I don't know, Jesse Kornbluth. *Interview* magazine wants to interview a young woman, he says, who has a book coming out of soldiers' wartime letters, and he can't do it because she's his fiancée. Would I be willing to interview her? Only six hundred words, and they will pay something, he goes on, and he thought I might be interested inasmuch as the very first few words in the book incorporate my name. He knows what kind of bait to dangle before this sucker. I agree, without even pausing to wonder if, personal letters seemingly being much involved, I should not emulate Jerry Salinger and call my lawyer.

Phil Hamburger, who I guess is about my age, was mugged at Grand Central yesterday by two hoods who threw him to the floor and then cut his pants pocket to get at his Mark Cross wallet. Later, a man phoned and offered to meet Phil at a drugstore and return his credit cards, for a reward. Hamburger wonders if he was in cahoots with the muggers. Phil says while he was lying down he did manage to kick one of his assailants in the balls. That was brave but could be dangerous.

Nothing much happened at the party, though I did get to show Alice Quinn my digs. Shawn was in today after all—I saw him hanging up his hat when I went to pick up Knapp for lunch—but he didn't attend. Ditto for Gottlieb, whom I haven't laid eyes on yet, except maybe at that party at our house. Down in the lobby, I was approached by Deirdre Donahue, of *USA Today*, who had apparently been assigned to stake out the joint. She looked beat, so I took her across the street to the Harvard Club for a drink. She wanted to know what the overall mood was among the staff. I gave her one sentence on the record.

We dine at Helen Frankenthaler's. A bunch of art dealers talking shop. I keep our Toulouse-Lautrec to myself. We don't sit down until ten and don't get home till nearly one. That will cut no ice with the dog-walker awaiting me at seven.

14 February

Valentine's Day, and while Ellie is still abed the dog and I sneak out to a florist who's just opened up shop two blocks away and buy a dozen roses, the price of which I don't want to put on the record because I'd rather not think about it any more.

In a rented Avis, with Hopi on board, we head for Princeton to spend the night at the Shaplens'. Young Jason, up for the weekend from Johns Hopkins, has decided to go kosher, so Jayjia has to prepare two kinds of egg rolls, one for him and one for the rest of us. Jason and Bob and I go off to an indoor club of theirs and hit tennis balls. I haven't touched a racquet in four months and meet the ball better than I thought I could, though of course if we were keeping score they might be putting it where I couldn't make contact at all.

At dinner, there is, obviously, much talk about the magazine. Shaplen hadn't been in since Tuesday, and hadn't yet seen his copy of Shawn's love letter, and berates me for not having tuned him in by telephone.

15 February

Hopi is an unexceptionable weekend guest. She prowled all over the house this morning and didn't rouse anyone but me. Hopi and all the others go out for a long walk, but I believe that to walk is—or would be if they could—for the birds, and elect to stay back and help Jayjia, or at any rate stand by and look on in awe, while she prepares a huge Chinese feast, to which the Shaplens have been good enough to invite our Princeton Ph.D. candidate son David, whose learned theological dissertations are getting dangerously close to being beyond my comprehension.

Tomorrow is Jaime's sixteenth birthday. How did I so quickly reach the point of having a near-adult grandchild?

16 February

Today is a national holiday—belated observance of Washington's Birthday. Bitter cold, zero temperature, when I deliver Hopi to Ruth the dog-walker, who already has another half-dozen critters in tangled tow, but Hopi seems as happy as a polar bear. Nothing mind-blowing can be happening at the office, because it's closed, so I stay home to wrestle with our income-tax data and only twice briefly venture out-of-doors. First time is to a newsstand to see what if anything is in *USA Today*. There's a photo of Bob Gottlieb, and Deirdre Donahue is to be commended, because the only quote attributed to me from our fairly long conversation is exactly what I put on the record: the prevailing office mood Friday was one of "great sorrow, and, to a lesser degree, of apprehension."

Second sortie, accompanied by Ellie, is to the florist, to complain that the Valentine roses were shriveled when we returned from Princeton, only twenty-nine hours after being purchased. The florist speculates that I kept them out in the cold too long, but when I rejoin that I don't consider a brisk walk of two blocks to be careless or life threatening, he yields and generously gives us a fresh dozen. Ellie promises him some future patronage.

17 February

Today is, I guess I should call it, G-Day. When I get to the office, I write Bob G. a note, to the effect that for the last ten or twenty years I've spent about ten minutes a year with Shawn and would welcome five with him. At 11:05 Sheila comes by, with a casually dressed young Gottlieb protégé in tow (*vice* McKibben?) whom she wants to introduce around—Adam Gopnik, who is going to be both editing and what he calls a "special kind of writing." Turns out he has a piece in the current issue. This new regime moves fast.

Ruth the dog-walker told me this morning that Hopi merely piddled yesterday. Evidently I am to describe the dog's voiding on delivery, so the lady will know what to expect, or to clean up. She wants me to tell her where Hopi's favorite spot is. It hadn't occurred to me that she had one, or ought to have. I guess it's all right to take note of all this. Hell, Ackerley wrote most of a whole damn book about his dog's dos.

I get a phone call from a reporter at the *Decatur Herald & Review*. He has been reading my Dwayne Andreas "Profile" and wants to know if Dwayne's public-relations honcho sat in—as he apparently does with the local paper —on my every interview. When I answer, with some surprise, in the negative, the *Herald & Review* man sounds envious. This is the first reaction I've had from anybody in the soybean world since my piece came out nearly a week ago. Since it was friendly, some say even flattering, I had rather imagined some word would be forthcoming from Dwayne and Inez.

Ellie is angry, and with cause. Both of the orthopedists Dr. Gorham referred her to are too busy to see her, and when she finally gets through to a third one his nurse says to be sure to bring along $200, because they want to be paid in advance.

Things are happening, inside and outside. Dusty Mortimer-Maddox says Gottlieb has told Martin Baron my Suzman piece may be running soon, and Dusty is going to check it, so may she please have my source material? And Joe Wapner calls from the coast. He has tracked down Pat Sajak, who's told the judge that he just turned down *TV Guide*, but that *The New Yorker* is different, and that he will phone me. Joe says to let him know if I haven't heard from the "Wheel of Fortune" man in a week, in which case he'll take further steps.

When I go out to lunch, at 12:20, out of habit I look for Shawn coming in to work, as he invariably does at about that time. But he isn't there. When I return, there's a giant wreath in the elevator. I make out the name of the addressee—Martha Kaplan, Gottlieb's administrative assistant. It's the kind of floral display one associates with gangsters' funerals, but I assume that was not its sender's intent.

A message to call the *Washington Post*, but enough is enough. Paula Span had a story there Saturday, about Shawn's farewell letter. She quoted McKibben as saying that nobody else could have got away with so many uses of the word "love."

Shaplen says gloatingly that while he was upstairs hanging around Knapp's office he got to meet Gottlieb. I will not demean myself by loitering on another floor.

Pat Sajak calls. He says he doesn't want his "Profile" done, though he is a longtime *New Yorker* fan. He gives no reason. It's hardly a piece that demands doing to the extent of doing it without cooperation. Sajak adds, before our ways part, probably forever, that when he got Judge Wapner's message on his answering machine, he thought for a moment it was about a parking ticket. I don't know him well enough, unfortunately, to be certain he is kidding.

At five, Gottlieb calls. He has a warm voice. He says we will talk soon but meanwhile wants me to know that he read my Suzman piece over the weekend and hopes to run it in mid-April. I say that I had proposed that date to Shawn out of sentiment, and Bob says there's nothing wrong with sentimentality. So we seem to be off to a good start.

18 February

There's a cocktail party to benefit the Yaddo colony this evening. Ellie and I both seem to be on the committee, though my only connection with the place has been to visit her when she spent a month there. I had to stay in a motel, because Yaddo does not condone conjugal visits, a state of affairs that amused both of us inasmuch as E. was quartered close to a couple of night-blooming gays who had discovered each other.

But I seem to have trouble reading when I return to the office after lunch, and I seek out a mirror in the gents', and lo and behold! my right eye is all puffed out. I phone Dr. Weisberg, leave a message on his answering machine, and head for home. (His office, conveniently, is in our building.) I am out walking Hopi at six-forty-five—nothing wrong with my arms or legs—when who should come along but Dr. Weisberg, carrying a bag lunch, or dinner. I hail him, and he says he will rendezvous with me in his office as soon as I get rid of the dog. He seats me in his high chair and exclaims almost instantaneously, with the enthusiasm of a man genuinely interested in his work, "The pink eye of the year!"

True, it is still only February, but I sense he feels that I am unlikely to be dethroned. He gives me some salve, one of his samples (the drug companies don't hand them out as freely as they used to, he laments), and a prescription for cortisone drops, and I hope that my absenteeism doesn't throw Yaddo's budget out of whack.

Ellie has been to a doctor today, too, a hand specialist. More X-rays of her wrist, and now a fiberglass cast around it. It cost her $455. Some of this will be recovered, we trust, from insurance, but even so how do poor people ever manage?

19 February

I stay at home to coddle my eye. I can see well enough to recognize the dog-walker from half a block away, though it might have been more difficult had she not been wearing a skirt of swirling quadrupeds. And my vision, though limited, enables me also to search through the trash for an envelope I threw away before realizing that the idiot who dispatched it put no return address on her letter. Jerry Cohen, writing from Hong Kong to let me know that my "Talk" piece has brought him $100 of the $3 million he needs for the Peking law library, has gone to the other extreme. His bilingual letterhead has five addresses in English alone: New York, Washington, Paris, and two for Hong Kong and its environs.

By hand, I receive *Lines of Battle*, by Annette Tapert, who is going to be my *Interview* subject. It turns out that she's leading off with a quote from a *New Yorker* piece of mine about getting mail when I was a soldier in New Guinea in the fall of 1942. Possibly because *The New Yorker* has become a cause célèbre, these days I seem to be more written about than writing. This week's *New Republic* has a piece about business books, which leads off with a mention of a privately printed biography I wrote in 1969 about Robert Winship Woodruff, the Coca-Cola man. (It was a birthday present to R.W.W. from his friends and colleagues in Atlanta.) The author of the *New Republic* piece says that by that time I was "well-known in certain corporate circles for his ability to dash off authorized work that made the subject proud to have lived a life of glorious accomplishment." Fiddlesticks. The only two partly subsidized corporate histories, of Eli Lilly and Arthur D. Little, that I've written—not dashed off, thank you very much—were both done after 1969. If I have such a sweeping reputation for flattering businessmen, how come there hasn't been a peep yet out of Dwayne Andreas?

20 February

We're having people for dinner tonight—since Peter Warner is coming, and he is publishing Ellie's *On Glory Roads*, he'll be the guest of honor— and this morning one man calls in sick. Ellie says maybe I should try at the last minute for Bill McKibben. When I ask Alison Rose, our eighteenth-floor receptionist and fount of information, if Bill is likely to be in today, she says he won't be around this week and—suddenly she is close to tears—maybe never again. The last couple of weeks have been tense all around.

21 February

Rita Gam, like Palmer Williams, has some sort of industry deal to review films, and we go with her this Saturday to *Crocodile Dundee*, one of Australia's latest exports, and a beguiling one. (Not an auspicious day for our companion. Tomorrow's *Times* puzzle's definition for "Rita" is "Hayworth or Moreno.")

Outside the theater, four Italian tourists (How do I know? a persnickety editor might ask; well, they looked like tourists) are laughing as they photograph the rear half of a bicycle chained to a No-Standing-Except-Trucks-Loading-and-Unloading signpost. I can visualize their friends in Rome or Genoa or Naples or wherever (I am being careful now) chuckling as they scrutinize projected slides of the deterioration of the quality of urban life in America.

Getting the Sunday *Times* innards on Saturday is not all gravy. We have looked up the movie's starting time and have arrived on the dot of six. But that is the Sunday time and today's was five-fifteen, and we've already missed the scene where the crocodile grabs the girl and the hero saves her from something unscreenable, so naturally we have to stick around for that, and by then it's time to get something to eat. Rita is just back from the coast, where she had a bit part in a forthcoming film, and got to ride around in limousines, like the old days. But to counter that she has just suffered a bitter blow; there was a flood in Petrossian's, the caviar emporium downstairs in her apartment building, and all her scrapbooks in the basement—reviews, movie-magazine spreads, press releases, fan mail—get soaked, and she isn't yet sure how much of it can be salvaged. No insurance, what's more.

22 February

I always thought "brunch" stood for a repast occurring between breakfast and lunch, but Martha Lear gives one today that doesn't start till one-thirty. For Hopi and me, that is practically afternoon-snack time. This meal, Martha says, was originally planned only for Pisces people—those born, I gather, between 20 February and 20 March. (I affect, when possible, the British way of setting forth dates.) Ellie and I are outsiders. She misses the select category, to be sure, by a mere eight days, but I am ineligible by nearly three months. I never can remember who, or what, I am astrologically.

Sagittarius? Capricorn? Something like that. Ellie is smarter than I am. She knows she is Aries.

Richard Reese is at Martha's, could be a break for me. Former Assistant Secretary of State for Africa, he's now with Shearson Lehman, but he still has good Nigerian connections and if I get there will give me introductions to the U. S. Ambassador and the head of the Central Bank.

Mike Levitas, head of something even grander to a writer, the *Times* Sunday Book Review, is on hand. He has heard, when the subject of *The New Yorker* comes up, as I figured it would, that Gottlieb wanted to cut two columns from one woman writer's piece and she blew up and he gave in. And who enters next but Phyllis Newman—now on Broadway in the new Neil Simon—whom I haven't seen in ages. Phyllis says that husband Adolph Green was talking about me just the other day. That gets me thinking that Adolph and Betty—Betty Comden, of course—have somehow never been "Profiled" in *The New Yorker*. I wonder if Gottlieb would be interested. I'd be, having known them since as part of the Revuers they played the Village Vanguard before the war. Second World War. My war.

In the evening, to the Irwin Rosses'. Rab Raphael is present, over from London, and Nancy Wechsler, who says that since Jimmy's death she's had three portable typewriters around that she doesn't know what to do with. More talk about *The New Yorker*. Irwin, who did Andreas for *Fortune* some years back, thinks my piece about him was favorable and can't understand why I haven't heard from Dwayne.

23 February

In a snowstorm, being as careful as I can, I ease the Toulouse-Lautrec into a taxi and deliver it to the picture framer where Martina Yamin awaits me. Once the frame is removed, Martina judges the print to be too delicate to risk trying to separate it from its backing. Now for the first time I detect a tiny green line on the white covering Jane's hand. We agree that the work should be rematted before it's reframed. I still don't know how much the *Divan Japonais* is worth (not that we intend to try to hawk it) but the estimate for having it appropriately sheathed comes to an impressive $350.

The *Decatur Herald & Review* reporter calls again. He says that Andreas didn't like the piece and has instructed all his people not to have anything to do with it. The reporter wants to know if I know why. Definitely not, but at least I know why I haven't heard anything. Good Lord, what would one have to write to please him! Wasn't it Harold Ross who used to warn us that a journalist can't expect or afford to have friends?

Laurie Witkin wants to know what I'm working on. I gather she is getting up a list for Gottlieb. (Sheila says Shawn called her half a dozen times last week and sounded very chipper.) Well, there's the Rotberg piece, and, after a fashion, the Nile perch and the food situation in Nigeria, and then of course the still unupdated Socialist Workers' Party litigation. Am I to be paid extra for the additions I've already made to that one? Laurie says I should take that up with Sheila, if she's a friend. She is. I take it up. Sheila says that when the piece is run there'll be a second word count; if it isn't that's another matter.

I really want to know whether or not I should plan to go to Africa within the next couple of weeks, so I request an appointment with Gottlieb. I see him at five. Shawn's old office, apart from a floral horseshoe of the genre of the one I saw in the elevator, is quite bare. Parts have been repainted. Gottlieb says there was an accumulation of dirt around one stack of papers that had been there for how many years he would hesitate to guess.

Bob is coatless and tieless, just as advertised. Also genial and extraordinarily relaxed, as if he had been producing this show for ages. He says that he's enjoying the job very much, doesn't feel overworked. Only problem is that he thinks so hard about the magazine—he says he has a "grasshopper mind"—that it keeps him awake at night. (Me, too, from a different perspective.) He wants to know where we've met. At my house, I say, party Nora Sayre gave there for her British publisher. He says he knows Nora but it couldn't have been then. It seems hardly worth arguing about at this moment.

Down to business. What am I working on? I tell him I'm poised to fly to Nigeria. He grounds me; he wants to think about that before he gives it his OK. Maybe later, once he determines what everybody is up to. He said that he was reading his way through every 1986 issue of the magazine and was about halfway there; and that he wants to keep the magazine the way it is while at the same time changing it. He says that Shawn purchased a slew of manuscripts just before he departed (I wish I'd had one ready to sell him), but he has no intention of using a lot of the inventory, old or new, that's lying around. He wrote a paragraph about Shawn, he goes on, with which he hoped to lead off this week's issue, but Shawn demurred, saying he didn't want his name in the magazine, and Gottlieb deferred to him.

Seven and a half minutes, by my unofficial count. We will talk further next week.

Ellie and I go to the City Center for a "Writers in Performance" evening, this one—"Darlinghissima"—based on letters from Janet Flanner to Natalia Murray. (The program lists, among "Donors," "E. J. Kahn and"—this is worse than the IRS—"Elanor Munor.") There are graceful introductory remarks by Phil Hamburger, among others, and then Marian Seldes plays Janet to Natalia Murray's own Natalia. (Ellie says that Flanner and friend once came to tea, circa 1960, when she was married to Alfred Frankfurter.) The letters are read chronologically, as well as—especially when Janet alludes to Ross's death—poignantly. Neither Gottlieb nor Shawn attend, though Cecille S. does. (I'd have thought there'd be quite a *New Yorker* representation in the audience, but the only person I notice is Dottie Lobrano Guth.) Cecille says that Bill is home, working. Just like old times.

Flanner, of course, spent most of her life in, and writing from, Paris. When Jinny and I took our three young boys to Europe in 1957, we had lunch with Janet at Versailles, and she got a chance to see her then five-year-old godson, my son Tony. Tony, for his part, had an opportunity granted to few children. My mother had died when he was only six months old. For years before that, people had remarked how much Elsie resembled Janet, and indeed more than once the one had been taken for the other. Now Tony could see almost exactly what his dead grandmother had looked like in the flesh.

24 February

It is David's birthday. I don't suppose I can call it celebrating when I begin the day with an hour and a half in a dentist's chair. Dr. Magnani seems to be digging into the same general area he enjoyed prospecting in the last time. That work, if I get what he's saying, was only temporary; now we're approaching the serious stuff, which seems to involve copper instead of plastic.

Shaplen says that at last week's art meeting Gottlieb bought only eight cartoons, in contrast to the usual twenty or thereabouts. Sounds as though he's going to use up some of the capital long since deposited in that particular bank.

Martin Baron says that Dwayne Andreas, while the piece on him was being checked, asked for ten copies, which were duly sent. Dwayne's son Mickey phoned the Checking Department and said he wanted to send something (Martin hoped it wasn't money, which would be unacceptable) to the magazine, but then nothing arrived. I say that if it does and turns out to be candy (a judge's wife almost got poisoned the other day from eating some sweets sent by a fellow her husband had committed to jail), Martin and his fellow checkers should have it analyzed first.

When I turned in my piece to *Yankee*, John Pierce, its editor, wrote questioning my use of "aval." He said he couldn't find it in his dictionary, and neither, in the first one I consulted, could I. I had apologized to Pierce, saying I'd always thought there was such a word, meaning "grandparental." One of the definitions in today's *Post* crossword, for a four-letter word, starting with "a" and ending with "l," is "grandparental."

25 February

Because Hopi went out fairly early last night, she demands a six-thirty departure this morning. I don't protest too much; I've heard every strike of that confounded aval clock from three on. So we get in a leg-stretching half hour before the dog-walker—who would inevitably pick the one morning to be late when I am early—comes round the bend.

Annette Tapert, whom I'm supposed to interview for *Interview*, stops by the office. She says that she sat next to Si Newhouse at dinner the other evening and that although he wasn't particularly communicative he did say that putting Shawn out and Gottlieb in had been an extremely difficult decision. She and I talk at considerable length about her book of letters and a proposed sequel—the next war she tackles is to be the Civil one—so I should have no trouble coming up with six hundred words.

At Gottlieb's request, I sent him a memo about the "Notes and Comment" and "Talk" departments in the current issue. I praise his opening paragraph—a replacement for his tribute to Shawn—about all the recent fuss at the magazine and how important our readers are to us; but I also say that I found a long, tedious "Comment" item about the weather (I have made sure that Bob didn't write it) embarrassing and that it reminded me of what some of my students at Columbia were wont to submit when they couldn't think of anything to write about except the weather.

Martin Baron phones. He did get a print, which he feels at liberty to retain, from an Andreas—a nephew of Dwayne's; it's a promotional piece for Corn Sweeteners.

To cocktails and German sausages at Vita and Peter Peterson's. Augie and Claude Heckscher are there; Claude says they moved from their town house to an apartment because it was getting to be too difficult to change light bulbs. Probably as cogent a reason as any. I have a chat with George Trow, for the first time, really, since he moved into the *New Yorker* office directly next to mine. I say with some embarrassment that our era of non-communication, which I am delighted has come to an end, must have lasted a good five years. No, says George, it has been twenty. How time does fly!

26 February

When I go downtown in the morning by Lexington Avenue bus and walk west to Vanderbilt Avenue through Grand Central, the number of weirdos I see in the terminal (the kind Italian tourists of a sociological bent might well pause to photograph) more often than not comes to an even dozen. I am almost across today and have bagged eleven when I bump into—no offense meant—Burton Benjamin. Bud, in from Scarborough on one of the Hudson River commuter trains I so long rode myself, walks with me to Forty-fourth and Fifth. He hasn't yet seen today's *Times* and doesn't know that Bill Paley, eighty-five, has been flown from the Caribbean to a New York hospital. There has been a lot of coming and going at the Columbia Broadcasting System. Bud, Walter Cronkite's perennial evening-news producer, says that not long ago he had lunch with Paley and Larry Tisch, and they offered him the temporary presidency of CBS News. But Bud didn't want that job and the headaches he well knew went along with it; he is going to be seventy in October, and enough is enough. Bud says, incidentally, that Walter is just back from South Africa; some people get visas and some don't.

President Reagan, asked a question at a meeting of business executives the other day, said it was possible to forget things, and added, "I'd like to ask one question of everybody. Everybody who can remember what they were doing on August 8, 1985, raise your hand." At eleven o'clock I turn in my first submission to Gottlieb—a detailed account of the minutiae I purport to recall from that long-ago day.

Most of the women at the office seem unusually dressed up today, and no wonder, for this evening is the magazine's birthday party at the Pierre. Bob Gottlieb gets there. He has compromised, sartorially; he is wearing a suit coat but no tie. I make a point of introducing myself to Martha Kaplan, his new chief of staff, and she tells me that from now on there's going to be free coffee on every editorial floor. It's not quite the same thing as an all-expenses-paid trip to Lake Tanganyika, but I suppose one should be grateful for small favors. Still, I wonder how this will impact the fortunes of the nice Chinese woman with the food wagon in our lobby, who knows her patrons' preferences without their having to utter a word: coffee, regular, no sugar.

Shawn does not put in an appearance at the Pierre. Nobody expected him to. "Most of us are here," Chip McGrath tells me, "because it would look bad if we weren't."

27 February

In the office library, to look up, for a memo to Gottlieb, how many "Wayward Press" pieces I've written (twelve), Helen Stark wonders if I happen to know how many times Wolcott Gibbs was married. Someone has called up who is working on a bibliography. A question, it seems to Helen, rather more biographical than bibliographical, but can I answer it for her? I think it was twice. She says Gibbs died in 1958. But that is nearly thirty years ago! She could of course have asked his son, back from Australia and from covering the America's Cup races for us, but Tony isn't in yet. He is due to depart from *The New Yorker*. I believe, however, that he decided to when leave-takings around here were voluntary.

At four o'clock, I get back my piece, which I titled "Speak, Memory!" about August 1985, with a note from Gottlieb: "I liked this a lot and was contemplating using it, but events overtook us. But THANKS!" Should I be happy that he thought it was good or sad that he rejected it?

28 February

The Smiths introduced us to a restaurant in Tribeca last night, jammed with yuppies and so popular Patrick had to settle for a 6:30 reservation. Pleasant and not too expensive, as things go nowadays; our half of the check came to only $115. But at least you can park down there, which represents a not inconsiderable saving. Ten years ago I had occasion to bemoan in print that the monthly rate at our Upper-East-Side garage had escalated to $90; now it's over $400. Yes, yes, I know; subway rides and candy bars used to cost a nickel.

Tomorrow is diagramless-puzzle Sunday, and once again I get stuck, because having determined that a letter sequence "ange" has to be correct, I conclude that the answer to the definition "citrus fruit" must perforce be "orange." But that throws the whole emerging diagram out of kilter, and it is a maddening ten minutes before I perceive that what is called for is "tangerine."

George S. Borchardt is throwing a wine-and-cheese party at his agency this afternoon for the authors he represents, and Ellie has asked if she may bring me along. Two of George's stars, Elie Wiesel and Francine duPlessix Gray, are no-shows, but a lot of nameless young men with beards are present, one of them telling another that he's a copy editor at *Sports Illustrated*, and adding, as if he had to justify that odd existence, "I don't know or care about sports, but it's a nice little sinecure."

Lis Harris tells me that when Gottlieb dropped in at her office the other day, he also plopped down on her couch. She seems to disapprove. But why shouldn't he? Shawn sometimes carried formality to extremes, and preceding him through a door was harder than getting a four-letter word in his pages; this new one, we are all going to have to learn, is different. Gottlieb wouldn't be able to stretch out on my couch, because it has a half-dozen piles of paper on it.

Strange coincidence: William Safire's word-usage department in tomorrow's *Times* magazine reminds us that the past tense of the word "dive" is not "dove" (that, he probably doesn't have to remind us, is a bird) but "dived." On the way out of Borchardt's office, I happen to notice, on one wall, a framed page from a fancy edition of something or other (#16 of 70 copies) signed by the author, Francine Gray. It is a page about a beaver, and what do my wondering eyes perceive but the words "then dove over and came out again and swam."

1 March

We are rid of February, and good riddance, if you ask me.

One of the parts of the Sunday *Times* we get on Sunday has a story about how Dartmouth and Princeton, now that they've gone coeducational, are changing their time-honored male-oriented anthems in deference to women. I wonder what Vassar has done, and what plans Mt. Holyoke has to make the men it's about to admit feel chorally at ease. The British, with their ready switch from "God Save the King" to "Queen," handle this sort of thing much better than we do. What, come to think of it, will we Centurions call our distaff members when and if they join our clubby ranks? Centurianas? No, that sounds too much like a collection of a hundred years' worth of musty prose.

At lunch, in artist Marcia King's Soho loft, a young woman says she can't believe it was just coincidence that the cover of the issue of *The New Yorker* that came out the week Shawn left, by Eugene Mihaescu, showed the back of a man, with a dog on a leash, walking off into the twilight. I am tempted to retort that there is about as much chance of that having been deliberate as of getting from m-a-g-a-z-i-n-e to g-o-t-t-l-i-e-b by changing one letter at a time; but I refrain and merely give her my word that it was indeed pure coincidence: many of Mihaescu's covers are somber, and besides, Bill doesn't have a dog.

2 March

The only time I've ever been the subject of a cover story in a magazine was when a young woman named Michelle Arnot featured me in a crossword-puzzle monthly. In today's mail, a letter from her, inviting me to a banquet at the conclusion of a crossword tournament in April. It might be fun to meet some of the hotshots.

At three-thirty, Gottlieb phones. He repeats how sorry he was he couldn't use my little piece and says *he* liked the "Comment" thing about the weather even if I did not. *De gustibus.* Anyway, of all the suggestions I've sent him, the only one he's taken a fancy to is Nicola Rotberg's near-fatal accident. "Wayward Press?" He's not sure he wants to revive that department; Shawn told him that the trouble was that New York had become—discounting the *Post* and the *News*—a one-paper town. (I would demur; the *Wall Street Journal* and the Manhattan edition of *Newsday* are in there slugging away daily at the *Times*, and the *Washington Post* is beginning to stretch its reach.) World's Fairs and Olympic Games? Bob wants to think about these a while longer, though he did watch part of the L.A. Summer Games and especially enjoyed—who by now has not heard about his balletomania?—the synchronized swimming. Well, I ask, casting about wildly, how about a long-overdue "Profile" on Betty Comden and Adolph Green? His response is troubling. That would be great, he says, they are old friends of his, but there's a problem: they've been under contract to Knopf for a book, took an advance, and haven't delivered. So it would seem that one part of Newhouse's realm can't touch them if they're beholden to another.

The conversation takes, to my relief, a less-disturbing turn. Bob's daughter went to a secondhand bookstore, he says, and came home with a copy of my 1979 book *About* The New Yorker *and Me*, which he hadn't known about. And the first name he chanced to see in the index—if he was looking for Knopf, it was there, too, I knew Alfred—was Cynthia Lindsay's. An intimate friend of his; Bob became her editor way back in 1957, and his wife Maria stays with her whenever she's on the coast. Cynnie! An intimate friend of mine for at least forty years! What a coincidence *this* is! Later, I look *her* up in the index. There are two references, one dealing with a book she was supposed to write but never finished—to have been edited, I would now presume, by Bob Gottlieb. (I hope she got a big advance.) When I mention to him that I am thinking of writing a sequel to my memoir, he says he's had a letter from someone who's planning a book about the Newhouse takeover of *The New Yorker* and who requested an interview. "You can imagine what I said to that," Bob says.

After we hang up (six minutes and forty-five seconds, but it was on the phone and maybe shouldn't count), I send him a note proposing that I try to do a piece on a crossword-puzzle tournament.

Just before I leave for the day, a young man stops by to whom, because he said he was like me the son of an architect, I said I'd be happy to give some advice he craved. He arrives with a sack containing three books of mine he'd appreciate my autographing—one, I observe suspiciously, bearing the bookplate of the Boston Public Library. He is interested in writing factual articles, he says, and the advice he seeks is: what kinds of things does *The New Yorker* want? I wish I knew.

I have a date to meet Tom Wallace, of W. W. Norton, at the Century, to discuss a possible book. The myth is that one never uses the club for business, but we both belong, so maybe that makes it all right. While I am waiting for Tom at the members' bar, a waiter asks Paddy for a Pimm's Number One, which Paddy says he hasn't had in stock for six years. When women join up, will they be ordering Grasshoppers and whatever you call all those other concoctions that require exotic ingredients? When Wallace arrives, he wants to know how many of my books Norton has published. I don't recall offhand. (Is that Ronald Reagan crying "Hear! Hear!"? Thank you, Mr. President.) I refresh my memory later: Four—*A Reporter in Micronesia*, *The Separated People*, *Harvard*, and *The First Decade*. I tell him about being stood up by Mr. Little, Brown at Le Perigord. Tom laughs; that, I imagine him musing, is part of life, too.

3 March

An out-of-town friend sends over a card he picked up while staying at the Algonquin: "Do enjoy this room copy of *The New Yorker*, which has been regaling us with wit and wisdom for over 50 years." At the Pierre affair the other night, Shaplen and Knapp were speculating grimly that the Newhouses planned to remove us to the East Side, preparatory to a merger with—Oh come on, now, things haven't reached this stage—*Vanity Fair*. If we cross town, will we become an ornament of our new neighborhood? Will the Algonquin continue to put us in its rooms? Should we make our own preparations and start cultivating East-Side headwaiters?

Gottlieb says OK on the crossword-puzzle tournament. Well, what do you know!

To dinner at the Kenneth Wilsons', with daughter Connie and Dan Aaron, down from Cambridge on Library of America business. Dan has an office in Warren House up there, and urges Ellie and me to drop in during my fiftieth reunion come June.

Kenny and his June are going to Santiago de Campostella soon, and we talk about our trip to Spain in July of 1984, when we were blessed enough to be there when all the pilgrims, among them Ellie doing research for her pilgrimage book, converged from far and near to do honor to St. James the Fisherman on his feast day. That was a special year—a holy year—and the King and Queen of Spain came, too. Ellie contrived somehow to get us into the cathedral only a couple of feet from Their Majesties, standing right in the middle of things when the incense-burning *botafumiero* swooped down from the ceiling and seemingly almost grazed the royal heads and ours, while thousands of the devout who were not as lucky as we were thronged the huge cathedral square outside.

4 March

I receive a copy of Dan Herr's new book, "Start Digging!" which I've been awaiting ever since one of the chapters in this compendium of pieces by the *Critic*'s "Stop Pushing!" columnist was hailed in a *Publishers Weekly* preview as a "gem of an essay." I'd written it in New Guinea after Dan was seriously wounded in a Japanese attack on a small boat offshore. Daniel Herr—prewar copyboy at the *News* in New York; wartime aide-de-camp to Edwin Forrest

Harding, the regular-army general who looked after both of us; and postwar spokesman, operating out of Chicago, for the liberal Catholic press—asked me some time back if he could use my piece in his collection, and I was glad to oblige. I don't stand to profit, but I'm praying, if I may, that Dan's sales are *big*.

New order of things: a note from somebody in *The New Yorker*'s Business Office goes, "Herewith a list of your current subscriptions. Those due for renewal have been circled. Please indicate with a check mark if you wish to renew." But nothing has been circled, and the only publication cited is *Newsweek*, to which I have always subscribed on my own and in respect to which, as this communication clearly shows, I am paid up through 09–89. Sheila and Natasha are the only people around our rocky establishment capable of making sense of this sort of thing, so I march up to their office.

They are both out, but on Natasha's desk I cannot help seeing a poignant note, scribbled on one of the yellow sheets generally used around the premises for messages: "Send magazine to Mr. Shawn."

5 March

The Shawns were at Joan's and Olivia's when we dined there last night. First time I'd seen Bill since he retired. He seemed relatively relaxed and even sipped a Campari. He says he is continuing to go downtown to the Algonquin for lunch, with whom I am too gentlemanly to ask. I do ask if he's seen the latest Century bulletin, in which John Russell's regular column is devoted to Bill. No, he hasn't, and he has no more intention of using the club now than ever, which was hardly ever at all. Bill only agreed to join in the first place, he says, because Brendan Gill asked him to.

The six of us watch President Reagan, on television, try to explain what gives with him and Iran and the Contras and the National Security Council and Colonel Oliver North. Bill says afterward that the speech is 30 percent too short. He has always believed in giving writers free rein. Only once in the course of the evening, though, does he allude, and then on short rein, to the trying events of the last few weeks. He calls them "unreal."

6 March

We are off to Cape Cod, first trip ever at this time of year (Bob, the 1095 Park doorman, who has a fenced-in backyard at home, will be boarding Hopi), because Ellie, in her capacity of vice president of the Truro Center of the Arts at Castle Hill, wants to attend a meeting of the town's Board of Appeals, which is scheduled to decide whether the center may renovate its premises to bring them up to code (Steve Williams, the Building Inspector, has already given the projected alterations his imprimatur) and thus be able to operate next summer on the site where it's been functioning without objection for fifteen years. But now some "abutters," principally one Robert Weinstein (who is chairman of the Appeals Board) and his wife, Monica Kraft (who is chairman of the Board of Selectmen, and—oh, what a tangled web they weave!—the ex-wife of Building Inspector Williams), are apparently trying to get the old place shut down. Ellie and I have had a lot to do with Castle Hill. We've both taught and lectured there, and she has arranged various evening programs. I have an additional modest stake in all the current brouhaha. I spent two whole months last summer superintending a building-fund drive for Castle Hill, to the exclusion of virtually all labor gainful for me personally. And now it is beginning to appear that whatever gifts and pledges Castle Hill gained may have to go for architects' renderings and lawyers' fees. It was Kraft who, last summer, the night before the center's traditional open house, had the cute idea of, entirely on her own, ordering the police to put up no-parking signs all along the road where Castle Hill's guests customarily parked.

The water at our Truro house has long since been shut off and the pipes drained, so we are going to stay with Tony and Judy and their kids at Wellfleet. Tony, I know, is worried about the evening's proceedings. He will be covering them for *The Cape Codder* and will have to balance his sympathy toward Ellie and me against his reportorial objectivity. His editors, bless them, are equally aware of this and have told him to use his own good judgment about possible conflicts of interest.

We rent an Avis car for the journey, forgetting until we are an hour on the road that we have a functioning vehicle of our own out in Princeton and that David could easily have given the keys to Bob Shaplen and let him bring the car to New York. But the 1978 Chevy wagon doesn't have those newfangled rear-window brake lights, and anyway David says it is beginning to make funny noises. I suppose you have to expect something like that after the first 120,000 miles.

When I set forth to pick up the car, Ellie suggested that I stop at the candy store to pick up something for the grandsons. What candy store? She was dumfounded. Why, the one I pass every day, on the west side of Lexington between Eighty-eighth and Eighty-ninth, just beyond the newsstand. I know the newsstand. I pause there most mornings to pick up the *News* (I've read the *Times* at home), and then I walk on south, either looking at the paper or to my left, to see if a bus is looming. Accordingly, I have never glanced to my right. That's where a candy store indeed turns out to be. How fortuitous for Ian and Matthew!

Ellie likes to listen to literary cassettes while we're on long trips. Today, courtesy of Books on Tape, we start in on Winston Churchill's *The Gathering Storm*. Ten cassettes, twenty sides. What an extraordinary man! There's been so much talk lately about Reagan's inattentiveness and lack of grasp of facts, and what did he know about what Oliver North was up to and when. Here is Churchill discoursing knowledgeably on the differences between 14- and 16-inch guns and the intricacies of the movements of their turrets. What's more, here is a refresher course in twentieth-century European history—rise of Hitler and Mussolini, execution of Dollfuss, Ernst Röhm, the Chamberlains. Here is Churchill warning us over and over, and not necessarily by hindsight, of the dreadful events that are imminent. What a privilege to be traveling our 290 miles in his company, and what an extraordinary felicity he has with words! Ellie is so carried away she says that people who waste their time writing novels (by coincidence, bound galleys of Marge Piercy's 651-page *Gone to Soldiers* has just reached us) are wasting their time.

We get to Wellfleet, where there's still a lot of snow on the ground, barely in time to make a candy distribution and eat part of a lavish meal Judy has produced. Matthew is clutching the tattered remnants of his security blanket. (When we all went to St. Bart's last year, there was a hideous moment when his parents erroneously feared the quintessential blanket had been left behind on the Cape.) Then it's off to Truro and Town Hall. Tony wants to make sure there is no misunderstanding of who says what, so he has brought along a tape recorder. Monica Kraft is similarly armed. Weinstein has had to disqualify himself, so there are five sitting members of the Board of Appeals. The audience is sparse. Ellie and I are just about the only summer people present. Is that what we are? We're nonvoters, definitely, but we're also taxpayers who spend six months a year here. Why, my grandson Ian was born in my Truro parlor. Does any of that cut any ice with the year-rounders? I doubt it. I'm afraid we are what on a campus would be gown to their town.

There is much talk, as the session gets under way, of how many cars Castle Hill can acceptably park on its own property. One of the five board members, a former policeman, who proclaims, "I'm here to do a service to the Town of Truro," says he has a son who's a volunteer fireman, and the ex-cop wonders theatrically what would happen if there was a fire "and my son died in it." It is clear that he and another man, one with all sorts of well-known links to Weinstein, are going to turn thumbs down on Castle Hill, but in my ignorance I am not worried; I calculate that we will carry the day—when the voting starts on a motion that the center be denied a permit to renovate on the ground that it is detrimental to its neighborhood —by a vote of three to two. It is only after the matter has been settled— in this jurisdiction, at least; there are courts of law superior to this panel— that I become aware that according to the rules of this particular game we would have had to win by four to one. So, defeat snatched from the jaws of victory, Ellie and I retreat to Wellfleet, where Judy tries to cheer us up with a delectable chocolate cake we didn't have time to sample earlier.

7 March

We'll be spending tonight at Cohasset with Terry and Rose and their three kids. To see five of my six grandchildren in a single day other than Thanksgiving, when the Cape Cod homestead literally becomes a family one, will be a rare treat. No rush to get there, so Ellie and I drive back to Truro. She has to pick up some red dirt she's had in her study since she and her sister went out West last summer; Betty needs it, apparently, for some piece of sculpture. Our driveway is so thickly covered with snow that I don't dare go down it; I would hate to have Avis charge me daily rates for a car stuck down there for a month. We park on the shoulder of the road, hoping Monica Kraft won't find out and have us hauled in, and walk down. We don't enter the house, but it looks shipshape, and the tennis court fence, blizzards notwithstanding, hasn't fallen down.

We head for the South Shore, with Winston Churchill's sonorities faithfully accompanying us all the way. Young Curtis is walking and talking. Well, at least he can audibly refer to his older brother Ely (Ely Jacques Kahn IV, if he ultimately decides to use the whole heavy name laid upon him) as "Eee-eye." E. J. III drives us to the Cohasset Common (where much of John Updike's *Witches of Eastwick* was filmed), so E. J. IV can test-drive a new scooter, and then Terry gives us a guided tour of some of the town's fine old homes. Rose and he, now that they are a family of five, hope to move to a bigger house, if they can sell theirs at a good enough price and buy ditto. (Tony said this morning that you can't get much of a house on the Outer Cape any more for much under $180,000, and I am glad that both he and I own ours.)

Terry reports that after we had dinner with the Shawns, he had a phone call from Joan, who said she had it in mind to take Bob Gottlieb to lunch and instruct him on dealing with me. I hope devoutly that it is true Bob never makes lunch dates.

8 March

The phone rings, Jacquelene answers and says it's for me—"your wife, Jinny." A natural enough mistake for a five-year-old; Jinny and I are her father's parents; but who on earth do you suppose my granddaughter thinks Ellie is? She dons a ballerina's costume and favors us with a sweet little dance before we leave. A lone female in my galaxy of five sons and five grandsons, I guess she could be what's called a sport.

We are about halfway through *The Gathering Storm* when we get back to the city, and it is beginning to seem that for Europe war is unavoidable.

9 March

Hopi is back. When I take her out for a walk at about six in the evening, there are two cops standing in front of the Dalton School. Not a bad idea, but why on a Sunday when it's closed? They are looking at 1105 Park, on the northeast corner of Eighty-ninth. Why? Bit by bit, the story gets pieced together. Using fire escapes and roofs, some prowler has been spotted at both 1105 and 1111, to its immediate north. He's now supposedly in an 1105 apartment. I overhear the dread word "Hostages." By the time I take the dog upstairs and take Ellie and me back down to Park Avenue, there is a swarm of police cruisers and other emergency vehicles. I count twenty uniformed cops, and who knows how many plainclothesmen are backing them up? Somebody says the perpetrator has tried to disguise himself by changing his clothes in one of the apartments he broke into. Somebody says he brought his own change of clothing along. Somebody else says he lost one shoe on a fire-escape landing. All at once a light-skinned Hispanic, handcuffed, in an ill-fitting sports coat, fully shod, is hustled out of 1105 and half dragged down the block into 1111. Ellie says he looks like a college boy. I'd have thought much older. She says he had a thin black mustache. I'd thought he was clean-shaven. About five nine in height, by her reckoning, a good four inches over my observation. Fine pair of eyewitnesses we'd make in a pinch.

A woman emerges from 1111 and says nobody can listen to an account an inspector's about to give of what actually transpired unless he or she lives there. She returns triumphantly inside. Lucky Louis Auchincloss! He'd been asking everybody what was going on. Is it worth my while to rush back upstairs and get my police identification card? I decide I can read all about it in tomorrow's papers. Ellie seizes the opportunity to tell a detective who's loitering around the scene that she saw some peculiar lights a few nights ago on the roof of the building where District Attorney Bob Morgenthau resides. "I deal in sex crimes," the detective says.

A fellow tenant of ours from 1095, chap I should say in his upper forties, maybe early fifties, chimes in (with a nervous laugh), "We're too old around here for that sort of thing."

The detective gives him a long and steady look and replies, "Guys your age are the most dangerous."

10 March

I should be dreaming about Gottlieb by now, but I seem to be stuck on a Shawn wavelength. In last night's episode, Bill was still at *The New Yorker*, though somewhere other than in his old office, and he had three important messages that he wished to impart to me: (1) a number of members of the staff had been declared surplus by the new regime (on awakening, I couldn't, I'm glad, remember which ones); (2) from now on, to save money, all "Talk of the Town" reporting is to be done solely by telephone; and (3) only one-third of all legitimate travel expenses will hereafter be reimbursed.

There is nothing in the *Times*, or even the *News*, this morning, about last evening's Upper-East-Side rampage of crime. Probably because nobody got raped, or even hurt.

When I take Hopi to rendezvous with Ruth Hoffman, the perambulator, in addition to her customary quota of dogs in tow, has a young woman with a notebook. It's a reporter for a high-school paper. Why didn't I think of this story first!

Organizing the trash before leaving for the office, I am about to throw out an unread *National Review* (with all the magazines we get, some inevitably have to suffer), when my eye is caught by an article about American robber barons. And who should the villain of the piece be but Dwayne Andreas! Wow! If I upset him, Bill Buckley et al. must be giving him apoplexy. Should any solicitor for the *National Review* Employees' Christmas Fund ask my advice in the months to come, I would strongly recommend giving Decatur, Illinois, and its environs a wide, wide berth.

There is a full-page ad in the *Times* for an Advertising Hall of Fame lunch to be held at the Waldorf-Astoria on April first. I do not think this is meant to be April Foolery. The ad is illustrated with a photograph of a Waldorf place setting: knife, fork, spoon, two empty wine glasses, salt and pepper shakers, and a sprig of parsley. Where did I read that the Mafia or somebody insists that hotels and restaurants decorate all their platters with parsley? Do people ever eat the parsley? Ellie thinks yes, but the parsley of my acquaintance is generally limp and unappetizing and looks as though it might have been recirculated. Just how many thousands of tons of parsley are consumed, or at least disposed of, every year? How high does parsley rank among uneaten foods? These odd musings bring back to mind a fellow I knew years ago, a playboy type, whose hefty unearned income stemmed from a mustard fortune. When somebody asked him how mustard could possibly have generated enough income to support a life-style like his, he replied, "It's not what they eat. It's what they leave on their plate."

The New Yorker has never had a masthead. Somebody told me that the satirical magazine *Spy* has made up one for us in its current issue, so I shell out two-fifty for it at the newsstand next to our candy store. We're not there, I must have the wrong issue, but there is a tongue-in-cheek Letters to the Editor of The New Yorker Department, contributors to which are enjoined henceforth to substitute, for "Dear Mr. Shawn," "Dear Bob."

In the mail at the office, a nice balance: requests for money from both the Gay Men's Health Crisis and the Republican National Committee. The former doesn't identify me in any respect, but the latter declares that I am a Sustaining Member and by way of evidence encloses a red-white-and-blue plastic card, with, for E. J. Kahn, the number 8,744,883. I was not aware that I'd ever asked to be admitted to this club and not sure that I wish to join it if it already has nearly 9 million members.

Sheila comes by, making her patient rounds, and says, *re* my memo about that *Newsweek* subscription, that it has long been *The New Yorker*'s policy to pay for subscriptions to magazines that might conceivably relate to its writers' work. How come nobody has ever mentioned this to me before? What if I were to send in a retroactive bill for a half-century's worth of subscriptions to a dozen or more magazines a year? I could be rich! I think I will at least put in for a two-fifty rebate for *Spy*.

I tell Sheila about last night's dream about Shawn, and she implores me not to breathe a word of it to another soul. Otherwise, she says, it will sure as hell be circulated all around before noon as the gospel truth.

11 March

Bud Benjamin and I take Shaplen to the Century for lunch. Place is full, as it so often seems to be these days, of journalists—John Chancellor, Cronkite, Lester Bernstein, Kermit Lansner, and look who's over there—Dick Hottelet, General Vernon Walters's incumbent flack. Hottelet strolls over to greet his onetime CBS colleague Benjamin, and when Bud makes introductions all around, says "How do you do" to me in the unmistakable tones of someone who thinks he has never laid eyes on someone else before. The *National Review* and Bill Buckley later come up in the conversation at our table, and Bud says he found a message on his answering machine the other day from Dick Clurman: "I am spending a week in Gstaad with Bill." Bud can't wait for Dick to get back, so he can ask him, "Bill who?"

I have known a lot of TV news people, some of them like Bud and Palmer Williams extremely well, but strangely enough I never think of getting my news from television. I scarcely ever turn it on in the morning, and when in New York, never in the evening. I have not yet got over the quaint old-fashioned notion that one gets one's news from newspapers.

12 March

In the latest *Cape Codder*, Tommy Kane has some interesting news to relate in his column, about sea clams: "We hear the tasty critters are plentiful, practically lying on the bars for the taking." That's good news indeed, because sea clams—the big ones, those with ashtray-size shells—mean a lot to our household. The first time I asked Ellie to go out with me I set the hour at 5:30 A.M. and proposed that she bring her two young sons along.

It was a morning with a good low sea-clamming tide. Nobody had ever made such a bizarre social overture to her before, and she was impressed. So, I guess, were David and Lexy, who though surprised were elated to be dragged out of bed to accommodate a barefoot stranger with a rake and a bucket.

13 March

At the dentist's, Dr. Magnani wonders why I prefer early-morning appointments. I explain that I like to get to him when he's fresh and steady-handed. While not overly gratified by that, he does thank me for having paid my bill; says most of his patients make him wait ten years. I should thank *him* for thus letting me in on a secret. Knowing I've just been on Cape Cod, the doc says he read in one of his trade journals about a practice for sale near me and is tempted to buy it, the reason being that you can play golf year-round, there being so little snow. If he didn't have both hands in my mouth, I could set him straight.

The small stretch of East Forty-third Street between Vanderbilt and Madison avenues gets a new name today: David Ben-Gurion Place. Some sort of ceremony is in the offing when I pass through—reviewing stand and flags and bunting and the like. Traffic Department agents have brought a tow truck around in the hope of removing a United Parcel Service van parked in the Place. Its absent driver locked it and left the brakes on. The traffic men are trying to remove a padlock on the driver's door with, at first, bolt-cutters, then a hammer, then a sledgehammer. But United Parcel vehicles don't give in that easily. When I move on the struggle is still unresolved.

Terry phones. He's just been told by a U. S. Attorney that Ed Meese is being asked to issue a subpoena for the tapes and transcripts of his interviews with some revolutionaries for *Boston*. If it's issued, the magazine may challenge it, on first-amendment grounds. My son could be our clan's pioneer prisoner, or martyr.

It is snowing. Three days ago, there were pictures in the papers of bikinis. Lunch with Gerry Piel and Dave Schwarz, to discuss some seminars we are arranging to give our fiftieth Harvard class reunion in June some intellectual tone. Dave is afraid we may have bitten off more than we can chew (the seminars, not the lunch); one of his crew has already submitted a tome of a manuscript that Dave is convinced will put his classmates and their spouses to sleep. I am relieved to be told that my group will be performing in mid-morning, which should ensure, before cocktails and lunch are served, at least a modicum of alertness. One of my panelists, Gibby Gibson, called me yesterday, by coincidence, to report that he feared the remarks he had prepared might be construed as misogynistic. I try to comfort him by pointing out that a substantial portion of any audience our age will probably be too deaf to hear what he says anyway.

Generation gaps: Dave and Gerry and I recall that when we lived in undergraduate houses (where we old-timers are going to stay in June), there were waitresses in the dining halls and biddies to clean the rooms. My family had servants when I was growing up, and I never had occasion to try to make a cup of coffee until I was a Bachelor of Arts. This morning, by the time I arrived at Dr. Magnani's for our 8:00 A.M. tryst, I had fed and walked the dog, dumped the trash, emptied the dishwasher, fixed Ellie's grapefruit, and made my own breakfast. Not all my skills are latter-life acquired. I have been tying my own shoelaces for as long as I can remember.

The elevator taking Shaplen and me down toward lunch halts to let Steven Florio aboard. He and I have never met, but I know who he is—the Publisher of the Newhouse *New Yorker*. Florio is accompanied by a woman swathed in mink and a man who looks as though he was en route to a guest shot in a Suzy column. Shaplen and I, waiting to cross Forty-fourth Street for a sandwich, look on admiringly as the chic trio eases itself into a stretch limo (hired; it has a "Z" plate), the likes of which hasn't been much seen on our block since Ivan Boesky became notorious and stopped having his chauffeur park *his* land yacht directly in front of the Harvard Club. Well, let's be fair. It is raining, and Florio's companions might be disheveled by the time they get to Lutece or the Four Seasons or even, if they are going to eat high on the literary hog, Le Perigord.

14 March

A fitful night. I tried to bring on sleep by bridging the lexicographical gap between "frown" and "smile," but that had the opposite effect and kept me awake until damn near what in other climes would be called cockcrow. (Cock-cook-cool-fool-foul-soul-sour-slur-slum-glum-glim-grim-gram-cram-craw-crow.) Eventually, just before the dog stirred, I got frown-grown-grows-glows-slows-stows-stops-stope-stole-stile-smile.

Bob G. phones. Of a number of ideas that I sent up yesterday, the only one he cottons to is an Alabama lynching case involving a judgment of $7 million against the Ku Klux Klan.

Although *New Yorker* readers are not told who writes the items in "The Talk of the Town," we usually know; Andy Logan puts page proofs of "Talk" on our eighteenth-floor bulletin board every Friday and identifies the culprits. Today's proofs bear two names I've never heard of before. Why not? Isn't it customary for a long-running show to bring in new actors?

In the mail, a plea for funds from—access to the *National Review*'s subscription list is my hunch—a conservative black outfit called Black Pac. It is proud of having, with the help of Roosevelt Grier, cajoled North Carolina blacks into returning Jesse Helms to the U. S. Senate. Enclosed is a glossy color photograph of Jesse himself, along with a card for me to fill out and send back if my souvenir is damaged, presumably so I can be sure to have one in mint condition. I autograph the photo, with flourishes that I hope look Helmsian, and send it to Sheila and Natasha.

To Daphne Shih's for cocktails. Brendan Gill and Whitney Balliett are among the guests. Brendan says he hasn't yet talked to Gottlieb, which, considering Gill's hard-earned reputation as a boulevardier, has got to be pretty good evidence that Bob does not go to parties. Whitney says he is depressed because he has heard that Gottlieb does not like jazz.

15 March

We decide to get rid of Hopi for a week, so I can sleep late. I call a kennel in Westchester. Thirteen or fourteen dollars a day, depending on the dog's size, plus thirty-two dollars for pickup and delivery. Our doorman Bob will take her without charging for transportation. To maintain our status with our dog-walker, Ruth is to get twenty-five a week even when we are not availing ourselves of her eoan services. People talk about how expensive it can be to live in New York City. I muse that if we had a car in town we weren't using and were paying the going rate for it in our neighborhood garage, as well as the going rate for a pet we were not patting, we could carry these two obligations for under a thousand dollars a month, though not much under.

Today is the day the new Castro Convertible for David's room is to arrive. When it does, I feel like someone in a TV commercial. The two men moving it in say they have sixteen other deliveries to make before nightfall. If they get a ten-dollar tip apiece for each, their probably untaxed take-home pay must be awesome. They could indulge themselves with cars and dogs—and indeed one of them does say he has a husky. He can afford a purebred.

Ellie said I could look over some of the contributions that have come in for the PEN newsletter. I propose only one alteration. A writer has referred to the painter as Adolph "Gottleib." I venture to suggest that that spelling looks wrong. How do I know? For the love of God!

To lunch at Lilo's. I suppose there must be plenty of women on upper Park Avenue with interesting pasts, but surely my stepmother ranks high among these. Forced to leave Nuremberg for Greece with her doctor husband when Hitler took over, forced as Nazism spread to leave Greece, starting a third life in America and having that cruelly disrupted by Dr. Myller's death and the loss of one of their two sons in Vietnam—she has come through it all, and more, with remarkable serenity. I wish I could borrow some of that. Among the other lunch guests is a very elderly gent whose daughter has evidently been trying to get Lilo to marry him. She confides to me that she has no such intention.

16 March

We have a date at our accounting firm to go over our tax data. I must remember to ask Mr. Fruchter if he knows a way of getting the IRS to correct its spelling of Ellie's name. What made me especially happy about switching to our present concern is that we've been promised we'll never have to appear personally at an audit. So far, so good.

17 March

St. Patrick's Day, and also grandson Ely's birthday. Grand Central seems fuller than ever of what I guess I should tactfully call misfits. In all likelihood, they've been driven off the streets this morning by the teenagers determined on this disintegrating holiday to ascertain which of them can get drunk enough fast enough to throw up first.

The March thirtieth *New Republic* (they really date ahead) jumps on the bandwagon with an item about Shawn's farewell letter to his staff and makes the unkind judgment, "Must everything end as a parody of itself?"

In the mail, an Office Catering Menu from Fisher & Levy. My first time on *their* mailing list. Can this be whence Gottlieb gets his sent-in lunch? Minimum delivery is twenty dollars, for which I could order an avocado, bacon, and beefsteak tomatoes sandwich, with herb mayonnaise, on Russian pumpernickel, seven-fifty; a smoked salmon platter with cream cheese and capers (nine ninety-five); and a two-fifty serving of Our Own Butter Cookies (choice of eight varieties, including lemon almond and pecan chocolate chunk); and have a nickel to spare. But I suppose anybody delivering a feast of such proportions would expect, maybe demand, a commensurate tip.

When I get home, to help Ellie prepare for dinner guests tonight, I find a curious document in the mail. It's a personal-and-confidential communication to me, sealed with red wax no less, from one David Miner of the College Republican National Committee. These Republicans! Why do they keep after me like this? The only one of them I ever voted for was the unsuccessful candidate (who was he now?) who ran against Bobby Kennedy (originally D., Mass.) when he was elected Senator from New York, and I did it because I was feeling high-minded about carpetbaggers.

My buddy Miner doesn't fool around. He wants me to return his letter and an accompanying report when I've dealt with them. "There are people on the Left who will want to see this letter. You must guard against its falling into their hands. . . . You were selected to receive this letter and the confidential report it contains because of your background. . . . You are widely known in conservative circles in Washington, D.C. . . . I assure you, I will never let the radical liberals know that I've written to you." The personal-and-confidential report declares that Colonel Qaddafi has given three hundred thousand dollars to radical leftist groups on American college campuses, "to turn innocent young students away from their parents and grandparents. . . so I must ask you for a contribution of $30."

But before I can respond to this comparatively modest beseechment, I must write a check for twice that amount to Columbia Student Enterprises, with whose ideology I am unacquainted, to pay for the services of a bartender we've engaged for the evening, to which I've already given a theme song—"Every Little Breeze Seems to Whisper Louise." We have Louise Bourgeois, Louise Dushkin, and Louise Talma. Also, among others, Ruth and Herbert Schimmel. Herb has had a chance to look over our unframed Toulouse-Lautrec. It is now his considered expert opinion that while we still have an original, "all kinds of people may have done all kinds of things" to it since it left its master's hand. Not in the last fifty-five years, I can assure him. Well, somebody did something sometime somewhere, and unfortunately Herb cannot even hazard a guess. I decide arbitrarily to eliminate all suspects except Toulouse-Lautrec, Picasso, Matisse, and my father.

The bartender, during a lull, asks if I went to Horace Mann School. Yes. So did he—class of '83. We are exactly fifty years apart. He is a conscientious servitor. He tells Ellie sotto voce that one of her guests has had four straight gins, and should he allow the chap any more? I haven't noticed any inebriety, and anyhow this is an urban party, no worry about anybody's having to drive home. The bartender lets *me* drink as much as I choose, either for old-school-tie sake or, more likely, because these students are aware that I am aware they may accept tips.

Among the other non-Louises present is Mary Stewart Allen. Arthur and she have come from Sotheby's, where the Duchess of Windsor's jewels are up for grabs. I cannot refrain from casually remarking—*casually?* I have to be restrained from telling it over and over again—that I once danced simultaneously with the Duchess and her Duke. The Allens look at each other, and I interpret their reaction to mean that surely that's not an exclusive. So, emboldened by the openhandedness of our H. M. bartender, I draw myself up to full height (five-six, though my old doctor Louis Bishop's nurse always used to insist I cheated by a quarter of an inch) and assert, "I'll bet you any amount you like that I am the only person in this room who has danced simultaneously with the Duke and Duchess of Windsor and has also shaken hands with Idi Amin." Arthur and Mary Stewart back off toward the buffet.

18 March

Any single game of backgammon may involve crucial decisions about timing, depending on whether one thinks one is ahead or behind, on the attack or defending—and sometimes, of course, like certain dancing, doing both simultaneously. When players of roughly the same capability are matched, the luck of the dice is an enormous factor, and if you have to quit when an opponent is on a hot streak (Palmer Williams never fails to run this sort of temperature), the outcome can be painful. Ellie and I are going to a lecture at the public library, and she is supposed to pick me up at the Harvard Club at 7:10. At that instant, in a dime game (ten dollars a point, that is), I am a grievous twenty-five points in arrears. But what a splendid wife she once again shows herself to be! She gets held up in traffic, for eighteen minutes, and I have a couple of lucky games, and when she rushes in and says we are late and have to leave at once, I have made a comeback and in fact am four points *ahead*. What is this thing called love?

19 March

Last evening Ellie and I had the kind of leftovers for supper one almost looks forward to the day after a party: smoked salmon, paté, melon slices, stuffed eggs. How thoughtful of our guests to leave enough untouched for us to gorge!

At 10:55 A.M., Bob Gottlieb is striding along an eighteenth-floor corridor, coffee cup in hand, looking like someone without a care in the world. He gives me a cheerful "Good morning, how are you?" en passant. An interesting question, and I do not know the answer. On balance, I guess I am feeling terrible, because I just had a call from Annette Tapert, who says my *Interview* interview never got to her (though it had a return address and hasn't come back to me), and this *would* have to be the time I didn't bother with a carbon. If she hasn't received it soon, I'll have to try to reconstruct it from my notes and memory, if I can find the blasted notes.

In the elevator earlier, John Bennet suggested that if I took up a new line of work it would add forty years to my life. But in the highly unlikely event that my life span is so generously extended, where would I turn? Some years ago, I had what seemed to me a novel and potentially rewarding scheme: to set up a business that would produce sound films of families, so that everybody could leave a meaningful biographical bequest to his heirs. I never made any headway with it. That was before the personal video camera came into vogue, and now—to borrow Bob Gottlieb's phrase—events seem to have overtaken me.

I have received an invitation to attend a Magazine Mergers and Acquisitions Conference, in May. Does somebody know something I don't know?

At lunchtime, when the down elevator stops at eighteen, Gottlieb and Hamburger are already aboard. They have been discussing, I quickly catch on, send-in lunches. Phil says that the place under their scrutiny is expensive (but not, I'll warrant, as dear as Fisher & Levy); Bob counters that that may be true, but the soups are good and the chicken pot pie is fantastic.

Across the street, Vartan Gregorian, a Hamburger "Profile" subject, is waiting for somebody in the Harvard Club lobby. I pause to say hello and tell him I was going to drop a note pertaining to my visit to his public library yesterday, in connection with my Rotberg research. Note about what? Well, if he wants to save me the trouble of writing, the thing is that the latest telephone directory he has for Jackson, Wyoming, is the 1981 edition. Gregorian frowns, and, without bothering to jot anything down, says he will certainly do something to rectify that as soon as he gets back. How I do admire people—of course he is considerably younger—with so trustworthy a memory!

John Bennet may already have decided, if in this era of mergers and acquisitions some career switch seems incumbent, how *he* is going to spend the next four decades. When I get back to the office, he is strumming on a guitar. I wonder whatever happened to my old set of drums. Would Shawn be interested in trying to revive our 1940 band?

I decide, to make room for private acquisitions over the next forty years, to clean some things off the top of my desk that have been there for, conceivably, the last forty. First on my agenda to go is a metal object, akin to the stamps that notaries public (I like that plural) use in their line of work. I squeeze a piece of copy paper in its jaws. What my thingamajig proves to be is an architect's seal from the state of Connecticut, undated, in my father's name. I think I'll save it for his great-grandson Ely Jacques Kahn IV. My father never knew the fourth Ely's mother, Rose Vella. Would it have surprised the progenitor of our small tribe to know that he had great-grand-children half-Maltese?

I spend part of the morning solving an acrostic sent to me by Eileen Lottman, with respect to my having mentioned, in my piece for the PEN newsletter, that out of disgust because Simon and Schuster had allowed a mistake to creep into one of their books of Double-Crostics, I'd written them a letter in the form of a puzzle with *two* deliberate errors in it. This is getting complicated. Anyway, Ms. Lottman's communication, not surprisingly, has two built-in flawed words: "mistaque" and "misteaks." I send her a thank-you missive in the form of a cryptogram, which should begin "To E. L. from E. J. K." but actually is "To E. K. from E. J. L." That should give her pause.

Brother-in-law Patrick Smith, who is also an acrostic buff (is it true that sisters tend to marry thinkalikes?), once told me that the biggest kick he gets out of puzzles is when he's solving a Double-Crostic and when, as the name of the author and title of the work from which the quotation comes slowly evolve, he realizes that it's a friend! I had an even more exciting experience once: when my own name erupted before my startled eyes.

We decided some time back to subscribe to the right-wing *Chronicles*, which in its come-on literature calls itself a "magazine of culture." The first issue has arrived. I guess by now I can take without flinching such generalities about *The New Yorker* as "a hothouse haven for a small group of writers who soothe each other's vanities and lullaby their readers to sleep with reassuring platitudes. . . . a geriatric hospital . . . a changeless and elegant package for withered and desiccated ideologies, a handsome political bible pressing the faded roses of the gracious intellectual left." But now, obviously referring to my series about food, here is a personal jab about " 'serious' discussions of . . . wheat crops in a dull style that made you long for the *Guardian* or the *Evergreen Review*." There are limits to even a ideologue's patience. Has anyone ever asked any magazine for a refund?

Bob Gottlieb doesn't get off unwounded, either. *Chronicles* delineates his role "as if a small boy had to spring a beloved grandfather from the state asylum."

I was beginning to get worried about receiving so much right-wing mail. So it is with genuine relief that I peruse an "Official Ballot" accompanying an "I-urgently-need-a-few-minutes-of-your-time" letter from Congressman Tony Coelho, Majority Whip. He is after me to take part in the Official 1988 Democratic Presidential Poll of the Democratic Congressional Campaign Committee. I am to judge which of eighteen Democrats (listed alphabetically, Bruce Babbitt to Mark White, whoever in the world they are) would make the "strongest possible nominee"; which of nineteen Republicans (William Armstrong to James Thompson, whoever ditto) would by my lights constitute "the greatest threat to a Democratic victory"; and which of a dozen campaign issues (from "Defend Social Security and Medicare for America's elderly" through "Enact stronger sanctions against Apartheid systems in South Africa" to "Halt research and development of Reagan 'Star Wars' space defense system") I deem to be "most important," "very important," and merely "important."

Inasmuch as there is no mention among the big twelve of anything relating to either Iran or Nicaragua, I decide that the gap between the Democratic Congressional Campaign Committee's priorities and my own is vast, and that even the minimum of fifteen dollars that Rep. Coelho is nagging at me to remit with my responses probably can't bridge it. There is nothing ascertainably confidential about his letter (save, possibly, "You can be sure that the Republican Right Wing [as if I didn't know!] is already raising funds for '88"), so I feel free to dispose of it intact.

Yesterday I espied a Traffic Department van, with a half-dozen uniformed men and women inside, and, written in big letters outside, "Booting Team."

On an uncrowded bus this afternoon, I see a Traffic Department man across the aisle, move over next to him, and ask if I am correct that such a team's function is to put boots on offensively parked cars so their owners can't budge them. Affirmative. He has had his job only for a year, he says, and is still Level One, which means he walks a beat. Level Two would be standing in one place and directing traffic. He would rather stay a One, he says, and have to face up to enraged citizens who've been given parking tickets, than a Two, because a One has far less chance of being run down by a bike.

We finally get to see *Platoon*. It is impressive, but I wish I hadn't already heard so much praise dumped on it. There are simply too many battle scenes in darkness or semidarkness. Ellie also wonders if there has to be so much raw language. I maintain that the way its soldiers converse is the way real ones talk (when I was in uniform the words were much the same, except that "motherfucker" had not yet come into vogue) and that that is the way, she might as well face it, many male civilians also often carry on out of ladies' earshot.

21 March

I am downstairs this Saturday morning doing the Sunday puzzles when Ellie summons me upstairs in a tone generally reserved for an invitation to a trip to a woodshed. Now what can I have done? Turns out merely that she has mislaid a check she had in her hands, she swears, not three minutes ago, and maybe I can help her find it. That's easy, she had stuck it between two pages of her desk calendar, but the memorable thing about the otherwise forgettable incident is that as I approached the upstairs landing I heard a familiar fond feminine voice cry out, as if ambushed by the Vietcong, "Jesus fucking Christ!"

We take off, on this first day of spring, in the first rain of spring, for some art galleries. First stop is at the midtown husband-and-wife-show of Wolf Kahn and Emily Mason. Wolf, whose full name would have served handsomely had my college roommate and I formed a business partnership, has a price list with no painting under five figures and one at $41,000. With ten days still to go, he has already grossed, judging from the ascribed worth of the works already marked sold, about $200,000.

On downtown to a Bleecker Street gallery, where Judith Malina has assembled a bunch of Julian Beck's watercolors, mostly sketches for their stage sets. The air is thick with pot. Ellie, who has thrice acted in Living Theatre productions—in Picasso's *Desire Caught By the Tail*, when she was just out of Smith, and again in Auden's *Age of Anxiety*, and yet again last fall when Judith put on a retrospective Obie-winning potpourri at Cooper Union—wants to buy one, but while bargains compared to more uptown art, they are still pricey enough to give one pause. Judith is getting ready to stage an opera in Frankfurt. She says that the Living Theatre has always scraped by because it appeals to a wide spectrum of supporters abroad, including Communists and anarchists. "If I did enough operas in Germany I could afford to live in New York," she tells us. One fellow present who has figured out a way to live here is a Zimbabwean who shared Judith's stage with Ellie last fall. He is the captain of a forty-two-foot yacht moored on the Hudson right next to Malcolm Forbes's; our skipper's vessel is used mainly for weekend cruises and in good sailing weather, he says, he can earn, tips included, a thousand a week.

We press on to St. Clement's Church, way over west on Forty-sixth Street, to see a Music-Theatre Group presentation of a drama about, and drawn from the writing of, Franz Kafka. It is played on a stage ostensibly covered with dirt (must be peat moss, we deduce, otherwise would be ruinous to costumes), and it features a dancer who, like the india-rubber men of old-time circus sideshows, can drape one long leg over his shoulder and walk on the other one. Then we go to one of those theater-district restaurants with celebrity portraits on its walls. The people at the table directly behind us are arguing loudly with a waiter about whether a certain likeness is or isn't that of Don Ameche. When the waiter comes to take our order, I point to a photo of W. C. Fields and say—I like to think deadpan—"My wife insists that that is W. C. Fields, but I know it's Henny Youngman. Which is it, please?" The waiter, who may well be an unemployed stand-up comedian, looks at Ellie, looks at me, and says, deadpan, "Next time your wife comes in we'll tell her." Ellie is forever complaining that I make her the butt of my so-called jokes; I try to explain that this time I'd made *myself* the butt. Earlier in the day, incidentally, she had chided me for being unacquainted with some poet with whose name at least I ought to be familiar. Now we are sort of even, because it turns out she has never heard of Henny Youngman.

22 March

There is a story in the *Times* about a military exercise scheduled to take place at Honduras in May. It will involve fifty thousand people and is supposed to replicate what might happen if we got into a real war with Nicaragua. The story says that in that event Guantánamo Bay would have to be evacuated (we'll be practicing that during the exercise), because Castro would surely attack it.

Small world: Leaving a Mary Frank show at the Brooklyn Museum, we are rushing to the subway so Ellie can make it to a chamber-music recital at the Lincoln Center, when she gets a side view of a man ahead of us and says, "There's Niccolo Tucci!" It isn't Bob Gottlieb's father-in-law, but that she thinks it was may show how our minds are running nowadays. Less than an hour later, after I leave her at Alice Tully Hall, I'm in a taxi and at Eighty-fourth and Fifth whom should I see waiting for a light to change but—and this is a head-on, unmistakable sighting—Niccolo Tucci.

A cocktail-buffet evening, back on the West Side, at the Kermit Lansners'. A lot of *Newsweek* people there, of course, he was its editor, also Max Lerner, who doesn't seem appreciably slowed down by the mere fact of being in his mideighties. Max wants to know, naturally, all about what's been going on at *The New Yorker*. So does Ed Diamond, for his *New York* press coverage. I am, through circumstances definitely beyond my control, a center of attraction. Could there be a spot for me on the lecture circuit?

23 March

For some years, I've been on a State Department mailing list. Not long ago, I received a Dear Sir/Madam letter from the department—specifically, from George B. High, Acting Assistant Secretary for Public Affairs. There were two printed enclosures: a circular titled "Strengthening Our Development Partnership with Central America" and the text of a March 3, 1987, message to Congress, on the same subject, from President Reagan. But what made me sit up was Mr. High's closing paragraph:

> When you have read these documents we would welcome an opportunity to have one of our experts on Central America discuss this matter with you. We would be pleased to arrange such a briefing or interview by telephone as part of our ongoing "direct line" program. Should this interest you, please telephone Kathleen Kennedy (202-647-2733) and she will make the arrangements at a time most convenient to you.

Well, sir, how about that! I had never heard of a direct line program, but I grabbed my phone, half expecting, in this grim electronic age, to get Ms. Kennedy's recorded voice. Instead, I got her secretary, live. She must not be a Conservative, because she had apparently never heard of me. A moment later, though, when I explained how I'd come to learn about this particular direct line, I got Kathleen Kennedy herself. I said I hoped she wasn't being buried under calls like mine. Ms. Kennedy, who before we parted also disclosed, with just a hint of ruefulness, that she wasn't one of the Kennedy Kennedys, said she hadn't been bothered at all; indeed, of some two hundred people who'd been sent the same letter from on High, I was the only one who'd responded. Would I like an appointment? I would indeed.

She called back a few minutes later. Eleven o'clock, the next Monday morning—that is, today. I should call such and such a number. Would a twenty-minute chat be time enough for me? I was glad, as a taxpayer, to be advised that it would be I, not the Department of State, who'd be expected to foot the bill. There was one more thing: "Backgrounder or on the record?" she inquired. I like my dealings with my government to be on the table. "Record," I said.

I still couldn't really believe any of this was happening. I figured that when I did keep my date, if somebody didn't call to cancel it, I'd be connected with some lowish-level perfunctory functionary, like as not a political appointee who had got to State by way of being the nephew-by-marriage of a Republican National Committeeman. (Kathleen Kennedy had already informed me, in answer to a question, that it would not be either George Shultz or Elliott Abrams, his by now well-known Assistant Secretary for Inter-American Affairs.) My briefer turns out, however, to be none other than Peter Whitney, a veteran of nineteen years in diplomatic harness as a Foreign Service Officer, currently Director of the Office of Regional Economic Policy of the Bureau of Inter-American Affairs.

I've known a good many FSOs around the world and have, with very few exceptions, a high regard for them and their endeavors. Whitney sounds not atypical and confidence-inspiring. He doesn't seem the least bit nervous, even though, he confesses, this is his maiden telephone briefing. For nearly all our allotted twenty minutes he discourses glibly and knowledgeably about some legislation he's helped draft involving United States aid to four Latin-American nations—Costa Rica, El Salvador, Guatemala, and Honduras—that's now being considered by the Appropriations Committees of both the Senate and the House. He goes into considerable detail, demonstrating an admirable grasp of his subject, and taking me at one point all the way to the year 1992. "Economics is not sexy," he says, "but what's fun about this thing is that we career Foreign Service Officers don't often get a chance, as with this opportunity, to do any long-term thinking about a situation. The story here is that despite Ollie North and the Contras, we are trying to take a long look and develop a consistent policy for the region. I hope we have a chance to make reasonable progress, if we can just stay the course."

Sensibly, I let Mr. Whitney do most of the talking. When I break in to wonder why, in none of the material I've received from State, has there been any allusion to Contras, he says, praiseworthily unafraid to come right out and speak on the record, "Everybody knows there are Contras. Anyway, we were told not to look at the security situation but to study economic, political, and social considerations and to try—in partnership, of course, with the countries affected—to transform their economics."

I have one more searching question to put to him before I let him get back to work, and I can't wait to hear how he will handle it: "How did Elliott Abrams get to know the Sultan of Brunei?"

He laughs—a Princeton B.A., Harvard M.A. laugh if ever I heard one. But then he answers, on the record, and unflinchingly, "I don't know."

After we've said good-bye and hung up, I kick myself for having blown my chance to ask if he knows where all the money went.

This afternoon, a call from a *Washington Post* reporter with the confidence-inspiring name of Trueheart. He wants to know what I know about the rumor that John Updike and some others are getting together to buy *The New Yorker* back from the Newhouses. John has got to be one of the best-heeled writers extant, but $200 million? That's what the Newhouses shelled out. I urge Trueheart to call Steve Florio.

24 March

Yaddo's Second Annual Spring Gala tonight, at the Starlight Roof of the Waldorf. Ellie is a vice-chairman, and I seem to be a patron. Even so, our table is far from the dais, so we cannot hear a speech by Jay McInerney, which may be fortuitous. His much-acclaimed (by others) novel *Bright Lights, Big City* was based in part on a stint he put in as a *New Yorker* checker, but he was there so briefly before he got fired that I have no recollection of ever laying eyes on him before tonight.

25 March

The things that can make one feel old! Today, an invitation to join the U. S. Horse Cavalry Association. Ronald Reagan (I wonder if he knows) is its honorary chairman. "Prior service in the horse cavalry is not a prerequisite for membership." I have been getting cavalry mailings, invitations to reunions, and so forth, for more than forty years, ever since I toiled for Army Ground Forces headquarters and was once sent out to cavalry headquarters at Fort Riley on some public-relations mission. But I don't think I'll go for a life membership ($225) or even the regular $15 one. I hope the President will understand.

Lunch with Shaplen and Knapp, to discuss whether we writers should give a tributary lunch for Shawn, and who, if we decide to and he agrees to attend, should be invited to join him. In the elevator, returning to the office, Lillian Ross wants to know if *Time* has called me yet about the rumored sale of the magazine to John Updike and Roger Angell.

Tom Whiteside says gloomily that Shawn bought Part I of an article of his and then he labored six months more on Part II and now Gottlieb thinks one part is enough. Happily, the mountain-climbing piece I'm working on never looked like anything other than a one-parter.

26 March

To a Board of Management meeting at the Harvard Club. We have two kinds: black-tie-full-course-dinner kind and—like today's—informal late-afternoon kind, with refreshments after we've handled our business. I have to leave unrefreshed because grandson Jaime is waiting for me downstairs. He's in town for his spring break from Concord Academy, and thanks to him—rare for me these days—I am going to the theater two nights' running. Yesterday was *Groucho*. The producers, presumably to save money, had a single actor portraying both Harpo and Chico Marx, and there must have been a very special casting call, for damned if he wasn't proficient at both harp and piano. And one actress handled Margaret Dumont and all the other female parts. I should have thought Actors' Equity would be furious. To-night is a Poets and Writers benefit performance of *Les Misérables*, with as big a cast as you could ask for, and Ellie has graciously let Jaime have her ticket. There's a cocktail party first at the Century, so I whisk him from my one club to the other and turn him loose on the oysters and crab claws and smoked salmon. Just before we board the bus that's been chartered to take us to the theater, Jerry Cohen walks in. He says the Chinese panda loan to New York is all set, so I arrange to discuss that with him tomorrow morning. The bus's route takes it past the Jack Kahn piano store on West Fifty-fifth Street, and Jaime sits up with a start: "Did you see that!" Yes, many times, and at dinner at the Paul Sperrys' the other evening, a bassoonist wondered, when we were introduced, if we were in the same general line of work. I have had on more than one occasion to explain that not only am I not Jack Kahn the piano man but also not the proprietor of the Sarasota restaurant that bears our far-flung name.

Les Misérables is big, and noisy, with some nice crowd scenes and marvelous scenery but much too long. There's an interesting death scene in which, Jaime and I agree, Jean Valjean carries on pretty much the way Groucho Marx did last night.

27 March

The *Times* had an engaging op-ed piece the other morning by a woman who was complaining, justly, about solicitors who have the effrontery to call up at dinnertime. When I rose from the table last evening to answer our phone's importunate peal, a woman asked for "Mr. or Mrs. E. Kahn." I did not recognize the voice and was suspicious of the overture. Correctly; she wanted us to subscribe to the *New York Times* and wondered if we were acquainted with it. I pointed out to her, with perhaps more asperity than the poor woman deserved, that her behavior was hardly consonant with the sentiments expressed with such clarity and verve not long ago on the op-ed page. On the what? She appeared not to have the foggiest notion of my term of reference. I was obliged to conclude, before I hung up on her, that she did not subscribe to the *Times* herself.

28 March

Ellie's birthday. I remember. So, bless him, does Lexy, who says on the phone from Santa Fe that he hopes the flowers he wired his mother will arrive on time. I buy her a hat. I can see her exchanging it right now.

Tomorrow's Sunday *Times* has a funny piece by Russell Baker on smoking and a neat one on Mary McCarthy by Michiko Kakukani. (Also a long review by Updike of two books. He has a two-book one in the current *New Yorker*. How on earth does he find time to read them all, let alone dwell on them at length and do everything else he does? And they say he plays golf, too.) I remember dining at Mary McCarthy's when she was married to Bowden Broadwater and they were spending a summer in Wellfleet. Over drinks, Mary sat in an easy chair, chatting with her guests and smoking a cigar, and every now and then Bowden would come out of the kitchen rubbing his hands on his apron and let her know how the meal was coming along.

At the picture framer's downtown, I pick up our refurbished *Divan Japonais*. It looks beautiful, and inestimably valuable, in its sturdy new frame, behind a shield of ultra-violet-ray-resistant Plexiglas that I am instructed is so sensitive it must be cleaned exclusively with silk, or did he say milk? I get it home unscratched.

Ann Garrity is down from Cambridge to spend the weekend. She accompanies us to Paul Resika's opening at the Graham Gallery. Blair R. says all the paintings in the show have already been sold—our painter friends are having a good month—except the big one over there. Ellie, with her expert's eye, guesses that its price tag is $40,000, and she is off by only $2,000. Ann, who is less familiar with the economics of the art world, guesses $1,500. She says defensively that that's the way prices run around Boston.

Along with our Toulouse-Lautrec, we possess a Resika of unarguable authenticity. We let Paul and Blair use our apartment once while we were traveling, in return for their looking after our dog Rainbow; and when we returned, Paul presented us with Rainbow's portrait, in pastels. We would never demean ourselves by attempting to put a price on her head.

We stroll down Madison Avenue and, at Seventy-second Street, enter Ralph Lauren's chalet to gape and gawk. A successful artist or anybody else could spend $38,000 there and probably fit all his merchandise into a single medium-size shopping bag. A block or two away, we reenter the real world: a bag lady on the sidewalk, all her earthly goods alongside her, and a few feet off a young woman artist, peddling her wares, the dearest of which has a $25 price tag. Ellie buys one of her sketches, to take to Patty Bosworth's as a housewarming present.

Patty, in widowhood, has moved from her town house to one of those new high-rise rental buildings. She's on the twenty-fourth of fifty stories. Only two closets, small elevators, narrow corridors, but good lobby security, and a first-rate view of the Hudson River, which Donald Trump hopes to obliterate any day now with a 150-story plaything of his own. Patty is working on a biography of her father, Bartley Crum, but has put it aside temporarily to make some magazine money—specifically, to go to L. A. for a piece about a movie actor. I am embarrassed to have to admit that I have never heard of him nor of the dozen or so films Patty says he's made.

The three of us are going, as a further treat after Patty's birthday dinner, to see *Coastal Disturbances*. Would you believe two plays in a few days on a bed of dirt? This time, the surface looks like real sand. The play is what would have been a three-acter in the old days, but now Boy Loses Girl halfway through the second of only two acts and near as we can make out never Gets Girl Back at all.

In view of all the shake-ups that are being attributed to *The New Yorker* these days, I wonder how many of our faithful readers have been startled, as Patty and Ellie and I were while riding down Ninth Avenue, to pass by the Andrew Porter Bar & Grill.

29 March

A hang-around day, mostly doing errands in anticipation of a small Sunday-evening-supper gathering that seems to have mushroomed: more than a dozen people now expected. With the Bruce Blivens and the Calvin Trillins among them, there is bound to be much *New Yorker* chitchat. When I mention to Trillin that Gottlieb was dubious about one long-fact idea of mine because it had already been written up in the *Times*, Bud says that he gets most of his ideas from the newspapers. (Some get more than that; the second part of a "Profile" of Cardinal O'Connor, in the current issue, is little more than a recapitulation of the *Times*'s accounts of His Eminence's visiting Israel and his letting a guy with AIDS get married in St. Patrick's.)

For a welcome relief, the conversation turns to Budd Hopkins and his obsession with UFOs. David Lind, who ought to know because Bess and he share a house with the Hopkinses, says Budd has another book coming out about the aliens he believes in and has been ushering a lot of peculiar people, some purportedly from outer space and some just plain spaced out, through the front door of their communal brownstone.

Even in bed one cannot escape the realities that beset the earthbound. I pick up the Winter 1987 issue of the *Authors Guild Bulletin*, which should have a predictably lulling effect, but makes me warily wakeful, at the start, with "Mr. Gottlieb is moving into a difficult situation, but he and the magazine are so widely admired that deep reserves of good will are available to them. Financial analysts and publishing experts asked to comment on the likely outcome at the magazine have by and large agreed that it is just possible that problems will be cured and success regained." I guess I can sleep on that.

30 March

The Dow-Jones goes down fifty-six points today. Would it be a good time to get in on that baking-soda stock George Gianis sent me a tip sheet about?

A woman in Florida who's been doing biographical research on my father phones to ask if she is right in thinking that one of my sons has a sketchbook of Ely's dating back to his youth in Paris. I doubt it, but I'll inquire, and if it turns up maybe there'll be something in it alluding to our Toulouse-Lautrec.

31 March

Isn't this the month that's supposed to go out like a lamb? It's raining so furiously at 7:00 A.M., umbrellas being turned inside out on all sides, that even Hopi seems reluctant to patter off with her walker.

At the Century, a book publisher wonders—this is the sort of talk we're going to have to get used to, or shrug off—if I am aware that one of the first long reviews in the Gottlieb *New Yorker* was of a book by a Knopf author and was written by another Knopf author.

One nice thing about being a crossword-puzzle nut is that you sometimes get reminded before many of your fellow citizens (save, of course, those who have children of the right age to put the salt in the sugar bowl) when April Fools' Day comes along. This morning's *Times* obligingly serves up the definition "Senator making a comeback" and the easy answer "Noitcele," so I will not be taken in when some purportedly concerned stranger tells me there is a rip in the seat of my pants. (A favorite first-of-April word of the dowager queen of crossword puzzledom, Margaret Farrar, whom I was once fortunate to meet, was "Yckowrebbaj.")

At lunch at the Harvard Club, G. Gianis brings over a man with, maybe, the world's greatest memory, unless he is indulging in timely foolery. He says I was responsible for his being put on KP at Camp Upton, Long Island, in September 1941. I remember Camp Upton. It was my first post after I was drafted, and I was given to believe, until I knew better, that regular-army corporals were the most formidable and powerful creatures on earth. This friend of George's is reminding me about a time when some GIs were shooting craps on a barracks cot, a plausible enough scene, and how a corporal or sergeant—now I am beginning to lose the thread of his narrative—seeking a slave for kitchen duty meant to collar me but somehow nabbed him instead. I tell him I am sorry but that we ought to rejoice that whatever happened then we both survived the war. He went on, he says, into luggage.

Camp Upton-Fort Bragg-Fort Devens-the Presidio and across the Pacific on the SS *Lurline*, a onetime luxury liner, except now there were nine bunks in a cabin designed for two. I might not have survived the war myself had not the battle of the Coral Sea diverted some Japanese naval vessels that were hunting rewarding prey. When the 32d Infantry Division, Maj. Gen. E. F. Harding commanding, landed at Adelaide in the spring of 1942, the natives gave us a warm welcome, because many of their own troops were committed to battle in far-off Africa, and the Japanese on New Guinea seemed eager to continue on down south, and we of the Red Arrow division, green as we were, at least constituted the first American foot soldiers to reach Australia. By that time I had become part of the CG's personal staff and, being able to invoke a major general's name, was no longer afraid of corporals, nor, when it came to that, of brigadier generals.

The other day Bud Benjamin, who's been a Fellow at Columbia's Gannett Center this year, told me he'd seen Bill Shawn on the premises. Bud wondered if he was on the verge of getting a fellow Fellow. Tonight, at Dorothy Sieberling's gathering (for bartending, *she* has a trio of nonacademic girl singers), Judith Gutman says she saw Shawn at the center, too, and she actually asked him what his plans were. She says he said, "I'm going to write something." Sounds reasonable; Bill has always wanted to, but aside from obits in *The New Yorker*, graceful but unsigned, has had little opportunity, and less time.

2 April

The *Times* says the American Association of Retired Persons, which I've thought on and off might make a "Profile" subject, has become the most powerful lobby in Washington. I must enroll to ascertain what kind of influence they exert on, if not Congress, me.

Big news of the day—the *News* gives it both front and back pages—is that Dwight Gooden is checking into Billy Rose's old house on Ninety-third Street for drug rehabilitation. Our neighborhood is getting to be more exciting every day. I don't like to name drop, but let's face it: it was our very own apartment building that Baryshnikov moved into, before he moved out; and our building too, what's more, that Dan Rather was emerging from when he got mugged. Jimmy Breslin writes about visiting a welfare hotel that has a huge portrait of The Doctor on an outside wall and asking its residents if, should they like Gooden earn a million dollars a year, they could keep off drugs. He says they say they could.

Tomorrow I head for Connecticut and the crossword-puzzle tournament. Should I enter it? I didn't when I did a *New Yorker* piece on a backgammon competition at Las Vegas. Roger Angell doesn't play for the Mets, nor Herb Wind in the Masters. Still, somebody was saying the other day that Gottlieb leans more toward participatory journalism than Shawn did. I'll play it—surely there's a better verb to use right now—by ear.

Gottlieb is unquestionably being tougher on "Talk" texts. My piece about Jerry Cohen and the pandas comes through in page proof, and somebody has deleted from it the fact that Jerry's recompense for fifty hours' of work on the project (what would his usual honorarium be: $200 an hour? $300?) was a City of Beijing necktie.

A note from Cynthia Lindsay, in California, to whom I'd written saying how pleased I'd been to learn she gave Bob Gottlieb and me something unexpected in common. I also offered her the use of my office any time she came east. (Sheila and I agreed, after a crazy woman writer actually lived in the office while I was on Cape Cod, and was a somewhat less than fastidious housekeeper, that henceforth it would remain, unless I chose otherwise, inviolate.) Cynnie writes, "I won't be needing your office as I can avoid working right here." Also, referring back to a sort of memoir I published in 1979, "I'm glad and proud to be in your book—put me in another." The woman is absolutely brazen.

Mark Singer wants to know how I feel about the changes in the editing of "Talk." Some of his pieces apparently have had radical surgery, too. I say I am not going to gripe about a mere "Talk" piece because I have a "Profile" going to press soon—my Suzman piece, and my request to appear in the April twentieth issue is evidently going to be granted—and I am more concerned about trying to keep *it* intact. We get to talking about writers' access to proofs, and when I say that I have a piece coming out in *Yankee* and have never laid eyes on it since I turned it in, Mark professes to be shocked and says that if he wanted to earn a living that way he'd go to Hollywood and write movies.

Penelope Gilliatt wonders, in another corridor colloquy, of which there have been more this fateful year than I can recall in any other, what *The New Yorker* will be like next year, by which time Gottlieb will presumably have shaped it in his image. Could Newhouse merge it into his *Vanity Fair*, which after all was itself once swallowed up, in an earlier incarnation, by *Vogue*? "Don't think that dreadful thought hasn't occurred," Penelope says. But to whom? I hope not to too many others.

3 April

We keep hearing that the Upper West Side of Manhattan is becoming as classy as our legendary Upper East, but all along I've scoffed at that. "Show me evidence," I keep demanding. This morning I get it. Our dog-walker habitually gives me an envelope on Thursday containing a reference to our weekly fee. Yesterday's charge was ten dollars higher than the ordinary. I ask her today how come she raised her rates without notifying her clients. But she hasn't, she insists. I show her my bill. "Oh, sorry," she says. "I must have given you a West Side slip by mistake."

Morris Dees calls, from the Southern Poverty Law Center, and I make arrangements to go down to Alabama and start looking into the Ku Klux Klan.

This afternoon, I am off to Stamford, on what I guess is a late commuter train. It's been a long time since I rode one of these. The Stamford Marriott, where I check in after dinner, is the kind of hotel that assumes you're going to steal its clothes hangers. Otherwise, why make them unremovable? My TV set goes on the blink during the final round of "Wheel of Fortune," so I repair to the lobby. It is filled with seated men and women bent grimly over puzzles. I spot Michelle Arnot, who once made me a cover boy, cruciverbially. She says about a hundred and twenty entrants are expected by the time formal competitions start tomorrow. "It's a very small inbred group," she tells me. She's just back from a Vegas convention of people who traffic with newsstands, and Official Publications, where she's now employed, would seem to be engaging in heavy traffic, with such titles as, to name only a few of twenty-seven, *Superb Word-Find*, *Superb Crosswords*, *Superb Word Twists*, *Superb Crosspatches*, *Teen-Word Finds*, *Soap Opera Word-Find*, and *Fill-It-Ins*. Michelle, thirty-three, who once taught a crossword-puzzle course at the New School and is working toward an M.A. at Columbia in, anticlimactically, eighteenth-century French literature, is the author of *A History of the Crossword Puzzle*; and she gives me a copy of her book inscribed in about as head-turning a way as I can imagine: to a "fellow puzzler."

There are some informal jousts this evening. Waiting for them to begin, I meet some of the giants of the sport: a thirty-four-year-old bond analyst at E. F. Hutton, Stanley Newman, who once reputedly solved a daily *Times* puzzle on TV in two minutes and twenty-four seconds (I don't believe I've ever got under five); Merl Reagle, thirty-six, a Californian who tells me,

"I'm the only one who makes a living just constructing crosswords full-time"; Maura Jacobson, the *New York* magazine constructionist, who tells me some of these racing pros are so hooked on saving fractions of seconds that they have figured out a way to write the letter "e" with the fewest possible number of strokes; and Will Schortz, editor of *Games* magazine. He is thirty-three and he retired from competition seven years ago, undefeated, after winning a crossword marathon.

It is time for fun and games. There is an empty chair at a table occupied by two ladies: Rebecca Wenger and her mother Renée. Rebecca, thirty-six, who does the daily *Times* puzzle in four minutes, is a three-time winner of the United States Open, which seems to be closed this year for lack of a sponsor. Over the last five years, she has taken home $4,000 in prize money—an exceptional record. (The *total* prize money here is $1000. "Games of the mind," Stan Newman tells me, "don't receive sponsorship like games of the body.") We take in a chalk talk by Mel Taub, the Sunday *Times* puns-and-anagrams man. He informs us proudly that he is the innovator of "stuttering" definitions. I.e.: "It follows M-may," ans., "Jejune"; and "C-car," ans., "Afford." Taub is wearing a necktie, as befits a good *Times* man. When he asks, "Is there anybody here who doesn't know how to solve a 'Puns and Anagrams'?" there are hoots of laughter. Does he think he's in a roomful of neophytes?

4 April

No dog to rouse me here, but out of habit I am wide awake at six. There's no Sunday *Times* here on Saturday, so I have a choice between Michelle's book and, on my resuscitated TV set, ladies' arm wrestling.

In midmorning, after some welcoming words from Ms. Arnot, the real stuff gets under way. The odds-on favorites for the highest cumulative scores in all events are David Rosen and his roommate Ellen Ripstein. They both work for the Metropolitan Life Insurance Company. His best time for the *Times* daily, he tells me, is two minutes and forty-five seconds; for the Sunday, he aims at ten. My best there is fourteen. I decide to retain my amateur status and remain a spectator.

There is little for me to do while the contestants are jabbing away all day long at one puzzle after another, so I join the fray, though unofficially, and am pleased to note that while no kind of match for the likes of a Rosen or a Ripstein, I finish each challenge round well ahead of two-thirds of the pack. Holding up one completed puzzle in simulated triumph, I am approached by a young woman who says she would appreciate an interview for a local newspaper. My adrenaline begins to flow. When she learns a moment later that I am merely another reporter, she turns on her heel and goes off to look for a more promising subject.

5 April

Page one of the Sunday *Stamford Advocate* has a banner headline: "It's Marathon Day!" But that refers, disappointingly, to some sort of outdoors rivalry among people on foot.

The top three finishers in yesterday's sedentary races will meet in a final this morning. Two of them, as predicted, are Rosen and Ripstein, and if they come in first and second (they tie for first), I already have a subhead for *The New Yorker* account I plan to turn in on the high drama: "The Dave and Ellen Show." I can't stay to the bitter end but hang around long enough to hear Maura Jacobson, who is presenting awards (mostly dictionaries), announce, "And in first place, of course . . . ."

6 April

At 6:30 this morning, I actually have to wake Hopi. Perhaps the weekend switch to daylight saving has disturbed her inner clock.

Dave Schwarz phones. He has been mulling over our lunch with Gerry Piel, about the class-reunion seminars, and has concluded that Gerry and I gave him a hard time—this is news to me—because of the difference of our cultures. How's that again? He is a scientist, Dave explains, and scientists take things seriously. Piel and I are different. We don't take things seriously. We are entertainers. Fine with me, but how would Gerry—the founder of the *Scientific American*—respond to that?

Today's *Post*, in an item about the impending arrival at Alfred A. Knopf of a successor to Bob, leads off with "Now that *New Yorker* staff temper tantrums are no longer noteworthy . . . ." Thank God.

Dinner at the Rolf Myllers', along with Lee Leggett, who translated the stage version of *Les Misérables*. How many authors get to see their works on sale in theater lobbies? I came close a couple of years ago, when the musical *Harrigan 'n Hart* opened on Broadway. It was based on my *The Merry Partners*. I'd been under the impression that I'd sold all my dramatic rights to Josh and Nedda (Harrigan) Logan years before. It turned out that I'd kept one percent of something, three-quarters of which I had consigned to my three sons. Broadway musicals gross so much these days that my sliver of the gate, had the show been a hit, would have come to a tidy sum. (Meanwhile, I had acquired and cut in two stepsons, so now David and Lexy each had a one-eighth stake in the proceeds.) Ellie and I went with Nedda and her daughter Ann Connolly, who'd done research for me on the book, to a tryout of the show in Connecticut, and while we weren't transported we had hope. So did we right up to opening night. I even hired a limousine to take Ellie and my sisters and me from the performance to a bang-up after-theater celebration at the Tavern on the Green. But there was never much chance for my book to be displayed in the lobby, for after a few previews and a handful of other stagings, the curtain went down for good. Even so, I believe each of the boys made enough to pay for a pair of good seats down front to some show somewhere.

7 April

I suppose it stands to reason that I dreamt about the Logans last night. Nedda and Josh were still living at River House, all right, but you had to approach the place (I had a guide with a flashlight) via a dirt path through a thickly wooded forest. That was one way, of course, of bypassing Le Perigord, which reminds me that it's been three months and a day without a peep out of the publisher who was a no-show at lunch.

I was going to start organizing my crossword notes, but along comes another page-proof revise of the Suzman "Profile," and I have to spend nearly the entire day fussing over that with Bill Knapp and Dusty Mortimer-Maddox. One section that I'd heard Bob wanted cut is still there. I hope he has so many other things on his mind that his memory's been cut.

Ellie picks me up in a cab on the northwest corner of Forty-fourth and Fifth, our usual rendezvous point for downtown passage, and we pay our respects to some Soho paintings of nudes Lachaise might have deemed overweight. Then we reverse our field and come all the way back uptown to our block, for supper at Judith Rothschild's, who has taken a four-story Park-Avenue structure and revamped it spectacularly. Many art people present, logically, digging into her no less spectacular buffet. John Bernard Myers is eager to share his version of the real story about the Van Gogh being auctioned off for close to $40 million. Myers says the purchasers must be the Contras, because they're the only people around who have that kind of money.

8 April

Palmer Williams phones. He is relieved to be out of "60 Minutes," now that some of CBS's people are on strike and that Andy Rooney, sympathizing with them, is publicly scrapping with Don Hewitt. Andy—suspended without pay, but, considering how well his books sell, probably solvent—has been getting flak for telling Larry Tisch, for all the world to hear that cares to listen, that CBS belongs, in spirit, to the people who work for it. What a relief, for a change, to have the crybaby label pinned on some other enterprise!

The *Village Voice*, in an April-Fool story about *The New Yorker* that I just now see, has Si Newhouse at a press conference on the street outside Elaine's, announcing that Gottlieb was only a stopgap and that Clay Felker is taking us over. The spoof bears the byline of Ellen Willis. In what was in my view one of Shawn's rare aberrations, evidently aspiring to trendiness, he hired Willis one summer as a rock-music critic. This was before my office was declared off-limits to transient females. When I came back in the fall, the room was tidy enough; the only visible alteration was an extra filing cabinet. I was sitting at my desk a few days later when a notably unattractive young woman walked in, and without saying by your leave or anything else, started rummaging through that cabinet. She kept at it for a good five minutes, and then, still without a "How do you do?" or an "Excuse me," or a nod, walked out. I learned then what it means to describe yourself as a mere stick of furniture. Or could it be that she's an uncompromising misanthrope? On the other hand, to give her the retroactive benefit of the doubt, maybe she was shy.

A communication from *Time* is not, as I'd assumed, a subscription-renewal notice. Rather, it's a *"Time* Subscriber Survey"—"For internal use only," in bright red—inquiring whether they have the correct listing for my title and industry status. My latter is "Publishing," and my former is "Technical Specialist." So that's what *Time* thinks I've been all along! *The New Yorker* doesn't much go in for categories, but the last time Sheila had some business cards made up, she was gracious enough to dub me a Staff Correspondent.

A triumph over the White House, no less! In my Suzman piece, I had the celebrated Zulu Chief Gatshar Buthelezi meeting President Reagan in the Oval Office shortly before Thanksgiving. Dusty, routinely checking that assertion, phoned the White House media office and was connected with a woman who (1) had never heard of Buthelezi and (2) said he hadn't been there since 1975. So Dusty, quite properly, had deleted my statement. But I can't believe I'd invented it. (Not that, over the years, I haven't unintentionally made things up.) So I go to our file of the *Times* on microfilm—luckily, our most up-to-date reel goes through last November—and there on the Tuesday before Thanksgiving is a picture of the two leaders precisely where and when I said they were. Dusty says she is going to call the White House back and give them hell. Checkers, by the time a "Profile" gets locked up, often know the subject as well as its author does. Dusty, who has been talking to Mrs. Suzman in Johannesburg, Cape Town, London, and elsewhere, says they've just had another chat. I suggest that by now she may be better acquainted with the lady than I am. "Yes," says Dusty. "We talk about our cats." I didn't even know Helen had one.

Maxine Sullivan is dead, at seventy-five. I go to the office library to see what, if anything, I wrote about her when I was the magazine's nightclub critic. The clippings are not in my own scrapbook, because we columnists used aliases then. Mine was "Check." (Appropriate, because *The New Yorker* always insisted that I pay my own way and not get beholden to any spot I frequented. I would often find myself fighting off free drinks.) The pages of the "Tables for Two" scrapbook are brittle. The first of twenty-seven such departments signed by Check—twenty-seven! I had no idea there'd been that many—is dated August 5, 1939, and in that column I discovered the Revuers (Betty Comden, Adolph Green, Judy Holliday, et al.) but didn't give any of them a name. (They were all then kids, like me.) My last coverage ran in the issue of July 12, 1941, by which time I'd already been sworn into the army. I'm curious to see how many times I mentioned Ms. Sullivan, to whom I listened purringly through so many smoke-filled evenings (my own smoke area of course included) at the Onyx Club. To my chagrin, I find that the only time I mentioned her (November 23, 1940) was when she was at the Beachcomber with John Kirby's orchestra. (I'd forgotten, until I saw her obit, that they were married then.) I complained in my critique that the place was too dark, but I'm glad now that I ended that particular column with "I would gladly listen to them even if I had a sack over my head."

9 April

I have been wanting to get my crosswords piece out of the way before I take off for Alabama five days hence, but today, like every other day this week, is largely consecrated to yet another scrutiny of the Suzman piece. Some of the major problems we have to come to grips with: should *The New Yorker*, like South Africans, use the British spelling "Minister of Defence?" And if we use the "c," how do we handle the phrase "defense-appropriation?" Some proofreader in an aerie unapproachable by mere editors and writers wants us, irrationally, to use both. Bill Knapp and I decide to go all the way with "defense," but of course we could be overruled by higher authority tonight. And I would hesitate to hazard how many hours are spent debating whether it should be, as I prefer, "The Gambia," or, as others contend, plain "Gambia." Eleanor Gould, the ultimate arbiter, comes up with another compromise—"the Gambia"—but only after Dusty has called the country's embassy and ascertained that nobody will take the hedge amiss. When *New Yorker* pieces that are far more complicated than this relatively simple account of one person's life are going to press, the finer points take much longer to resolve. Did Shawn warn Gottlieb it was going to be like this?

A Harvard '37 dinner tonight, kickoff for the June reunion. Bill Bentinck-Smith, Bill Haskins, and Steve Stevenson down from Cambridge for the event, bearing the first copy of our 50th anniversary class album—a thick one. Nathan and Anne Pusey favor us with their prestigious presence.

Steve—who's running our reunion, as he ran the university's 350th anniversary last fall—tells us that the president of West Germany is going to be the chief speaker at Commencement. I always thought that was supposed to be kept secret till the last minute. Nate Pusey, who'll be attending his 60th reunion next year, says of our 50th, "Enjoy it, because from here on, the road is down."

10 April

Last evening may have provided a clue to Dwayne Andreas's disaffection. I had described him as saturnine, thinking—without any remonstrances from Eleanor Gould and her vigilant cohorts—that the word means "dark." At the Harvard dinner, Fred Comins, who must have read the piece with unusual thoroughness, handed me a slip of paper with two definitions for the adjective: "having a sluggish, gloomy temperament" and "suffering from lead poisoning." Oh, dear. First thing this morning, I consult my Oxford. "1.a. *Astrol.* Born under or affected by the influence of the planet Saturn. b. Hence, sluggish, cold, and gloomy in temperament. 2. a. Of or pertaining to lead 1669. b. *Path.*, Of disorders: Caused by absorption of lead. Of a patient: Suffering from lead poisoning." Maybe I owe Andreas an apology.

One publisher I always like to have lunch with is Mac Talley—prompt, hospitable, and genuinely interested in promoting his writers' wares. (He was responsible for a book I wrote about the 1970 census—*The American People*.) We meet, as is Mac's wont, at his club Doubles, where he introduces me to a woman whom he identifies sotto voce as the reigning queen of Cuban society in New York. She announces right off that she has been married twice and that that's enough, before either of us, both happily wed, has even hinted at a proposal. Mac has two books of his for me to take away—one about dogs and one about cats. The cloakroom attendant at Doubles apologizes for having merely a Lord & Taylor bag to tote them in; says on better days he'd have a Tiffany. I assure him that I can manage all right, because by coincidence I am heading for Tiffany's, there to buy a bar mitzvah gift for Daniel Traum. My eye is drawn to a silver baseball, with sterling stitching, but I don't dare even ask the price of it; he will have to make do with a money clip.

Ellie and I were bemused by an ad in yesterday's paper for one of Donald Trump's places, this one on Central Park South, with apartments starting at two and a half million and going up. We examined the accompanying floor plan meticulously and could discern no service entrance. Does this mean that the Bill Buckleys or Dick Clurmans or whoever the owners' dinner guests turn out to be will have to enter just as the garbage and trash are going out? I had a letter from a retired army colonel I know out

West, saying he'd had a mild heart attack, and grousing that condominiums advertised in *The New Yorker* start at the ridiculously high price of two hundred thousand dollars. If he ever saw a Trump ad, it could be fatal. Could it be that it was he who arranged for me to hear from the chairman of the Mayor's Veterans Advisory Committee of the City of Los Angeles, who would like to know if I'd be interested in entering a float in a forthcoming parade? It sounds too involved: The use of paper treated with tar or petroleum-base flammable products, for instance, is prohibited, and I would have to flameproof, in an approved manner, all my papier-mâché, corrugated paper, wrapping paper, newspaper, cloth, vegetation, leaves, grass, and palm fronds.

While trying to write about crosswords, I've been mulling over Stan Newman's claim to polish off the daily *Times* one in two minutes and twenty-four seconds. The Suzman "Profile" has finally gone to press, and I know that Bill Knapp has nothing urgent to do for the nonce, so I ask him to hold a stopwatch on me while I fill in letters—there are 187 squares—*at random and without looking at the definitions*. Writing as fast as I can, it takes me one minute and thirty seconds.

We have a couple of small Paul Bowens at Truro. He used to make sculptures out of driftwood, because he couldn't afford any other materials, and he never sold much. At today's opening of a show of his downtown, how heartwarming to hear—what a year for artists!—that it's already sold out. We go on to the 1987 biennial at the Whitney, where the photographs are far more interesting than the exhibits in other media. Richard Tuttle, who once got away with murder here—he tacked a single piece of string across a bare wall and called it art—is back again with more substantial goods, but he hasn't fashioned them into anything I'd want to take home, or buy for a museum, either. We stop for a bite at a little Russian place on Madison Avenue, across the street from a trendy establishment called EATS. Ellie took David there for lunch recently and spent thirty dollars on a couple of sandwiches. You want to be with it, you've got to pay for it.

11 April

Lexy has an opening today, of his photographs, in Santa Fe. I say we should send him a telegram. Ellie: "Can you still send telegrams?" A good question. When did anybody last see a Western Union courier?

Daniel Traum's bar mitzvah runs the gamut from Temple Emanuel to the Tavern on the Green. Dick Waters, who has come down from Newton for the occasion and has changed at our apartment, is amazed to hear that this is only my second bar mitzvah. I had a ball at the first, many years ago in Westchester, in my much younger and much more foolish days, by falsely identifying myself as a second cousin once removed and thus being able to kiss almost anyone in sight. At the Tavern, I am seated next to a woman who is a second-and-once herself, but that, I now discover, can't be an especially close kinship, for when all Danny's relatives are summoned by name to blow out a candle on his cake, she does not get a call. Whoever was hired to write out the table-assignment cards for this emphatically Jewish rite of passage has a beautiful script but has made the same mistake that Ellie and I have grown accustomed to encountering in the Moslem world: we are "Mr. and Mrs. E. J. Khan, Jr."

12 April

It's amazing what one can do under pressure. I have a self-imposed deadline this Sunday to get my puzzle piece written so I can turn it in tomorrow; and I make it, five thousand words' worth, and time left over to help prepare for a dinner party. Columbia sends a girl bartender this time, high-school affiliation undisclosed. The William Jay Smiths are among the guests, and Sonya takes me aside for a confession: I gave them a vial of my beach-plum brandy when they stayed with us on the Cape last summer, and instead of sharing it with Bill she drank it all. Fortunately I still have some, and I pour Bill an ameliorative nip. One has to be careful, dealing with drink. In my Suzman piece, I had her sipping a sherry at the members' bar in Parliament, but she told Dusty she doesn't drink sherry, only Scotch. Knapp and I felt that sounded too strong for a working lady legislator, so we settled on her having "a drink."

13 April

It is Joan's birthday, also Eudora Welty's and—along with the Shawns and a few select others—they are both at my sister's for a celebratory dinner. So is our stepmother, and at one point Lilo says to me, enigmatically, "Your father used to say, 'Nobody knows who wants to sleep with whom.' " Bill S. says he has taken an office in the Brill Building, the songwriters' enclave that Joe Liebling used to write about—within easy walking distance of the Algonquin. He doesn't volunteer what he's using the space for, and nobody puts him on a spot by asking him.

14 April

I am off to Montgomery, Alabama. I check my bag all the way through at La Guardia, and then kick myself, because we leave late, and there is an

Atlanta connection, and getting from one part of that airport to another is like commuting. We are delayed because this is one of those flights that are overbooked, and the airline is trying to bribe already boarded passengers to yield up their seats.

I buy *New York*, to occupy myself in transit with Maura Jacobson's puzzle and also the more challenging one it borrows from the Sunday *Times* in London. The magazine's "Intelligence" column says that Gottlieb has commissioned a couple named Stern to write about a convention out West of people who collect things relating to Scottish terriers. I wish I'd thought of it first. I read that these Sterns are kitsch people, and that they wrote a book about Elvis Presley for Knopf and that they gave Bob the ceramic head of Him that, we all know by now, adorns his desk.

This is my first longish plane trip for Bob, and if he should ask me how it went, I must remember to tell him that nothing has changed: there is yet to be found an airline stewardess—sorry, flight attendant—who when selling drinks has change for a five-dollar bill.

The Southern Poverty Law Center, where I'll be doing most of my research in Montgomery, occupies a new building just up a hill from the Dexter Avenue church of Martin Luther King and just across from the state capital, where the Confederates' Stars and Bars shares flagpole space with the Stars and Stripes. But before going there, I have a get-acquainted lunch with Morris Dees, its director, and Bill Stanton, who runs its aptly named Klanwatch offshoot. We eat at the Elite, which features crab claws, and which is indigenously pronounced, I am urged not to forget, "*Eee-lite.*"

Back in my hotel, late in the afternoon, I talk to Ellie, and we agree that I am tired and should go to bed early. When I hang up, the phone rings. It is Morris Dees, inviting me to a seder at the home of his lawyer friend and colleague J. Richard Cohen. The Cohens' nine-year-old daughter, a northerner from birth, is a manifestly adaptable child, as evidenced when she gives a rollicking imitation of a really deep deep-South accent. Morris's wife is not present. She is attending medical school, and he implores me, since the homicidal right wing has long had him and his on its hit list, not to divulge which one.

15 April

Travel is broadening. At home, I would never think of starting a day by watching Jimmy Swaggart on television. The Reverend is disappointing; he doesn't even directly mention Jim and Tammy Bakker, though in his orisons there are veiled suggestions that even estimable preachers can be seduced.

All day at the center, talking, reading, and setting aside mounds of trial transcripts and other documents to be Xeroxed and studied back north. There's already been one murder conviction, stemming from Klansmen having picked up a young black man in Mobile, torturing and killing him, and then stringing him up on a tree limb; but the trial in which a jury— an all-white one—found the Klan itself institutionally accountable, was a civil procedure. Now Dees and his associates are trying to find out what assets the Klan may have that can be seized to meet at least part of the $7-million judgment levied against it.

I have lunch with Dees in the basement cafeteria of the courthouse down the street from the center. When he began practicing law in Montgomery, the courtroom upstairs was segregated, and no blacks could use the cafeteria. After integration laws were passed, instead of the cafeteria being opened up to all, it was simply closed. Now, in the new South, chumminess seems to prevail—more so, indeed, than in much of the North; black and white cocktail waitresses giggling together at my hotel; a white bar girl deferentially serving a black customer.

Morris Dees, about whom at first I wanted to write a "Profile"—Gottlieb said he'd rather have a piece about the lynching and its aftermath—probably does not fit anyone's preconception of a civil-rights attorney. He can afford to be individualistic, having sold a flourishing direct-mail company for something like $7 million. He affects (except in court) determinedly casual dress. He has spent most of the recent years trying to right wrongs against blacks; he also took out after a black university for denying tenure, apparently on grounds of color, to a white professor. He scorns what he calls fern bars, preferring to shoot pool at redneck ones. Over the years, he has been on affable enough personal, if not professional, terms with a few far-right-wing ideologues. To most of them, however, he is anathema. One noted extremist once challenged him to a duel to the death. Dees's former headquarters was severely damaged by arsonists, and according to some of the Ku Klux Klan literature I've read while rummaging through his files, he is the very incarnation of evil.

16 April

Another day mostly hunched over a Southern Poverty Law Center desk. Very tight security here, and no wonder, considering the ardor of some of its enemies. Electronically controlled iron gates for automobiles, closed-circuit television for scrutinizing individuals, bullet-resistant window glass. I've been given an office next to Morris's and note that another of his quirks is that although the place is well appointed and well staffed he elects to do his own typing. Greetings, brother. I suppose every human being of a certain age or more entertains fantasies—involving travel, money, sex, whatnot. Mine is now and then to wonder how my working life might be improved, or at any rate different, if, like most of my contemporaries, I had a secretary. But when I come back down to earth I force myself to admit that if I had one she would be spending a good deal of her time twiddling her thumbs or looking out of a window.

17 April

One more day at the center, more reading, more briefing. Patricia Clark, chief of research, overcomes my weak demurrers and drives me to the airport. "Southern hospitality," she says, though she knows that I know she comes from New Jersey.

On the Delta flight out of Atlanta, you can make a phone call from your seat, with a credit card. Whoever in the phone company thought this one up deserves a bonus, but I suspect that in the long run the innovation may not benefit any airline; surely a fair number of the calls made will be to convey the information that the goddamn flight has once again been inexplicably and insufferably delayed.

The woman sitting next to me is a fund-raiser for a university, and we swap some memorable experiences in her line of work. One of my contributions to the exchange is painful to relate: how last summer, when I was soliciting for our Truro art center, I managed to make a date to call on a reluctant prospect unarguably gilt-edged; Harvard had him listed in its $100,000-or-more category of supporters. I visited him at night, in a driving rainstorm, and after making a pitch that, I thought, moved him from cold to at least lukewarm, I started backing down his steep narrow driveway. I slid off and knocked over a fencepost. He sent a check for $100. It could have been worse, I suppose; he could have billed me for the damage.

18 April

The New Yorker with my Suzman piece in it is awaiting me at home. For my sixtieth birthday, Bill Shawn had thoughtfully dug up a copy of the magazine with my very first piece in it and had encased it in a handsome cloth portfolio. I want this April 20, 1987, issue to snuggle up against what I've been describing to everybody, Bob Gottlieb not excluded, as my debut issue of April 19, 1937. I remember where in a living-room bookcase the folder has been shelved. When I open it up, I am stunned. I'm supposed to be a *reporter*? I'm supposed to be able to handle *facts*? The date on that 1937 number is not even close to April nineteenth; it is April third. I am mortified. That is the bad news. The good news is that I began writing for *The New Yorker* even longer ago than I thought I had.

We go to see James Earl Jones portraying an old-time Negro baseball player in *Fences*, getting, our ticket broker has told us proudly, the last two seats in the house for this Saturday matinee. (It has just won the Pulitzer Prize.) Very moving. Nancy Milford grumbles in the lobby entr'acte that the blacks depicted in it are stereotypical, but then the play is set in 1957, when things were different, and if Jones's role doesn't upset him, it'll pass with me. Strange to be seeing this while I'm immersed in the affairs of the Ku Klux Klan. Ellie expressed surprise on the way to the theater that I was unfamiliar with the name of a so-called artist whose "art" consists, it seems, of masturbating beneath floorboards that his audiences are treading. I feel less embarrassed about my ignorance when it develops that E., who has never pretended to be a sports fan, is equally unfamiliar with Josh Gibson and Roberto Clemente.

When we get home, we find a cluster of balloons outside our door. They are from Ann Garrity, in honor of my fiftieth anniversary at the magazine. I see no reason to advise her that, because of my own stupidity, she is more than two weeks late.

19 April

We had a scare in the middle of the night. Hopi, highly unusual for her, began growling and barking. Then Ellie whispered to me that there was somebody standing in our bedroom doorway. It turned out to be Ann Garrity's hydra-headed bouquet of balloons, which had drifted over from the hallway ceiling. But how reassuring to discover that our placid pet can be a watchdog after all!

Today, while it has proven to be no anniversary of mine, is both Easter Sunday and Patriot's Day, and maybe for one or both reasons the *Times* hasn't yet been delivered when I take our ferocious guardian out at seven. When the paper finally arrives (ours had been misdelivered, and the one we get has a Sunday *News* tucked inside it, like contraband), there's a story in it to the effect that volunteer fire companies are dwindling and may in this part of the world soon be extinct. I was a member of the Scarborough Fire Company for several years, kept the minutes of its meetings, was entitled to a flashing blue light on the front of my car, actually fought a few fires, and, as long as I remained in good standing, was exempt from jury duty. Since moving to New York City, I've been summoned time and again. I got nailed for a whole month on a grand jury last year. We were offered nothing but narcotics cases, and nearly every one consisted of nothing more exciting than a couple of cops—usually plainclothes ones, looking in their disguises as disreputable as any pusher—testifying about picking up so and so (to us jurors, never a body, always a mere name) with so and so many grams of such and such substance on his or her person. After the age of seventy, I am happily aware, one has the option of serving or not. My contemporary, Palmer Williams, whom I have always thought of as omniscient, was surprised when I informed him of his rights.

The April 20, 1987, *New Yorker* costs one dollar and seventy-five cents (the price got raised—hardly his fault—for the very first Gottlieb-edited issue), and it consists of 104 pages, each slightly smaller, both horizontally and vertically, than its 1937 (fifteen cents) counterpart. The current table of contents promises, after the "Talk of the Town," an Updike short story, poems by John Ashbery and Susan Mitchell; Edith Oliver, Andrew Porter, and Pauline Kael on, respectively, theater, music, and cinema; and a "Reflections" piece about Freud, by Janet Malcolm. Cover by William Steig, cartoons by him and twenty-one others. Plus my Suzman "Profile."

The April 3, 1937 *New Yorker* had 102 pages and a cover by Alajálov. The very first advertisement was for the Hamburg-American Line, North German Lloyd, owners of the *Bremen* and the *Europa*. (My grandparents sailed on both.) There was no index of signed articles, but Bill Shawn helped me out in 1976 by enclosing a birthday card that said, in his so recognizable cramped hand, "Recalling page 82 and hundreds of other beautiful pages . . . ." There were cartoons by Rea Irvin, Peter Arno, and Charles Addams, who isn't in my 1987 issue but is still very much on our scene. Theater by Robert Benchley. Signed articles by John O'Hara, James Thurber, and Wolcott Gibbs. Gibbs's "Profile" of Burgess Meredith runs only fourteen columns, which nowadays would be merely an extended lead. Since all pieces tended to be shorter then, there was room in this issue for a host of contributors: Lewis Mumford, Howard Brubaker, Richard Lockridge, Lois Long, Robert A. Simon, John Mosher, Margaret Fishback, Clifton Fadiman—what an all-star cast! I don't remember when *The New Yorker* banned cigarette advertising, but it was less than half a century ago; the center spread is a two-page ad for Camels. Each of the four women in it is lunching with a man at the Marguery, and each is wearing a hat. The ad seems to suggest that what fashionable ladies do is to light up a Camel between—people lunched well then—the caviar and the squab. There were 184 columns of advertising altogether. This week's issue has 130½. But I'm sure our rates have gone up.

Tony and Judy are going to be in New York next weekend, and I've decided to take Ian and Matthew to the circus. I call their paternal grandmother and ask if she thinks I can handle them by myself. Jinny says it might be foolhardy, but I am willing to risk it. Matthew is a year older than he was at St. Bart's, and there should be no trouble if I don't lose track of his security blanket. I have a strategy. I aim to announce at the outset that I will be in charge of Ian and he will be responsible for his younger brother.

20 April

I get to the office at nine, and at ten Gottlieb calls. He likes my crossword-puzzle piece but wants to discuss the lead and the end. When? Is right now OK? So I go upstairs, and we have a talk so leisurely that I neglect to clock it but that must have lasted close to fifteen minutes. I had put Rita Gam and her incessant appearance in puzzles into my piece; Bob says surely we can dispense with that, inasmuch as I'd already done that in *About* The New Yorker *and Me*. I had? He knows my book better than I do. So it's good-bye Rita. Bob ruminates. He says it feels strange after book publishing—where there are reviews and author tours and queries about foreign rights and paperbacks and everything—to be in a business where there's so little feedback. (Of course, if we had a letters-to-the-editor department there'd be more.) Another difference, he says, is that in book publishing authors and editors work together both for glory and increased profits, whereas a magazine writer's goal is simply to get a piece written and paid for and printed. Seems like a worthy enough goal to me, but I don't interrupt. Bob goes on to assure me that it is erroneous, as some people have alleged, to think of him as having preconceptions against lengthy articles. In fact, when he was plowing through every 1986 *New Yorker*, there was at least once when he wished a "Profile" had been even longer. He wants my opinion of how things are going in general. I say all right, as far as I know, but we down on the eighteenth floor aren't really much in on things. I gather from his relaxed air that in his view everything is going along as well as could be expected.

Ellie phones. She's just heard from her publisher that her *On Glory Roads* is being given an excellent review in next Sunday's *Times*. Thames & Hudson will get it for her tomorrow. The hell with tomorrow. I call Edith Oliver, but our copy hasn't arrived yet. Sheila gets one by sending a messenger over to the *Times*. It's a handsome review indeed. The publication party I am going to be co-host of is beginning to look more and more festive.

21 April

Matthew Smith is spending a week with us, while his parents travel. I don't know what Betty and Patrick have told him about our reliability, but he has brought along his own alarm clock.

It's a springlike day, so hoping it will make a "Talk" piece, I take a stroll from Forty-fourth Street up the west side of Fifth Avenue to Fifty-seventh, and back down the east side. I note en passant that Fifty-second Street, where the *New Yorker*'s prewar Check stubbed out so many Camels, is still known as Swing Street, though it hardly warrants the designation any more. Word is going around that Gottlieb is going to be much more tolerant of strong language than Shawn ever was, but in writing up my notes I don't think we're quite ready yet to quote verbatim what a male motorist just south of the Trump Tower says to a female traffic cop as he revs off in a rage. In case one of my children or grandchildren should ever peek at this, I'm not of a mind to record it here, either.

I have lunch with Alma Triner, of Arthur D. Little. She was largely responsible for my writing its history. *The Problem Solvers* was a Little, Brown venture, and Alma's opinion of the book's publisher is no less heartsick than mine. Alma has quit smoking and says that I—along with, she adds deflatingly, a hypnotist—deserve a lot of credit. Her timing was perfect, it seems, because no sooner had she stopped than the city of Cambridge began cracking down on smoking in workplaces.

I run into Jimmy Greenfield, and he asks me to tell Bob Shaplen he has done the *Times* a favor. Obituaries are one of Jim's responsibilities there, and Shaplen had complained that some worthy citizen's obit seemed unconscionably brief. After looking into the situation, Greenfield concluded that some of the people he had working in that field were too young to have heard much about anyone over the age of fifty. So he has mixed in with them more mature writers—closer-to-senior citizens to whom when the grim day comes the name of a Robert Shaplen, or someone else with a career that deserves earthly memorialization, will at least stand a chance of being recognized.

To Ann Sperry's show at the Sculpture Center. I tell Paul S., whose recitals often consist of *lieder* and the like, that while in Alabama I caught him singing some Rodgers and Hart on "Today." Paul says he wishes he could allot more of his performance time to that kind of music, but I gather he is fated to give his audiences what they're accustomed to. Ellie and I proceed to the Herb Schimmels' apartment, where we are stunned. It's practically a Toulouse-Lautrec museum. Almost every inch of wall space boasts a Lautrec, and there's a library exclusively devoted to writings, Schimmel's among them, about him. Is Herb going to leave this trove to some museum? No, he says, he figures it's his children's and grandchildren's inheritance. And a tidy one indeed it should come to, judging from the appraisal we know he's given to a mere one of the now so visibly prolific master's works.

22 April

I make a round-trip to Cambridge for Return to Harvard Day. It's anything but my first return. There've been three books by now—*The Staffs of Life*, *The Problem Solvers*, and, of course, *Harvard*—that have involved extensive residence in the well-known surroundings. I take the 8:00 A.M. shuttle up and the 6:00 P.M. back, which means I have to forgo an evening lecture at Memorial Hall by Dr. Ruth on "Safer Sex," sponsored by the Harvard/ Radcliffe AIDS Benefit Committee. I assume Dr. Ruth doesn't have to be told, as a bulletin board in the Harvard Hall vestibule soberingly informs rubbernecks, that one out of every thirteen women will be raped in her lifetime. We homecomers are offered a plethora of courses to audit. One that appeals to me is Afro-American Studies 130, partly because it's being given in a Sever Hall room where once I fought the good battle against irregular Greek verbs. But the young woman instructor can't have been expecting many guests (I am her only one); when she passes out copies of a poem she spends her fifty minutes analyzing line by line, she doesn't have one for me. Her closing words, as chapel bells next door began to peal, are "Love poems tomorrow." All this and Dr. Ruth, too!

There's some hideous gray-green stuff smeared over the grass in the Yard—fertilizer, I imagine, to help prettify the area for Commencement. I'm surprised no student environmentalists are picketing the lawn. This day was supposed to have been attended by alumni—members of reunion classes—who graduated in years ending in seven and two, so I am further surprised, when I go back to Sever and a much better attended classroom for American Intellectual History, 1900 to the Present, to see a friend of mine, a celebrated Boston man-about-town, brazenly wearing a 1941 class tie. "Don't tell anybody," Martin Slobodkin says when he realizes I've spotted him, "but I've been taking this guy's course for five years."

Donald Fleming, the doyen of History 1690b, quotes Bill Buckley to the effect that he'd rather be governed by the first two hundred names in the Boston phone book than by the Harvard faculty. After waiting for the predictable laugh, the prof adds drily, "which I must say after attending a great many faculty meetings I do not find preposterous." He gets his second laugh. His third comes at the very end, when after observing that the three American Presidents with the strongest ideological bents—Jefferson, Wilson, and the incumbent—had all found themselves beset by contradictions when they took office, Professor Fleming adds, "If you want to preserve the purity of your ideology, don't become President. Papers due Friday." I wonder if Martin will turn one in.

After lunch, four undergraduates are trotted out on the stage of the Science Center (according to *its* bulletin board, one out of every *eight* college women has *already* been raped), to answer questions about contemporary Harvard. One of the quartet is in an ROTC program and says that at Fort Bragg he had to jump forty feet into a river. "This is the sort of experience that many Harvard students don't take part of," he adds.

Q. from old-timer: "Why don't more undergraduates go to the football games?" Ans., from tall young woman, on track and basketball teams: "We're doing all we can. We need some help from all of you out there."

Q. from another codger: "You people are so much more wonderful than I was. I wonder if anybody like me could get into Harvard nowadays." Ans., tactful, flattering, from young man active in track, basketball, *and* soccer: "I don't think the standards have changed."

Why can't anyone invent a paste-on name tag that won't fall off? There's a fortune to be made out there.

23 April

Gottlieb is giving my crosswords piece to Knapp for editing. Bob says it is time for *The New Yorker* to shed some of its old-world phraseology—specifically, in my case, "I betook myself."

The Fiftieth Anniversary Report (778 pages) of the Harvard Class of 1937 has arrived. I realize that in my entry, while I mention having written books (twenty-five I guess by now), I forgot to say that one of them was *Harvard*.

At the Harvard Club's management meeting this afternoon, Walter Isaacson is kind enough to say my "Profile" on Averell Harriman was very helpful when he and Evan Thomas wrote *The Wise Men*. Broward Craig informs us of new smoking regulations. In the main dining room, smokers will be sequestered next to the sushi bar. No restrictions at the main bar; Broward hopes that will bring it more trade.

To dinner at the Roiphes'. Herman and Anne had a brownstone, but they sold it and bought an apartment. They figured the difference would constitute their children's inheritance. Everybody I encounter seems to be inheritance-minded. If only I could remember where I put my stamp collection and baseball cards!

24 April

It is time to vote for Harvard Overseers and Alumni Association directors. I've been one of the latter, and our class has a proud record when it comes to Overseers: at one time or another, Gerry Piel, Mogie Lazarus, Brent Abel, Ed Gignoux, and maybe one or two others whom memory eludes. This year's ballot lists several candidates who've been nominated by petition, and they've been endorsed by Archbishop Desmond Tutu. These are single-issue candidates, of course, the issue being Harvard's divestment of stocks of corporations that have South African connections. (I was writing in *The New Yorker* about the Reverend Leon Sullivan and the Sullivan Principles long before the current crop of Harvard undergraduates could throw a decent Frisbee.) The Reverend Tutu's right to get involved in our election is explained, tortuously, by his having been the recipient of an honorary degree.

But this seems to be a dangerous precedent to be setting. Are we next going to have nominees for the Presidency of the United States openly supported by the Pope, the Archbishop of Canterbury, or the Lubavitcher Rebbe?

For some years now, a dozen or so members of the class of 1937 have been gathering for a pre-Christmas lunch. We began in the private dining room of the Bowery Savings Bank, when Rusty Crawford was its CEO. Then we moved downtown, where arrangements were made at some posh Wall-Street-lawyers' club by Fag Goodhue. Francis Abbot Goodhue, Jr., and no cracks, please. Lately, it's been a private dining room at the Harvard Club. Last year, Gerry Piel was talking about the Russian edition of his *Scientific American*, and Archer Trench proposed that with our fiftieth reunion coming up maybe we should consider taking a trip, ensemble, with our wives, to the Soviet Union. Gerry has been following up on this, and now he says that if he can recruit seven couples, we may be on, for mid-September. He hopes he can arrange a visit to Novosibirsk, in Siberia, and to its suburb Akademgorodok, a scientific city carved out of the wilderness twenty years or so ago. I've been to the USSR twice—in 1958, with Jinny, and in 1980, to cover the Moscow Olympics—but it would be a novel experience for Ellie, and I tell Gerry to put us on his list.

25 April

Another Return Day—this time to Horace Mann, to celebrate the school's hundredth anniversary. One of the discussion panels on the program features four alumni who are *New Yorker* contributors: Bruce Bliven, Gerry Jonas, Ed Koren, and myself. Ed said yesterday that he was going to retrace his steps and take the subway to the end of the line at Van Cortlandt and walk up the hill. Bruce and I are older and opt for a cab and get lost—well, it's been fifty-four years and we didn't go to school by taxi—after turning off the Henry Hudson Parkway and don't get our bearings until, after quite a bit of circumnavigation, we espy the familiar old subway station. Lots of familiar old faces, too, when we finally make it up the hill: Al Josephy, Tony Lewis, Justin Kaplan, Larry Lader, and Morris Lasker, who has suddenly evolved from a kid in Mr. Nagle's Greek class to a senior federal judge.

Lawrence Van Gelder, H.M. '49, of the *Times*, has been designated moderator of our session. He says beforehand that he wants us to talk seriously about the relationship between the contributors to and owners of the magazine and what pressures, if any, may be exerted by the one faction on the other. That was not what any of us had in mind. We'd intended to be anecdotal. We do our best to please both our mentor and ourselves. Later, somebody says that a woman sitting down front is married to a Newhouse. She was attentive enough but kept mum.

26 April

This is turning into something of a children's weekend. Yesterday afternoon there was a show of Laurent de Brunhoff's Babar illustrations, and today is circus day. Tony assured me that Matthew won't need his security blanket; they didn't even bring it to New York. Ellie reminds me as I'm about to take off that the last time I made such a safari, with my stepsons when they were at the Babar stage, I escorted them out toward the street afterward without noticing that David had left one of his shoes behind and that we had to breast the stream of exiting traffic to retrieve it. I make a mental note to check on that before we leave our seats.

Jinny would have been proud of our grandsons. Both of them behave beautifully, no fussing, no demanding souvenirs, though this indulgent grandfather would have felt remiss in not noticing Ian's covetous look at a fright mask and Matthew's imploring reach toward a sword. And there is no gluttonish gobbling of refreshments—merely a hot dog here, some Coke there, a sampling of snow ice, a plunge into cotton candy, that sort of routine thing. As for the circus itself, there are the usual tigers and tumblers (Olympic gymnasts are just as good, if not better) and a lot of fancy costumes and blaring music. Ian is learning to be skeptical: we are introduced to an elephant billed, nay trumpeted, as the earth's largest land mammal, but Ian wonders how they can be sure there isn't another one somewhere in Africa yet to be discovered, let alone delivered to a circus. The clowns don't strike me as being as funny as yesteryear's (whatever happened to the miniature car that disgorged a dozen of them?), and maybe NOW has got after Ringling Brothers, because we are treated to none of the traditional Maggie-and-Jiggs-type stuff, with men and women engaged in mock battle. A surfeit of bicycles (but, curiously, nary a unicycle), and commendable aerialists. But not until I get home and Ellie asks how the high-wire acts had been do I realize there wasn't a single one. I did remember to count shoes.

27 April

Inasmuch as Gottlieb wants to stay away from fancy words, like "peruse" for "read," when Knapp and I are going over Bob's own proof of my crosswords piece, I do him the favor of deleting a "gratified" that he had inserted somewhere and substituting "pleased."

Publishers Weekly says that Little, Brown is going to celebrate its 150th birthday—here's an anniversary I didn't even know about when this telltale year began—with a bang-up party at the Metropolitan Museum on April thirtieth. My invitation must have gone astray.

Lunch with Bob Wolf, who hasn't made a class reunion yet, but says

Peggy and he are going to the fiftieth. We catch up on children. His physician son Tommy, living in Tucson, has a specialty new to me: neuroophthalmology. Bob says they may not be able to stay for the entire reunion because there's an overlapping gathering in California of the American Clock Association, which he naturally would not wish to finesse. (There cannot be too many of my acquaintances who boast a grandfather's clock that actually belonged to a grandfather. I've always believed that mine—an English Tiffany one, no less—was an engagement or wedding present to my maternal grandparents. Let's see: my mother was born in 1892, so we are talking about circa 1890, and our clock—assuming it was brand-new then—will soon be a centenarian. When Jinny and I were divorced, she got all the furniture, not unreasonably, from our Scarborough house. She had the clock at her city apartment for a dozen years or more, and never wound it. When she moved to Boston, she gave it back to me. Through my college roommate Bob Wolf, a clock buff from way back, we found a man to get it running again. Ellie had one caveat: it was to be allowed to strike only on the hour and not, as before, on the quarter and half hours. Different wives, different strikes.) Bob's also scheduled to visit Vienna, in connection with a Freud museum he's been instrumental in launching in London. Apparently Kurt Waldheim was helpful when he was at the United Nations. But just today the president of Austria has been declared persona non grata by the United States, and Austria has recalled its ambassador to Washington, and Bob's Vienna excursion may be less *gemütlich* than he'd anticipated.

The *New York Woman* has a long feature, aptly titled "Koch's Nemesis," on Andy Logan, who is quoted as saying that she has the rare privilege of being allowed to call Shawn "Bill." The magazine also says that Bob Gottlieb once laid out a toy town, called Normalsville, at Knopf, and it wonders if he'll do something of the same sort at his new location.

I'd invited Mona Simpson for a drink at the Century today, having forgotten until I went there that this is a jazz-concert evening. So when she arrives we repair to the Harvard Club. Her novel *All the Way Home*, which has forty thousand copies in print, is published by Knopf, but while she likes Gottlieb he wasn't her editor. Mona reveals that she is the offspring of a Syrian father and a Jewish mother. She also says, wistfully, that all the men she dates seem to be Jewish and watch Monday-night football. Do I have any available sons? Well, Joey is going to be in town next week for Ellie's book party, so I ask Mona to stop by. Only trouble is, if I know Joey, any Monday night he's not tied up he's probably going to be watching football. And although it could be argued that he's not Jewish (if you want to be technical, this is a maternal inheritance, and Jinny's solid Gentile lineage has been traced back well into the seventeenth century), his surname isn't Khan, either.

This evening, at home, Ellie and I discuss how much liquor we should order for the book party. I propose that we calculate what I'm apt to consume and multiply by two hundred—roughly the number we've invited. Ellie says, not unkindly, that if we did that we'd have so much left over we'd never have to stock up again as long as we live.

28 April

Jinny phones. She's going to be in New York next week, staying with the Palmer Williamses, and can we have lunch? Of course. While I am at it, I invite her to the party for Ellie. Why not? I doubt, though, that I'll ever get to where Phil Hamburger is. He sometimes shows up at parties with his wife on one arm and his ex-wife on the other.

We'll be going to press soon with my crosswords piece, and I step into the Checking Department and ask whether there are any major hang-ups. Only that Michelle Arnot has advised that David Rosen and Ellen Ripstein have split. Bill Knapp says not to worry; we are reporting an event that took place at a specific time; but even so, we make a few changes, including a reference to "his Ellen." Young people being the way they are, mind you, they may have made up before we go to press.

When today's first-run issue is delivered, I note with pleasure that the issue—healthy for this time of year—measures 158 pages. My enthusiasm ebbs when I perceive that 44 of these make up a single advertising insert, for European travel. Once I've tugged this out and thrown it away, the magazine seems dismayingly thin.

29 April

On the bus going downtown, there is a nasty exchange between a beggar in a wheelchair and the driver, whom the handicapped man accuses of failing to have let him off, by coming around and lowering the step, at his chosen destination. They are both black and apparently have had run-ins before, because at one point the driver yells at the passenger that if he ever pulls out a screwdriver again, he'll leave the bus more precipitously than he expects to. I suspect there's more of this sort of confrontational dialogue in New York these days, regardless of race or color, than in, say, Montgomery, Alabama.

Well, what do you know? In the mail, a letter from the Little, Brown guy. He has instructed their credit manager not to send me any more bills. "I still owe you a lunch," he writes, "but am leaving for Europe and will not be back until the middle of May, when I will call you to join me for a repast." (Bob G. would not go along with that "repast.") But going to Europe? Don't tell me he didn't get invited to the Little, Brown shindig at the Met, either.

The latest edition of *Winners & Sinners*, the commentary on proper usage that Ted Bernstein initiated for his colleagues on the *Times* years ago and has since been made accessible to us hangers-on, goes into the question of the appropriateness of putting ethnicity into articles. Bill Knapp and I have had to come to grips with that. Of the three finalists in the crossword-puzzle tournament, one was black. What made him even more special was that among the 118 paid-up entrants, he was the solitary black. Even so, did the color of his skin have anything to do with his puzzle-solving talent? Without consulting anyone else, Bill and I decide that it didn't.

When I return to the office after lunch, there is a substitute receptionist, girl I don't know, at our eighteenth-floor desk. She is chatting with messenger-in-chief Bruce Diones. She has a message for me and calls out, "Hey, sir!" Bruce looks at her and looks at me and—Gottlieb has infested this place with a heady informality—says to her, "Sir? *Jack!*"

Helen Suzman phones from South Africa. She likes the piece. She seems to be suffering as only an authentic liberal can. Radical students at her alma mater, the University of Witwatersrand, have protested against her speaking there, on the ground that she is too conservative; and her right-wing adversaries have called her a Communist. She expects to be reelected notwithstanding, but by a narrower margin than heretofore, in part because *Time* has run a photo of her with Winnie Mandela's arm around her.

I am off to Cambridge again for, as Helen was interested to hear, a meeting on the South African press sponsored jointly by Harvard's Nieman Foundation and the African-American Institute. I have to make a phone call at La Guardia, because coming down in the elevator at the office, Joe Cooper, our house lawyer, said he was worried about that "Dave and Ellen Show" subtitle. It doesn't matter that they broke up after I left Stamford, Joe says; people offended by the out-of-date subtitle could accuse me of—he didn't specify how long the jail term might be but he looked grave—prior knowledge. In a hasty airport conference with Bill Knapp, we agree to switch to "Cobble and Tenk," two crossword answers to which few people could object, since who in his right mind would have heard of either of them before?

Funny coincidence department: Looking for a taxi to take me to La Guardia, I called out to one cab driver who was disgorging a fare, "Are you free?" When I got in, he turned—he may be an unemployed magazine editor—and said, "I wasn't free. I was available." At the airport, I pick up a copy of the *Financial Times* and turn to its crossword—usually, for me, a tough one. The definition for 11 down is "Available, if the price is about right," and the answer is "free." ("Fee" around "r" for "right"—get it?)

Cocktails and dinner in Cambridge at the Faculty Club, where one of the Niemans tells me that Bill McKibben is not coming back to *The New Yorker*. I greet Kay Fanning, our hostess in Alaska in 1976, when she edited the *Anchorage Daily News*; now, as editor of the *Christian Science Monitor*, Kay is consequential in mainland journalism. (She is, among other things, president of the American Society of Newspaper Editors). But the newspaper person I am most anxious to meet is Joseph Lelyveld, once the South African correspondent of the *Times* and now its foreign editor. I have a special reason for introducing myself; twice over the years he has reviewed books of mine for the Sunday *Times*, and both of them left him cold. I want to get to know him so that if and when he's offered another such assignment he can say that he probably shouldn't take it on because we're acquainted. Before the evening is out I am obliged to admit to myself that he seems a very decent sort.

Senator Paul Simon, the dinner speaker, apologizes for having to rush off immediately after having his say to catch a plane, which is probably as good an indication as any that he is running for President. He thinks change in South Africa is possible. He cites Montgomery, Alabama, and Martin Luther King as one example. He calls South Africa a "great testing place today" for the survival of humanity.

30 April

This conference is, to be sure, one of those exercises where believers are trying to exhort the already persuaded; but even so, the participants are well worth listening to. Some black South African journalists who might have been particularly illuminating weren't allowed to leave home. But Anthony Sampson, former (and white) editor of *The Drum* magazine, is here. So is the Afrikaner Harald Pakemdorf, who says, "I think very soon— within my lifetime—we will have a black government." Zwelakhe Sisulu, editor of the *New Nation*, one of the liveliest of the so-called alternative papers over there, is in prison, but his business manager has made it to Cambridge and reports that to avoid running afoul of the law—there are, of course, scads of relevant laws—a prudent journal submits its copy, before publication, not only to its own attorney but to its printer's lawyer and its distributor's lawyer.

During a morning coffee break, I chat with a Nieman Fellow from Thailand, chief subeditor of the *Bangkok World*, who says he expects to get home for his King's sixtieth birthday, when the Royal Barge procession will be held. Ah, yes, I say, Jinny and I happened to witness the parade along the Chao Phraya River of dazzling red-and-gold dragon-shaped vessels in 1964, purely by good fortune; we'd only arrived at Bangkok the night before the annual spectacle. It turns out we were luckier than we'd realized. The subeditor says it's not annual at all; the last one was in 1983.

Nadine Gordimer, whom I first met in South Africa in 1966, when I was persona grata, is the lunch speaker. Beforehand, she asks about Bob Gottlieb, who was her editor at Knopf, and then says she liked my Helen Suzman piece with one exception—that I echoed the opinion that if any South African deserved the Nobel Peace Prize, Helen might have been a worthier choice than Bishop Tutu. In her remarks, Nadine speaks of the South African authorities doing violence to the human word as well as to human bodies—physical violence, too. She is a director of a liberal publishing house, the Raven Press, and it was bombed, and when she went to an emergency board meeting she was struck by the smell of burnt paper, and there was one pile of charred books on the floor, titled *To Kill a Man's Pride*. "This is what they were trying to do," she says, "trying to kill the word."

At lunch, I am seated next to a young black woman from Virginia, working for the African-American Institute, who knows how to catch an ear. She says *The New Yorker* changed her life. An older sister gave her a two-year subscription to the magazine, and after reading every word of every issue (I'm not sure anybody except Bill Shawn has ever done that for 104 straight weeks), she decided to head north and go to Princeton.

After lunch, Lelyveld comes over and sits next to me. I interpret this to mean he is sorry for his past sins, seeks atonement, craves absolution. Since he is the son of a distinguished rabbi, I will try to proceed cautiously. Joe tells me—see, I am calling him "Joe" already, he is all but home free—that when he was in South Africa and had a date one time to visit an Afrikaner farmer, he was invited to spend the night. But, he told his prospective host, he was bringing along a friend. Fine, fine, both of you stay. Well, Joe went on, let's decide that after we arrive. The friend was black. They arrived, were greeted hospitably, and were well fed, but there was no further talk of staying the night.

I decide to skip a windup cocktail party, take the T from Harvard Square to Logan, and discover on arriving at the Eastern terminal at six-twenty that the five o'clock shuttle hasn't left yet, let alone the six—something about winds at La Guardia. I am one of the earlier check-ins for the *seven* o'clock, though, and thus manage to squeeze aboard the six o'clock when it leaves its gate at seven-twenty.

1 May

Terry phones. He spent time—agreeably—with Jimmy Carter last evening, in the course of some research Ter's doing for a piece on Evelyn Murphy. Evelyn who? He is surprised at me. Evelyn Murphy, that's who—Lieutenant Governor of Massachusetts, first woman ever elected to statewide office there, and if Governor Mike Dukakis ("You've heard of *him*, Dad, I hope," said with a trace of pity) goes to Washington in some high capacity or other, she would of course become. . . . Terry switches to a subject he knows will be more familiar to me, I having raised five sons: between soccer and Little League baseball, his Ely has four games and three practices coming up this week alone.

At the office, Bill Knapp says one of our feminist editors complained that he and I are male chauvinist pigs because in my crossword-puzzle piece, referring to David Rosen, I used the phrase "his Ellen." Bill was able to retort that we'd already changed that, though he saw no need to explain why. I ask him whether the woman involved would have bitched if I'd used "her David." If anybody were to refer to Ellie as "my Ellie" or "his Ellie" I would be flattered, and I don't think she'd be cross.

I thought my spring-walk "Talk" piece was about as uncheckable as anything you could come up with, but Hal Espen is going to repeat my up- and downtown stroll. It is nice and clear today, temperature in the mid-sixties, and he agrees when I opine that he might not check the piece so conscientiously were it raining. Since many of the figures I used (number of stretch limousines illegally parked, number of people on steps of St. Patrick's), are uncheckable, he can have a nice, relaxed day.

A Coca-Cola lawyer phones from Atlanta. In connection with a lawsuit involving bottlers' contracts signed in 1921, can I refer him to somebody familiar with the history of diet syrup? Sorry, no.

It's been quite a time for the Coca-Cola people. First there was the death last year, at ninety-five, of Robert W. Woodruff, of whom *Fortune* once said, in an article about the top fifty business leaders of America, "Fortunate indeed is the corporation whose bosses have the courage and objectivity to sense the need for change before it is forced upon them by disaster." Then there was the change—in Coke's formula—that became a disaster, when the public wouldn't go for it. Woodruff had passed on before the new drink was launched. Not that the formula hadn't been altered since Coca-Cola's debut in 1886. There was a time, very early on, when Coke, whose inventor thought of it primarily as a headache cure, contained infinitesimal traces of cocaine.

I've written a couple of books about Coca-Cola: a history of the company that first ran in *The New Yorker* and a commissioned biography of Woodruff that his Georgia colleagues gave him as an eightieth-birthday present. Some of his underlings down there, conceivably grateful that I never divulged the secret formula (I couldn't have; I've never seen it) once sent me a gold-plated Coke bottle, *sous cloche*. Ellie keeps trying to get rid of it, but I refuse to; I want to have something unique to leave to my kids. My resolve faltered when the new Coke was introduced. As war veterans displeased with the President sometimes dispatch their hard-earned medals to the White House, so was I tempted, to evince my grief and dismay, to return my treasured gilded relic to Atlanta. I had a hunch Woodruff would have approved. He had a high sense of right and wrong. He believed so staunchly in the Golden

108

Rule that when such friends of his as Dwight D. Eisenhower met his criteria (he liked Ike), he would reward them with solid-gold six-inch rulers.

The New Yorker library is using a new kind of paste, with the result that scrapbook pages now lie flat instead of being wavy, and more pages than was the case can fit into a single book. Considering that a twenty-thousand-word "Profile" can now be accommodated on both sides of only four sheets of paper, it is getting harder and harder to fill up an album. I complain to Helen Stark that her improved technology has probably forever ruined my chance of getting to a sixth volume. She replies that I already have more books than anybody else. Some people, I can hear her thinking to herself, are never satisfied.

Ellie has her own American Express card and wants it included in our hot-line roster—place to notify when credit cards get lost or stolen. I have no address, only the phone number 1-800-HOTLINE, and the woman I get connected with there, wanting to make damn sure I am whom I purport to be, asks a number of searching questions. The clincher, which would presumably trip up a common cutpurse, is: "What was your mother's maiden name?"

2 May

Ellie has afternoon tickets for *Les Liaisons Dangereuses*, reviewed just yesterday. How many years has it been—if ever—since I went to two matinees in a season? Anyway, this one, Royal Shakespeare Company import, is a delight from beginning to end, and our front-row seats have us virtually mixed up in the action. A play about two of the most charming incarnations of pure evil—one male, one female, as you could hope to cheer for.

One reason why I wanted to do a "Profile" on Pat Sajak: in today's "Wheel of Fortune," a girl stands to win a fifteen-thousand-dollar diamond necklace, or some such, if in fifteen seconds she can fill in the rest of "S__LTS_____ER." The answer, obviously, is "saltshaker," but the contestant hazards—it doesn't even have the right number of letters—"saltpeter," whereupon the insouciant Sajak, before putting his hand to his mouth in an apologetic "Oops" gesture, mutters, "Thought I was back in the army for a moment."

3 May

Palmer Williams phones. Sidney Simon is sick, and can I fill in at tennis? I go down to the Eighth Avenue-and-Twenty-seventh courts. Palmer and some big guy named Harry are still a body shy, so they recruit the house pro and give him to me, inasmuch as I am clearly the weakest of the lot. The pro's drop shots are unbelievable. We—not, I am emboldened to add, without some help from me—take three straight sets, 6–3, 6–2, 6–0, and our opponents quit, though they still have seven minutes of prepaid court time coming.

At Palmer's afterward for some backgammon, he exacts revenge. I have a closed board, and he has *four* men on the rail. I need only a 4, a 5, or a 6—odds three to one in my favor—to escape from his board. I throw a disastrous double-3, followed instantly by his double-6, and he goes on to win. Whoever said this was a game of skill?

4 May

Lunch with Jinny, as is our wont now and then. Much talk, naturally, about our sons and grandchildren. Jinny has been to dinner at Charlotte Ricks's, with what's left of our old Westchester crowd: Reimans, Benjamins, Nina Engel, Mary Cheever. J.'s mother is ninety-five and has just had her driver's license renewed up in New Hampshire. There may be more to Christian Science than I've ever yet been willing to concede. On the other hand, when Harold Rice passed on—in a hospital, after surgery that was deferred too long—he may have been younger than Jinny and I are now.

Once a year, every member of the Board of Management of the Harvard Club is supposed to tour the premises, looking for deficiencies and recommending improvements. Today is my turn, and I am determined not to be accused of being slipshod. In one otherwise immaculate guest room, accordingly, I pounce on a Manhattan telephone directory that has been too much thumbed, and I strongly urge that it be retired. Otherwise, the old place looks commendably shipshape.

During my tour, our manager imparts one disquieting bit of intelligence. A taxidermist was around not long ago, on a consultative mission, and he pronounced our stuffed animal heads—some or all of which I've always assumed were bagged by Teddy Roosevelt—to be worthless.

5 May

Ellie's book-party day. It's amazing how many people, when they know or should know that you have a lot of things to do, persist in phoning to ask what cross street your Park Avenue apartment is at. I mean, you can find that out from even a scuffed phone book. I begin the day by hauling ten cartons of liquor into the kitchen. Then Ellie and I borrow Elisabeth Smith's car and head downtown to a pâté place on Greenwich Street, getting lost because there is no Canal Street exit off the East River Drive, and fighting our way through Little Italy and Chinatown and Jewish town and God knows what other ethnic enclaves. By the time we get back up to East Seventy-eighth Street, where there seems to be a whole block of bread stores, it is beginning to rain and we are beginning to wonder where more than one hundred people are going to put their coats and umbrellas.

The party seems to go well despite the weather. Ellie says the orchid corsage I ordered for her is the first of its kind she's had since Homer took her to the junior prom. Mary Stewart Hammond (Allen) says there were several mistakes in the last poem of hers in *The New Yorker*. The apartment so crowded that I never get to lay eyes on several of the guests Ellie says were here. But all seems to go smoothly enough, as any party should with two bartenders and three maids.

Guest George Gianis wants to know about melanomas. He has a spot on his back and wonders how extensive surgery may be if it's required. I take him into an upstairs bathroom and let him look at the gouge on my back. George offers to bare his, but I decline; I never looked at my own spot, either, before it was carved out. I urge him to make an appointment with a dermatologist pronto because one shouldn't dillydally about these things.

Gerry Piel says the preliminary arrangements for our trip to the USSR call for us all to fly first class. I demur; we're talking about a couple of thousand dollars extra here per couple. Gerry argues that when people get to be our age they need more leg room while in aerial transit. Not me; I probably have some of the shortest legs in the class.

There was a time, back in the sixties, when *The New Yorker* routinely let us travel first class on foreign assignments. But then retrenchment set in, and we were supposed to use first class only when we were really pressed for time and no other space was available. I took comfortable, leg-stretching advantage of that loophole once on a truly long flight—via Lufthansa from Frankfurt to Windhoek, Namibia. That was when the government in Pretoria would grant me a visa to South West Africa but not to South Africa itself. I saved the magazine some airfare money, though, before that trek was over. I wanted to get up to the very northern edge of Namibia, at the Angolan border, where South Africa had and has a military base. But the South African authorities in Windhoek kept raising all sorts of objections. Finally, presumably hoping thus to get rid of me, they said the only way I'd be able to make the trip—they never dreamed I'd go *that* far—would be to charter my own plane. Fine, I said, and I did. I don't remember now what the tab came to—many hundreds of dollars, for certain—but just before I was about to take off Anthony Lewis blew into Windhoek (blew into Ellie's party today, too), and he said the

Times would be willing to split the cost of the charter if I'd take him along. So whatever that trip might have cost *The New Yorker* was cut in half. I've been accused from time to time of taking extravagantly good care of myself when I'm on a remote assignment, but this incident strikes me as evidence of my innate frugality.

6 May

Gottlieb has installed a Xerox machine in the hall near his office. When I go to the nineteenth floor to check out the free-coffee situation, there's a small crowd around the machine—Bob, Martha Kaplan, Chip McGrath, Pat Crow, and Tony Hiss. Hiss has figured out a way of using the contraption to make Xeroxes of people's faces. He offers to do me. I decline, and as I depart they are laughing and Bob is crying out, "Cuteness is all." We have definitely left the Shawn era for a new one.

Letter from a woman in Susquehanna, Pennsylvania. She is a genealogist, saw my name in *Yankee*, and wants to know if I am descended from a couple of clans she's been looking into—the Ely and Jacques families. "I liked your 'Cape Cod Evolution' and frankly you *sound like an Ely*," she writes. (Emphasis hers.) One learns new things about one's self every day.

7 May

For anyone who has a daily date with a dog-walker at seven, making an eight-fifteen dentist's appointment is a breeze. Ruth H. is glad to be able to advise me that she knows of a newfangled electronic flea collar—it emits some kind of buzz that humans and dogs cannot detect but that makes fleas run for their lives—that she can procure for us for only fifty dollars, plus tax. I tell her to go ahead; exterminators charge even more.

Gary Hart and his girlfriend are much in the news, along with General Richard Secord, who clearly loves to testify before Congress and to relate, for instance, how Ollie North, being a good marine, always stands at attention while talking to President Reagan on the phone. I once wrote a "Profile" about an elderly gent, Gridley Adams, a superpatriot who was the founder and, I sometimes suspected, only member of the United States Flag Foundation. He had all kinds of quaint, lovable beliefs—one being that the colors of the national standard should properly be described as "blue, white, and red." Adams would have cottoned to Colonel North, because every time the old man heard the "Star-Spangled Banner" played on radio or television he would haul himself out of his chair and stand ramrod straight until it ended.

Ellie reminds me to call Mike Curtis and wish him a happy birthday. Mike says he is beginning to get old. He is fifty-three.

Joan Cohen invites me to go to Forest Hills to watch some tennis—a Legal Aid Society benefit program. (One of Jerry's law partners is John McEnroe's father.) I haven't been out there for more than forty years—not since I covered the sport for the magazine, back in the days of Donald Budge and Bobby Riggs and Alice Marble and Sarah and all the other Palfreys. We have to turn back because Joan has forgotten the tickets, and then we run out of gas, and then her glove compartment won't stay shut, and then we get lost, and it's six-forty-five by the time we find the tent where the tickets entitle us to food and drink between five and seven. Young McEnroe doesn't seem to be playing in what is billed as a Tournament of Champions, but we do at least get to watch Boris Becker beat some Argentinian. I am nervous about staying out too long, because Ellie has gone to Cincinnati for a feminist sculptors' conclave, and I have to walk the dog. When I get to Hopi at ten-fifteen, she has evinced her displeasure at my tardiness by tearing up the *Times* all over Lexy's room. Last time she used David's room. At least she is impartial.

Talk about coincidences! Page one of the *Times* has—or had before it got shredded—a story to the effect that Gary Hart, because of his revealed hanky-panky, is going to pull out of the Presidential race. The crossword puzzle offers for its 15-down definition "____-night stand."

8 May

I call Ellie in Cincinnati at eight-thirty and rouse her. I've been awake for three hours myself. How I envy her being able to sleep late! Wait till she gets to be my age. I pass along some messages for her from our phone-answering machine; they all seem to be from women with common names like Mary or Ann or Margery who don't bother with surnames and assume, I assume, that they are *sui generis*.

Boy, did I ever apparently blow it! Today's gossip page of the *Post*, quoting some publication I never heard of called *Media Industry Newsletter*, has as its main headline "Writers' Stampede at *New Yorker*." It seems that Shawn, in revenge for his abrupt dismissal, commissioned a raft of manuscripts from us "pampered intellectuals" at the very last minute. Bill is said to have "assigned $750,000 in long, feature-type pieces" to "lofty writers, who disdain deadlines as the curse of lesser mortals." Where was I when all this peaches-and-cream was being dispensed? And I always thought Shawn was my friend! Of course, there always is the possibility that the *Post* is talking through the *Media Industry Newsletter*'s hat.

9 May

Really small world department: Dave Schwarz phoned the other day, to urge me to ask any of my college-reunion panelists whether they'll be wanting audiovisuals for their presentations. So I dutifully instructed myself not to neglect to make inquiry soon of tire-company exec Gibby Gibson (who I believe is all set), philosophy prof John Ladd, and federal judge Eddie Gignoux.

This Saturday afternoon, I am walking the dog in Central Park when we are hailed. I look down at Hopi, because she is the one of us who always attracts attention. But no, this rare time it is I who am being accosted, by no less than J. Dinsmore Adams, Jr., the attorney and the secretary of the Harvard Club. (I have a sneaking soft spot for all adults who cling to their "Jr.s.") Dinny and I quickly get onto and off the subject of Gary Hart; that leads him to ask me who, had I the choice, I'd prefer for President. I say that in the light of his native intelligence and experience over the last six years—forgetting, if you like, the four before that—I think the person probably best qualified is Jimmy Carter. Well, Dinny rejoins, if he had his druthers it would be a federal judge up in Maine I've undoubtedly never heard of—fellow by name of Edward T. Gignoux.

As we are parting, I beg a favor. Gary Hart has put us all in mind of distinguishing between appearance and reality. I have a choice today in my wife's absence, I explain, of either walking the dog in the park, as I am patently doing, or not walking the dog and pretending to Ellie when she returns, should she inquire, that I did. Would he be prepared to testify on my behalf? Counselor Adams says he'll give me an affidavit, and I hope it won't make him change his mind that, as a young daughter of his runs up, my strong, ill-trained four-legged walking companion leaps affectionately upon her and knocks her down.

10 May

The Actors Fund of America wants me to spend $1,000 on a theater ticket in celebration of George Abbott's 100th birthday. If Warren Munsell, who ran the fund for years after retiring as the Theatre Guild's business manager, were still alive, he'd be just about 100, too. I'd have bought a ticket at almost any price to honor *his* centenary. Warren, who was like a second father to me and whom I always called "Pop," did hang on at that to a creditable 90.

Joey calls. He is feeling old. His son Jaime went to a prom last night in a tuxedo. *He's* feeling old! How about me, with a black-tie grandson?

Our Gary Hart conversation turns to Morris Dees. Joe reminds me that when Hart managed the George McGovern campaign in 1972, Dees handled its direct-mail fund-raising; and that Dees and Hart, being of comparable age and temperament, may well have double-dated.

It is Mother's Day, and David greets Ellie on her return from Cincinnati with fresh strawberries. She shows me the text of a little speech she made in a public square out there, a graceful oration about God creating woman and woman creating sculpture. Ellie pays me a welcome compliment. She says she got a few nice laughs, and she attributes that in part to my having persuaded her that an almost surefire alternative to solemnity is levity.

11 May

In the mail, from North Dakota, an unsolicited book, apparently first of a series of two on world literature, with a "Dear Classmate" note. The author, whose name doesn't ring any bells, is sending me the volume as a fiftieth-reunion gift, but if I want to contribute to the cost of its publication he'd appreciate twenty dollars. If he gets that from each of the other 692 of us who, according to our redoubtable class secretary Bill Bentinck-Smith were still alive when he last took count, he won't need my pittance. I look him up in one of our reunion albums. He was born on October 22, 1917. Nearly a year younger than I am, and I've always thought I was one of our youngest.

I can't help wondering how our classmate Floyd Haskell feels about the Gary Hart extravaganza, considering that Floyd was once a Democratic senator from Colorado himself. Considering, too, that Haskell is now married to the topflight Washington journalist Nina Totenberg (I used to have a crush on Nina's mother, but we are getting sidetracked here), Floyd must be amused by all the difficulties Hart is having with the inquisitive press.

Lunch—this is becoming classmates' day—with Paul Killiam. He needs material—levity, here we come, I hope—for some reunion entertainment he'll be putting on. We try hard to think of some Bentinck-Smith jokes we haven't used before. Paul is an indefatigable researcher and says that Bill B-S is our only hyphenated classmate. OK, but close to a half-century's one-liners about a hyphen? I ask Paul if he has received the "Dear Classmate" literary work. Not yet. He doesn't think, by the way (this guy has researched *everything*) that the author is our class baby. Someone whose name starts with a "T," Paul recalls, and was born in 1918. I am skeptical.

At 3:00 P.M., Killiam is on the phone. "Herbert Tabor, November 29, 1918." Damned if he didn't get a magna and another magna from the Harvard Medical School. In his class biography, Tabor doesn't mention being our youngest. Maybe he doesn't know it. But he surely knows that when he entered Harvard he was fourteen.

Joan Colebrook is staying with us for a couple of days, en route between Mexico and Cape Cod. While she's in New York, Roger Straus is giving her a dinner party at the Lotos Club. Now that's the sort of publisher any writer could learn to get along with. Like most authors, Joan is idiosyncratic. At our apartment, she makes what she calls a cocktail by throwing lettuce leaves into a blender.

Ellie and I dine, à troix, at Lilo's. She wants to show us photographs she's unearthed of her banker grandfather's big house in Nuremberg. Apparently when my stepmother and her first husband left Germany for Greece they had no trouble taking worldly goods along; here is a photo of two loaded freight cars, with a limousine parked alongside. But how different must it have been when she and Dr. Myller (she thirty-five, he fifty) embarked from Athens to New York with two young sons and few possessions and only $500 in cash! She met my father, I learn for the first time tonight, when the Myllers were strolling along Madison Avenue one day and passed by his sister's store—Rena Rosenthal's—and went in because they saw a chair in the window like one they'd had to leave behind in Greece, and Ely happened to be there and so—soon making introductions all around—was Lilo's onetime next-door Athens neighbor, Marina Ladas (Mrs. Cyrus) Sulzberger.

12 May

I feel pretty smug, because the morning paper says that the two Broadway shows with the most nominations for Tony awards are *Fences* and *Les Liaisons Dangereuses*, and we have seen them both.

I have won the Harvard Club's annual backgammon tournament three times and am feeling pretty smug about that, too. Today, I play in the first round of this year's competition, on my way to making it four. Tener Eckleberry, who may be the club's only member of genuine Basque origin, eliminates me so fast I hardly know what hits me.

I talk to Gottlieb. He expresses guarded interest in a piece I may try on a Riverside Drive couple, Glen and Mildred Leet, who are running their own foreign-aid program out of a penthouse apartment. He tells me about a new policy he is instituting. He no longer intends, à la Shawn, to buy whole finished books and then serialize them.

I run into John Brooks. He is giving up on a "Profile" on Malcolm Forbes. I am welcome to him, but John doesn't think I'd want him. John also says that somebody is writing a book about all the recent changes at *The New Yorker* who would seem to have an inside track because she used to sleep with—I am relieved to hear—a man who has not previously appeared in this journal.

A full house at home. J. Colebrook still on hand, and Terry is down on a big-city assignment for *Boston*. Ter wonders what I thought of Bing Bingham's retirement piece in *Sports Illustrated*. I had missed it. But Bing, that kid, *retiring*! He still runs the marathon. I can remember him in an air force uniform. We won the men's doubles in Lee Falk's annual Truro Invitational Tennis Tournament twice, at eighteen-year intervals—1963 and 1981. I had figured we were a shoo-in for 1999 (unless T. Eckleberry moves to the Cape with a friend and a tennis racquet). But now I am not so sure.

To dinner at the V. Henry Rothschilds', with a Cape Cod crowd. When the subject of Presidential prospects inevitably comes up, Sidney Simon says that Bill Bradley has often been seen at art galleries, which, considering what many of them now choose to exhibit, might be grounds for charging him with depravity, or at the very least poor judgment. We move on to more serious matters: setting fire to Amoretti wrappers and watching them float mysteriously to the ceiling.

13 May

A package from Little, Brown! No note from anybody in it, merely the Spring 1987 issue of something called *Telecommunications Book Review*, of the Center for Telecommunications Management of the School—hang on, we're getting there—of Business Administration of the University of Southern California. Twelve whole pages are devoted to my Arthur D. Little book *The Problem Solvers*, with quotes I couldn't have crafted better myself: "fascinating," "well-written," "entertaining," "remarkably comprehensive." There is a summary of every chapter. Most beguiling to me is "Reading Time: 9 to 12 hours." Never before, to my knowledge, has a book of mine been clocked.

14 May

Working at home on the Ku Klux Klan. Makes sense because I have to change for a black-tie dinner dance at the UN for the African Student Aid Fund, on whose board I once sat. Ellie isn't coming along, she has a PEN thing, but before we go our separate social ways brother Mike Curtis is coming by for a drink with us both.

Things are the same all over. There's more and more testimony evolving about how a lieutenant colonel is running the United States, and now another of his ilk has pulled off a coup d'état—unlike Ollie North's forays it was bloodless—at Fiji. The rank of lieutenant colonel is at best nothing but a stepping-stone toward colonel. Since it seems to breed troublemakers, maybe we should simply do away with it (and some of them). I'll bet there isn't a major extant who'd object.

New York magazine has a full-page color ad—will *The New Yorker* be similarly graced?—for Rose's Lime Juice. It features Arthur Schlesinger, Jr., seated in a book-lined study, conceivably his own. Tama Janowitz is standing on his desk. "And so they meet," burbles the text, "the chronicler of the historical and the chronicler of the hysterical." His red bow tie matches her shoes. There is a piece of paper in his typewriter. Yesterday, when the Business Department at *The New Yorker* sent a young woman up to take my picture, I remembered to stick a sheet of paper in mine, so I'd look like a real writer. I must ask Arthur the next time I see him how he sweet-talked Janowitz into scrambling up there. The girl who snapped me yesterday was cute, and if I'd had the guts I'd have urged her to scale my desk. But if she had, to put a quick end to this hallucination, who'd have been left to take our picture?

Sister Joan phones. She had lunch with Bill Shawn. She says he is writing a novel. Is she going to publish it? Joan doesn't know, and anyway, she says, she never gives an advance on a novel till she's seen it. I suggest that in view of the extraordinary nature of this one she should send Bill a blank contract and let him fill in the figures.

Mike comes by, and Ellie decides not to go out after all but to have some Chinese food sent in, and it isn't hard for me to conclude that the United Nations will probably not disintegrate if I stay home, too. The Student Aid Fund may emerge from my truancy ahead of the game, because as we all know there is nothing more conducive to generosity than guilt.

15 May

There's a review in the *Times* of a new biography of Brenda Frazier, by Giola Diliberte, and I guess I'd better pick up a copy. Brenda, back in 1939, was one of my earlier "Profile" subjects and one about whom I got to know the least. But then how much more could there have been to learn about an eighteen-year-old who did not have time to read far beyond her dance card? When I reach the office I find a copy, compliments of the author, who calls me, as of forty-eight years ago, "a young reporter," which is certainly unobjectionable.

Sidney Simon's seventieth birthday party is being celebrated in his downtown studio tonight, same place I lived in for several months between marriages. Ellie wants me to write a poem for the occasion, but I can't come up with any doggerel sufficiently inane, so I settle for a "page 17" from an alleged book, a page all about Sidney that begins "na says" and ends "said Donna as." Gary Hart would probably not think it funny.

When we get home, our building is aswarm with uniformed police and plainclothesmen. Apparently the Alan Tishmans are entertaining some Israeli big shot. The self-service passenger elevator on our side, which wasn't working at all this morning, now has an operator aboard. Maybe its earlier malfunctioning was just a ruse so the Secret Service or whoever could check it out, or keep it inviolate.

16 May

We take the train to Scarborough—Doorman Bob is happy to board the dog again—to spend the night at the Burton Benjamins'. Bud has only a few more weeks to go at Columbia as a Gannett Center Fellow. He says Shawn has been around a couple of times by now and that Lillian Ross, who's apparently extremely bitter toward *The New Yorker*, may be applying for a fellowship herself.

Nina Engel, Ginger and Don Reiman, and Katie and Dick Witkin have been invited to dinner. Nina, who has spent a good deal of the last few years visiting a daughter in Australia, confesses that she has never really much liked that continent and, family or no family, is going to Alaska instead on her next long trip. The Reimans are buying a place, for eventual retirement, on the Maine coast. Dick Witkin, who as the *Times*'s aviation expert ought to know, has scary things to say about the Provincetown-Boston Airline, which I have been blithely patronizing all these years.

The trial of Bernhard Goetz for shooting four blacks on the subway is in progress, and the table talk turns understandably to racism. Why is it that Korean and Vietnamese families can come to New York and work hard and prosper, we wonder communally, whereas so many native blacks cannot? One reason surely is that the Asians have intact families, with a paterfamilias, and much stricter upbringing. We agree to a man and woman that nobody can mention this sort of thing publicly without being accused by black racists of being racist.

I manage to change the subject long enough to recount my Oliver North dream. He is on the witness stand, and I am cross-examining him, making a point all the way of addressing him not as "Colonel" but as *"Mister"* North. In a low voice, I inquire offhand what sort of clothes he was in the habit of wearing when on White House duty. Why, conventional civilian garb, he replies. I suddenly glare at him and change my tone and raise my voice and snarl, "Then why are you appearing in this courtroom today in that uniform with all those medals tacked on it?"

17 May

We sat up talking and drinking brandy till nearly 1:00 A.M., very late for me. Ellie said not to worry, we don't have the dog, I can sleep as long as I like for once. But the alarm clock inside my head rousts me out of bed at 6:30 notwithstanding. It was worth it; Aline's dazzling azaleas are right outside our window.

Ellie stayed up even later, reading Susie Cheever's new novel. There was talk yesterday, incidentally, of a sale of John's journals—apparently Knopf outbid everybody else—for a cool million.

Over to the Reimans' for Bloody Marys, and we walk back to the Benjamins'. I peer into our old driveway but don't trespass. There seem to be some totemlike statues on the back lawn.

We take the train home and retrieve the dog. The temperature is in the eighties, and she is beginning to shed something fierce.

18 May

The South African government has told the Rev. Leon Sullivan to forget about a trip he was planning to take there next week, because he isn't going to get a visa. Welcome to the club.

I started reading the Brenda Frazier book last night. Some of it sounded awfully familiar, so when I got to the office I looked up my 1939 "Profile." The author has made liberal use of my material, but why not? We journalists all do it, and facts are facts. (Not that there could be too many about a girl just turning eighteen.) But hold on, now. Maybe sometimes some of us go too far. My piece ended with Brenda *saying*, "I don't deserve all this. I haven't done anything spectacular. I haven't done anything at all. I'm just a débutante." The book's Chapter Eight ends with Brenda's *thinking* to herself, "I don't deserve all this. I haven't done anything at all. I'm just a débutante."

I also learn from it, interestingly, that when Jock Whitney died, he bequeathed his flying-boat hangar, in the loft of which his old pal "Shipwreck" Kelly lived rent-free for so many of his declining years, to Brenda's ex-husband. It was noblesse oblige characteristic of Whitney at his finest.

By the time my biography of Whitney was published in 1981, Jock was too sick to read. So a number of his relatives and friends—I among them—were recruited to record chapters of the book, in case he felt like listening to them. Some day I hope to indulge in the privilege of listening to a few pages of my prose recited in the familiar tones of Walter Cronkite.

Overheard conversation in the men's room, between two longtime *New*

Yorker writers: "How are you reacting to the circumstances?" "That's a long question." "Have I ever been known to ask a short question?"

The December 1986 issue of *Guam & Micronesia Glimpses*, to which I've been a nostalgic subscriber because of my long-standing concern for and writing about those far-off realms, has a photograph of the Governor of Yap, addressing a gathering of church and secular dignitaries. The governor, now gray-haired, is none other than John Mangefel, who so far as I know is the only Yapese ever to have visited Cape Cod, or at any rate Truro. He came to spend a few days with us in the sixties, and there are old-timers around (me, for instance) who still marvel at the memory of his swimming prowess.

19 May

It is raining. When I turn Hopi over to her walker, I am made to realize what high-class canine circles we move around in. Ruth has only six dogs in tether today, and she explains of the truants, "One of them decided to sleep in, and another went to Boston."

As I am leaving the office with a bag full of homebound reading matter, I run into Sheila, who relates a warm story about Emily Hahn and herself. Mickey H. told Sheila that she had availed herself of the magazine's limousine service to transport her to her installation as a member of the Institute, and would Sheila please send her the bill when it came in. Sheila responded that according to *The New Yorker*'s Bylaw 42A, any staff writer over eighty who comes to the office regularly whenever she's in town is entitled to a free ride every time she's installed at the Institute.

I dump the publications I've lugged home on the dining-room table. This one single day's haul includes *Publishers Weekly*, the *Atlantic*, *Chronicles*, *Time*, *Newsweek*, *Manhattan, Inc.*, the *Scientific American*, the *Economist*, and—yes, *The New Yorker*. How is one ever supposed to get through them all?

20 May

A call from Greg Katz, at *USA Today*. He wants to check out a rumor that young writers at *The New Yorker* are abandoning ship to launch a magazine of their own. I ask George Trow next door. He has heard nothing, but then, as he's reminded me, he isn't all that young. Jim Lardner would qualify, but he isn't in. I find Alec Wilkinson, who must be about thirty-five, which should suffice. Alec says he did hear such a rumor—involving Schell and McKibben, as he recalls—but a couple of months ago. *He* isn't leaving, and he knows that Mark Singer isn't. Alec has a rumor of his own:

that Shawn is going to Farrar, Straus, with his own publishing imprint. I do not pass this along when I call Katz back.

Fred Shapiro, whose age is now immaterial, asks me to step into his office. He wants to show me a "Talk" piece he did a couple of years ago, about a walk he took on Fifth Avenue. I'd forgotten all about it, if indeed I ever read it. I apologize for having borrowed his idea and promise that the next time we cover that story it'll be his turn.

Ed Diamond is doing a *New York* piece about changes at *The New Yorker*. He seems mostly beguiled to learn that we have an editorial coffee machine. He says he has heard that the cartoons under Gottlieb are both better and worse. I point out that unless they're timely ones, while Gottlieb obviously put them to press, they may have been bought by Shawn.

21 May

Nicaragua is planning to boycott the 1988 Summer Olympics unless they're held in both Koreas, with opening ceremonies in both Seoul and Pyongyang. That's hardly likely to happen, of course, but if the Sandinistas carry out their threat, what an opportunity for the Contras! Reagan could fit them out with uniforms and send Oliver North along as a coach. The March 1987 issue of *Olympic Review*, which arrives (somewhat belatedly) today, has a good deal to say about International Olympic Committee negotiations with the North Koreans and of a possible agreement to give them archery and table tennis and some cycling and football, but there is no mention of Nicaragua.

Lunch at the Harvard Club with a young woman publisher, who says after a bit that she has to ask me a question that she asks of everybody: "Would it bother you to know I'm twenty-four?" Not at all, I say, perhaps too hastily. I am a pushover; it doesn't even bother me when she asks would I mind if she smoked. She has been smoking, she goes on, since she was seven, when a seventeen-year-old brother came home with some chums and they talked her into it. She is one of five children of a Debevoise and Plimpton lawyer and has known her father's partner Roswell Perkins since she started smoking. I am happy to be able to tell her that when Rod Perkins was president of the establishment she is smoking in, he integrated it.

Max Lerner's column in today's *Post* tells of his getting an honorary degree at Adelphi University and how about three-quarters of the faculty members present rose and turned their backs when Edward Teller was similarly singled out. "In our liberal culture, which presumably celebrates openness to ideas," Max writes, "it is almost always those with conservative ideas who get disinvited. . . . What is it the faculties fear?" the doughty octogenarian goes on to ask, and answers, "They fear the very freedom of ideas they are sworn to guard." I remember Harvard in 1969, when certain faculty members egged students on to all kinds of disruptive action but then somehow vanished while the students were getting arrested. Max does not, in this column, go into one matter that has long bothered me: why should higher education be virtually the only field in which people are granted tenure? It has been in all too many instances a license for negligence or abuse.

Bernard Taper is in town from California, and we meet back at the Harvard Club for a drink. It's been years since Tape left *The New Yorker* to become a professor of journalism (once out West when he had a tennis date he let me take over his class); but apparently he's going to do some more writing for the magazine. When he asks what I'm working on and I say it's a piece about a young black man who got lynched by the Klan when he went out for a pack of cigarettes, Bernie startles me by saying that his older son, who lived in a largely black neighborhood, went out for a pack of cigarettes five years ago and several hours later was found shot to death. Bernie is remarried again—third wife—and he now has one living child from his first marriage, two stepchildren from his second, and one stepchild from the third. But he does not see his second wife any more, and the two sets of stepchildren have never met. When I get back to my office, I look up at the picture on my wall—left to right, arms linked, son, stepson, me, son, son, stepson—and I feel blessed.

Bernie says, incidentally, that he talked to Gottlieb about the editorial transition and that Bob told him he'd heard Newhouse's version of what happened and had heard Shawn's version and that he suspects neither of them grasped what the other was saying. Bernie suggested that maybe the trouble was that Shawn told Newhouse he was going to be retiring "soon"; and that Newhouse, unlike so many of us writers who've tried over the years to get our pieces in the magazine, didn't understand and thought that when Shawn said "soon" he meant "soon."

Taper has been talking to another staff writer, Dick Harris. I tell Bernie that it had long been my impression that Harris left *The New Yorker* because of some misunderstanding with Shawn over eligibility for a dental plan. Taper says that Harris told him that Shawn told *him* at the time, "I think of Saul Steinberg as Matisse, and Matisse didn't have a dental plan."

A Harvard Club bartender, not knowing I have a black-tie Board of Management dinner tonight, hands me an open letter to all members, asking us to use our influence with the club president for a modest increase in wages. I am early and before going upstairs stop to chat with Morris Lasker. The Judge and I get to reminiscing about the Horace Mann centennial day and how impressive a group of alumni the old school was able to corral. Being by now a senior federal judge, Monty now handles only—only!—about one hundred cases a year (in one of them, he will be pronouncing sentence on our fellow club man Ivan Boesky), so he can spend a whole summer month on Martha's Vineyard. He asks if I know the place, and I find it awkward to respond without name-dropping, because the only time

I've been there in the last decade was when Palmer Williams and I flew over from the Cape to play tennis against Mike Wallace and Art Buchwald. They beat us, largely because Buchwald, over the years, has trained the Vineyard winds to bend to his infernal lobs.

I can't help wondering what our disgruntled staff ("Negotiations have not broken off," President Craig assures us) might think of our dinner menu: cold baby lobster with ginger-lemon dressing (Meursault Jaboulet-Vercherre 1985); medallion of veal tenderloin with fresh morels, asparagus, and salsify (Morgon Georges DuBoeuf 1985); salad of radicchio, frisee, and field lettuce; brilliant Savarian cheese; individual fruit bavaois—and, before all that, the usual tempting array of canapés, including oysters, shrimp, and, yes, caviar. I am seated next to a young woman, class of 1977 and friend of son Joey's, whose household appears to have taken advantage of the club's admitting women in a way Rod Perkins may not exactly have anticipated. When she was allowed to join, her Harvard husband resigned, because he could use the place spousally now and not have to pay dues of his own. They both work, she in real estate, he in law, but they have a nine-month-old baby so they do not qualify, she tells me, as dinks. Beg pardon? DINKS—dual income, no kids.

22 May

A phone call, a long one, from a man who says he is eighty-three and has been constructing crossword puzzles since 1925. "I'm of the old school— the dictionary type," he says. He is full of venom—his word—about Eugene Maleska, the *Times*'s high priest of puzzledom. My caller knows all the young solvers I wrote about, he says, and thinks they are brilliant, but still there's something missing. "There was a better camaraderie sixty years ago than there is today." He believes *The New Yorker* should run a cryptic puzzle every week, and he would be happy to send along a sample. I urge him not to spend too much time on it.

Still, maybe I should push this. Gottlieb might make me the first *New Yorker* Crossword Puzzle Editor ever.

When I get home, a welcome message from George Gianis. He's been to the dermatologist, and there's no malignancy. Now he doesn't have to fret about anything save the World Backgammon Championships at Monte Carlo, in July, a handsome invitation to which I myself have just received from the Societé des Bains de Mer. But I don't want to spend six days there in July, let alone spend the six thousand dollars or so it would cost me even if I somehow managed to keep out of the casino.

"Wheel of Fortune" runs unaccountably short this evening, and for the first time in my considerable experience Pat Sajak and Vanna White wander

124

across stage to have a time-filling chat with Jack whatever-his-name-is—the fellow who describes, off-camera, how marvelous all the prizes are but to my knowledge has never before been made visible. Jack turns out to be an older man, a model of dignity, and I can't help speculating whether he'd have been more careful selecting his necktie if he'd dreamed forty-odd million of us were going to have a glimpse of it.

23 May

Time was when holidays fell on holidays. But this Saturday seems to be the onset of the Memorial Day weekend, and the day itself is going to be celebrated on Monday the twenty-fifth. I suppose the parades will be held then. I am glad Tony has grown up, because otherwise it might be hard to explain to him why the firemen and police and Legionnaires no longer strut their stuff on the thirtieth—in honor, Jinny and I used to pretend, of his birthday. This arbitrary fooling around with the calendar can have unexpected, even cruel, consequences. When I go to the tailor's at 1:00 P.M. today to have my dinner jacket cleaned and put into hibernation for the summer, two very elderly women with canes are walking—hobbling rather—down Lexington Avenue toward a fast-food joint that is almost always open. When they reach it, it is closed. The looks they exchange are almost as painful to watch as it must be for them to make their slow way back to wherever they came from.

Bel Kaufman calls. Sidney and she have four tickets to an American Ballet Theatre production of *Don Quixote*, and at the last minute can we go with them? They also have a limousine to take us all back and forth. Who could resist *that*? Kevin McKenzie is the star dancer, Martine van Hamel his partner. There is a splendid windmill. It has never been entirely clear to me why Don Q. is tilting at one in the first place, and nothing that occurs this evening helps clarify matters, but the dancing is first-rate, and I suppose a ballet should consider itself lucky to have a plot at all.

Bel says entr'acte that she and I must have met back when she was dating Arthur Kober. Arthur, who would be about eighty-seven if he were with us, was a close friend for some twenty years and a frequent houseguest of Jinny's and mine—the only one, I daresay, who sometimes brought along his own maid to help with chores. And of course he'd been a *New Yorker* contributor, with his memorable Bella Gross stories, long before I came on that scene. (The only mention of him in a recent biography of Lillian Hellman, to whom he was married for a while, is when their union was described as "lacklustre." He deserved better.) A revival of his *Wish You Were Here*—his and Harold Rome's, it goes without saying—was put on recently, and it was pleasing once again to see the Kober name among the credits. I wish Arthur were here.

24 May

I call Palmer Williams, who'll be returning to Truro ahead of us, to let him know that our tennis court will be ready for him on arrival. Palmer asks if I've heard about the net thieves. It seems two nets have been stolen from Harry Kahn's court—Harry's, and the one Malcolm Preston installs off-season. The perpetrators didn't unwind them, either, but cut them loose. Who in the world would want to do a thing like that? I know some losers who've behaved badly, but this is something new, and ugly. I may find myself having to take out a net-insurance policy before summer's over.

Joan and Olivia come for dinner. Joan has now, by her rough calculation, edited eight hundred books, the titles of quite a few of which, not surprisingly, she does not recall.

25 May

To Jackson Hole, Wyoming, via Denver, to gather material for my mountain-climbing-accident piece. We fly Continental, despite dire warnings the other night from Dick Witkin, who is identified on the society page of today's *Times*—a son is getting married—as its Transportation Editor. That page also mentions a son of divorced parents who's taking his mother's name. Ellie says this isn't so rare any more and confides while she's at it that she's just ordered her very first ever "Eleanor Munro" business cards.

No in-flight problems to Denver, possibly because as we're advised over the intercom it's our pilot's birthday. When we deplane, to use that awful word, Ellie gives him some lemon drops, part of an emergency-rations package pressed on us by sister Joan, who has long been convinced that everybody dear to her who is going anywhere will starve to death en route unless she provides adequate sustenance. Some toffee of hers once cost me two teeth between N. Y. and L. A.

Jenny Lake Lodge, a fancy Rockresorts enclave where Jinny and I stayed with the boys when we drove across the country and back, hasn't opened for the season yet. We are booked into Colter Bay Village, a somewhat more Spartan resting place. Both, of course, are within the Grand Teton National Park, and at one ranger post I am, because of my senectitude, presented with a Golden Age Passport, which entitles me to free passage in and out of all national parks for the rest of my presumably limited life. There is something unimpressive about this new privilege; after all, our Truro home, where we now spend about half each year, is smack dab in the middle of a national park, and any old Tom, Dick, or Harry can wander in and out of it at will without a passport or even a visa.

On our way to Colter Bay, we stop for a look at Mt. Moran (altitude: 12,594 feet), the scene of the accident I'll be writing about. Its Skillet Glacier—the exact stretch down which Nicola Rotberg fell—so-called because it resembles a frying pan—is scary enough just to look at from ground level, and I have no intention of getting carried away enough by my research to try to set foot on it.

We dine at Signal Mountain Lodge with Angus MacLean Thuermer, Jr., managing editor of the *Jackson Hole News*. (Journalists habitually seek out their own kind.) He calls himself a "climbing bum" and says a descent of Skillet is no big deal if you know what you're about.

26 May

First interview with a couple of rangers, Pete Armington and Scott Birkenfield. When we wonder if climbers in trouble could be more quickly rescued if they were obliged to carry radios, Armington, who's been a ranger since 1971, points to his radio and says it cost eighteen hundred dollars. If they were in general use, he adds, that would undoubtedly contribute to a lot of false alarms. But more important is that mountain climbers don't *want* too many safety nets. "People come here to pursue the wilderness experience," he explains, "to challenge nature on its own terms." And Birkenfield, when Ellie wonders if there could be some way of park officials' preventing inexperienced climbers from taking rash chances, tells her, "How are you going to ask a ranger to play God?"

27 May

We drive to Jackson, a city of four thousand that grows to thirty thousand in season. We're still out of season; it's chilly enough for Ellie to buy some wool gloves. The center of town looks like a wild-West stage set, and if for a souvenir you'd like a stuffed jackrabbit head with deer horns attached, Jackson is your place. We are more interested in meeting a doctor, Brent Blue. He treated Nicola, whose temperature was down to eighty-two when a helicopter brought her to his hospital's emergency room. Dr. Blue is a climber himself. He almost died one August when, clad only in shorts and a T-shirt, he fell into a snow crevasse, was too cold to move, and drifted into unconsciousness before a companion hauled him out. "I couldn't figure out why I was falling asleep in this critical situation," the doc recalls thinking. He has become an expert on hypothermia, although he didn't have to come to Wyoming to learn about it. There was plenty of *that* in San Francisco, he says, where he got his medical training—scantily clad drunks lying on the street. He remembers one hypothermia case in Minnesota where a young woman plucked from a snowbank was so stiff that her body couldn't be bent to put her in a car. Her eyeballs were frozen, and IV needles also bent when they were thrust into her, but she survived.

We are late for lunch with the helicopter pilot who picked up Nicola, but I had forgotten this is the Far West: Dr. Blue picks up his radio and calls Ken Johnson on his and says we're on our way.

Ellie and I have seen a lot of wild animals—we've heard lions howl in Uganda and hyenas do whatever they do in Tanzania—but she is concerned out here about bears, and at the Colter Bay Visitors' Center she bought *The Grizzly Bear*. Brent Blue mentioned elk, buffalo, antelope, and moose (Moose, indeed, is the name of the town where Grand Teton park headquarters is located), but so far we've seen nothing except, through the picture window of our lunchtime restaurant, two frolicking mongrel dogs.

Ken Johnson has had six thousand hours in helicopters and describes his airborne life as "long, long times of intense enjoyment and moments of sheer terror." His evacuation of Nicola Rotberg, which was carried out in almost total darkness at a point where he couldn't land, had to hover, did not come under intense enjoyment, but he tells us, in retrospect, "Something like that happens, it makes you feel real good."

Colter Bay Village has a big beaver on its letterhead, but we haven't seen one of them, either. On a walk Ellie takes through the woods there, though, she does come upon, and manages to sidestep, a clump of what she takes to be moose scat.

28 May

We have Idaho plates on our rented car. At the Visitors' Center, a retired locksmith and his wife, apparently taking us for authentic Idahoans, wonder if we know the place in the river at Shoshone Falls where Evel Knievel fell. "We climbed up a hill to watch him," the man says. "It sure was something." I didn't know he had fallen. Was it deliberate?

Still pursuing wildlife, we take a long walk on a woodland trail and come upon one chipmunk, one squirrel, some northbound geese in an imperfect V, and some fresh prints that we think may be elk. Ellie says I should make a loud noise, so we won't inadvertently take some antlered critter by surprise.

The only paper around with national and international news is *USA Today*.

("Today" is not always today. This is a Saturday, and what we get is a Friday-Saturday-Sunday edition.) There's an air-traffic feature in it: the busiest American airports are, in order, Atlanta, Chicago, Los Angeles, Dallas-Fort Worth, and Denver. It's good every now and then for us New Yorkers to learn a little humility.

29 May

Ellie has never been to Yellowstone Park, so we drive up there, in part to talk to the leader of Nicola's climbing expedition, in part to see Old Faithful. There's a lot of faith out here in the mountains. Ken Johnson, the helicopter pilot, was telling us that although a Baptist by birth he is now a Mormon and that his beeper always seems to go off in church. Steve Adkinson, whom we've come to Yellowstone to interview, started off as a Catholic but is now, he says, pantheistic. "I can't look out of a window and see a storm without seeing the face of God behind it," he says.

Ellie often chides me, not without cause, for saying we've "done" the Parthenon, or the Prado, or whatever. Driving away from Old Faithful, she murmurs that we may be the only couple in history who did Yellowstone —she pauses to rebuke herself for acquiring my bad habit—without buying a single souvenir, not even a postcard. Before leaving the big park, we do chalk up some sightings: one female moose (no antlers), several badgers and chipmunks (or were they prairie dogs?), two bluebirds in a tree, many buffalo, many deer, one possible elk. Not a bad day's bag.

Back at the Colter Bay bar, we have a drink with a man who may well be the only Illinois banker in history who was Elvis Presley's army sergeant and whose wife is the daughter of a Czechoslovakian who served in Hitler's army.

30 May

The breakfasts these tourists eat! Today's Colter Bay special: one pork chop, two scrambled eggs, hashed browns. But I am a tourist, too, I am reminded, when we do our laundry, first time ever for me, in a launderette, which spurs us on with a sign reading "Have a Grand Teton Day!"

As we drive to the airport, the Tetons are rising, glisteningly, out of collars of mist, as if these truly grand mountains had been demurely dressed to go to a party. The guy who parks next to you at the scenic turnout is always the one who, unlike you, though you have driven past the identical spot at practically the identical time, has just seen a herd of fifty elk.

Inasmuch as tomorrow is Lexy's birthday, and we are so relatively close to him, what the hell, we might as well stop off in New Mexico on our way home. He meets us at the Albuquerque airport and we take the scenic route, past old mining towns, to Santa Fe. Lexy has a beard. He and his mother stop at a Madrid café for what Lex, after his by now long immersion in the quaint customs of the old Southwest, has come to call a "soda," and I am left to watch the car and its contents. One of these is his subscription copy of *The New Yorker*. I turn by chance to the "Briefly Noted" section—anonymous short book reviews—and there I am hit between the eyes by a paragraph about Ellie's *On Glory Roads*. I'd had no idea the magazine was even going to mention it. I take a deep apprehensive breath and begin to read but don't get beyond four words: "This quite wonderful book . . . ." I forget all about my custodial duties and abandon my Wyoming research and our luggage, not to mention Lexy's car itself, to rush inside as a messenger with extremely glad tidings.

31 May

In the book review section of the Sunday *New York Times*, which the hotel newsstand at La Fonda del Sol obligingly carries, there's a long piece by Paul Goldberger about a new history of architecture, and here illustrating the article is a photograph of my father's Squibb Building and a mention of him along with his eminent contemporaries and friends Raymond Hood and Ralph Walker. Seventy-five dollars, but clearly a book I want to get.

Lexy's car breaks down—how come these things only happen when parents are around?—and while waiting for a tow truck, fortunately I have the *Times* Sunday puzzles to finish, having resolutely put them aside earlier to type up five thousand or so words of Grand Teton notes.

Birthday dinner at a place called the Coyote Café with Lexy and three of his local friends. One is a young woman who has been studying labor unions from Sweden to Yugoslavia and points in between. We all agree that American unions don't have the political clout that once was theirs.

1 June

We rent an Avis car and proceed to the International Folk Art Museum, where Lexy has been working part-time. He takes us on a tour of the basement, where four-fifths of the extraordinary Alexander Girard Collection—it contains one hundred thousand objects—is stored. Then on to Chimayo, a Spanish-Colonial sanctuary and a pilgrimage place, featuring a shrine with a pit containing healing sand and trusses and crutches significantly arrayed on a wall just beyond it. Also handwritten notes stuck into the corners of holy pictures—like one from a mother about her daughter: "She is going through some problems right now and is pushing herself. I don't know what to do no more, Jesus." Lexy has heard that a priest blesses a whole mountain at a clip, so he'll be sure there is always enough sanctified dirt to keep the pit filled. Ellie rubs some of the gritty stuff into my hair, which I shampooed just this morning.

2 June

Time to go home. By bus to Albuquerque, where a courier places on the check-in counter a box with a label new to me: "Human tissue for transplant."

At home, an eight-day accumulation of mail. (There will be even more, for me, at the office, where I elect to receive most of mine, largely because it is conscientiously forwarded—God bless Natasha Turi—when we're living on the Cape.) Most welcome communication—most flattering, anyway—is a letter from Harvard classmate Dick Schultes. He hopes to see me at the reunion, but what he wants at the moment is a copy of my *The Staffs of Life* ("this remarkable volume" is his head-turning phrase) for his Botanical Museum library. I spent weeks and weeks there, doing research for it, grabbing at his richly laden shelves like a kid in a candy store. God bless Justin and Anne Kaplan for giving shelter to the transient homeless.) Dick, who is probably the world's leading expert on tropical hallucinogens and who has spent something like fourteen years in Amazonian jungles, writes that Harvard can't fit my book into this year's Botanical Library budget, so would I consider donating it? A few minutes later, I return a phone call from Pete Allen, cochairman of the Class of 1937's fiftieth-anniversary gift to our alma mater. Pete says we need another $100,000 quick to reach the $3 million we are supposed to be presenting to Harvard at reunion time. He has labored so hard and seriously to attain whatever sum we come up with that I refrain from asking him if we can add the $19.95 price tag on my book to the total.

One of the *Cape Codders* awaiting us at home reports that David Luhman is dead, at sixty-four. He was one of a group of us who, back in 1968, bought the next-door newspaper, the *Provincetown Advocate*. As I recall, I owned one-third of 49 percent. A couple of years later, after a number of editors had come and gone, who should be editing the *Advocate* but my son Terry, barely out of Harvard, and his contemporary John Short. They invited me to write a column, and I contributed ten of them, signing myself "Snowberg." (The "Snow" was supposed to be in recognition of one of the old Outer-Cape families; the "-berg" of all the psychiatrists and psychoanalysts who had latterly infiltrated the region.) Because I am a professional writer, I insisted on being paid, and when Terry and John asked how much, I said I didn't care as long as I got as much as one of the paper's longtime columnists, Tom Kane. Boy, were they relieved! Turned out they were paying him five dollars per piece. But I never received even a pittance, and because the *Advocate* has since changed ownership a couple of times more, I am getting close to the point of asking our accountant if I may deduct that fifty dollars as a business loss.

3 June

I hardly recognize any of the names any more affixed to the "Talk of the Town" pieces on our bulletin board. A half century ago, "Talk" was a much more modest operation. For a while, until I was allowed to write my own pieces, there were just four reporters: Eugene Kinkead, Charles Cooke, Milburn McCarthy, and me. We would hand in our notes to St. Clair McKelway, then the managing editor before he decided to switch to writing, or to Bill Shawn, then Mac's deputy, and they would pass along this raw material, if they felt it had enough merit, to Russell Maloney, who had the rewrite franchise. I would never know, hanging around the corridors on the day "Talk" copy went to Make-up, whether an assignment of mine had worked out until Maloney emerged from his office. If he handed me a carbon on the yellow copy paper we then used (he was a meticulous typist and never even seemed to have to strike over a comma) I was in—assuming, of course, that Ross, the final arbiter of these and all other matters, didn't demur. Nowadays, I wouldn't be surprised if in the course of a year as many as fifty individuals contribute to "Talk."

A young woman who once worked in the *New Yorker*'s Checking Department is doing research for somebody writing an unauthorized biography of Irving Berlin, and she phones and mentions two "Talk" pieces of mine about the composer. I recall only the ninetieth-birthday one. So I check with the library. Yes, there was a piece in 1952, about Berlin's revamping the lyrics of "I Like Ike" when Eisenhower decided to run for president. But this time apparently I was merely the rewrite man.

Roberta Pryor phones. My agent has had a request from some Harvard fund-raisers to use my *Yankee* piece—which by now just about everybody has seen save me—for their own worthy purposes. Sure, but can't some of the money collected be credited to the Class of 1937?

Michelle Arnot writes, first time I've heard from her since my puzzle piece came out. This editor of a dozen or so magazines says, "I want to thank you for elevating crossword solving to a sport worthy of national press coverage." And an upstate man who says he has been "patrolling my flanks" since my first book, *The Army Life*, came out in 1942, writes that my getting Major General Harding to write an introduction was, for a private, "an elegant piece of enlisted effrontery." He goes on to say that, judging from pictures of me that have decorated book jackets, "you have the face of Everyman, a face that can be trusted, the face in a crowd of strangers one asks for directions." I hope in a way I never get to meet Fred McMaster; he would surely be disappointed. Ellie maintains, incidentally, that one of my major character flaws is that, however hopelessly and palpably lost I may be, I resist asking directions.

The Wise Men, which coauthor Walter Isaacson is gracious enough to have sent to me, is an enormous tome—853 pages. But I think I am more likely to read it—and not merely because Walter says some works of mine were helpful—than the no less robust volumes of David Halberstam and Marge Piercy, which have lately been vying for my inattention. I am surprised not to find myself in the index, but my bruised spirits are somewhat healed by two mentions in the list of sources—once, oddly, with my "Jr." and once without.

Another party for Ellie's book—this kindly given by Daphne Shih. Nice turnout: Charlie Addams, the Whitney Ballietts, Peggy Day, Harold Taylor, the Arthur Schlesingers. Arthur says his class, 1938, is going to have spies at our fiftieth reunion, either to learn the ropes or to profit by our mistakes, I'm not sure which. I tell him about our forty-*fifth* and how we let classmates' wives, for a change, occupy the spotlight, and he sounds interested, but of course it's too late for Alexandra et al. to try to emulate that innovation. He says he's going to read *On Glory Roads* en route to China.

4 June

From London, a copy of a Jay McInerney piece in the Sunday *Times* about *The New Yorker*. Its title is "Goodbye, Mr. Shawn." McInerney was fired from Shawn's magazine for being a lousy checker, and his article presents evidence of why that was a good idea: "And somewhere in the mind of every young man or woman who has ever sent a short story or a resumé to the shabby offices on West 43rd Street was the knowledge that J. D. Salinger's *Catcher in the Rye* had first appeared in these pages." 'Twould have been nice if it had, but it hadn't.

It is raining this evening, and Ellie has cleverly hired a limousine, inasmuch as we have to go to a birthday party for Judith Malina over on West End Avenue, thence way down to Thomas Street for a Beverly-and-Bill-Pepper dinner, and finally back up to the Cooper Hewitt for a farewell to director Lisa Taylor. The car costs only twelve dollars an hour, and taxis

—if we'd been able to find any—would have set us back twenty-five at the very least. We dismiss the car at the museum, because from there it's a short walk home; but I hadn't reckoned that, after a vigorous hour of dancing, I'd be burdened with three heavy bags of party favors: marmalade, mineral water, truffles, an ashtray, perfume, and a tin chocolate box that's a small-scale replica of the institution.

5 June

Stepson David once asked me when I thought the New Age had begun. I think it began this morning, when I board a Lexington Avenue bus that's air-conditioned and has an empty seat and, to cap it all, a driver who greets new fares with "Good morning, passengers," who announces each stop, who stops without jerking, and who releases us all to the outside world with a "Have a good day." Or am I dreaming?

6 June

Last night I watched Dwight Gooden's return to action for the Mets; and I was, I am constrained to report, singularly unmoved. Those fans who did cheer him on were in large measure envious of him, I suspected, because they couldn't afford either his sickness or his cure.

To dinner at Joanandolivia's, with Ruth Prawer Jhabvala. I bring up the matter of India and Sri Lanka, the latter a country of concern to Ellie and me ever since we covered much of it—except Jaffna up north, Tamil country where so many dreadful things have happened lately—when we met in Colombo in the course of her research on India and its pilgrimages. We'd been booked into our hotel through the good offices of Joe Smyth, of the Harvard-Backgammon Smyths. I found awaiting me, while I awaited Ellie, some hotel stationery with my name imprinted in gold (I have always been careful about getting Joe S.'s surname straight; you'd think they could have done better than "Khan"), but before I'd had a chance even to dash off a postcard the phone rang, and a jewelry salesman wondered if I'd care to inspect some of his dirt-cheap wares just off the lobby. I've always followed the news from Sri Lanka—all the more so the recent sad tidings—with special interest. But Ruth seems totally uninterested in what's going on among the Tamils and the Sinhalese and their big Indian neighbor next door, and Joan and Olivia give the impression of never having heard of the lot of them. They are worried, though, about whether they should celebrate Olivia's birthday next month at the Ritz, where St. Martin's Press is putting them up this time around, or at the Basil Street, their perennial choice for this particular rite of passage. I am glad I don't have to make decisions like this.

8 June

Driving up to Cambridge for my fiftieth reunion (the Chevy wagon hasn't been around quite that long, but it does have a hundred and twenty-odd thousand miles on it and a generous veneer of rust), we reflect that Ellie started in on a memoir of her youth, which she learns just this morning has been accepted for publication, exactly seventeen years ago. So her gestation period would seem to be not unlike that of certain locusts. She is going to show it to all her siblings, which could be awkward if they ask for too many changes. I showed E. my journal ten years ago, and a lot got deleted. The only other person I showed it to was Bill Shawn. He asked to have only one entry removed. Since it apparently would have hurt his feelings then to have the item printed, I see no reason why I should resurrect it now.

At a gas station, we pull up alongside a psychedelically painted van, with a sign on back: "Caution, wierd load." The trouble with so many contemporary weirdos is that they are so illiterate they can't even correctly identify themselves.

Our reunion name tags, perhaps for geriatric reasons, have space on the back for "Medical Information." Thank God for name tags. Otherwise how to distinguish Tom Jones from say, Tristram Shandy? Ellie's has to be edited, they made her "Munroe," but she's no worse off than Bill Bentinck-Smith and Ed Gignoux, who, respectively, have been robbed of a "c" and endowed with a superfluous "i." Several people at the registration desk mention my *Yankee* piece, so I nip over to the Square and buy myself a copy. I hope the Secretary of State never sees it. Somebody has made me make him—is *that* what happened to Bill B-S's "c"! —"Schultz."

We are assigned to a ground-floor suite in Kirkland House of unalloyed austerity, but it does have, in case I snore, two bedrooms.

To Boston for dinner at the Aquarium, with Derek Bok the principal speaker. Next year, he informs us, 20.8 percent of the incoming freshman class will be made up of "minorities." Derek gets started so late that at nine-fifty he is still talking, and there are two more courses to be served, and I shudder to think of what kind of reception a show will get at the Science Center back in Cambridge, where Paul Killiam and Natalie Stone and Danny Keyes are poised to regale us. They don't get to go on till after eleven, which seems rather late for a curtain to go up before an audience of any age.

9 June

What is the purpose of these spring gatherings, anyhow? To raise money, principally, of course, and now we know that 1937 did in the clutch pass that 3-million mark, and then some. But to renew old friendships is surely an objective not to be sneezed at. Last night we sat at a table with the Bob Wolfs and the Bill Canns. I've known Bob since kindergarten, and Bill, a comparative Billy-come-lately, since the fall of 1934. But reunions don't have to deal entirely with the past. Most of my classmates whom I now number among my friends are ones I never met until our twenty-fifth reunion, though we all sort of now pretend we were close as undergraduates.

This morning's *Crimson* has a story about our class with numerous quotes from Bruce Bliven, who hasn't yet made a reunion. He had better hurry. Bruce, another kindergarten throwback, mentions that in our undergraduate days I was turned down by the *Crimson* because of my "religion" and that the *Lampoon* rejected him because he dined with too many Jews, one of whom of course was me. So I seem to have jinxed us both.

I'd never been to the Kennedy Library. After breakfast I choose a tour of it from among the options offered. Different people obviously react in different ways to the myriad exhibits at such shrines. What makes this visit especially appealing to me is the discovery that Jack Kennedy—though probably not after his place of work became the Oval Office—used an Underwood standard nonelectric typewriter absolutely identical, near as I can make out through the glass of the case it's in, to the one I'm typing on right now.

Back to Cambridge for cocktails and lunch, back to Boston for dinner at the Harvard Club and a Pops concert at Symphony Hall. A fellow who lived in Eliot House when I did looks at my name tag, which reads "Jack Kahn," and asks if by any chance I am related to Ely Jacques Kahn. I tell Ellie that this is my first encounter with the Pops, but Phebe Bentinck-Smith corrects me gently (I wonder how many times any part of *her* name gets by orthographically unscathed): Jinny and I were here at the twenty-fifth reunion, with our children, like those of classmates, up in the balcony. The only member of the orchestra who looks old enough to be of our vintage is a double-bass player who spends a good part of the evening—I hope it doesn't mean anything—demonstrating his virtuosity with bubble gum.

10 June

We are joined at breakfast by the Maurice Sapienzas, they holding the distinction of probably having come as far—from their home in Hawaii— as any couple present. He also holds the distinction—no mean one, in a class that boasted Robert Lowell and Peter Viereck—of having been chosen, when we graduated, as our Class Poet.

We all troop to Memorial Chapel, for a service honoring dead classmates—some three hundred of us, so far. Their names are listed on the program (I hear that our class treasurer, Gorham Brigham, who is notoriously tight-fisted, allocated a hundred dollars for crimson program ribbons, which I'm sure he'd have done even had he not been Head Usher), and as my eye skims the sobering roster I see Bob Bridgman, Al Butterfield, Irving Fine, Dave Lindsay, Nat Sanders—but enough. This is depressing even to think about.

Back to the Science Center, for the seminar I'm presiding over, and since there is no competing event this morning, we have a full house. The behind-the-scenes organist at the church has inadvertently provided me with a socko opener; he started banging out a postlude without realizing that one clergy-man was still trying to speak; now I can assure my audience there will be no intrusive Bach. I say further that we have checked out the walking time from where we are to the Holden Quadrangle, where drinks and lunch are to be served, and that it comes to four minutes, and we will therefore adjourn at 12:26. And so we do.

At lunch, I run into, among dozens of others, Dick Schultes. His name tag says fittingly—the man all but visibly exudes dignity—"Mr. Schultes." Schultes (who will be introduced at one of the afternoon seminars as "one of the greatest explorers of this century") has just won some enormously important international science prize, and he says he's sore that he's going to have to pay income tax on it. "But you're a Republican," I say, wondering how he can go against his party's imposts. "No," Dick says, "I'm a mon-archist."

Curt Prout wonders, should Diane and he accompany us to the Soviet Union, whether the Russians would let him visit any of their prisons, and when it comes to that, whether it would matter if they knew about all the time he has devoted, as a physician, to the practice of medicine in American jails. Quite apart from Curt's being a nice guy, it would be pleasant—remembering the request for medical information on our name tags—to have our own doctor in our group.

11 June

This is the fourth day in a row of ideal weather, and we do not even have to think about removing our Harvard 1937 souvenir umbrellas from their crimson sheaths. We arrived without an alarm clock, but don't need one, for at 6:50 A.M. two fifes and a drummer, in Colonial garb, are Yankee-Doodling around the Kirkland House courtyard.

Terry's fortieth birthday. Another milestone in this year of multiple an-

niversaries. I manage to get him on the phone. He is canceling some previously made birthday-dinner plans in order to watch the Celtics play a
crucial game in the NBA playoffs. I understand perfectly; as one gets older,
one must increasingly recognize and respect priorities.

It's Commencement Day here in Cambridge. These reunion people work
fast; outside the Faculty Club, where we're being served breakfast, there's
an array of photographs of us taken over the last couple of days, and we
can order copies. I spot one of Ellie with old friends Bob Bishop and
Mogie Lazarus and splurge on it. Then after assembling in the Yard,
we of '37 march toward our reserved seats through ranks of capped-and-
gowned young men and women, politely applauding us old duffers. But
what can these young children be doing here, all dressed up like college
seniors?

The conferring of degrees is enlivened by the release, from the seats
occupied by Public Health graduates, of a shower of condoms, each imprinted with *"Ad venerem securiorem"*—"For safer sex." When it is the Business School's grads' turn, and President Bok says MBAs are supposed to
go on "in service to society," he evokes considerable laughter, even more of
it than when, conferring an honorary degree on Yale's new president, Benno
Schmidt, Jr., his Harvard peer alludes to "one of the nation's great insti-
tutions of learning."

We decide to skip the afternoon's alumni exercises—I want to get home
in time to catch the Celtics—but do take in lunch at Memorial Hall. I ask
Dick Schultes what necktie he is wearing—a truly resplendent one, with a
gold crown on it. The doughty monarchist explains that he spilt something
on his Harvard tie yesterday, so had to make do with this other institutional
one—Royal Society, London.

Reaching New York City, and driving down Second Avenue, we notice
something amiss but can't at first figure out just what. Then it dawns on
us. Skipper's Mobil station has become a parking lot! But whatever will we
do now when our aging car needs surgery, or even a checkup? We've relied
on Skipper, who always—like Dick Schultes in his botanical bailiwick—
wore a spotless white physician's tunic and who never in our presence dirtied
his hands on a wheel or an engine, leaving such chores to underlings. I'm
afraid we'll never see his like again.

12 June

The New Yorker has a traveling art show—covers and cartoons—and while
it's at the Athenaeum in Boston, next week, I've been asked to give a talk
about the magazine. Licia Hahn comes up from the Business Department
to inform me that they've reserved a room for me at the Ritz, but I tell her
to cancel it; I'm going to spend the night at Cohasset with Terry and Rose

and the grandchildren. Here I am saving *The New Yorker* pocketsful of money once again! Ms. Hahn says that my lecture is already sold out, but she will make every effort to obtain admission for Terry and, at their request, the Prouts.

Sheila presents me with what she describes as the very first press identification card signed by Robert (no "Bob" here, this is serious stuff) Gottlieb. It is Number 112. It has been a longtime policy of the magazine that nobody should be made to appear to outrank anybody else; and I'm glad to see that the tradition has been continued.

In the morning papers: the Algonquin has been sold to a Japanese woman, but Shawn was seen at his usual table at lunch yesterday notwithstanding. Yet another tradition that has praiseworthily resisted change.

13 June

Reagan is in Berlin, urging Gorbachev to tear down the wall. It was just a couple of days ago, at his library, that I heard President Kennedy's voice memorably utter *"Ich bin ein Berliner,"* and now here's an upstart actor trying to play his role.

I talk to Tony, in Wellfleet. Ian's Little League team won one game (he is playing first), but had the victory taken away when it developed one of his teammates had been born three days too soon and was thus ineligible. Competition is clearly just as fierce as it was when Tony and his brothers were Little Leaguers. I was never much more than a bystander (and, of course, rooter) at those tilts, but the next generation has taken big strides forward: Terry has been coaching a team his Ely's on, and because nobody else would volunteer to do it Tony had to umpire a game the other day—a difficult task, considering that his son was playing in it.

14 June

Since for the time being we have our car in the city (our neighborhood garage has consented to house it for us at a mere seventeen dollars a day), we take advantage of its availability and drive over the George Washington Bridge to have lunch at Bud Vervaet's woodland place at Oakland, N. J. Most of the other guests are women. One is wearing a T-shirt that I guess she finds amusing; its inscription reads "Old Fart." Another, nursing a baby, says on being introduced to me that she takes exceedingly strong exception to a recent "Profile" of a man in *The New Yorker*. He was depicted there as a rather engaging, if eccentric, chap, and the young mother says that was a totally false representation, that the man is unredeemedly obnoxious. As a Little League coach should loyally defend his players, so do I rally to the side of my colleague, and I demand of this woman by what authority does she have the presumption to take a tack so diametrically opposed to that of our reporter? "I lived with the son of a bitch for two years," she says. I feel like asking the other guest if I can swap shirts.

15 June

Today is Flag Day, also Income-tax Installment Day, a yin-and-yang orbit of the sun if ever there was one.

I thought I was going to get my new teeth emplaced permanently today, but no, only temporarily permanently. Jules Leaf, who has been holding them more or less together for over forty years, is practicing less and less nowadays. He works only three days a week for six months a year. For the other six, he has bought a house at Palm Springs, on the edge of a golf course—a waking dream for him. He has a golf cart in his garage there and drives it around his pool to the eighth hole, giving him a chance to warm up on it and the ninth before joining the rest of his regular foursome.

Jules asks after Jinny. I say she was at a party at our house not long ago. Dr. Magnani seems amazed that my first wife should be on speaking terms with my second. I am lucky in that respect. I remember one friend whose second wife's first husband, when he had occasion to correspond with her about their children, would never deign to write her name upon an envelope, relying instead merely on a post-office box number.

On the way to the office, I stop off and buy *New York 1930*, the architectural book that mentions my father. And in its 846 pages, what a heady profusion of mentions! Page 340 tells of a dinner that year for Frank Lloyd Wright, at which one of the speakers was Ely Jacques Kahn. I decide to have the principal section about my father Xeroxed for me and assorted grandchildren and to give the big book itself to E. J. K. III as custodian for E. J. K. IV.

I learn a lot about my forebears from this book that I'd forgotten, if I ever knew it: that my paternal grandfather, for instance, who I've always thought of as French, was born in Austria; and that my paternal grandmother was the daughter of an architect. And that it was my *maternal* grandfather who got my father into his first architectural firm. And that when Ely went to China, during the Depression, when eminent architects were vying for such commissions as remodeling bathrooms, the Japanese police followed him all the way. If my grandchildren ever read everything herein about their great-grandfather, they'll know more about him than I did until today.

Rooting around aimlessly in one of my unindexed file drawers, I unearth a letter, 1973 vintage, from Caspar W. Weinberger, then Secretary of Health,

Education, and Welfare, congratulating me on having been admitted to the Century and adding—this was long before he or I anticipated he'd become Secretary of Defense—that "I first read your articles on the war in the Pacific shortly after I returned from that area and I always felt that you captured more of the real experiences than anyone else I have read." How enjoyable a surprise to come upon a letter one would have confidently wagered large sums one had never in one's life received!

But wait! Down at the very bottom of this dusty drawer is a pile of yellow manuscript—a color *The New Yorker* must have abandoned for its standard copy paper about when Bob Gottlieb was in high school. What can this be, anyway? What it turns out to be is a long-since forgotten journal, begun, reasonably enough, on one of the most meaningful days of my life—my first son's birth date.

11 June 1947. Today I am beginning a diary. I have decided to keep one because in time to come I hope the little events of my life will be of real interest to me and to my family, and, pursuant to reflecting on those events, I should like to have a fairly accurate record available. The more time I spend as a reporter, the more aware I become of the imperfection of human memory. Sinclair Lewis once said to me—I am throwing him in early, so that in years to come the egotistical part of me may take distorted pleasure in the memory of my associations with Important People, even though the cynical part of me may point out, reasonably enough, that I am dragging in a reference to my only meeting so far with Lewis, and perhaps my only one forever—Lewis once said to me, then, that history of any kind is bound to be full of distortions, because of the frailty of memory. Lewis said he had once asked a group of reporters—among them Vincent Sheean, I believe, Dorothy Thompson (of course), and several others whose names I have already forgotten (see?)—to describe to him an incident—I think it was a speech by Dollfuss, or something—of which they had all been eyewitnesses. Their accounts of this incident all differed wildly, depending partly on their philosophies of life, partly on their political beliefs. If the world's leading reporters cannot agree on an important scene they have all actually seen, history's reliance on the statements of eyewitnesses, as recorded in the press, etc., is bound to be somewhat faulty.

If I must keep a diary, this is as good a time as any to begin. For one thing, I am now thirty—perched precariously between my past and my future. For another, at 11:45 this morning, in Room 1207 of Leroy, my son ????? was born. He weighed 6 lbs. 14 oz. Length: 19½. In years to come, he may derive more pleasure from this extended manuscript than I. Children never really know anything about their parents' lives; to most children, it is unthinkable that their parents had much in the way of life, before they, the children, were born. I know that I find it difficult to think of my own parents as having had much of a life unrelated to my own. Children are awfully young when they're born, moreover, and their memories of their early years, as they grow older, become increasingly dim. As a doting and proud father, I shall undoubtedly jot down in my diary [I quit after less than a year] all sorts of things affecting the growth of my child; in years to come, perhaps this diary (if he inherits from his mother, certainly not from his father, sufficient patience to enable him to read it) will prove even more valuable a stimulation to his reflections about himself than it will to mine about me.

16 June. I was told yesterday that I could take pictures because there are no prominent babies here now. When I tried today I was summarily rejected. This clear proof to me that Terry is a prominent person, and I am cheered no end. Grandpa and Mima [my maternal grandparents] in. He looked for ten seconds and wanted his lunch. Never did focus on Terry, any more than Terry could focus on him. In nearly eighty-eight years, he has never missed his lunch, but he always acts as if people were trying to keep him from it.

17 June. Fifteen vases of flowers in Jinny's room this evening. Brendan Gill, a father of some standing, told me about a much-hailed lecture by Spock, saying that women should now do the things they wanted to do by instinct—nurse their babies, fondle them, let them sleep in the same room, pick them up, let them dawdle over feedings, etc. A complete revolution.

29 June. Terry will be surprised at how much his father goes to ball games, just as I was by my father. I will be able to tell Terry that one summer I saw two no-hitters and I hope he will be impressed. Today I am concerned, as are many others, whether or not Jackie Robinson can continue a hitting streak. I hope that by the time Terry gets to go to a ball game he will see nothing unusual about a Negro playing in the company of white men.

16 June

Ellie and I go to the Barbizon (now fancily named the Golden Tulip Barbizon), where she lived as a young single woman, for a joint radio interview with Caspar Citron. As Judge Wapner knocks off a week's worth of "People's Court" programs in a single day, so apparently does Citron make the most of his time. He knows us both, and indeed was at Ellie's book party, but when we enter the room fitted out as his studio he barely has time to look up and thinks at first, from looking down at some schedule in front of him, that we are what he calls "the apartheid couple." While we were waiting our turn, E. showed me a passage in *On Glory Roads* that she'd added to the book since I last read it. She is describing how a companion on her trek to Santiago de Compostela was quick to shout, after the fashion of footsore pilgrims on first sighting the distant spires of its cathedral, *"Montjoie!"* I was pleased, because although she didn't identify her traveling mate, I was the only one along that day.

Lunch with Sheila and Natasha. They tell me about the farewell party for Johnny Murphy, which I had to miss because I was out of town. Gottlieb and Martha Kaplan, who produced two cases of champagne, told Sheila to spare no expense; and her prodigality at Zabar's apparently impressed even its blasé staff. Both Sheila and Bob made a point of inviting Shawn, who came early and didn't stay long, but the important thing was that he was there. Johnny has been at the magazine for forty-five years. I'm not sure, now that Bill S. is gone, who holds the longevity record. A toss-up, maybe, between Mickey Hahn and Gene Kinkead?

The Bernhard Goetz jury has acquitted him of all charges except carrying an unlicensed gun. People are wondering how young blacks will react to that. Jeannette Rohatyn comes by, and she and Ellie and I go to Central Park for an alfresco afternoon presentation of *Tosca*, with Placido Domingo. There's a huge crowd—quite yuppieish: picnic baskets and bottles of wine. All we have is a blanket and some cherries. Central Park, reputedly a sneak thief's paradise, is teeming with cops, maybe would have been Goetz or no Goetz, but here I am lying on my back with Ellie's purse as my pillow, as ripe a target as any miscreant could ask for. To be sure, we have Hopi with us. Were an alien hand to reach for my pillow, though, she would probably wag her tail and lick it.

There is an early-evening meeting of apartment owners from our building. One person in attendance, who seems not to believe in the inviolability of private property, argues that before any apartment is sold to an outsider we insiders should be offered first crack. I tend to keep quiet at these gatherings, but in an endeavor to lighten an atmosphere that is beginning to darken, I rise and pledge solemnly that I will not put our 1978 Chevy up for grabs until everyone in the room has had a chance to bid on it.

17 June

Pat Crow has a "Profile" in the current *New Yorker* about a man who makes fishing rods. There are mentions of Leonard rods. I am not a fly fisherman, not a fisherman of any caliber, so why is this so familiar? On a hunch, I go to the office library and discover that the very first "Profile" I ever had in the magazine, back in 1938, was of a fishing-tackle store that sold Leonards.

Larry Adler phones. He's in town for just this one day—the "Today" show this morning, a gig at the Ballroom tonight. We have the Blivens coming to dinner, so we won't get down there. Larry says he worked hard for the Labour Party in the recent British elections, which Mrs. Thatcher, of course, won, and thumpingly. Are Americans, I wonder to myself, allowed to, or supposed to, play active parts in foreign election campaigns? It doesn't bother me especially, but it might bother the Tories, or might have if they'd lost.

At dinner, there is much talk of Naomi B.'s having sold her first long-fact piece, about a mountain upstate somewhere, to Gottlieb. Naomi and Bruce are among the few couples we know who still smoke. (I went to Dr. Gorham this morning to have my blood pressure checked; it was OK, 142 over 80 or 140 over 82 or some such, and he reminded me again of the time I almost had a smoking relapse.) I give Bruce the *Harvard Crimson* article quoting him. Reminiscing about the past prompts Naomi to reveal that she has become a good friend of a girl whom Bruce dated in our college years. I remember her well; although the term "jailbait" was not then in vogue, she always seemed to be about twelve. Bruce's old friend, now Naomi's new one, has while I wasn't paying attention reached the implausible age of sixty-eight.

18 June

There have been riots in Seoul again. George Miller, the executive director of the U. S. Olympic Committee, says it's too soon to consider an American boycott of the Games. Meanwhile, Jesse Jackson, who is increasingly making himself a force to be listened to, if not actually voted for, has warned the South Korean ambassador to Washington (if Larry Adler can get involved in extraterritorial politics, why not the Reverend?) that if his countrymen don't shape up a boycott is certainly possible. Whether Bob Gottlieb intends to boycott the Olympics—it would be for editorial, not political reasons—is still up in the air.

I head north for my talk about *The New Yorker*. On the way, I stop off at *Boston* magazine, to see Terry's new office, and then we stop off together at a bar partly owned by his barber. Standing room only at the Athenaeum, where after an introduction by Penn Brown, of *The New Yorker*'s Boston office (business), I'm expected to speak for forty-five minutes. I realize halfway through that I've outlined more than an hour's worth of material and cut myself off at fifty minutes, so there'll be time for a few questions before we move on for sherry and cheese. The Prouts got in all right, and so to my surprise did daughter-in-law Judy and her sister Sharon, who's just flown in from Florida. Judy didn't know the lecture was sold out. She just marched up to the front door and identified herself and continued on in. The talk seems to go well enough, I am assured by a number of people who accost me over sherry, among them a woman subsequently described to me as a "Waspi" ("Wasp indeed!") and a man who's a collector of autographed photographs and presents me with a copy (autographed, naturally) of a book of his pictures.

19 June

Bedded down in Terry's and Rose's guest room at Cohasset, I am awakened at dawn by a door being softly opened and whispering voices enjoining all within earshot to silence. Jacquelene is the first to try to ascertain whether Pa Jack, as this batch of grandchildren have elected to call me, is asleep. Before departing for Boston and the airport, I get to visit her classroom and to watch Ely play soccer in a school yard. It was my impression at breakfast that Curt, who at two is just beginning to talk, uttered a reasonably intelligible "Pa Jack."

Reading the *Times* on the shuttle, I learn that President Reagan has awarded some big-time civilian medal to, among others, Ella Fitzgerald. I first heard her, while I was an undergraduate, at an Eliot House dance. She was Chick Webb's singer. I remember the occasion well because my date's parents sent a chaperone up from New York with her to share her hotel room.

At two-thirty, back in New York, a knock on my office door. It's Bob Gottlieb, who'd heard I hoped to see him. We discuss a couple of pieces I'd like to work on, and then we talk at some length about the magazine in general—and about changes already made in the "Talk of the Town," book reviews, theater criticism, etc., etc. He says he wants to encourage some staff writers (I do not think he means me) who've just been sitting around to become more productive. He says he thinks of me as a fast writer. Well, I explain, there are people around these premises who equate *The New Yorker* with the Bible and believe everything that appears in it has been carved, as it were, out of stone, but in my view it has always been a magazine, albeit an exceptional one, that comes out fifty-two times a year. I wonder, while I have the floor, about one of Bob's recent innovations: for the first time ever, if I'm not mistaken, a "Profile" did not appear ahead of all other long-fact pieces. He explains that the issue in question was one of those with an advertising insert of sixteen pages or some such, and he didn't want to have a piece so robustly interrupted, so there was no alternative to what transpired. Bob seems incredibly relaxed, and indeed says he's going to take a couple of weeks off next month for a tour of some of the nation's flea markets. I hope he lets me know if he's planning to look over the one at the Wellfleet drive-in.

20 June

Our semiannual move. This time, we break the trip to Truro with an overnight stay at the Patrick Smiths'. Sharon, Connecticut, is not exactly on a straight line to Cape Cod, but when we leave there tomorrow the car will already have been packed. *Getting* it packed, ever since Ellie switched to a computer and printer and whatever else it is that fills her big bulky boxes, is no easy matter, but somehow we always seem to fit everything in, dog included, though rarely with more than a few cubic inches to spare. At least I don't have to carry a typewriter. I am the privileged possessor now of three old-fashioned standard uprights; *The New Yorker* has become so addicted to word processors that it's been urging contributors to take typewriters off its hands. I was happy the other day, accordingly, to remove from the premises a lovely old Underwood—same kind Jack Kennedy used, though he probably had no more than one. These days, no prudent magazine publisher would think of throwing assets, however venerable, to the wind. Accordingly, my latest treasured acquisition, which was delivered cleaned, and with a brand-new ribbon, set me back ten dollars.

Patrick S. says that George Steiner is furious at *The New Yorker* because under the new regime somebody had the temerity to change two of his words. I have a hunch that if the complaint reaches Bob G., he won't lose any sleep over it.

21 June

Longest day of the year—summer solstice and all that. It has to do with the sun, which remains stubbornly invisible from early dawn to late dusk. On the road, I see a Massachusetts automobile with an "Ex-POW" license plate, which is probably as surefire (and deserved) a way as any of avoiding traffic tickets. At Truro, the tennis-court fence has been repaired and the court is ready for action. The roses are doing poorly, though, and the porch screens need attention, which will have to wait, I suppose, until the eggs hatch in the nest a robin has chosen to build just off the kitchen door.

Lexy phones. He won $300 in a photography contest. Also (he has an ordinary license plate, and a beard), he got stopped by some New Mexico cops who, suspicious of a package of cinnamon he was transporting, scoured his car, fruitlessly, for drugs.

22 June

Ellie says she found a tick on her last night. So first thing this morning on goes Hopi's tick collar and her microelectronic flea collar. I had a restless night myself, being unable in the middle of it to remember the combination for the lock on our post-office box. At dawn, I suddenly realized it isn't a combination lock at all (that had been back at Scarborough, a generation ago) and that the key to it was on the same ring as our car keys. The day when I can't sleep for being unable to recall my own name can't be terribly far away.

There's a familiar pattern to the first day back on the Cape. A trip to Wellfleet, of course, to stock up on groceries. But when I ask, at Lema's, after Maggie, my special friend there for check-cashing and other perks, I learn to my dismay that she's moved next door to the drug store. At the post office, eight large bundles from *The New Yorker*. The ones Bruce Diones and his crew have wrapped arrive in tip-top shape. The ones I wrapped myself are falling apart. It's one of the agreeable characteristics of small-town life (Truro's year-round population is still not much more than fifteen hundred) that only rarely can one go to the post office without running into friends and neighbors. This morning, for instance, I encounter a couple of Joans—Cohen and Fox—Bud Stillman, Linda Traum, Etta Connor, and Palmer Williams. No time to linger long, because I have my Town Hall errands to pursue: beach sticker, dog license, clamming license. Senior citizens can hunt sea clams, assuming there are any around, for free.

At Town Hall, I also pick up the annual report, for 1986, of the Town of Truro. Our three Selectmen each get $9,000 a year. Highest paid official, at $37,401.17, was our school principal, who was more than $10,000 ahead of the Chief of Police. Fire Chief Ray Joseph—he doesn't have to work every day, blessedly—received $5,800, far less than the $18,000 earned by his son as a full-time truck driver. Arthur Joseph was paid $980 for his services as moth agent, Malcolm Preston $100 as Town Moderator, and Cindy Worthington—I must remember to ask her how this figure was derived—$18 as Police Department Matron.

Last year, in Truro, there were ten cases of forgery, two drug-law violations, fifteen missing persons, five annoying phone calls, three suicide attempts, eighty-eight arrests, 222 instances of suspicious activity, and one sex offense. There were twelve births, twenty-two marriages, 282 licensed dogs, and ten new private swimming pools. Ten pools, in our seashore community! That one staggered me. Where in the world can they be? Clearly, there are a lot of people who get mail at our post office who are not in my social orbit. Otherwise, though, sounds like a healthy, vital town to me, even though the average cost of a new home (not counting land and, I assume, not counting swimming pool, either) has reached $110,000.

Dinner at Judy's and Tony's, and since they own their house, I hope that the value of Wellfleet real estate, old and new, is accelerating like ours.

23 June

Fred Astaire died yesterday, at eighty-eight. Palmer Williams says that when "60 Minutes" did a piece on him, they found him as inarticulate as I had in my turn. But, oh, those feet!

Marie Joseph, whom I haven't seen since she was a little girl living across South Pamet Road, comes by with a husband and two sons. She is bearing a petition she wants me to sign—expressing concern about a proposed National Seashore bicycle trail. The people who drew up the petition fear that tens of thousands of cyclists will descend upon us, with no bathroom or refreshment facilities to ease their passage. I sign, but with misgivings; the National Park Service has been awfully good to those of us who are lucky enough to have houses inside a park, and national parks should after all be not for the privileged few but for the nation. How tiresome to think of one's self as a liberal and forever be examining both sides of questions!

First tennis this year on our court, with Ellie, Joan Fox, Sidney Simon, and Palmer Williams. That "our" ought to include Palmer, who probably contributes more to the upkeep of the court (and don't let anyone tell you that a clay court doesn't demand huge amounts of upkeep, both in time and money) than its nominal proprietors.

24 June

It was chilly last night, and the furnace wouldn't switch on. I went down into the cellar with a flashlight and couldn't get it going, although I thought I was pressing all the right buttons. There was a curious smell—a winter's accumulation of mustiness, I reckoned. I phone Mooney's this morning, and they send over a repairman, and by daylight the trouble is visible and dismaying: a dead animal, probably a decomposed raccoon, its hind legs, or what's left of them, protruding from the furnace. Mooney's man won't even try to dislodge it, says just being near it is making him sick. We phone our longtime animal exterminator, same chap who once got the squirrels and chipmunks, dead and alive, out of Ellie's study. He says he'll be right over. What he's going to have to do will be disagreeable, but what the hell, it's a living. (He has more in common with most writers than he may realize.) On arrival, he borrows (and fails to return) three of my best screwdrivers, removes part of the furnace housing (and throws it away as hopelessly contaminated), and charges us $100 for his half-hour's work. But who else would have done the job at any price? Yes, he says, it was a raccoon, must have come down the chimney. I make a mental note to have that chimney capped before next winter.

Ding Watson is giving Linda Sturner Traum a birthday party tonight. Jerry T. can't make it. I point out to Linda—not very graciously, or logically, I am bound to concede—that he could have chartered a plane for less than what it is undoubtedly going to cost me, before the furnace gets cleaned and reconstructed, to dispose of a dead raccoon. The Simons, Kaplans, and Foxes are present. Also April Hopkins, but not Budd; he is promoting his new book on UFOs tonight on the Ted Koppel show, but even if I'm still awake then I have no intention of tuning in; why go out of my way to make myself irritable? Frank and Joan Fox are about to take off for a wedding at such a high-class (and, I gather, heterosexual) section of Fire Island that the guests have been instructed that anyone who anticipates playing tennis should bring along whites. At our court, we are much more easygoing, and just about the only rule I try to enforce is: no children or dogs on the playing surface while a point is in progress.

25 June

A pleasant, sunny day. We wouldn't need the furnace if we could use it. At breakfast, I look over yesterday's "Living Section" in the *Times*, which has a feature story, "The Soybean Eaters." It's all about Central Soya, of Fort Wayne, Indiana, which the paper thinks is a big outfit because it has $1.37 billion in annual sales. Over in Decatur, Illinois, Dwayne Andreas and his Archer-Daniels-Midland cohorts, whose gross is about four times as large but who are nowhere mentioned in the article, must be amused.

Annie Dillard comes by, and when she hears about our raccoon trouble, she tells of an even more harrowing experience of the Hamburgers'. A pair of the animals have apparently built a nest inside their Wellfleet house, are raising a litter there, and are grudgingly permitting Anna and Phil access to only a severely limited part of their own domain. Because the Hamburgers are more softhearted than I'd be in such a circumstance, they want the whole family evicted alive, and apparently the people they recruited to do that are charging them thirty-two dollars a head. We may end up getting off more cheaply, unless we have to buy a new furnace.

Annie D., whose life I had always believed to be reasonably eventful, startles me by saying that playing anagrams with me was the highlight of her entire 1986 summer. I am so touched I invite her over to play again next Monday evening. Meanwhile, in belated appreciation of my crossword-puzzle article, Anne Bernays, who I suspect put up with me when she and Joe were putting me up in Cambridge because I was always a compliant lamb for her leonine version of Scrabble, has sent me an anagram: "Copy a live eel." The solution, obviously (and flatteringly), is "A lovely piece," but no word-games nut worth his or her salt (remind me some day to look into just how much salt is worth, anyway) would respond so straightforwardly, so I pretend she stumped me and write back that I had to throw myself on the mercy of a retired admiral, who provided the correct answer: "Leave policy."

26 June

I am organizing my piece on the mountain-climbing accident out West— the hardest part of nonfiction writing, in my view, though it may not entail the putting on paper of a single imperishable word—and am encouraged by the receipt of a letter from the William Mackeys, parents of the girl who died. They are at their summer place, in Woods Hole, and I may drive down there tomorrow and call on them. It could be difficult for all of us, but how can I write about the incident without touching base with them?

Terry and Rose and the kids come by, en route to Provincetown. Jacquelene is proud to demonstrate that she can spell her name. (She'll find as she grows older that virtually nobody else can.) She can also spell "Ely" and "Curt," but her prowess seems to stop with siblings; when I test her, it turns out she has no idea how to spell either "Terry" or "Rose."

The Mooney truck arrives, but the men who are supposed to repair the furnace contend that there are still bits of raccoon lodged inside it, and they won't touch it until it's thoroughly cleaned. They don't seem to realize that at this time of the year it's difficult enough to hire cleaning people to clean the ostensibly *clean* parts of one's house.

27 June

Old age can't be all it's sometimes cracked up to be. Today's guest list at the post office includes D. B. When I ask about her husband, he's in an up-Cape nursing home, and while he has all his marbles, at ninety-odd, he's no longer ambulatory and needs constant attention. It would have cost more to have round-the-clock nurses in Truro, D. says, than what the nursing home charges. I refrain from requesting figures.

I work on my accident outline all morning and then with some trepidation head for Woods Hole. The Mackeys have been checking up on me; they know that the *Globe* had a story yesterday about a course in memoir-writing Ellie and I are scheduled to give at Castle Hill in August. I had programmed myself to be solicitous to the bereaved parents; instead, they go out of their way (even cookies) to demonstrate their awareness of how awkward an interview this may be for me; and way beyond that, they let me see a number of invaluable letters and other material that are bound to enrich my account.

It is a rainy Saturday, and that means more people on the roads than on the beaches, and even though July hasn't yet arrived, it's a two-and-a-half hour drive each way to and from the far end of the Cape. But the trip was eminently worthwhile, and I tell the Mackeys that I'll be sure to let them see the piece before it runs—if it runs. Some of us who would like to know more about Gottlieb's tastes are still uninformed about to what extent they're formed.

28 June

I am starting to write. As a motorist might check his oil before embarking on an arduous trip, or a channel-swimmer his goggles, so do I ritualistically put a fresh typewriter ribbon into my trusty old Underwood.

It is a Sunday, so there will be no shortage of tennis players, even though Palmer is hors de combat with the gout. He has some prescription pills, which is good news, because I have a hunch that before the summer's over I'm going to beg him to lend me a couple.

29 June

It's beginning to look as if all systems are nearly go for our journey to Russia. In today's mail, visa application blanks from Gerry Piel. He says we may not have to travel first class after all, which could save us thousands of rubles. And who are "we" finally going to be? After several changes of cast—this classmate's wife is ailing, that one's mother-in-law —we're going to be six couples and one stag: Gerry and Eleanor, Brent and Corinne Abel from San Francisco, Dave and Jeanne Schwarz, Fag and Dede Goodhue, Archer and Hope Trench, Rusty Crawford, and Ellie and me.

Annie Dillard comes by for our anagrams date. She trounces me handily, but it has been a long day at work, and I am tired. Excuses! Excuses! It turns out—for safekeeping in our coincidence files—that in writing, this very day, we both had occasion to use the word *bergschrund*, which I at least have never trifled with before.

The Soviet Union will have to wait its turn. Annie and Ellie are booked in advance of our trip there to head for Calgary, not to preview the Winter Olympics but to embark on a horseback safari up into the Canadian Rockies. Here am I writing a piece about people ill-prepared to climb a mountain, and here is my wife, who hasn't been on a horse in the eighteen years I've known her, planning a near-vertical ride—she who in recent months has fractured limbs while (1) trying to mount a bicycle and (2) walking a dog. Well, she's a grown woman and knows what she's doing. I am spared the necessity of apologizing for not accompanying them because I have not been invited to go along.

30 June

Our eighteenth wedding anniversary. I hope the roses arrive. They do, fortunately, even before Ellie is up and about.

We need rain, and the tennis court is dry, so I go to Mooney's and pick up some calcium chloride. The smallest measure they have on hand is 100 pounds. I bring home a couple of sacks, and it's typical of Palmer that although his gout has reduced him temporarily to the role of spectator he nonetheless drags them to courtside. Several of the players who turn up today suddenly remember that they have bad backs, but Doug Huebler and Jerry Cohen and Bob Lifton all pitch in anyway—they had witnessed Palmer's limping heroics—and soon we have the stuff adequately spread. (Naturally, only a few hours afterward a heavy thunderstorm dumps more water on the court than it can come close to absorbing.) Bob says it is the first time that he has ever indulged in heavy labor like this and makes me promise not to tell his wife.

We foregather at the Cohens' for, once again, a joint celebration of two wedding anniversaries. The Gerry Holtons are there, and when our trip to Russia comes up, I sense that he is surprised that the likes of us would be traveling to Russia in the company of someone with the scientific credentials of Gerry Piel.

Meanwhile, Brent Abel has phoned. A retired Austrian cop, one of the crew of the U-boat Brent's ship rammed and sank, is going to be in the States for a few days, and would I be interested in meeting him? Also, more important, how would Ellie and I feel, after our trip to the USSR, about accompanying the Abels to Germany, where other Second World War veterans whom he plucked from the Atlantic are talking about giving him a hero's reception? I say at once that we'll go along. Such a meeting could immeasurably strengthen whatever I might write. And I'll try to catch up with the policeman while he's over here.

1 July

Joan Colebrook calls. Her book is going to press, and her publishers have challenged her assertion in it that her son Jay was named after John Jay, the first American Secretary of State. Can I help? Do I have a reference book? I know, having written John Hay Whitney's biography, that John *Hay* was McKinley's Secretary of State, but I'm not sure about John Jay. (And I should after all be surer than Joan, who's Australian.) I find that I do have, in my study, an ancient *Information Please Almanac*. John Jay isn't even in the index. And he isn't in a roster of all Secretaries of State, either. I tell Joan when I impart the news to look at the good side of it; she's in time to correct her book, and it's much too late in Jay's life for her to worry about rechristening him.

In the mail, a welcome refund check from the New York State income-tax people, and a letter from the Internal Revenue Service saying there was a mistake on our return so we'll get no refund from *them*. But this would seem to suggest that they've examined the return and that we're not going to be audited. In view of that, it might be foolish to draw further attention to ourselves by bringing up that "Eleanuor" business.

2 July

Eleanuor's mother is due to arrive from Cleveland this afternoon, escorted by grandson Kevin and his German girlfriend. Lucile, we've been warned, may have a slight fever, which gives us pause inasmuch as she's over ninety and the *Cape Codder* has just run a story headlined "Medical Situation Becomes Critical as More Cape Doctors Depart."

Helen Suzman writes, expressing disappointment in the recent South African elections. She got returned to Parliament, predictably, but her Progressive Federal Party lost seven seats and is no longer the official opposition. "All those big hopes of an alliance of like-minded people in the post-election period appear to have disappeared like the morning mists," Helen says. "Ah well, we soldier on with 19 Members instead of 26 and will just have to hope that we can survive during this very depressing period."

E. and I drive to Logan Airport (Amanda Williams will walk the dog), stopping off at Orleans to have photos taken for our USSR visas, and to have some Xeroxes made at the *Cape Codder*. Tony shows us through the paper's new wing, very impressive, and we receive high-level greetings from Mal Hobbs and Greg O'Brien. At Logan, the plane from Cleveland is—did you expect early?—quite late, and it's close to eight before we leave, and another hour before we get through the tunnel, and eleven before we reach Truro. But Lucile seems astonishingly well, in better shape really than last summer. And Hopi has not yet jumped up and knocked her down.

3 July

An in-memoriam card from Berte Taube, about a contemporary of Lucile's who's just died—Max Granich (1896–1987). We hadn't seen much
of Manny in recent years, even though he was a Truro neighbor, but we
remember well being in a group the old Communist shepherded around
China in 1973—so far back that the great underground statues at Sian
were just beginning to be excavated and that the bookstores in Peking
(not yet Beijing) and other cities contained little indigenous reading
matter other than the works of Chairman Mao. (Shawn never ran anything I wrote about that trip—in part, I've always believed, because I'd
made all the arrangements myself at a time when the magazine was trying
hard but in vain to get other writers over there.) If there is a special part
of Heaven reserved for undeviating Marxists, Manny Granich is surely
there.

4 July

I probably should go to Wellfleet for the Fourth of July parade, because
the Judy Wallace Group is going to be playing on a flatbed truck. But I
want to finish the first draft of my piece, which I hope to get to Gottlieb
before he goes away. Rain seems imminent, so the Cohens come by for
morning tennis with their houseguests the MacFarquhars. Emily M. is
covering the Dukakis campaign for the *Economist*. That journal doesn't believe in bylines, of course, but she says she once contrived to have her
name appear in a story of hers; she was interviewing President Zia of
Pakistan, and in the course of answering a question of hers he was kind
enough to interject the name of the asker. A small triumph, to be sure,
one about which most readers couldn't care less, but the sort of thing that
warms journalistic hearts.

Rod MacFarquhar, now a Harvard professor and director of the Fairbank
Center for Asian Research, once sat in the British Parliament with Shirley
Williams, the incumbent head of the Social Democratic Party over there.
She's around this weekend, too, thanks to Dick Neustadt, and she joins our
group at Corn Hill for the traditional holiday beach picnic. Ms. Williams
and Gerry Holton and I discuss the two-party political system and its
chances of surviving in the United States. (Fair to middling, we concur.)
She says she is traveling incognito and is giving no interviews to journalists,
but it's all right to talk to me because she's just been informed that after
fifty years at *The New Yorker* I have finally retired. I never do ascertain her
source.

5 July

So many tennis players show up this Sunday—Joey, Cy Post, Renée Simon, John and Mary Bunker, Cindy Worthington, Ray and Lee Elman, Palmer, now gout-free, I forget who all else—that we could use a second court. But where are they all on those days when we desperately need a fourth for doubles? The Bunkers are here from California for only a few days, getting their house ready for tenants, and Doctor John gets worrisomely winded running back after a lob. Physician or not, he should be careful; he is no kid any more, just had his forty-fifth Harvard reunion.

When he gets his breath back, John, on hearing that we'll be going to Russia with Gerry Piel, says he knows and admires Gerry because of some medical publication he's been putting out. At courtside, John favors Palmer and me with his two favorite professional reminiscences: how he almost treated a Pope for hiccups (anesthesiologists do it by deadening some nerve in the throat or cheek or thereabouts) and how he almost put to sleep a rhinoceros with an infected horn. In neither instance did he have to test his skills. The Pope, perhaps through prayer, stopped hiccuping before John could minister to him, and the rhinoceros's veterinarians decided to let nature take its course, which was an enormous relief to John, for he had no idea what would be the proper dosage to knock out a rhino, and if something went wrong, how would you resort, as in an emergency you might have to with a Pope or any other human being, to mouth-to-mouth?

6 July

I typed my piece—about eight thousand words—nonstop between breakfast and lunch. (I may have to fiddle around with it a little more before I send it in—by, naturally, overnight express mail, which I always use to try to make my work look urgent even when it isn't—because Ellie has suggested a few much appreciated changes.) I can type at a two-thousand-words-an-hour clip for four or five hours, without faltering. I suppose it's comparable in a way to marathon running or channel swimming: you get going and after a while you keep on without knowing exactly where you are, although you're aware of your ultimate destination.

At the post office, Ann Keezer says her dog of fifteen years has died. I've never, thank God, had to cope with a child's death. A dog's can be bad enough. I remember tearfully when Jinny took poor crippled Barge off to the vet's (I didn't have the guts myself) for terminal anesthesia; and how anguishing was the news of Rainbow's succumbing to a hit-and-run driver. Why do we let ourselves get so attached to dogs that their re-moval is so wrenching? Hopi runs at large for up to six or eight hours a day. If anything happens to her this summer, I'm not sure I'd ever want another dog. How much potential suffering should one bring upon one's self, anyway?

You know what can make a person feel old? I enter Ellie's study in search of an eraser—a bit of rubber, remember? at the opposite end of a pencil from the lead—and there's grandson Ian sitting at her computer. I say, "You know how to work this machine—eh?" (I haven't the foggiest notion how to myself), and he replies, with just a hint of condescension, "It's not the machine. It's this stupid game." I guess he is playing some electronic game, or perhaps inventing one. Well, I think I can still hold my own with him at chess, though by the time he turns twelve, who can tell?

Larry Adler phones. He seems genuinely and touchingly sorry that we won't get to New York for the party celebrating the publication of the American edition of his autobiography. I look at it again and am reminded that he describes me therein as "my best friend." That makes me feel guilty about being here instead of there.

The current *New Yorker* says that Knopf has brought out a collection of Kennedy Fraser's pieces for the magazine. I didn't know there were enough of them. I sometimes think I may be the only *New Yorker* writer not all of whose pieces have eventually come out in a book.

7 July

The May-June issue of *Olympic Review*, a publication of the International Olympic Committee, of which Juan Antonio Samaranch is president, con-tains sixteen photographs of Samaranch.

Oliver North's crimes include at least one for which he will probably never be indicted: unfairness to morning workers. His televised testimony starts today, and how can one draw away from so powerful a magnet merely to write? The *Times* has a story today explaining what all those ribbons he sports represent. It's one of the few accurate debunking analyses of fruit salad I've ever seen and is written by John Cushman. I wonder how many readers of the *Times* know that that recently designated military correspon-dent is a retired Marine Corps general—a reporter who truly knows his stuff. How splendidly imaginative of the editors to have piped him aboard! He outranks North in more ways than one.

Appended to Bruce Cagwin's plumbing bill is a note stating firmly that he has repaired the downstairs toilet for the last time. We need a new one. I tell him to get us one. I wonder how much a toilet costs. Here is a facility we all use at least a couple of times a day, and I have no idea what it is worth. I am sure Bruce will be glad to enlighten me.

Big crowd again for tennis. Robin Howard says that her Caitlin stepped on something—clamshell, glass, razor blade, whatever—at the Fourth of July beach picnic and sliced off part of a big toe. Turned out that if mother and daughter hadn't waited until the next morning to consult a doctor they might have got it sewn back on. Robin says that when they wondered how Caitlin could go swimming now without getting her bandage wet, somebody said that was easy: use condoms. Safe swimming, safe sex—what a versatile convenience!

8 July

Dinner last night deep in the Wellfleet woods, at the Jack Phillipses' pond. We got there all right, having to stop only once to beseech guidance from —well, look who's here!—Chrissie Schlesinger; and we got home all right, too, because Paul Resika led us through the maze to an exit spang on the way to our house. I wish I could remember the way for next time. Our hostess forgives me for not having hung around Cambridge long enough on Commencement Day to see her father, Mason Hammond, be awarded the Harvard Medal, which in terms of recognition for achievement (the eminent classicist has also long been a source of Harvard lore) probably outweighs most of Oliver North's chestwear.

On the stand today, North is bragging about how the American people love him. I wish I knew of some useful way of going on record to the effect that it is not unanimous.

That spoiled my morning, but the afternoon proves to be rewarding when, only twenty-four hours following the receipt of my manuscript, Bob Gottlieb phones to say he likes the piece and hopes to be running it within the next six weeks. For *The New Yorker*, that's quick. Bob has scarcely hung up when there's a call from Pat Crow, who's going to be handling the piece. I'm especially glad now that I wrote Pat the other day complimenting him on his fishing-rod "Profile."

9 July

We took Lucile to Wellfleet's Masonic Hall last evening for a recital—songs, readings, everything Irish—by Robin Howard. A first-rate turnout—SRO. Robin does not treat this crowd to an engaging yarn she shared with us the other day; about a woman who hated her husband and took care of him after his death by mixing up his ashes with some marijuana. At one point, while talking about some Irish writer, Robin described him as "rather like Jack Kahn," because he wrote on just about every subject on earth except bucket handles.

Dear Robin:

Have you ever given any serious thought, if you have time for any considering your intense preoccupation with the wearers of the green, to the significance to our civilization of bucket handles? Just how far do you honestly think mankind could have progressed without the invention of the wheel? And what good would the wheel have done man without receptacles for wheeled vehicles to cart around? And if you agree, as surely you must, that no receptacle has been more evolutionarily utile than the bucket, pray tell me just how far this bucket would have got *without a handle*. As an *unattached* object, to be sure, a bucket handle may not perhaps stand up under long scrutiny as well as, say, the Parthenon, but in point of fact there is so much to be written about the bucket handle (Jack and Jill would have been foolish starting up that hill without one) that I hardly know where to. . . .

Maybe it would be easier to take it up with her in person.

We seem to be hanging around the Masonic Hall a lot, these days, for noninitiates. David Shainberg talked Ellie and me into going there not long ago for an all-day yoga session, which was supposed to increase our muscle flex, or something of the sort. We remained for the morning session and then at the lunch break, when the guru in charge was being served his pickled yogurt or whatever, we fled.

The *New Yorker* that arrives today contains the first of two articles on South Africa and the South African press, by one William Finnegan. I say "one" because I've heard of him only once before. That was when Frank Ferrari of the African-American Institute invited me to that Cambridge symposium. Frank said some guy named Finnegan purporting to be connected with the magazine wanted to be invited, and was he legitimate? I said the name meant nothing to me, as indeed it didn't, and Frank said in that case he would turn the fellow down; anyway, one *New Yorker* person who'd written about South Africa was enough. But now I realize that Finnegan would probably have been a better qualified representative of the magazine than I was. If he exists and I ever get to meet him, I must try to remember to seek his forgiveness.

At the Lewis Bergmans' cocktail party, I compliment Renate Ponsold on a striking-looking black object pinned to her breast, which I take to be some kind of exotic jewelry. No, she says, it is a device—not unlike, perhaps, Hopi's pulsating flea collar—to repel mosquitoes. Chris Busa takes Stanley Kunitz and me aside, out of Norman Mailer's earshot, to ask if we think Chris and Ray Elman should let Norman see proofs of a Peter Manso interview with Mailer they're about to run in their *Provincetown Arts*. We both urge them not to; Mailer is, has made himself, a public character and has given evidence over and over that he can take care of himself when offended. If Chris and Ray have checked for libel—they have—that would seem to be enough.

10 July

Sikhs have waylaid another bus in India and slaughtered a few dozen more Hindus. When I made my only trip ever to India—with Ellie, after joining her in Sri Lanka—I knew better than to hope to be able to write much for *The New Yorker* about the country. Ved Mehta had long since come to grips with it and had a stranglehold. I did manage to wangle a "Talk of the Town" piece out of the trip, about India's first serious attempt at a nationwide census. (Having published *The American People*, my book about the 1970 United States census, I had at least some familiarity with the subject.) I also sold Shawn a "Talk" piece about some monkeys hanging around the American Embassy in Delhi, but he never used it. He may have had a thing about animals. He also bought and let languish a "Talk" piece of mine about some live bulls—for a Merrill Lynch television commercial—on Wall Street.

We stayed in Delhi with Cornelia and Herb Levin, who was then posted to our embassy. I never made it to Calcutta (Ellie did, on her own), but we did get to Bombay and to Poona, where we were lodged right next door to the then citadel of Bhagwan Shree Rajneesh, who had not yet carted his disciples off to Oregon. When we wandered over to watch him mesmerize them, Ellie enjoined me to stay absolutely quiet, which was not easy because I was still smoking and had an irrepressible cough. Not that any of the guru's flock seemed to care. Near as I could make out from personal observation, the young men and women sprawled on the floor of a big open chamber or dancing—if that was the word—on the perimeter of the room, seemed mainly interested in sex. If sneezing was out, snuggling was certainly in. Later, we introduced ourselves to the Rajneesh's publicity woman, a no-nonsense South African who insisted that contrary to what the outside world might think, he had no personality cult—a statement that hardly seemed to jibe with the no less observable fact that all the members of the gang, male and female, were wearing their leader's picture strapped around their necks.

On our way back from Agra, one day, when we'd rented a car to pay our respects to the Taj Mahal, the car broke down. It was late in the afternoon, darkness was imminent, and while our driver tried to reincarnate his vehicle, Ellie and I got out and looked across the road, to where some women and children and a bullock or two were laboring in a rice field. "*That's* the sort of thing you ought to be writing about," she said. I had already written about it, in a way—having done an article on the International Rice Research Institute while passing through the Philippines on another mission—but I took her words to heart and when I got back to New York proposed to Shawn, not that I really believed for an instant he'd respond affirmatively, that I do a series of articles on foodstuffs on which the human race was chiefly dependent: rice, wheat, corn, and so on. To my surprise, Bill said, "That's the best idea you've had in a long time," and I was off and running to, among other ports of call, Switzerland, Italy, Mexico, Peru, and Harvard's Botanical Museum library, in pursuit of data that evolved into a five-part *New Yorker* series and the book *The Staffs of Life*. A fortuitous breakdown, and an intuitive wife.

The Mike Curtises are in Truro. They've rented a place for a week and both toilets are malfunctioning, and there's something wrong with the electricity. I invite Mike and Jean over for a restorative drink. They come without son Hans, though they assure me there is little chance he would try to repeat what he did the last time they stopped by: to set off firecrackers under my station wagon. Mike has the big architectural book that tells so much about our father, who I now learn probably met Ms. Curtis when Ely was lecturing at Cornell in the mid-1920s. Mike says he can't get his daughter Hilary much interested in the volume, because she complains that her only legacy from that grandparent was short arms and legs and a barrel chest.

11 July

In the mail, a fund-raising letter from Gus Tyler, who's now chairman of the American Veterans Committee. The AVC, on whose national board I sat forty years ago (I am reminded by the discovery of my ancient diary that I took off for one of its national conventions when Terry was only a couple of days old), is in desperate straits and needs $1,000 from me instanter. But so does Castle Hill, to which I'm already on the hook for a substantial pledge. Oh, what high hopes we had for AVC back then, with its estimable slogan, "Citizens first, Veterans second!" Take that, American Legion! So much for you, Veterans of Foreign Wars! But we foundered on a reef of internal friction—non-Communist left vs. Communist left, for summary oversimplification—and the Legion and the VFW continued to dominate the field we'd had the audacity to, if not take over, at least get in on.

A fellow in the Philosophy Department at Northeastern Illinois University has been asking authors, over these many years, to inscribe their books to him with their opinions on the meaning or purpose of life; and now he proposes to put his accumulation into a book titled *On the Meaning of Life*. He craves my permission for him to use what I sent him nearly seven years ago on the flyleaf of *About* The New Yorker *and Me*—". . . who will teach me some day, I hope, what life means." I am not sure I am proud of this, but I was younger then, and I deduce from his communication that I'm in good company: Elizabeth Hardwick, John Hersey, Gilbert Highet, Christopher Isherwood, Bel Kaufman, and both Aldous and Julian Huxley.

To the Bill Webbs' for dinner. There's a woman present, never did get her name, who says she's working on a book about Mrs. Thrale. She says James Boswell lived in Scotland and really didn't know Dr. Johnson at all well. Also, Boswell contracted gonorrhea nineteen times, which presumably kept him occupied. Dr. Johnson, my informant adds, was scrupulously faithful to his wife.

Everybody is wondering what might happen to Oliver North, assuming that (1) he isn't indicted, (2) he doesn't become the *Times*'s military correspondent, and (3) he doesn't get elected President. Inasmuch as the gung ho gyrene seems determined to have a continuing confrontation with what he perceives as the forces of evil, I propose to the assemblage that he be promoted to full colonel and put in command of the marines arrayed against Castro on one side of the fence that separates the rest of Cuba from Guantánamo Bay. I flew down there once, late in 1979, to report on a marine training exercise, involving a mock amphibious assault on the enclave with no casualties, except for one marine officer who suffered a heart attack during the pseudo-excitement. The Cubans in their watchtowers overlooking the American base seemed unperturbed.

12 July

Dorothy and Mel Horwitz by for tennis. Mel has added a J.D. degree to his M.D., and Dorothy says she now calls him—my spelling—"Midgejid." We talk afterward about the Baby M surrogate-mother case. Mel thinks the surrogate parents' rights should prevail over the natural mother's, because a contract is a contract. His "jid" seems to have carried the day against his "midge."

Cocktails at Lucy Chaplin's. I learn for the first time that Lucy's father was a court clerk in Dedham, Massachusetts, and that it was he who read aloud the death verdict against Sacco and Vanzetti. Lucy is convinced that Sacco was guilty, but she appears to harbor some doubt about Vanzetti. Here is a woman who, when she talks about Judge Thayer and his courtroom, is not indulging in history but personal reminiscence.

New York magazine, in one of its periodic competitions, wants its readers to send in titles for the world's shortest books, and by way of example of the sort of thing they're looking for the sponsors offer "*Willkommen, Bienvenue, Welcome: New at* The New Yorker—*by Robert Gottlieb.*" I myself would prefer something along the lines of *My Last Haiku.*

13 July

To the Hamburgers' for cocktails, and then to the Badillos' for Caps Wilkinson's birthday party, but between the two I have to sandwich in a run to Hyannis to pick up Lexy at the bus terminal. (In all my experience, admittedly limited though it be, I don't recall ever seeing a sadder-looking bunch of people than those at the station, either waiting for somebody to arrive or for themselves to depart.) Kirk Wilkinson says he's going to have to give up tennis. Knees. I guess he must be well into his seventies. Even so, it's a pity, what with his own court sitting right there outside his door.

The *Globe* says that King Hassan, about to arrive in England with an entourage of 150 and his own five-foot-wide bed, is turning up a day early so he won't again get in Dutch with Queen Elizabeth, whom he once apparently kept waiting for two hours in a broiling desert tent when she was visiting Morocco. When Ellie and I kept His Majesty waiting, it was only for a few minutes. Hassan was wearing a Western-style sports coat when we called on him at his Fez palace, and it was hard to think of anyone within thousands of miles who less needed identifying insignia, but in his buttonhole, we were enchanted to notice, was a small gold crown.

Oliver North says he is definitely not going to run for President. Guantánamo Bay, here we come!

14 July

At 10:19 this morning, after three days of what an honest person would call shilly-shallying, I finally manage to put the first two sentences of my Ku Klux Klan piece on paper. For me, this is the equivalent of an A-O-K NASA liftoff.

Katharine Kuh, who gets the *Times* earlier than we do, tells Ellie there's a big story about Shawn in it. I make tracks to Lema's for our copy. Bill is going to be an editor at Farrar, Straus, which I interpret to mean he is probably not going to write that book for Joan. He is going to edit two books, for starters. I assume that some blockbuster of a revelation is coming next—perhaps The Return of J. D. Salinger. But before we get to titles, Ed McDowell gives us a direct quote from Roger Straus, Jr.: "I'm the only person you know who calls him Bill." In one sense—I can see Ollie North nodding approval—this might be accurate, because McDowell may not know many people. But come to think of it he knows me, and I would hardly have asked William Shawn to be best man at my first wedding forty-two years ago, nor would he have been likely to assent, if we weren't on a first-name basis.

And now at the end of the *Times* story it's revealed that the two books in question are by Edith Iglauer and Lillian Ross, and I know that whatever either of them calls him, it is certainly not "Mr. Shawn." At the Holtons' cocktail party this afternoon, Phil Hamburger says he knows for certain that Edith, to whom he was married for many years, calls Bill "Bill." So does Phil. Maybe the quote in the paper was a veiled plea to Farrar, Straus's new editor to address his new boss as "Roger."

All-Star game tonight, and Ellie asks me which team I am for. I am not for anybody and don't even wait up for the finish. I stopped caring about major-league baseball when more than half the names in the lineups of my hometown teams were those of strangers.

15 July

Tom Begner and Rickie Harvey, of The Stephen Greene Press, need a jacket photo for their inside-guide-to-Cape-Cod-and-the-Islands book, to which I've contributed a preface. So most of the other contributors convene *chez nous* for drinks and lunch and posing. Begner may turn out to be our family publisher. Tony has written the chapter on Provincetown for his forthcoming guide, and Tom and Rickie bring along a copy of *Net Results*, of which Terry is coauthor.

Tom gives it as his inside-guide-to-publishing opinion that Bob Gottlieb is the only book editor who could possibly have made a go of taking over *The New Yorker*.

16 July

Judge Francis W. Keating's obit is in the *Globe*. It was he who, hearing that Joe Wapner was going to be staying with us last summer, asked if he could come down and meet the "People's Court" luminary. Our guest graciously consented. Joe and Mickey spent a week in Truro, and it was amazing how many of our neighbors turned out to be ardent fans of his and were no less eager than Judge Keating to see him in the flesh. I seem to recall that we got a lot of cocktail-party invitations that week. As soon as word spread of Joe's legerdemain on the tennis court, players of higher caliber than usual began showing up, too, hoping to get in a set or two with or against him.

Just as there are levels of justice, so there are of tennis. Juliet Waters, who's in Wapner's class, comes by today but won't step on the court, because two men of demonstrably inferior ability are already present. But they are both genial people, and they know that we have an open-house policy, and

I haven't yet figured out a diplomatic way of telling some of our friends that they simply aren't competent enough to serve and receive with some of our others.

A strange evening. A man Lexy met in Santa Fe comes over to present a slide show, with music and commentary of his own creation, on our VCR. His Truro hostess has advanced Alzheimer's, sits on our couch, and never once even glances at the TV tube. The only words she utters are when, a half hour or so after their arrival, she turns to me and said, "Who are you?" Very sad. Lucile's mind works in strange ways, too, but she can carry on a lively enough conversation, though she has no recollection of it soon afterward. She has lived for the last sixty years or so exclusively in Cleveland and Sarasota, yet when Jerry Hermanson asked politely at the tennis court the other day where she was living now, she replied instantly, "New York." But my mother-in-law is much older than the other woman, and simply has a fading memory, and if she chooses to call Hopi "Rainbow," what if she is one dog off? If I were to say "Rainbow!" in my usual "Hopi!" tone of voice, I imagine our incumbent pet would respond.

17 July

I get galley proofs of my mountain-climbing piece from Pat Crow, and I send off sets of them, as promised, to Nicola Rotberg and the Mackeys. By and large, I've learned from experience, this can be risky, because things people say in conversation sometimes look different to them in cold print. Our redoubtable checkers at *The New Yorker* run into this sort of thing all the time. I lost an important paragraph a few years back when a checker asked a man to verify a quote and he flatly denied having uttered it. I remembered exactly when he had, sitting alongside me at lunch at the Algonquin, and I had the notes I took that day to back me up. But once he had gainsaid me, what could we do? Oh, I suppose we could have used the paragraph nothwithstanding, but he was a person of some consequence and the magazine didn't choose to get into a hassle with him about it.

I spend part of the evening browsing through Larry Adler's book. He does seem to go on a bit much about his sexual conquests, but then maybe I have underestimated the aphrodisiac properties of the harmonica. In a reference to our prewar band down off the Bowery (Wm. Shawn, piano; E. J. K., Jr., drums; L. Adler, harmonica; Bruce Bliven, Jr., clarinet, et al.), Larry has converted Bruce into a bass fiddler, but then at the very start of the book he confesses that nobody is perfect, and he has used the get-me-off-the-hook title of *It Ain't Necessarily So.*

18 July

Deborah Eisenberg has a short story in the current *New Yorker* that's full of "shit"s and "fuck"s. I wonder if it's one that Shawn bought and if so whether he would have run it as she wrote it. I wonder too, naturally, inasmuch as she is Wally Shawn's roommate, whether Debby will appear on his dad's Farrar, Straus list. I suspect she is another of the growing legion of us who do not call Bill "Mr. Shawn."

19 July

The car seems to be sputtering, and I'm a little concerned, because I'm supposed to go to Fall River tomorrow to meet one of Brent Abel's shipmates and the Austrian policeman their destroyer escort rescued when they sank his sub.

To Provincetown for a cocktail party, in Susan Sinaiko's colorful garden, for the board members (and spouses) of three Lower Cape groups that may coordinate their fund-raising: Castle Hill, the Fine Arts Work Center, and the Provincetown Art Association. Ethel Edwards seems surprised when I tell her how disappointed I was with last summer's Castle Hill building-fund drive. She apparently believes that I would be willing to devote a couple of months to that endeavor once again. No way, José.

The *Globe* has a feature story about Truro. It quotes Tom Kane, ex-town clerk, ex-schoolteacher, columnist, trombonist, man of many parts: "There's a real dichotomy in this town, perfectly illustrated when you go to the town dump. You watch the summer people throwing away their *New Yorker* magazines, New York *Times* and Brooks Brothers jackets, and here I am throwing away my Provincetown *Advocate* and an empty bottle of Jim Beam." At least Tom doesn't accuse us of being martini drinkers. (I gave up both gin and vermouth a long time ago.) Teresa Hanafin, the writer of the piece, calls Truro "the last bastion of rurality left on Cape Cod." Good for us.

20 July

I drive off out of the bastion, and when I stop at the end of the Cape for gas and ask to have my oil checked, a kid says somebody has loosened two of my spark-plug connections. My eight-cylinder car has been struggling along on six. He fiddles around with the engine and I assume he has made the necessary repairs and tip him extravagantly. (But at the end of the day, when I limp back to Truro and to Sonny's service station, the home port for my ship, Sonny says there is more trouble than meets the eye, and he will have to take the car apart and put it back together again. Meanwhile, he enjoins me not to drive it. I dare not tell him I've driven it a couple of hundred miles just today.)

I have a date to meet Joe Aucoin, Brent Abel's man, and Vinzenz Nosch, the U-boat survivor from Austria, and Robert Bell, who brought the onetime enemies together more than forty years after their fight on the high seas, at Battleship Cove, a Fall River outdoor museum with a battleship, a destroyer, and a submarine, among other vessels, available for public inspection. But my car's errant behavior makes me late, and I don't have a chance to do much more than get acquainted. What little conversation we have time for takes place on the deck of the submarine, directly under the Fall River bridge, which is undergoing repairs, so we are all but drowned out by riveting. No matter; we will presumably reconvene when Brent arrives in Germany.

21 July

I haven't been following every word of the Iran-Contra hearings, but to the best of my knowledge nobody has yet asked Admiral Poindexter one simple question: if you and your man North were so totally aboveboard and loyal and legal and patriotic beyond the comprehension of most mortals, how come he got fired and you resigned?

23 July

At Cindy Worthington's request, I agree to serve on a Truro committee with Ansel Chaplin to raise money to repair the Town Hall steeple. We so-called summer people—"Washashores," the year-rounders sometimes call us—get more involved in community affairs than some people realize. Whatever I do in this capacity should be a lot easier than the burden Ellie has agreed to shoulder: she's been persuaded by Charles LeClair to succeed him as president of Castle Hill—and this at a time when the art school has a brand new director and a lawsuit pending against some of the town officials who do their work beneath the steeple I am supposed to be helping to resurrect. Ellie reminds me, by the way, that one day soon she and I are going to have to sit down and decide what we're going to do about the Castle Hill course in memoir-writing that we've agreed to teach together next month. She's already decided where she's going to be for half of the four sessions we are scheduled for—on a horse in the Canadian Rockies. If only Gottlieb would ask me to undertake a rush assignment someplace equally remote!

To dinner at the Frank Foxes'. Robin Howard is there and another guest just back from a folksinging course in Scotland (maybe I could fly over there and write about that), and before the evening is out, inevitably, a lot of Scottish and Irish ballads are aired. Eventually, more or less out of politeness, I am asked to render my version of "Lazybones," but I am not exactly in the mood and would rate my performance distinctly below snuff, although I have never known for sure just how high "up to snuff" actually is.

24 July

Frightfully hot day—95 in Boston, only in the 80s here. So far, no fleas. Many years ago, when we rented the Truro house for a month (we had taken another place at West Cornwall, Connecticut, where we once tentatively planted some roots), the temperature went up over 100, and there was an eruption of fleas in the house, and we had to pay for our tenants' stay in a motel until the exterminators came and went.

26 July

New faces for tennis: Fred and Buster Glimp, who are staying in Truro with Mimi Aloian, whom we have somehow never previously met. I did know her late husband David, who ran Harvard's alumni office. And I've known the Glimps since we sat together to cheer for the Harvard crew at the 1968 Olympics in Mexico City. (Fred knew my son Joey even before that; interviewed him when Joey was at Andover and applying for Harvard.) Fred left the university soon after he and I became friends, following all the troubles of 1969, but has come back and is now vice president in charge of alumni and fund-raising and all that.

Buster and Fred remind me of the time when I was working on my book *Harvard* and the three of us were supposed to have dinner with some undergraduates. We plodded through a blizzard to our destination, but all the students chickened out, so the Glimps and I, with nothing better to do, countered the chill by polishing off a bottle of gin. This recollection gives me a clue as to when I switched from gin to vodka; less than twenty years ago. And when we get to harking back to those Olympics, they remind me that I introduced them then to Red Smith, Roger Bannister, and the British journalist Brian Glanville. The Glimps subsequently had dinner with Brian in London, they report, and say he used the foulest language they'd ever heard. That reminds Buster that I told her twenty years or so ago that women employed a lot raunchier language in ordinary conversation than men do. She laughed at me then but says she's beginning to come around to my point of view.

As I look back—way back—at my undergraduate days at Harvard, I don't recall having spent much time in any of its libraries. Mea culpa. I have endeavored in much of the last half century, however, to atone for that remissness. Three times in my postcollege life it's been my pleasure and privilege to be able to use the Harvard libraries for research. I never checked to see if I was eligible. For a while, I planned to refer anybody who might challenge me to a friend of mine who happened to be the chief Yard cop. Then he retired. Since then, while using Harvard libraries I've always worn an ancient tweed jacket so tattered and torn that I am assured by Ellie— though she frowns upon my wearing it anywhere else—that it is a perfect academic disguise. Once, when I was gathering material for a book about theatrical history, the New York Public Library proved adequate for a time, and it had—and has—the added convenience of being located just a block from my office. But the Harvard Theater Collection, I eventually discovered, was much better, and I have been trying ever since to think of another book subject that would require a return visit. Then when I wrote the book *about* Harvard, I was introduced to, and cheerfully rifled the contents of, its marvelous archives. The fall of 1982 was my third time around. I had embarked on a massive enterprise: to write about the staple food plants of the earth and how they grew. As I was getting under way, I ran into my classmate Gerry Piel, who became an Overseer of Harvard, and I asked him if he had any ideas about where I should begin my research. "Go see Dick Schultes," Gerry said. "Richard Evans Schultes," he went on. "Professor Emeritus of Botany, director of the Botanical Museum—your *classmate*." So I returned to Cambridge and called on Schultes and explained what I hoped to be up to. Dick led me past his fragile glass flowers over there and up a flight of stairs and flung open the door of the Oakes Ames Ethnobotanical Library. I'd never before known it existed. "Now then," said Schultes, "what was it you were interested in?" Well, I said, trying to remember the names of what I hoped were staple food plants, "Wheat, corn—" "maize," he interrupted gently—"rice, and, you know, the others." "Here's wheat," he said, pointing possessively to a couple of crowded shelves. "And there's rice, and there's maize, or corn, if you like." I felt like a child on the White House lawn who's found all the Easter eggs. And thus for nine rewarding weeks I holed up in that splendid repository of botanical lore.

Later, I spent a week at each of three international research centers in Latin America. At every stop, I made a point of visiting their libraries. As I was bidding farewell and thanks to my hosts at the International Potato Center, just outside Lima, Peru, an administrator asked me to tell him candidly if I had any criticisms of his establishment. I said, yes, it was the International Potato Center, and should have harbored the world's greatest collection of potato literature, but I had read a dozen or so books on the history of the potato that he lacked. And just where, he inquired—his affability cooling—could I possibly have encountered this trove? "Why, at

Harvard, of course," I said. "Where else?" They engender loyalty up in Cambridge.

Why do women have no sense of time? There is a 9:30 dance at the Budd Hopkinses' in Wellfleet. But Ellie and Betty Lifton took off for three art shows in Provincetown at 6:00, and it is now 8:05, and we haven't had dinner, and they haven't returned. The question is: do they do this sort of thing deliberately, or are there differences in gender that make it difficult, if not impossible, for them to think ahead more than one step at a time? Is anticipation exclusively an attribute of men? Come to think of it, who was the last world-famous woman chess player? All the ones who'll play you for two dollars a game at Harvard Square are male.

27 July

Nancy Webb stops by to pick up, for its annual polishing, the staffs-of-life bronze plaque Ellie commissioned her to make for me when my book came out.

We've all heard about the escalating value of Truro real estate. When our tax bill arrives today, I learn that our three acres—which, being in the National Seashore, we can't split up and sell off—have been appraised at $166,500, while our house itself is worth a mere $64,800. When we go to dine at the Kaplans', they reveal that they have nine acres outside the park, which they envision as their legacy—it should be a hefty one—to their daughters. Annie beats me twice at Scrabble. She has the advantage of knowing most of which two-letter words are acceptable and which are not, while my such vocabulary does not extend far beyond "ai"—the good old two-toed sloth (or is it three-) so entrenched in crossword-puzzledom.

I finish the first draft of my Ku Klux Klan piece.

Walter Bingham and his son Eric turn up for tennis. Bing is doing more writing for *Sports Illustrated* now—those wordy advertising inserts that he calls advertorials—than he did before he retired. Eric has retired from the marines, where he was a helicopter pilot, and he covers the court like one.

Many of our Cape friends are in Wellfleet for a Hall family art exhibit—Marty and Jack and I forget what others of their kin. Ellie and I can't linger, because we agreed a long time ago to perform for a "Couples in the Arts" evening at the Provincetown Art Association. We are supposed to plumb some such highfalutin' depths as, "What are the dynamics of a relationship when both partners are artists?" Nobody at the art show rushes to follow us, and when, taking Lucile along, we get to Provincetown, I am at once disgruntled, because the signboard in the lobby announcing our appearance misspells Ellie's surname and leaves the "Jr." off mine. So much for trying to establish a byline. Malcolm Preston, the only person in the room I've laid eyes on before, has been prevailed on to introduce us, which he does with his customary grace, but aside from Ellie's mother—who though a nonagenarian appears to be one of the younger people on hand—there are precious few for him to present us to. Ellie insists afterward that we had an audience of twenty, but I count only seven, refusing to include the elderly man front row center who sleeps throughout.

29 July

Sheila, at my request (is there anything that can be salvaged from the old piece?) sends me galleys of my Oxfam America "Profile." I note that it was set up in type in October 1985 and was edited by "McK." Obviously not McKelway, has to be McKibben. So this was when Shawn was grooming Bill for editorial greatness, or at any rate giving him a chance to widen his sphere of influence. I don't think that his handling this ill-fated piece of mine had anything to do with the partial eclipse of his rising star.

Judith Malina is coming to stay with us next week, and Ellie is organizing a beach picnic in her honor. I only learn of this when I happen to take a phone call from Rochelle Owens, who says George and she are sorry they won't be able to make it—mutual theatrical interests notwithstanding—because, as Rochelle puts it with refreshing candor, "I hate beach picnics!"

30 July

Ray Elman comes by for tennis, on a bicycle. He has got a third speeding ticket, and his license has been invalidated for a month. He seems unaware that while it's easy enough to ride a bike from his place to ours, the return trip will be in large part uphill.

Barbara Kerr, en route between Newport and the Vineyard, has detoured to Truro to visit Jane de Rochemont, who's taken the Fred Nelson house. It develops, when Ellie's horseback tour comes up at the cocktail hour, that Barbara has quite an equestrian past, and there is much talk—in, mind you, a strictly ladylike way—of saddle sores and the effectiveness of silk underwear in avoiding them.

The priorities that television networks ascribe to their own offerings are illuminatingly revealed in a *Times* piece about a lawsuit against ABC-TV: "The jury rejected claims that the Los Angeles-based cameramen earned as much as $16,649 a year less than some of their white counterparts because they were routinely assigned to low-prestige jobs, such as news, rather than situation comedies or soap operas."

31 July

Leo Salzman has been in Alaska, on some sort of psychiatric mission, and in that haven of big-game hunters he has bagged a rare trophy: a copy of *The Voice*, my ancient biography of young Frank Sinatra. Just how the book got way up north is unclear; a flyleaf says that it was donated, year unspecified, to the Milwaukie, Oregon, Public Library by the Milwaukie Junior Chamber of Commerce Auxiliary. I had forgotten that my preface contained a warm— deservedly so—tribute to Bill Shawn, who edited the book when it was serialized in *The New Yorker*; and also my allusion to Sinatra's having told me that he was going to write me a letter saying he liked the magazine pieces and my having told him not to bother. I could just as easily have kept quiet.

Peter Rand stops by. He reminds me that after Ellie and I went to Indonesia, I urged him not to fail to go to Borobodur; but when he'd got to Bali he couldn't bring himself to budge. He asks if I have kept up my membership— answer: affirmative—in the Flying Doctors Society, which his mother has so long been running out of Nairobi. Peter says Maddy, now seventy-six, was hit so hard by an automobile (its driver, just back from the U.S.A., had forgotten that Kenyans, after the British fashion, drive to the left) that she broke most of her bones; but her Flying Doctors put her back together again and she's playing tennis three times a week. I'd have seen her this year if Gottlieb hadn't turned thumbs down on my Nile-perch story.

To Judy's and Tony's for drinks. They are excited because folksinger John Hammond is going to attend their gig tonight. When his father, John, Sr., died not long ago—he was seventy-six, but only twenty-eight when I wrote his "Profile"—the music world must have been justly proud when the *Times* gave him a page-one obit.

I had complained to Tony some time back about the *Cape Codder*'s making its weekly cryptogram too easy to solve by putting a clue to one letter directly beneath the puzzle itself. Now the clue has been moved to another page, so that people who don't want that sort of help don't have to see it. Tony advises me that this change in editorial policy is directly and exclusively attributable to me.

I haven't quite stopped congratulating myself on that achievement, though its value to an obit writer might be moot, when Ian now beats me at chess, handily.

1 August

John Beeker has come from Cleveland to escort his grandmother back home, and at 1:45 P.M. is still not out of bed. How do the young do it? He makes his return to the rest of the world emphatic by devouring an entire package of sausages for breakfast, or whatever you call a 2:00 P.M. meal when it's the first of the day.

2 August

Lucile's last words to her daughter, before she boards her flight to Cleveland, are to the effect that she is concerned about whether she'll be met by her mother, deceased these forty years. By the time she gets to Cleveland, she may have forgotten that she's just spent a month on the Cape with her own daughter. How strange it must be to be living literally for the instant!

The wedding in Newton of Anath's sister Maya and her young man is, in a sense, a rehearsal for the impending nuptials, whenever they finally occur, of Anath and our David, who've already decided to be married by the same rabbi officiating today—a young woman who's never before performed this ceremony. White silk yarmulkes are distributed to those of us who, unlike the bridegroom, did not bring along their own. I have never owned one—nor, for that matter, have I ever attended Jewish services of any kind. (My maternal grandparents did have some connection with the Ethical Culture Society, which is about as close as any of us ever got to any sort of organized worship.) It may be symbolic of my apostasy that when Jinny and I were married it was by a domestic relations judge, and that Jet Thomas, the minister who pronounced Ellie and me man and wife, is a Southern Baptist.

In this age of specialization, it probably should have come as no surprise to me to learn—it did, anyway—that the bridegroom's sister is gainfully occupied giving dance therapy to Catholic nuns and priests who've been determined to be—by whom I don't know—in sore need of it.

On the way home, we listen to part of T. E. Lawrence's *Seven Pillars of Wisdom.* He writes in such graphic detail that as a reporter who often has trouble deciphering what I jot down in a taxi, I cannot help wondering how he managed to take notes while thundering across the desert on camelback.

3 August

Judith Malina and her young man, Hanon Reznikov, arrived during the night to spend a few days. He is too tall for our eighteen-twentyish house. The ceiling hooks that hold the kitchen swing when the grandchildren come to call are below his eye level, thank God, so if they wound him at least they won't blind him. Judith, on a kind of buswoman's holiday from her Living Theatre, is fresh from having portrayed the Duchess of York in a Joseph Papp Central Park version of *Richard II*—first time, she says, she has worked under another's direction, and she loved every onstage minute of it.

No tennis, Judith and Hanon having brought rain with them. Anyway, I have page proofs of my Rotberg piece to wrestle with. I observe that some editor has taken out my snide assertion that the total amount of money spent by the government on training National Park rangers for helicopter rescues ($12,250) is less than the cost of the security fence around Oliver North's home. Would Edmund Wilson or George Steiner—both of whom allegedly resisted any changes in their copy—have squawked at the deletion? On the other hand, if my comparison was inappropriate, or indelicate, would they have had the sense or the taste not to have put it in to begin with?

The New Yorker has a signed piece this week, about presidential candidates, by Richard Harris—presumably the same one who quit the staff in a huff nine years ago. When I talk to Pat Crow this afternoon about my page proofs (I don't bother to bring up Ollie North, I know a losing cause when I see one) I ask if Elizabeth Drew isn't furious at this seeming incursion into her territory. Pat, who is taking a smoke-enders' course that the magazine is treating him and others to—they get their forty-dollar tuition reimbursed if they lay off for six months or a year or whatever—measures his words in the best tradition of careful and responsible editors. He says, "Yes."

Oliver North is on others' minds, too. Today's mail yields up both a *National Review* and a *Peelings*, the journal of Washington, D. C.'s, Potato Museum. The *Review* is the first publication, so far as I know (*New Yorker* writers tend to shy away from flat statements and to armor themselves in qualifiers), to use North's full name in an acrostic puzzle; and *Peelings* reprints a cartoon in which the light colonel is shown telling one of his coconspirators to use "potato" for "money."

4 August

Sue Tolchin calls. Marty and she have just arrived for the month. He is doing a thing for the *Times* about Bob Dole, and he wants to talk to me about the Senator's relationship with Dwayne Andreas. Any time. They've just finished a book—could hardly have picked a more up-to-date subject —on foreign investments in America.

Brent Abel phones. He's starting to make arrangements for a reunion in Germany toward the end of September.

Judith and Hanon are writing an opera. She gets up early. I found her sitting out on the lawn this morning, if you can call our patch of dead grass a lawn. Ellie says they have been lovers for nigh unto fifteen years, starting when Hanon was just out of Yale.

We go to Ryder Beach this evening for a picnic in their honor. Small crowd: the Kaplans, the Foxes, Annie Dillard and her Gary Clevidence, Robin and Caitlin, and the Tolchins. Marty has spent a good deal of time talking to Andreas, he says, but Dwayne has never mentioned my "Profile." An unfamiliar woman living just upland of our fire (yes, I got a permit for it) starts yelling at us that we are on her private beach—something about sand between mean high tide and mean low tide—and that she is going to call the cops. She does, and a Truro policeman who knows us comes by and wishes us a pleasant evening and departs. By the time I return to our car the headlights are malfunctioning. Vengeance? Sabotage?

5 August

I didn't sleep well, worrying both about our car (Sonny says we simply need a new sealed-beam lamp) and our memoir-writing class, which begins this afternoon. At the post office, I gaze in horror as a woman who appears not to be aware that her automobile has a rearview mirror backs briskly into my parked car. She misses my brand-new, never-yet-switched-on headlight by a whisker.

Pat Crow phones. I quoted a Park ranger as saying that the helicopter rescue of Nicola Rotberg, as night was falling, was a "balls-to-the-wall" race against time. Pat says some editor, and when it comes to that he, too, wants to know what that means? It's not a question of choice of words—*The New Yorker* can stomach that "balls"—but of sense. Damned if I know myself, but I do know that the ranger said it. Pat and I decide to go with "backs-to-the-wall."

Tony has a nice piece in the *Cape Codder* about neighbor Lee Falk. He says the creator of Mandrake and the Phantom is eighty-two. But he also states that when Lee wrote his first comic strip, in 1934, he was only nineteen. Palmer W., who is better at arithmetic than I am, says there's something wrong here; that would make Lee only *seventy*-two. It turns out that Tony consulted a reference book that mistakenly had Falk born in 1905 instead of 1915. Fortunately, by the time Lee returns to the Cape, the *Cape Codder* will have had a chance to print an apology and correction.

Our memoir class has thirteen students—twelve women and one man, Don Sparrow, whom I met while writing my book *The Problem Solvers*, about his onetime company Arthur D. Little. He won't be able to make next week's session, and Ellie will be in Canada, so I'll have a harem of sorts all to myself. I happen to mention this morning's balls-to-the-wall incident, as an illustration of something or other, and our students all exclaim that "backs-to-the-wall" isn't at all a suitable substitute for the situation I'm trying to describe. So while the class is scribbling away at an assigned exercise ("Write the first few sentences of a memoir") I find a phone and call Pat Crow and we once again modify our modifier. Pat says that whoever's checking the dratted piece is running into troubles, because several people I talked to are altering their versions of what happened on that mountain that night— understandable and probably inevitable when you are dealing with memories of stressful moments, but tough on a checker and on an author, too.

Tomorrow, Ellie and I are to take off on a northern-New England tour —first to the farm at Old Brownfield, Maine, of which Joey and Jet Thomas are part owners, and then to the Bread and Puppet Circus in Vermont, where Lexy and his friend Kristin are involved in this summer's festivities. So Roberta and Joe Lema, who are going to tend to Hopi in our absence, come by to pick her up. While we're all preparing our separate dinners, Judith (she and Hanon are vegetarians) says they are working on an opera about the Trojan War, which is not easy for professional pacifists. "I'm the only person I know," she says, "who loves television and hates chess and considers herself a civil libertarian." Apparently her late husband and collaborator, Julian Beck, first met her when they were both fifteen, and for a while played a lot of chess together, but then they concluded that the game brought out aggressions in them and, what was even worse, anti-anarchist emotions.

Judith goes on to recount how, back in 1957, she once spent thirty days in a women's house of detention cell with the celebrated Dorothy Day and how Judith got into trouble by breaking a windowpane so they could get some fresh air in their dreary cubicle. She goes on to say, for my benefit, that *The New Yorker* figured importantly in the Living Theatre's history. For after Ken Tynan gave their 1963 production of Jack Gelber's *The Connection* a glowing review, Brooks Atkinson, who'd let a second-stringer cover, and pan it, for the *Times*, went to see it, with a favorable reaction, for himself. Even before that, it seems, Bob Rice, my longtime friend, classmate, and *New Yorker* colleague, wrote a "Profile" about Julian and her, but it never ran because, in her recollection, the magazine wanted an unforthcoming statement from the two of them that their radicalism was purely theatrical and not political.

After dinner, David's newspaper-reporter friend Irene Coletsos (who has been awarded a scholarship at the Columbia School of Journalism) comes by with a young man, a teacher at the University of Connecticut. Talk about coincidences! Hanon and he, like a couple of sniffing dogs, size each other up for a bit and then realize that in the fall of 1968, as Yale freshmen, they roomed together for a few weeks. And now here unexpectedly they meet again.

6 August

In the mail, a Catalog of Publications from the Cherokee Publishing Company, which published my *New Yorker* pieces about Georgia in book form. I am gratified to learn that unlike most of my more substantial books this one ("delightful glimpses of the state and its people," the catalog asserts) is still in print.

At noon, after stopping in Orleans to buy Ellie a couple of pairs of jeans to help her cushion her saddle, we head for Maine. Joe and co-owner Jet, the nearest thing to a Marryin' Sam our family can boast, welcome us to the farm, which is delightfully rustic. Joey flushed a bear while blue-berrying the other day, and Jet has a pet crow, which rides around on the preacher's head, and also on Jet's dachshund's head, and even deigns for a moment to perch on Ellie's.

7 August

Joe drives me to Brownfield, for the newspapers. I can't resist buying Ellie a *Sun* with one of those wild come-on headlines, this one reading (she threw it away before I could record it precisely) something like "Half Boy Half Girl gives Birth to Own Child." By the time we get back, Jet is closeted with a couple he's booked to wed. (He refrains from introducing E. and me as examples of ties he's bound.) This is an easy pair, he says after they leave; he's got a more ticklish situation to confront in Virginia, where the mother of the bride-to-be is insisting that her daughter can't wear white because she's not a virgin.

We leave, too, to drive across the White Mountains and into northern Vermont, close enough to the Canadian border for stop signs also to read *"Arrêt."* We check into a motel that's a bargain these days, twenty-five dollars for two, though it's fairly Spartan, with no hot water at night. (Kind of place, also, where you have to pay cash in advance. A lot of Canadian-American babies may have been conceived on these very premises.)

Lexy and Kristin are volunteers at the Bread and Puppet, paying twenty-five dollars a week apiece for their food, which they say is plentiful—especially the all-you-can-eat sourdough rye bread with garlic butter that Peter and Elka Schumann, Mr. & Mrs. Bread and Puppet, are known for far and wide. (We've heard somewhere that a special flavor is imparted to the bread because the ovens in which it's baked are stoked exclusively with the Sunday *New York Times*.) We drive over to Glover, where the circus has been based since 1974, and when I try to park near the main building, a guy tries to shoo me away. But when I point to a "Reserved for the Elderly" sign he takes another look at me and, somewhat more quickly than I might have wished, shrugs and lets me stay. We walk in the dark to a stage in a pine grove, where a dress rehearsal of some kind of show is about to start, but it doesn't get far before it's rained out.

8 August

The *Burlington Free Press* says of the people who regularly attend Bread and Puppet affairs, "Some described it as a '60s crowd talking'80s politics—Nicaragua, El Salvador, Reagan and real estate." If Ellie and I feel a bit out of place, our automobile doesn't; David and Lexy have decorated it over the years with all sorts of trendy stickers—"No Nukes" and the like—but haven't yet gone as far as one I saw not long ago at the Truro post office: "Nuke a Gay Whale for Jesus." The Bread and Puppet clientele, Lexy briefs us further, are almost universally against Reagan, against Contras, and against—because he supposedly had children by a slave—Thomas Jefferson. I run into Truro friends Joan and Bud Stillman and promise that I won't tell anyone I saw them if they'll keep equally mum about me.

We get to the amphitheater where most of the action will be at 11:00 A.M. and don't leave until 10:30 P.M. (En route, some volunteer firemen are stopping all cars and soliciting donations. They say as long as we have one of their little stickers on the back of our side mirror, they won't bother us further. Why did we volunteers in the Scarborough Fire Company never think of anything as effective as this? We used to try to raise money through the mails!) I have never enjoyed sitting on the ground—I'd be hopeless as an Indian, American or Asiatic—but that appears to be the only alternative to standing up. We brought along some bread and cheese and roast beef and plums and a six-pack of beer, so we'll survive, and there's always sourdough rye and garlic butter to fall back on. But at least, at the very end of it all, we do get to watch Lexy and Kristin put on a shadow play they've created, and after all their work they surely deserve to have a full moon watching over them.

9 August

I wake up at seven, as always, but since there is no dog to nag me onto my feet, I fall back asleep, and the next thing I know it's nine-thirty, which is when we said we'd meet Lexy and Kristin for breakfast. But we get to them only thirty minutes late. Then it's off to Boston and to Logan, where Ellie boards the Pan-Am shuttle on the first leg of her trek to the Canadian Far West. I reach Truro in time to go to a cocktail party where the hosts, oddly, are giving their guests a choice of (1) gin, (2) jug wine, and (3) pretzels. Their attendance may sag next year. Dick Waters takes me aside. The Castle Hill nominating committee is to meet tomorrow, for Ellie formally to be named the new president. He wants to talk to me about that off-the-record. I say that anything I say about Ellie and Castle Hill will be entirely on the record as far as she and I are concerned. Dick next wants me to know, as an old friend, that if she's nominated and accepts it's going to be a tough year, and he adds—I hope this is on the record—that if it was his wife and she took the job he'd divorce her.

When I get home, finally, and have a chance to look at the Sunday *Times*, the lead book review is of a collection of S. J. Perelman letters. The critic, Mordecai Richler, says "There's a lot of juicy stuff in the letters for *New Yorker* buffs." For openers, he tells us—whenever will the *Times* stop chewing at this old bone?—that Sid addressed the editor who succeeded Ross not as "Mr. Shawn" nor as "William," but plain "Bill"—"which I should have thought," Richler burbles on, "was only God's prerogative."

10 August

The girl we hired as a companion for Lucile, or sitter, or whatever exactly she was, takes her things by taxi to Provincetown but leaves behind a young woman friend whom I meet for the first time when she comes down this morning. She wonders if she can stay a few additional days until she finds a comparatively permanent residence. I say two more nights at most, pretending I'll need all beds then.

There's a benefit dance at the Inn at Duck Creek tonight for the Wellfleet library. Judy and Tony and the group are providing the music, so I ask Palmer and Barbara to go with me, but we don't stay long. Why do I ever permit myself to drink stingers?

11 August

Ellie calls at seven, from some airport. She forgot her camera. It was under the front seat of the car. Do I mind being in the house alone? I hesitate for a second. What she does not know about the current population of her home cannot hurt her. I say I'm getting along just fine. But what a blow to my ego these last twenty-four hours have been! What a shredding of my pride! Here I am living à deux with a nubile nineteen-year-old and nobody even raises an eyebrow.

By eight-thirty, tennis players have begun showing up for some matches scheduled on our court in Lee Falk's annual invitational tournament. The court is still too wet, though, from a Sunday downpour, to be playable. When I send Cy Post packing, he seems happy and says now he can have breakfast. He has a lot of theories about fitness, one being that people play their best tennis on empty stomachs.

Brent Abel phones. The German-American reunion is taking solid shape: dinner at Frankfurt, 29 September. I will be there.

Terry phones. He has hurt his back. I point out that at forty he is no youngster any more and should look out for himself. He says he can still beat me, at tennis, from a rocking chair. I like a kid with spunk.

To the Kaplans' for some Scrabble—Annie is getting to be unbeatable, or maybe I am aging—and then on to dinner in P'town. Tomorrow should be a pretty good morning tide for sea-clamming, so we agree to meet at their place at seven-thirty. We are served by a creature Joe K. calls a "wai-tron," because there is no way of determining by observation, short of a strip search, whether it's a male or a female. Ellie and Lexy and I had a similar experience out in Santa Fe. Ellie voted female, Lexy male. I, the old-fashioned liberal, couldn't make up my mind.

12 August

Palmer was supposed to pick me up to go sea-clamming at seven-thirty, but he forgot. No matter; Lexy and Kristin arrived last evening (very shortly after which my young female housemate abruptly skedaddled), and Lexy accompanies me. A good thing he does, for he is the only one who finds any clams.

Lexy wants to know if I have ever heard of harmonic convergence, which is very big in Santa Fe. It seems that according to the Mayan calendar, Cortez conquered the Aztecs in 1540 and that on 15 August 1987 a Mayan god is scheduled to rise from wherever he has been hibernating and smite us all in retaliation. I've been trying for some days to make up my mind whether to continue working on my foreign-aid article, and if I never finish it at least now it won't be all my fault.

The memoir class comes off all right, though two hours can be a long solo teaching stint. I had suggested to the class, for homework, that each of them write something about Oliver North and herself. Most of my students produced solemn quasi-editorials about what a bad person he was, but there were two interesting responses: one about a woman's ninety-three-year-old father distributing Ollie North souvenirs, as a gag, to his assorted relatives, but their not being quite sure at first that he wasn't serious; and another about a debate between her left-leaning eighteen-year-old son and *her* father, a Yugoslav emigré extremely bitter about Communist oppression.

We cook up a clam pie for dinner and are just about to dip into it when, vainly hunting for "Wheel of Fortune," I get some New England news on television and hear that Massachusetts shellfish have been declared polluted. On a map of Cape Cod that's next projected, no town is identified beyond Dennis. So Lexy and I resolve to take a chance, reckoning that surely we have poured enough brandy onto the clams to kill off most germs. People who have seen youngsters staggering about after sampling one of my clam pies sometimes ask me for my recipe, and if they don't appear to be from the Children's Aid Society I am always glad to oblige. Not that there really *is* a recipe. Once my clams have been shucked and cleaned (you have to squeeze out the gizzards, or whatever you call the stuff that lurks inside), and I have sautéed a mess of onions, I throw both batches into a frying pan with—no fixed measurements—butter, lemon juice, Worcestershire, Tabasco, pepper, white wine, and, as aforementioned, brandy. Then after briefly cooking it all, I dump it into a piecrust and let the oven do the rest. That's all there is to it, and you're welcome.

There are no aftereffects, which is just as well, because I have to moderate a seminar in Wellfleet on the responsibility of the press. Reagan is making his first television address this evening since the Iran-Contra hearings began, so I assume we—Morton Dean, Therese Steiner, Palmer Williams, and I—won't draw much of a crowd. But the Masonic Hall is flatteringly jammed. I am always awed by Palmer's knowledge of television, which goes back to the Ed Murrow days. When I did a two-part "Profile" on "60 Minutes," I wanted to watch one segment being put together, and when I learned that he was going to be the on-the-spot producer of a Harry Reasoner piece on Scotch whisky, I decided to accompany the two of them to Scotland. We had a heady few days there, drifting from one distillery to another, and from early morning till late evening, out of politeness, sampling (we left the driving to others) the output at every stop. This was not as easy as it may sound, because none of the three of us was particularly fond of Scotch. The call of duty prevailed, however, as for responsible journalists it always should; not until we'd reached whatever hotel it was that we'd been booked into for the night did we permit ourselves so much as a nip of vodka or gin.

13 August

Robin and Caitlin slept in Ellie's study last night. Robin says E. gave her permission to before she left, in an emergency; and there was one. They had to decamp from the Rothschilds' because there are black snakes in their bedrooms. Robin has brought along her cat, which I can't believe Ellie authorized. She is allergic to cats, and a live one in her study may in the long run raise as much havoc as a serpent in Jacqui Rothschild's boudoir or a dead raccoon in our heating system, or—quondam gardener Jenny has just rushed up with the bad news—a nest of yellow jackets in the woodpile Hopi was nosing into an instant before she seemed to throw a fit. Jenny proposes mud packs and a paste concocted from meat tenderizer, but after a bit Hopi calms down and I guess she'll recover on her own.

Lexy says that at midnight, walking from a P'town movie to their car, Kristin and he saw a couple approaching of such scruffiness that they might have been denied admission to a Janis Joplin concert—young man in dirty shapeless garment with guitar, young woman in equally nondescript costume, both stoned to their ears, or their feet. When they drew closer, Lex recognized the female. It was the one I lived with, in a manner of speaking, for three days. I must remember to count our spoons.

We dine in style at home: a clam bisque made from leftover juice and heavy cream, a peach pie baked by Kristin, and in between some broiled swordfish. The rest of the household watch a New Zealand movie on the VCR. I retire to read Pamela Painter's book about an American doctor's experiences in Saudi Arabia.

Glen and Mildred Leet, whose private foreign-aid program has me preoccupied these days, are now operating in at least ninety countries. I once tried to compute my own total (does one count Palau and Yap as separate entities?) and got somewhere into the sixties or seventies. Saudi Arabia is not among them, though I could have gone there on a publicity junket not long ago. But Shawn (or could it already have been Gottlieb?) was not interested. One of these days, just to tidy up my travels, I must try to think of some good reason for touching down in the only two of the fifty United States I've never been to—Mississippi and Louisiana.

14 August

Terry and Rose and their three are due this afternoon. There's an extra car outside this morning, with Michigan plates, so I guess David and Anath arrived during the night. If you count Robin and Caitlin, we have eight people in residence even before the anticipated five more materialize. But then what do you expect in mid-August?

Some women's-doubles tournament matches are under way on our court. What would Lee Iaccoca make of the following? Of the eight cars parked at the moment in our driveway, the only American one is my 1978 Chevrolet. The others, all much newer, are a Volvo, a Honda, a Volkswagen, two Toyotas, and two Mercedes.

But wait! What is this newest automotive crisis? Frank Fox, I quickly learn, has won the broken-racquet trophy for being the first motorist this month to get stuck in and have to be towed out of our driveway.

When I pick up the mail, Jack Kelley says, out of the blue, "How's your friend McPhee? Haven't seen him in the magazine lately." So, in the praiseworthy person of our postmaster, we do have at least one local reader after all! Somebody left the current issue—the one with my mountain-climbing piece in it—at our tennis court, but so far nobody hereabouts has mentioned reading it, let alone being aware of its existence.

15 August

One of the more agreeable aspects of having Terry in residence is that he gets up early, with Curt, and goes off and buys the *Globe*; so it's available —a rare treat—at breakfast.

Lee Falk, evidently having forgiven Tony for adding ten years to his age, invites me to preside at one of tomorrow's tournament finals up at his court. Lee wonders whether "umpire" or "referee" is correct. I believe it is "umpire" (a referee supervises an entire tournament), and I am happy to have Terry, whose tennis book is due out soon, in the vicinity to confirm my supposition.

16 August

I am assigned to the mixed doubles. Ray Elman wins, but questionably, for he has a partner, in this purportedly friendly neighborhood competition, who isn't from Truro and whom nobody has heard of before—a nineteen-year-old Wellfleet Amazon who could beat most of the men around here at singles. Afterward, Lee asks me to drive his daughter Valerie and him to the Charles LeClairs' cocktail party. John Worthington, Jr., is among the other guests. When I ask after his parents, both now well along in years, he is reminded of the time when Lady Bird Johnson, as part of her highway-beautification program, had something like Scotch broom planted all along our very own Route 6, whereupon John's mother, Tiny, because the species was not indigenous to Truro, with her very own hands uprooted every last one of them and tossed them out onto the highway.

17 August

This morning's *Globe*, courtesy again of Curt and Terry, says that every freshman at Tufts is henceforth to be given a world atlas and a *World Almanac*, as part of that university's effort to educate its students for future life in a "global village." How refreshing to learn that at least some students somewhere are going to be taught something beyond How to Be Anti-Apartheid Without Giving Up Your Diamonds and Gold.

In the mail a "Personal and Confidential" envelope. Good! After a long drought, I have finally been put on some pornographic list! But I rejoice too fast. The contents are merely a solicitation from the alleged chairman of the board of something called the Silver Bow Resources and Chemical Corporation, who is inviting me to become an Accredited Investor (his capitals) in Silver Bow. I can get in at $46,000 a unit, on a first-come, first-served basis. My correspondent says Harvard University has $50 million invested in the "Texas Oil Patch," but he doesn't specify how much of that is in his units.

Whitney Balliett phones. Nancy and he are in the area, and may they stop by before they return to New York? Of course. Interesting, because the Ballietts have been coming to the Cape for years, and he has never called like this before. Can it have to do with the Shawn-Gottlieb transition? Is it because of Tony's feature story on Whitney in the *Cape Codder*? Or because he and I both happen to be in the current *New Yorker*? Maybe there isn't any special reason at all. A lot of people on earth waste a lot of time searching for motives that didn't exist to begin with.

All the crossword-puzzle people are jumping on the current-events band-wagon. I pick up, belatedly, the August third *New York*, and here is Maura Jacobson's 70-across, "Oliver Burnett-Balin," which it doesn't take the CIA to figure out requires the answer "North Carolina."

I tell Terry, before he and his brood depart, about Tiny and Lady Bird. He says that while working for the *Cape Codder* one summer long ago he noticed men planting and that when he mentioned that to Malcolm Hobbs his boss said to look into it and write about it, so it may well have been his story that spurred Tiny into action.

Who should call but Ellie! She is back at Calgary, safe and sound and only a little stiff. How was her trip? Great, she even trotted. She will tell me all about it when she returns; for now, she has to trot off and have a couple of beers with the cowboys.

But Ellie doesn't *drink* beer.

18 August

Tony has an interview with Norman Mailer in the *Cape Codder*, in which Ray Elman is quoted as saying he is a journalist and Mailer is no saint. Mailer himself has a few abrasive things to say about Elman. Ray phones me, for advice, and reads me a letter he has written, but not yet posted, to Mailer, in which somebody or other is characterized as an old lion with fleas on his ass. I gave him the best advice I can dredge up from my own experience: don't do anything for forty-eight hours.

Barbara Williams, who apparently thinks I might otherwise starve till Ellie arrives, sends over a CARE package: delicious zucchini soup and some cherry tomatoes. That's sweet of her, but I'd have managed. I still have a hamburger patty left over from Sunday's family cookout.

19 August

Ellie, driving a rented car from the airport, got home at two-thirty this morning. I had meant to greet her with a "Hi, Pard," but was too sleepy to remember my line. While we have been sweltering here, she has caught a cold from trotting through snow.

I have some *New Yorker* subscriptions to renew. I see that the postage-paid business-reply envelope bears the zip code 10109–0138—a set of numbers I never noticed before. When the Postal Service first tried to get people to use nine-digit codes, I went down to Washington to interview the then Postmaster General about the innovation and was so carried away by his assurances that it was going to amount to something that to test it out I mailed an envelope to myself at Truro. Our five-digit zip here is "02666," and our box number is "212," so all I put on the outside of the envelope was "02666–0212." The envelope never arrived. Fortunately I had only included a blank sheet of paper.

Some mail does get through—a forwarded New York, N. Y. 10036 Registered Invitation to me at the address (no *"New Yorker"* included) 25 West 43d Street. The outside of the envelope declares that "IF THE RECIPIENT residing at the above address is anyone other than E. J. Kahn Jr. the law expressly prohibits such recipient from opening this invitation." Well, I am in Truro and I have never resided on West 43d Street, but I am not afraid to take risks, and I open the envelope anyway, fearing that its delay in reaching me may mean that my free trip for two to Hawaii has come and gone. Alas, all that is involved is a free trial subscription to *Business Week*. I hope that *The New Yorker*, for all the changes that are taking place there, hasn't yet stooped to this kind of nonsense.

A memo from Nancy Little, of Whitney Communications, to all us members of the Greentree Stable Naming Committee. Of seventeen Jockey-Club-approved names for two-year-olds, I am credited with only one: Summit Meeting (Secretariat-Stepping High). Nancy thinks that merits a "Bravo," but I don't know: Betsey Whitney, Peter Duchin, and Nancy herself got two apiece; Kathy Ritchie and Terry Blanchard a whopping four. Bravissimo!

Archer Trench calls. Hope and he, en route to Moscow next month, are going to take a day flight to London and sleep over at Heathrow. Ellie and I are already booked on a night flight. Archer wonders what clothes to take along and how expensive caviar is going to be. When I say that the last time I was there (1980) caviar was so plentiful and reasonable that more than once I left some on my plate, he seems much relieved.

Ellie doesn't come downstairs until one-thirty, which gets her out of showing up for our two-o'clock memoir class. I had asked, as today's assignment, either for some typically Cape-Coddish incident or for a description of someone memorably hateful. One student combines the two by writing about the time she rented a made-over barn with a ceiling so low she had to move around on hands and knees, a non-stop-flushing toilet, a malfunctioning cesspool, and a landlord deaf to her entreaties. I manage to fill up the entire two hours, though not without resorting to desperate measures, such as asking one young woman in this ostensibly nonfiction group to read a piece of her fiction that she's brought along. It's a short story telling in rather graphic detail of the incestuous relationship of a father and daughter. The author hopes to have it published and insists it is not based on any true-life happening. Another member of the class wonders if the author's father is still alive. Oh, yes. Well. . . .

The questions publishers keep asking: Tom Begner, for reasons unexplained, wants to know *The New Yorker*'s circulation figures for the United Kingdom. I put it to Natasha Turi, and she to John O'Brien, and before the day is out I am in a position to convey the intelligence that the numbers are England, 2,387; Ireland, 177; Scotland, 146; Wales, 20; Northern Ireland, 12; Channel Islands, 7; Isle of Wight, 2; Isle of Man, 1.

20 August

Trying hard not to work, I look around my study, which has hardly changed in more than thirty years except for the importation of a bunch of kitchen cabinets from our Scarborough house. They became surplus when Don Reiman designed a fancy new kitchen for Jinny and me—one completed so near the time we separated and sold the house that I hardly remember its appearance. It's been close to twenty years since I've looked inside the cabinets. Some of the things my wandering eyes detect outside them: a photograph of my maternal grandparents, my mother, my sisters, and me, taken on 24 August 1928, in front of the house where Grandpa was born, in Eschwege, Germany; the 1950–51 edition of *Who's Who in America*; a wicker-backed rocking chair with most of the back rotted out; a Palauan love stick (young man would poke it through side of young woman's sleeping hut, and she could tell by feeling the design of its edges whose it was; if she wanted him to join her, she'd give it a tug); a screen Janet Tenney gave me ages ago, papered with *New Yorker* covers, all blue and all from the nineteen-thirties; a photograph of me on a boat, taken by John Swope (he was also fond of placing his camera in one corner of a squash court and getting a time exposure of both of us at play, or in combat); a photograph (cameraman unknown) of an eland and me in South Africa; a 1940 clam license for S. Robert Large, whoever he is or was. He is authorized to take clams from restricted areas on Mondays and Thursdays between sunrise and sunset, but no more than twenty-four quarts in the shell a day.

Whitney and Nancy Balliett arrive. He and I have been colleagues at the magazine for thirty years or so, but this may be our first protracted chat. Whitney says that he looked up my old John Hammond "Profile" while writing an obit that'll probably be running in next week's issue. Then, to my surprise, he says he used to play the drums in a group with Shawn on the piano and Bruce Bliven on clarinet. But that was what *I* did, at our apartment. Bill and Bruce were leading a double life, without telling me. Whitney says he was the drummer at the Shawns' apartment a long, long time ago, because since his second marriage he hasn't been invited back there. Come to think of it, neither have I.

I ask Whitney if I'm right in assuming that he, like Bruce and me, has always called Shawn "Bill." No, he says; it's always been "Mr. Shawn" and on Shawn's part "Mr. Balliett." But wait; back in the old days when they were making music together, Bill did once call him "Whitney."

I have a sievelike memory—what was the answer somebody told me only yesterday to "How many feminists does it take to change a light bulb?"—but I do remember some of the figures Natasha gave me on *New Yorker* readers in the U.K.; so when we go to the Dick Waterses' for cocktails I tell our hostess, perhaps the most thoroughly British person on the Cape, that the Isle of Wight has a circulation double that of Man's, and what would she guess their totals are? Juliet reflects for a moment and comes up with Wight, 2,600; Man, 1,300. How about that, Mr. Newhouse!

21 August

Do I have no strength of character at all? I get out some of my foreign-aid notes, stare at them, do an acrostic puzzle, clean my typewriter keys, and open up, against my better judgment, one of those kitchen-cabinet drawers. What do I find at first (beneath a chaise longue recover kit) but some architectural blueprints—Kahn & Jacobs, 9–8–50—for the very kitchen that these very drawers once graced!

Now that I have opened Pandora's box, I am a goner. Here is a 2 August 1945 letter from the American Red Cross to *Mademoiselle*, thanking the magazine for $100, which Chief Warrant Officer Kahn could not accept for writing a piece about army insignia because he was in public relations. A copy of the February 1948 issue of the magazine '*48*, containing a piece of mine about Bill Mauldin. I don't know how much I got paid for that one, probably not much over $100, but I sure do like the description of the article's writer: "a member of *The New Yorker* staff who specializes in shrewd and pithy portraits of well-known contemporaries." And here I am ("Biographer Extraordinary") in a January 1956 New York University publication, portrayed in my *New Yorker* office, "rummaging through piles of letters and hastily scrawled notes arrayed in a sort of systematized confusion." A not inaccurate depiction of what I seem to be doing right now.

I was making the columns in the old days. Both Danton Walker and Louis Sobol ran items about my breaking a leg skiing. Westbrook Pegler, who could not abide Frank Sinatra, felt impelled also to savage "one E. J. Kahn, Jr.," when I had the temerity to write about the singer. Pegler, who devoted at least three whole columns to one Frank Sinatra and myself, wrote, for instance, "Any group of Republicans might be 'pro-Fascists' to Kahn and Sinatra." (I like the way he put us in alphabetical order.) A 1 August 1955 letter from Bennett Cerf, after Random House published my *Merry Partners*, asking, "What are you going to do for us next?" A 5 May 1961 letter from James A. Farley, who was Chairman of the Board of the Coca-Cola Export Corporation (do you suppose his autograph, or Cerf's, would be worth much today?): "*The Big Drink* is a truly remarkable book, and I know that it will maintain its place in American literature." A 1961 royalty account from Bodley Head, about the English edition of that one; so far I'd earned only a little more than a third of my £150 advance. An editorial-personnel list dated May 1957. Forty-four of the names on it are also on the November 1986 roster. At *The New Yorker*, we tend to hang on.

22 August

Dinner last night at the Foxes'. Pamela Painter says she didn't much like the doctor whose life in Saudi Arabia she wrote about. Frank F. says, surprisingly, that he didn't much like Benny Goodman, who once, when invited to Frank's for dinner, brought along practically his entire band and then hardly said a word all evening. I didn't know Benny well—saw him around the Century from time to time—but had no reason to fault his volubility.

Tony and Judy went to the fifty-dollars-a-head preview of the Mailer movie. Tony says Norman complained to the audience there that the *Provincetown Arts* story about him had his relationship with the late Roy Cohn all wrong, though why anyone would want to admit to having had any kind of relationship with that man is hard to fathom. Tony, as broad-minded as any of my sons, says the film has so much dirty sex in it that despite so many of its settings being familiar he would never take *his* sons to see it.

The New Yorker has Ved Mehta, as a young man, in California. How fortunate he is to be able to remember every word everybody said to him every day of his life! And here I am struggling to recollect what I had for dessert last night.

I change my typewriter ribbon, spurred on by a letter from an elderly woman (well, she says she has been a *New Yorker* subscriber for over fifty years), whose postscript says, "Did you ever use my typewriter ribbon?" Ved Mehta, unlike me, would probably recall that she once sent one, and why. She is concerned about changes at the magazine and writes in the main body of her text, "I hope the newcomers walk gingerly down those halls as I'm sure Ross is there somewhere, baring his fangs." (She actually had it "bearing," but I am taking the liberty of editing her.) And her closing paragraph, just above that unsettling P. S., is almost enough to make me her slave: "I have just been wallowing in a re-read: you, Sullivan, Thurber, Gibbs, Perelman, and of course E. B. White. What a grand bunch you are, but I guess you're the only 'are' left, aren't you?"

At tennis, Bing, modestly ignoring his own deft drop shot, gives it as his opinion—and after all his years at *Sports Illustrated* who is going to gainsay him?—that two of Truro's most memorable ground strokes are Palmer's sliced backhand and Ellie's windmill crosscourt forehand.

Chris Carduff, E.'s editor at Addison-Wesley, is spending the night. There is no Addison and no Wesley, he confesses, and never has been. The firm was founded by two unrelated men named Cummings, and they used their middle names. Chris brings along the first copy we've seen of Annie Dillard's forthcoming memoir. We go to Annie's—to Annie's and Gary Clevidence's, that is, of course—for dinner. Judith Thurman is there; she's been commissioned by Gottlieb to do a piece for us on Nicaragua. She's also reviewing books and writing an occasional "Talk" piece. So I get to meet another leading player among the new dramatis personae.

23 August

A typical late-August day: tennis brunch at Lee Falk's, plain tennis at our court, Castle Hill fund-raising yard party, Ray Elman-Nancy Webb show at Group Gallery in P'town, dinner back in Truro at Tim Dyk-Sally Katzen ménage. Lee's daughter Diane also works for a magazine, *The World & I*, which I've never previously heard of, even though, when she shows me a copy, it proves to be a whopping seven-hundred-page monthly, ten dollars a copy, and practically no advertising. She speaks of living in a Washington, D. C., commune with ten fellow *World* workers. What can this be all about? Then I notice, on its cover, "A Publication of the Washington Times Corporation." Oh, now I get it—Moonies!

24 August

Hopi has found a turtle and is carrying it around, as a plaything. Ellie manages to pry it from her mouth, and Palmer says he'll release it somewhere way off the dog's beaten track. That may not be as simple as he thinks; Hopi has been spotted far and wide.

This is a Monday, but no word yet from Gottlieb on my piece. Maybe he is so relaxed an editor that he spends weekends with his family instead of telephoning impatient writers. I wonder if he has seen—and how he would react if he has—the current *Vogue*, which of course is also owned by the Newhouses. Ellie has brought home a copy, and I start leafing through it. I pause at a full-page ad urging people to subscribe to *The New Yorker*. Why should they? Because, I read on, of the contributors—my name agreeably among them—they will find therein. Then as I scan the ad to see who else has made this honor roll, my blood begins (as surely Bob's would too) to curdle, for this ad by *The New Yorker* for *The New Yorker* has misspelled the names of two longtime eminent writers: V. S. Pritchett and Whitney Balliett. I must hide *Vogue* from Bob Shaplen, when he and Jayjia come to stay with us this weekend, because he didn't get mentioned. If he had been, come to think of it, they'd probably never have got the name right.

25 August

Now, what can I do this morning to avoid getting to work? I *have* it. Inspect our beach plums! Tommy Kane was on the button in his column. The crop is plentiful. It should be a good year for beach-plum brandy.

Dick Harris was in last week, had apparently reenlisted in our forces, and a couple of days later fell, or jumped, from a window. When I pick up the *Times*, there is an obit. Dick left *The New Yorker* in 1978, it says, and at his death was writing a book about the magazine. Shawn has been asked for a comment and credits him, in the story, with "intellectual grandeur and great moral depth."

26 August

At 6:00 A.M., Ellie to me, sharply, "Turn that damn thing off!" My new wristwatch's alarm has begun buzzing under her ear. But how could it have? I haven't yet figured out how to set it.

Marian Javits on the phone. She is going to send us a memorial book she's been putting together about the Senator, whom I first got to know when I wrote his "Profile" way back when Jack was merely a member of the House. Marian says that once he fell ill and needed a wheelchair and a respirator, he became less feisty and more lovable. In his very last days, she adds, he was an angel. He was certainly one of the best public servants of our era.

Our last memoir session, and the entire teaching staff is on hand to put on its act. Ellie and I are not exactly Burns and Allen, but when we perform together she tends to play it straight and let me make the jokes. Our students seem to think we are going to give this course again next year, but by then Ellie may be too busy running the whole school to serve as an instructor, and I'm not sure I want to take on the job alone.

When we get home, we find Palmer and Bing on the court, playing Joan Fox and Ellen Hawkes in an innovative contest. The men are giving the women six points a set, which they may use at their discretion. Ellen and Joan have apparently already made a serious tactical blunder by taking two of their six early on, at deuce.

27 August

Brent Abel phones. Corinne and he will be flying from Boston to London and will meet us at Heathrow. They have been reading up on me. I suggest they read up on Ellie, too, or, better yet, read *On Glory Roads*. After hanging up, I decide I'm a cheapskate and should send them a copy of it, and do so. You talk of coincidences! I have scarcely packaged the book for dispatch to San Francisco 94111 when the phone rings again. It is Herb Levin, in San Francisco. He says his marriage is breaking up because Ellie promised Cornelia a copy of the book when we were staying with them in New Delhi, and after all this time it hasn't yet arrived. So off goes another copy to S. F. 94115.

To drinks at the Leo Capronis'. The Ben Reads are at the party, and when I mention that we're going to Russia, Ben, who used to be Dean Rusk's right-hand man at State, says we should call on the U.S. Ambassador, Jack Matlock. "He used to work for me," Ben says. I join Malcolm Preston at the shellfish bar (actually an ice-filled rowboat), and he says, "Remember when you showed up at seven in the morning with oysters?" Of course I don't remember. "We were talking about them one evening long ago," Malcolm goes on, "and I said I would eat them at any time, and you took me literally. It wasn't easy to get them down at that hour, but we both did." Ah, youth!

After we're in bed, the phone rings. It is Cynthia Beeker, in Cleveland, with news for Ellie about their mother. Lucile has fallen and broken her hip.

28 August

Arthur Schlesinger calls. He has been talking to Myer Feldman, and they want to know if I'd be interested in writing a biography of Roger Stevens. I have known Roger ever since I wrote his "Profile," back in 1954, before there was a Kennedy Center or even a Kennedy, and will be happy to discuss the matter. But I'm not certain how much general interest there'd be in such a book.

Old friend M. J. phones. She is grateful to me for having had *The New Yorker* sent to her all these years, forty-odd of them, but there's no need to any longer, because she is moving from Greenwich Village to Brookline. Does she think the magazine is only for New Yorkers and not for the Old Lady from Brookline? But this is a refreshing novelty; I've found over the years that once you put people on your private free subscription list, it's hard to get them off.

The Shaplens arrive, Jayjia bearing smoked turkey and homemade pâté. They have become, at a glance at their provender, ideal houseguests. Joey and Jaime materialize, too. Now for the first time I have a grandson taller than I am. Jayjia and Bob accompany Ellie and me to cocktails at the William Phillipses'. It surprised Ellie years ago to learn that Stanley Kunitz was a sports buff. She didn't believe a poet could be like me. Now it turns out that Bill loves pro football, and before the afternoon is out he proposes that I try a sports piece for *Partisan Review*. Top that, Shaplen!

Afterward, Bob feeds me a few tidbits of news about *The New Yorker*. His wife's pâté is tastier and more nourishing. Still, it is interesting to hear the rumor that there is by now even a name—*The Turn of the Century*— for the magazine Schell and McKibben supposedly have on the drawing board; and that it is going to feature, whatever this may mean, eschatological articles. Shaplen also says that Dick Harris, who always struck me as dour, actually had a funny streak. Viz.: He once told Bob he'd had a shouting match with Shawn, and when Shaplen expressed surprise that Shawn had ever raised his voice, Harris said, "You could hear him all the way across the room."

Reading *Publishers Weekly* in bed cannot, for many writers, induce sleep. The issue that arrived today reports that the first print order for the next Garrison Keillor book, apparently a collection of his radio scripts, is seven hundred and fifty thousand.

29 August

Sister Joan phones. Shawn will be eighty tomorrow. She is going to send him a telegram, and maybe I'd like to also. I have always refrained from mentioning the anniversary, lest Bill think his staff was thinking he was getting old, or older. It's different now, so Shaplen and I decide to send joint felicitations. I let Bob write the first draft so I can have the pleasure of rewriting him.

Shaplen has been covering the Philippines for nearly half a century, so it seems appropriate to take him along to Wellfleet, where Judy's sister Tina, just back from a year outside Manila on a student-exchange program, is celebrating *her* birthday. (From eighty to eighteen at practically one swoop.) Shaplen and I have long been competitive; Tina makes my day, after a fashion, when she addresses a few words to him in Tagalog and he doesn't understand. She is thinking of spending a year in Kenya, a quondam stamping ground of mine, and I hope Bob isn't within earshot if, after she returns, she hails me in Swahili.

30 August

The sun is out, for a change, but the court is still too wet for play. There are strange animal tracks square in the middle of it. How did the beast get there without leaving a trail? Flying squirrel? Joey says the footprints are definitely not those of a deer or—he has the place in Maine and ought to know—moose. Speaking of large animals, I had a note yesterday from a Harvard classmate, anent my mountain-accident piece, saying that the climber who told me bears hibernate was wrong; they take prolonged sleeps, but since their body temperatures don't go down, it's technically not hibernation.

At the Elmans' housewarming—a staggering variety of vegetarian foods —Paul Brodeur says there's going to be a memorial service for Dick Harris in New York on the tenth—the one day Ellie and I will be there, en route to Russia. We escort the Shaplens on to the Webbs' book-publication party for Joan Colebrook. It's typical of what seems to beset Joan's work that not a single copy of the book has arrived in time to be displayed. Shaplen gets to meet, and later admits he had never heard of, his longtime fellow *New Yorker* contributor Arturo Vivante. As far as that's concerned, Jayjia chimes in, until she met Bob she had never heard of him as a writer but only as— this makes *his* day, if not year—a sex symbol.

31 August

The Shaplens depart early, before I have a chance to recount to them my first major Gottlieb dream. For several days I have been standing in a long line, awaiting an audience with him, and finally over a loudspeaker I hear "Mr. Kahn," and I approach and sit, very briefly, across his desk, and then I am dismissed and handed a mimeographed sheet, with writing on both sides: on the one, a list of pieces, and on the other (was I supposed to see this? did I get it by mistake?) an efficiency rating—what I have written, what I am thought capable of, an overall candid and barely satisfactory assessment. Bothered by this, nonplussed, I repair to the Century for lunch.

Women are members, though they must drink in a corner. Ellie joins me, and so, I assume to explain what was going on earlier down the block, does Gottlieb's second-in-command, except that it's not Martha Kaplan but Colonel William Hones, the Chief of Staff of the 32d Infantry Division, who has had it in for me ever since, editing a mimeographed newspaper for the passengers on a trans-Pacific troopship, I invented a yarn about a flying fish landing in his bathtub. I wake up before he orders lunch.

No word from Gottlieb yesterday about my piece. That may have triggered the dream.

Three generations on our tennis court at once: Joey, Jaime, and yours truly. Earlier, Jaime, with the characteristic eagerness of a newly licensed sixteen-year-old, volunteered to drive to Wellfleet to fetch the papers. That gave me more time to pick ripe plums—on some bushes so thickly clustered, like grapes, that they've bent their branches to the ground. (Problem is that some people, Joey alas among them, are beginning to hint as delicately as they can that they aren't overwhelmingly fond of the distillation I concoct and call beach-plum brandy.) On the tennis court, everybody is amazed that, considering I am giving Jaime fifty-four years, I get to and manage to return one of his drop shots. I am amazed, too.

At the Howard Wises' dance (music by the Judy Wallace Group, seven strong tonight) Joel Meyerowitz has some kind words for Lexy's architectural photos now on display at the P'town Art Association and thinks they ought to be sent to the *Architectural Digest*.

1 September

To all those skeptics who say nobody can survive August on Cape Cod: We've done it again!

Gerry Piel calls. He is sending us a batch of literature about the USSR. Our visa applications are in Washington, he says, and there should be no complications. He adds offhandedly that he and his Eleanor are leaving for Russia tomorrow (I guess they have *their* visas) and will be meeting the rest of our gang at the Moscow airport.

Bob Gottlieb phones! He says he tried to reach me a couple of times when he first read my Ku Klux Klan piece, never got through, then decided to wait until he read it again, now would like to have the ending amplified and strengthened. I cannot tell from his tone whether he is actually buying the piece or not; I guess I won't know until we're back from Europe.

Most of the afternoon at the Truro Congregational Church—built in 1827, later than our house—for Castle Hill's annual meeting, in the course of which Ellie is formally installed as president. The disposition of the school's court case against the town officials who are impeding its operations has been put off at least until January. There is no mention in the organization's financial report of the pledges I obtained when I ran its building-fund drive last summer, and I urge the new president to have somebody look into this. Ellie makes a graceful speech, mainly about the history of the place during its fifteen years of existence. A lot of praise is showered, during the meeting, on all the school's board members, but I can't help wondering where many of them were last summer when I needed them.

2 September

We have four telephone extensions on the Cape, and it's our practice not to pick one up until after the second ring. Otherwise calls, especially long-distance ones, tend to get aborted. Now that Ellie is involved with Castle Hill, though, she is pressed for time and has been answering after one ring, so that by the time I get on the line I hear a man's voice say, "Is this Virginia Rice Kahn?" Ellie says that this must be for me. It's Bill Cook calling. He used to be stationed, as were Jinny and I toward the end of the war, at 90 Church Street. He was in navy public relations. Now he's a columnist, he says, for the *Cape Cod Chronicle*. Bill reminds me that he and I used to exchange notes way back then, in the form of cryptograms. We agree to aim at a reunion later in the fall. If Brent Abel can get together, after forty-odd years, with his onetime enemies, why can't the American army and navy? I wonder if anybody ever broke our code.

3 September

In case anybody ever asks me what a new toilet costs, today's mail provides the answer—$140.50, exclusive of labor to install it. Also, if you're buying in Truro, a $4.00 fee for disposing of the old one at the town dump.

The homework Gerry Piel has sent, presumably for us to attend to before we convene at Moscow, arrives today: the bundle includes the Russian-language edition (*V Mire Nauki*) of his *Scientific American* and also a book, *Classic Russian Idylls*, with introductions by three noted American Sovietologists—Armand Hammer, Donald M. Kendall, and Gerard Piel.

We dine with Juliet and Dick Waters at the Blacksmith Shop. After having had their water tested at both their Newton and Wellfleet homes, they have finally learned the reason for their daughter Liz's baffling blackouts. It occurred to somebody that, however dizzy she sometimes became while driving, she seemed to recover soon after getting to her destination. So they had the car tested, and it developed that her exhaust system was malfunctioning and that she'd been suffering from recurrent carbon-monoxide poisoning—committing day in and out, as it were, involuntary suicide.

4 September

More coincidences: The latest and tenth-anniversary issue of *Chronicles*, the Rockford, Illinois, publication that is amazingly reactionary (its editor writes, "The feminists, homosexuals, and creeps own the universities now, and taxpaying parents who send Johnny and Suzie off to State should realize into just whose hands they are entrusting their children and count their blessings if their precious darlings are seduced by a professor of the *opposite* sex"), is dedicated to the late Leopold Tyrmand, my onetime *New Yorker* colleague and friend. "Having once escaped from Warsaw's Communist rule," *Chronicles* relates, "Tyrmand had more recently fled from an oppressive New York literary scene. Now, he was to make Middle America his home for his assault on a decadent liberal culture." Tyrmand came upon that scene—*The New Yorker* scene, I assume *Chronicles* means—toward the end of 1967 and before his final appearance in the magazine, in the winter of 1970, wrote five long, reflective pieces, consisting mainly of pithy paragraphs. But his political views were apparently too far to the right of those who helped Shawn determine whatever editorial policies we had, and Leopold vanished from our roster of contributors almost as quickly as he'd joined it. According to a Tyrmand obit in the very conservative *Human Events*, Shawn kept on buying his stuff, but with no intention of using it, and he didn't.

But that's not the coincidence. A few pages further on, this provocative magazine has an article titled "Scientific American Goes to Moscow." It starts off with "Who is Mr. Piel?" And it goes on to say, among much else, "If Mr. Piel's support of Communism has no objective basis, why does he sound like a Soviet propaganda mouthpiece? Can there be a subjective explanation? Does he have some reason for resenting the U.S. or the free enterprise system? This is hardly likely . . . ." If I take this diatribe to Moscow, will the Russians impound it before I can deliver it to Gerry?

That's a trivial question. Here comes perhaps a more profound one: would Leopold Tyrmand have become so embittered and swerved so far to the right if *The New Yorker* had continued to be hospitable to his views, or at least tolerant thereof, or at the very worst not hostile?

5 September

In bed last night I read John Hersey's *New Yorker* piece from Moscow. (Gottlieb had warned me this was coming in and that he had so much other

Russian stuff in the works that I shouldn't expect to get anything for the magazine out of our trip.) Bob is concerned about the endings of pieces, and obviously he was satisfied with Hersey's, but it seems an odd one; the whole piece has a decidedly *glasnosty* tone, but then it concludes with an anecdote about a brutal Soviet general that might well appeal to the editor of *Chronicles*.

The end of summer manifests itself in mysterious ways. At the Paul Resikas' twentieth-wedding-anniversary gathering (nature gave them quite a present: a breathtaking sunset and a full moon), Judy Shahn discloses that on August thirty-first, the very last day it was needed, the beach sticker on the window of her car fell off as she was leaving the beach.

6 September

A modified version of the end-of-summer party we've traditionally given with Ding, at her place, is scheduled for this evening. It used to be an open house, but it got out of hand; a couple of years ago, after dark, some kids made off with all the liquor from our outdoor bar. And then there was the guest who accused us, in a *Vanity Fair* story about parties of the year or some such, of serving nothing to drink other than cheap Spanish wine. I want to exclude her from this year's affair—which Ding seems to have proclaimed a bring-your-own-food shindig—but Ellie and she have more forgiving natures than I do.

The party goes well. J. C. is a no-show. Nobody gets objectionably drunk. Styrofoam cups don't hold much. The Meyerowitzes bring along Ed Koren, who tells me the news, disturbing if true, that Bob Gottlieb reputedly wouldn't let a certain writer praise a certain person "in my magazine" because Bob happened to dislike the individual in question. (I can't believe either Ross or Shawn said "my magazine." They said "the magazine.") Ed adds, however, that so far Gottlieb has seemed more receptive to novel cartoon ideas than was his predecessor.

The Mike Snells provide the music tapes for dancing, and Mike also brings along my Cameron. *My* Cameron? His daughter, that is, the Cameron who was my secretary during my Castle Hill fund-raising efforts last summer. She was a daily one-woman fashion show—never the same outfit and each one more dazzling and colorful than the one before. Watching her come to work for a month beat riffling through *Harper's Bazaar*. Tonight she is a vision in off-the-shoulder black. She wants me to find her an inexpensive loft in Manhattan. She should know from having observed me importuning deadbeats last year that I cannot perform miracles.

7 September

Labor Day. The tennis-playing ranks are being thinned. The Binghams are gone, Bing having left behind a canoe paddle with a portion of it painted red, so that we can employ it to tell if our net has been adjusted to the correct height. The Hueblers are on their way West. Doug, bidding me farewell at the post office, says that the marines, contrary to what I stated in the book of mine he borrowed and is now returning, did not suffer reverses at Peleliu. He says he should know because he was there. After he's gone, I scan *A Reporter in Micronesia*. I made that assertion on page twenty-eight. I must try to remember to ask Doug next summer whether that's as far as he got. Maybe he quit there out of disgust.

I construe it to be one of my roles in life to be helpful. Never having been a Boy Scout, I got off to a late start, but as an example of how I've tried to catch up, look at my good deed for today. Palmer comes around bemoaning that he couldn't get a single word at the top of yesterday's *Times* crossword. It appears to come as a staggering revelation to him when I suggest, in a kindly, Scout's-honor tone, that he try beginning at the bottom or right hand of puzzles, because the ends of words are usually easier than the beginnings. Words are apt to end in letters like those people going for the bonus car on "Wheel of Fortune" generally select—r, t, s, n, d, l, e. Palmer seems unconvinced, like a little old lady not entirely certain of the motives of the lad whose tight grip on her elbow is propelling her across the street.

Brent Abel phones. We are probably going to have one more day in Germany than he'd anticipated, and would Ellie and I be interested in accompanying Corinne and him on a visit to the American military cemetery in France where her brother is buried? David Waybur, who I gather from Brent's mention of a blue-and-white striped shoulder patch was in the Third Division, was, until a German sniper killed him, one of the most decorated heroes of the Second World War: Medal of Honor in Sicily, others in Italy Brent can't cite offhand. I would very much want to tag along.

8 September

At noon today, after more than two months of staying in place, my temporary dental bridge comes loose. I manage to shove it back in all right, but I suppose some glue would help. Why didn't Dr. Magnani and his staff caution me about cream cheese?

Looking over the material I've accumulated so far about Brent Abel, I note that his destroyer escort's epic battle with the U-boat took place on his twenty-eighth birthday. How young he was to hold such high command! How young we all were in that bygone war! It may be that there's nothing like a war to make a generation grow up fast.

Taking advantage of my relative idleness today—indolence might be more accurate—I head for Provincetown to see Lexy's photos at the art museum. (Happily, he can mature at his own pace, in mufti.) He has twenty-three pictures on display by my unofficial count, and an impressive lot they are. I enjoy driving to P'town at this time of year. I park only a few feet from the Art Association door, thumbing my nose, figuratively, at the lot across the street, with its five-dollar berths all vacant.

Writers learn early on that you can't copyright the title to a book—only its contents. The latest issue of the *Times Literary Supplement* carries an ad for *The Glory Road* (has to do with the British and French fighting along the Nile in the late nineteenth century), and while this isn't an exact duplicate of Ellie's *On Glory Roads*, it's close enough, so on the what-they-don't-know-can't-worry-them theory I tear out the ad and throw it away. I am reminded while doing so of the time she and I went into a midtown Manhattan bookstore and, not seeing my *The Problem Solvers*, asked a clerk if it was soon going to be in stock. She went off to consult some reference work and on returning asked which book with that title did we have in mind? She had found a listing for two such—neither of them mine.

9 September

Will Hopi be able to forgive us for abandoning her for three weeks? When we drop her off at a kennel on our way to Boston and the airport, is that a reproachful look she is giving us? How are you supposed to be able to explain to a dog, anyway, that you can't take her to Moscow? I wish it were possible to let her know at least that we are as much concerned about her welfare as about our not yet having received our Soviet visas.

We have barely reached our New York apartment and begun pawing through the heaps of second- and third-class mail when the phone rings. It is Bill Shawn, to thank me for the birthday telegram. How glad I am that Joan suggested it! He sounds cheerful, and when I mention his new job at Farrar, Straus, says the *Times* story was premature and that he's just going to be doing a couple of things there, informally.

10 September

There must have been a story in *New York Woman* attacking Shawn and *The New Yorker*, because the current issue has a letter praising him and describing it as "vital and important."

Our visas and tickets and some yellow ribbons to tie to our luggage have been delivered to my office, along with two Russian Travel Bureau flight bags—their color a cross, appropriately, between Soviet red and Harvard crimson.

I ride down to the Village and the Judson Memorial Church, for Dick Harris's service, with Sheila McGrath and Joe Mitchell. Joe is one of the few people I know who still wears a hat. There's a big crowd—just about everybody in *The New Yorker*'s extended family, including both Shawn and Gottlieb. Bob has donned jacket and tie this sweltering afternoon. Bud Trillin speaks, also Tom Wicker and Roger Wilkins. A young woman unknown to me reads a tribute from Shawn. Now I know what it must be like to be deaf. The acoustics are so bad and the audio system so inadequate that nobody can hear what anybody says.

Afterward, Sheila and Joe and I move on to a neighborhood bar for a testimonial drink or two and watch the Pope arrive on television. We get to talking about restaurants, and the name of the Red Devil crops up, and Joe recalls the time I ate some glass there and offended Freddie Packard, the longtime head of the magazine's Checking Department. Joe believes it was octopus or squid that was my undoing. Anyway, when I discovered that what I was chewing on was not exclusively seafood, and furthermore that it induced bleeding, I was not only taken aback but indignant; and most of the others at the table concurred with my request, nay demand, that I be given a substitute dish less challenging. Not Freddie, though. He clearly felt that whatever inconvenience we had all been put to by my interrupting the meal was not the establishment's fault but mine. I never went back to the Red Devil again and don't recall that Freddie ever again consented to break bread with me (or glass), either. He was a hearty eater, and I guess I spoiled his appetite.

11 September

Maybe I have been hanging around *The New Yorker* too long. A man sending me a postcard about my mountain-climbing piece says, "Your father E. J. Kahn Sr. once wrote a like type story about a crossing he made with a convoy—either shortly before or shortly after we entered World War II. Great reporting." Both of me thank you.

I call on Gottlieb. He is gung-ho about the Brent Abel piece. He isn't sure I should proceed with the foreign-aid piece. He is buying the Ku Klux Klan one. He doesn't think much of World's Fairs, but he might consider Brisbane if another Australian piece in the works doesn't pan out. He has more Russian pieces in the works than he cares to think about. He agrees that this time around we can skip the Winter Olympics and just cover the Summer Games in Seoul next fall. He cannot run my Socialist Workers' Party piece soon, because he has another story coming up that involves the FBI. He says, astonishingly, that of all the long-fact pieces Shawn has bought and hoarded, there are only fifteen or twenty on the bank—my UNICEF "Profile" not among them—that Bob deems publishable.

The night flight to London lasts six hours. Takeoff at nine, dinner at eleven, breakfast before you know it. Forget sleep. In the departure lounge, a woman confides to me her anti-jet-lag diet: no coffee for three days and then huge last-minute infusions of it. Or was it the other way around? Among our other fellow passengers are a black woman with three small children, on the first leg of a flight to Kano. She is bringing along enough television and stereo equipment to stock a boarding school. Remembering the greed of Nigerian customs and immigration officials, I can see their hands outstretched now as she approaches with her otherworldly goods.

The Class of '37 assembles at Heathrow—five of the seven of us who survived all the shakedowns and are actually going to Russia together. Gerry Piel's already there, we hope, and Archer Trench, held back at the last minute by Hope's indisposition, will meet us, with or without her, in Moscow. Ellie and I greet Rusty Crawford, also sans wife; the Brent Abels; the Fag Goodhues; and the Dave Schwarzes. Four respectable classmates: a big-bank CEO, two lawyers, and a biochemist—all now retired or semiretired. Two hearing aids and two canes among us. Well, let's face it, we're not kids any more.

The Piels are at one of the two Sheremetyevo airports—#2 was brand new when I landed there for the 1980 Olympics—to welcome us. (One of the first jokes we hear in Moscow is that the spot at Red Square where that young West German landed his small plane is now called Sheremetyevo #3.) Eleanor P. has bouquets of red flowers for Jeanne Schwarz, Dede Goodhue, Corinne Abel, and Eleanor K. Rusty's luggage didn't get through, and he has to fill out what the USSR, which evidently doesn't like to use words like "lost," calls a "Property Irregularity Report." We are urged to enumerate, on a regular property report, every bit of jewelry we have, lest there be trouble about getting it out when we depart. I neglect to itemize my cuff links but will worry about that later. We are booked into the six-thousand-room Hotel Rossiya, which I remember well from the 1980 Olympics, when security people checked credentials on exits from the building as well as on entrances to it. The bell tower of Ivan the Great, in the Kremlin, is eighty-one meters high, and nothing taller may be constructed inside Moscow; the Rossiya was topped off at seventy-nine. Ellie has brought along, at the suggestions of various more or less informed sources, Scotch, pepper, soap, wash-and-dries, and Kleenex. We should have packed some bath towels.

13 September

The only English-language publication on sale at the Rossiya newsstand is the *Morning Star*, the Communist weekly published in London. Free of charge are booklets saying we are guests of the Soviet Union and should behave like guests. (That we are paying guests is evidently irrelevant.) The guide who's been assigned to our tour for the duration—Moscow, Novosibirsk, Tashkent, Tbilisi, Leningrad—is a no-nonsense young woman named Irina. She escorts us forthwith to the Kremlin's Armory Museum. Asked there for the English word to describe a metal animal on exhibit, Irina says "ounce." Others try to explain to her that that can't be right, but crossword-puzzlers know better; it is a large, leopardlike feline, and not at all, as some people think, a mythological creature comparable to (surely all Harvard men know *this*) the yale.

At lunchtime, we learn something about a practical effect of Gorbachev's *perestroika*. Hotels and restaurants may not serve drinks until 2:00 P.M., and bottle shops can't open till then, either. (Bars close at 11:00 P.M.) Irina tells us, as our bus takes us around, that on Saturdays, like yesterday, 1 million Moscovites volunteer to tidy up the city (what happens to those who don't step forward nobody asks), and in her view Moscow looks cleaner than it did Friday. She points out the railroad station where trains arrive from Kiev, and while the building doesn't ring any mnemonic bells, I'll never forget that rail line.

Jinny and I and the rest of our 1958 Intourist group took a night train from Kiev to Moscow. Many of our companions were students, on slim budgets, and by the time we reached Kiev we'd all come to a tacit understanding that the Kahns, one of whom at least was traveling on a *New Yorker* expense account, could be counted on in emergencies, specifically when there was a shortage of vodka. We ran out not long after departing from Kiev. Then after dark the train stopped, not at a terminal but out in the countryside. A couple of hundred yards from the tracks, we could see a row of stalls, presided over by women in babushkas. Here, presumably, was a chance to replenish our supply. It was a hot summer night, and I was in shirtsleeves. I jumped off the train with a fistful of rubles, leaving my passport and all other credentials aboard. I found a stall selling vodka, bought two bottles, and was strolling debonairly back toward our car when the train began to move. I stopped strolling. I sprinted to the tracks before the train outdistanced me, and a couple of students, arms outstretched, grasped my hands and hauled me aboard, but not until they had first grasped the bottles. A few seconds longer, and I might still be out in the Ukrainian countryside, trying to explain with gestures why I wasn't wearing a necktie.

Irina has arranged for us to dine at a restaurant called the Slavonic Market.

Chekov ate here, also Stanislavsky, Tchaikovsky, Rimsky-Korsakov, and Chaliapin. Nowadays it is popular with the younger set. *Glasnost* is rampant. The youths at the table alongside ours are celebrating a girl's birthday. "We don't want war to be," she says in English. It doesn't take more than that for me to be prevailed on to make a birthday toast. Then we all mingle and dance. Before the evening is out, our table is singing "Fair Harvard," and some Germans a few feet away are singing the "Star-Spangled Banner"— *im Deutsch*. But at exactly 11:00 P.M. Gorbachev takes over. The lights flicker, the party is through, and everybody goes home. Ellie says there were tears in my eyes when I made that toast. Well, why not? I am not running for office and don't care if I'm called a wimp, and if I want to cry I'll cry. I cry at bad movies. I am crying right now just thinking about crying.

14 September

We had such a good time fraternizing last night that Fag left his cane at the restaurant.

At breakfast, Dave Schwarz says he has been reading the Soviet constitution, which seems appropriate, inasmuch as he is the only member of our team with a Ph.D.

The day gets under way uneventfully: a visit to a not very modestly named Exhibition of Economic Achievements on the outskirts of the city, with an enormous space pavilion among them; and then to a no less grandiose art show (Russian art, 1920–1987), with more Lenins than nudes. One beguiling exhibit here is a *1987* painting by D. D. Zhelinsky of a *1937* scene: Russian soldiers invading the home of his father, Dmitri Konstantinovich Zhelinsky, who was arrested on trumped-up charges and sent to Siberia. There are others than our Harvard '37 contingent who are thinking in fifty-year terms, and someone has placed a bouquet of flowers on the floor beneath this filial tribute.

Rusty Crawford has a television set in his hotel room, but like the refrigerator in ours it doesn't work. His frig does, though, so—also because he is for the purposes of this trip a bachelor—his room becomes generally accepted as our group's premeal water hole. At the *Beriozka* in our hotel— hard-currency shop barred to indigenes—a small bottle of Stolichnaya costs $8.10, which is even more than Joe Duarte charges back in Truro.

The evening is more interesting. The Piels have arranged for us to dine at an elegant rooftop restaurant with a dozen Russians, among them Sergei Kapitza, the editor of the local *Scientific American* and a TV personality; Nicolai Enikolopov, the director of the Institute of Polymer Chemistry; and Boris Belitsky, a correspondent for Radio Moscow. The woman at my left, whose identity I never do get, speaks a little English—enough for me to infer that when her children were growing up she gave them daily, as

American parents were once wont to do with cod-liver oil, a dose of caviar. There is also a Jewish molecular biologist, a refusenik whose mail, both incoming and outgoing, is routinely intercepted, but he says he isn't un-happy; he is at least allowed to write for foreign publications. Irina says afterward that he could leave the country all right, any time he wished to, though of course if he did he might not be able to come back.

15 September

At the America-Canada Institute, we are the beneficiaries of a briefing by its director, Georgi Arbatov, a frequent high-level exponent of his govern-ment's position to foreigners. We men get tea in glasses, our ladies in cups. Arbatov complains about the Allies not having sooner opened a second front during the Second World War. (None of us brings up the Nazi-Soviet Pact.) He says *glasnost* is an old Slavic word for "voice"—so it has to do with people speaking out. He complains further that an important speech he made has been ignored by the American press, and we should look for it in the weekly English-language *Moscow News*. Any questions?

Rusty Crawford says that public opinion got the United States out of Vietnam. What about the Russians and Afghanistan? Answer: Gorbachev wants a political solution and doesn't need public opinion to tell him so. Arbatov blames the troubles there on drugs and Pakistan, and anyway Afghanistan abuts the Soviet Union, he adds, which is hardly the case with respect to Nicaragua and the United States. Are we aware that Washington, D.C., is no closer to Managua than Moscow is to Gibraltar? When he alludes to Reagan's having called the Soviet Union an "evil empire," he pounds a fist on the table.

Over a prelunch sip in Rusty's room, Dede Goodhue, a New York State Senator from Westchester, says that when she first ran for office she ap-proached some men at the Ossining railroad station (my old neck of the woods) and said, "I'm running for the Assembly and I'd like your vote," and they said they'd be delighted to oblige but unfortunately had just been released from Sing Sing and as convicted felons couldn't.

We visit Moscow State University, where Gerry, who has lectured here (in a room called Communist Hall, known before the 1917 Revolution as Theological Hall), had hoped the administration could round up some of *its* 1937 graduates to meet us. But apparently none could be found. For one thing, the war had taken a dreadful toll of that age group (only 3 percent of all Soviet males born between 1920 and 1925, for example, were alive at the end of it), and for another, the institution doesn't maintain alumni records as carefully as does Harvard, having no need to fund-raise. We do get to meet the dean of the school of journalism, which now turns out four hundred graduates annually. He says the Soviet press had until recently been on a short tether, but now it's been unleashed and is barking at everybody. He says hotels like ours are supposed to stock the *International Herald Tribune* and *Le Monde*—there are special arrangements for obtaining them for rubles instead of hard currency—but the Rossiya has a reputation for inefficiency. He says with a straight face, in further dogged pursuit of his canine analogy, that the Soviet press, which he knows we know is 100-percent government controlled, serves as a watchdog of the public's interests.

Archer Trench arrives from New York, without wife but with the *Trib* and, as a special gift for me, a Xerox of the *Times*'s Sunday crossword. He also has the *Times* of Monday, the fourteenth, which reports on the arrest, here in the USSR, of twenty Soviet dissidents. Whether any of the people's watchdogs also reported that we will probably never know.

16 September

Because Gerry is our leader, our trip is naturally science oriented, which for someone like me, to whom physics and chemistry are by and large as incomprehensible as Tagalog and Swahili, can be challenging. This morning we are escorted to the Institute of Molecular Genetics, where Professor Enikolopov happens to mention a "Garvard" University professor who won a Nobel prize in science in 1946. For all my ignorance, I know well who *that* was—the late Percy Bridgman, father of our very own and also unfortunately late classmate Bob, who roomed across the hall when we were freshmen. Comrade Enikolopov is carrying on, while I muse about the days in the Yard on the fourth floor of Stoughton Hall, about pulverization. He says it is the most ancient of all sciences, and he brandishes a picture of a Neanderthal man crushing something to prove it. He himself pulverizes used automobile tires. Now he passes around a jar of crushed rubber that looks like coffee. He has patents in the United States, Japan, and West Germany. He has radically altered the technology of soap manufacture—first real innovation since Babylon. He makes soap without water.

Few visitors get to see much of Russian homes. We're all invited to tea at Sergei Kapitza's apartment. Tanya and he have laid on a tea that's really high: cheese sandwiches, pears, plums, watermelon, grapes, half a dozen kinds of cake, Georgian wine, vodka, and—oh, yes—tea. Some of our party, who may not have another opportunity to ride the Moscow subway, elect thus to return to the hotel. I've done that and welcome a much more exclusive mode of transportation: Tanya's driving Ellie and me back in a stately 1978 limousine bought with the money her late father-in-law received when he won *his* Nobel. The Kapitzas call the chariot their Memory Mercedes.

17 September

Our last day in Moscow. Huge swarm of tourists in the hotel dining room for breakfast. We get an inkling of Brent Abel's stature in California legal circles when a federal judge from Sacramento comes over to pay his respects and, on learning that Corinne's eyeglass frame needs adjusting, kneels at her feet to fix it. In the dining-room lobby, I am accosted by two Syrians, I hope of nonterrorist stripe. They are on their way to the Moscow Circus and solicit my opinion of it. I say it was first-rate when I saw it last, twenty-nine years ago. After they leave, I wonder: could it have been the Kiev Circus?

A big eye-popping Chagall retrospective at the Pushkin Museum, including some of his works painted from 1911 to 1914, which have never before been publicly shown here, apparently because they've long been judged not to be in harmony with Soviet realism.

Lunch at the Aragvi. The Piels are going to have to leave us soon; some emergency in the States that requires their presence.

Like the British, the Russians delight in showing off their palaces and their jewels. Unlike the Chinese, they don't show off their factories. So far, we haven't had a sniff of the Soviets' industrial strength, nor, when it comes to that, of their military. In keeping with our hosts' priorities, we're taken to the Castle Ostankino, once owned by a count—Dmitri Nikolaevich—who, a guide says, almost proudly, also owned two hundred and ten thousand serfs. It's the kind of shrine where, to preserve the floors, sightseers have to put slippers over their shoes.

Dede Goodhue puts in a call to Albany. Mario Cuomo, she is told, is going to be in Leningrad at the same time as we are. Dede knows him well—when the governor was merely lieutenant governor, he presided over her senate for four years—and she's going to try to arrange for all of us to get together when the noncandidate for the presidency crosses our path.

18 September

It's a measure of the vastness of Siberia that there are four time-zone changes between Moscow and Novosibirsk, and a measure of the mystique of Siberia that though like most Americans I have long been aware of its labor camps, I knew little before we flew there last night about Novosibirsk ("New Siberia"). It turns out to be a bustling Ob-River metropolis on the Trans-Siberian Railway with a population of nearly a million and a half and a Bolshoi Theater larger than Moscow's.

On our way from downtown Moscow to the airport last night, we passed one huge apartment complex after another, some still abuilding. It's hard to believe that there'll ever be a housing shortage thereabouts. We were sequestered in a waiting room for foreign tourists only. Our flight was not posted, but on our way to our private chamber we saw a list of other romantic-sounding destinations: Baku, Khabarovsk, Nizhnovartovzk, Karaganda, Cheljabinsk, Novokuznetsk, Ufa, and Tomsk. (Has anybody ever computed the total of the world's airports?) "If it's possible, try to have some rest during the flight," Irina told us. "It could save your life."

Novosibirsk, where we check in at dawn at the Hotel Tsentralnaya, on Lenin Street, was founded in 1893, when the Trans-Siberian was under construction. It is the largest city in Siberia and the eighth largest in the whole USSR. It has a temperature range from ninety-seven above to fifty below zero. It's always fun for natives to try to scare hicks like us. In July and August, we're told by a local guide, the mosquitoes (like so much else relating to Siberia) are gargantuan. We hear later, not from any emissary of Intourist, that in bygone days a favorite summertime form of execution was to tie a poor wretch naked to a tree and let the mosquitoes tend to him.

Today's agenda calls for us to make the first of several visits to a Novosibirskian suburb called Akademgorodok ("academic township"), which since it began to be carved out of virgin forest in 1957 ("by party and government decision," according to a Russian-cum-English booklet issued in 1982 in observance of the enclave's twenty-fifth anniversary) has become a citadel of Soviet scientific and technical research and achievement. Thirty miles south of Novosibirsk, Akademgorodok, also on the Ob (the big river has been dammed here to generate power, and a fair-sized lake, with a sandy beach, has evolved), is a sprawling, tree-lined think tank with a population of fifty-five thousand, more than a thousand of whom have doctoral degrees. It has its own schools, shops, cinema, library, hospital, hotel, and concert hall—this last in a splashy edifice called, perhaps inevitably, the House of Science. The air is so pure—no heavy industry—that the snow that blankets the community from October to April stays white. Akademgorodok lies in what aeons ago was mastodon country, and its Institute of History, Philology, and Philosophy, one of the few of its centers devoted to the humanities, has a skeleton of a mammoth on historical display.

Akademgorodok has a slew of institutes, specializing in, to cite just a few examples, thermal physics, semiconductor physics, pure and applied mechanics, automation and electrometry, and chemical kinetics and combustion. The director of the Institute of Economics and Industrial Engineering, Professor Abel Gelevich Aganbegyan, was recruited last year by Gorbachev as a consultant on the *perestroika* of the limping Soviet economy. (It was Aganbegyan who wrote a *Pravda* article that is said to have influenced Gorbachev's decision to scuttle, on ecological grounds, a grandiose scheme to reverse the drift of the country's major rivers, which, the Ob among them, flow northward into the Arctic Ocean.) Scientists at the Institute of

Cytology and Genetics, for their part, have made considerable headway—crucial for the future of Siberia, with its long, cold winters—in breeding quick-ripening wheat and quick-maturing sheep; Gerry Piel tells of one exceptionally enterprising and patient member of that faculty, now dead, who contrived over twenty-five generations of watchful procreation to come up with a fox tame as a dog.

We push on to the Institute of Geology and Geophysics, where the lady curator shows us a boxful of Siberian diamonds. (One diamantiferous pipe is called Peace.) Siberia, she tells us, has so far yielded up every known mineral and also one—charoite—unknown until it was discovered in 1960, near the Chara River, by a geologist from an Irkutsk outpost of Akademgorodok. Charoite is a lavender-colored silicate used mainly, so far, for decoration and adornment. Two of the museum's exhibits, none of which are for sale, bear valuation tags: seven thousand rubles (about ten thousand dollars) for a vase, and fifty rubles for a finger ring. (I never spot any of the precious stuff, though, at any of the *Beriozka* stores in which I go souvenir hunting.) Scientists at Akademgorodok's Institute of Catalysis and Inorganic Chemistry, incidentally, have managed to synthesize opal, beryl, and alexandrite, along with a superfine gold—99.999 percent pure—and a superfine tin so precious it's as costly as gold, though as far as I know has yet to be counterweighed with Siberian butter.

Intourist is forever trying to get its overseas charges to attend folk-music concerts, and tonight we are conned into forking over ten dollars apiece (no rubles accepted, only real money) for one. It boasts a versatile participant —a man who first turns pages for a pianist and then reemerges as a soloist both on a tambourine and what I take to be a Jew's harp, though in the Soviet Union today its virtuosos may find it prudent to give it another name.

19 September

Buckwheat blinis with curd, from boiled sour milk, for breakfast. The rest of us are so enthusiastic that Dede Goodhue for once forswears her imported cornflakes.

Today is a Saturday, and on our way to the V. I. Lenin All-Union Academy of Agricultural Sciences, we pass quite a number of people crouched over in potato fields. Our mentor, when we arrive, is the agronomist Roald B. Kondratjev, Corresponding Member and Chief Learned Secretary of the Academy's Siberian Department. Mineral water and beer on his conference table. He asks each of us for a brief self-description, and when Corinne Abel says she's a rancher, which she is, I sense that her companions have rapidly diminished in relative consequentialness. Kondratjev's institution, which has been at Akademgorodok since 1969, has fifty research outposts scattered around Siberia, among them reindeer farms in permafrost areas. Reindeer meat is very succulent, he says, and has more vitamins than beef. The reindeer population of Siberia is 3 million—two-thirds wild and one-third domesticated. On one wall of the room in which we're received by Chief Learned Secretary Kondratjev, whose forte is seed-grain quality, is a painting, on reindeer skin, of two reindeer—shades of electrons and positrons! —butting their heads together. In no small part owing to the endeavors of this academy, he says, Siberia has become self-sufficient in grain, potatoes, meat, eggs, milk, and such frost-resistant vegetables as beets, carrots, and cabbages. The academy has also bred a small, frost-resistant apple (there are only about a hundred frost-free days a year at Akademgorodok), which grows on trees so stunted apple-pickers have to stoop at harvest time.

If the Harvard Class of 1937 ever publishes another album, we now have a potential illustration: a photograph of seven members sitting at Lenin's statuary feet in the main square of the capital of Western Siberia.

There's a bookstore on one corner of the square. In English, it stocks Maugham, Wilde, Faulkner, Tolstoy, Waugh, Bierce, Washington Irving, and a biography of Lenin's mother. In anticipation of the 1988 Olympics in Korea, I buy *Sports*, published in both English and French in Pyongyang. The only reference to the United States is a picture of an exultant winner in some undefined contest and head-bowed loser with the caption "Ku Yong Jo, a People's Athlete, defeats the American rival."

At dinner, Archer Trench, one of whose daily papers was the *American Metal Market*, gets to talking about the late Charles Engelhard, the precious-metals man, whom I got to know well in the sixties, and whose biography, which Jane E. commissioned me to write and paid for handsomely, is still, by her choice, unpublished. I have a lot of memories of Charlie I could share with Archer: how Jane had a metal message affixed to the back of the front seat of one of their limousines, reminding him in solid gold to fasten his seat belt; how he once impressed everyone at the Provincetown airport by sending a private plane to pick up my son Joey and me and whisk us to an Engelhard fishing camp in Canada, how at their New Jersey estate I once danced à trois with the Duke and Duchess of Windsor, and how. . . .

But it is time, Irina says, to stop this prattle and head for what she calls a nightclub. It is a large room in the basement of a nearby building, with no music, no dancing, no liquor—merely apple juice, cake, and coffee. The rest of our group soon heads back to the hotel. But there is music to be heard upstairs, and Ellie and I climb toward it. Here is a bona fide nightclub, with dancing and drinking and a uniformed sentry at the door, some sort of junior officer, who at first firmly denies us admittance. He speaks some English, though (and on learning we live in New York and Massachusetts says knowledgeably, "Ah, yes, on Atlantic Ocean"); and after a while he relents, lets us in, and resumes a chat we interrupted with a Cuban in mufti who told us, while we were waiting, that he had a brother in Angola.

20 September

We have an authentic Siberian lunch scheduled, with wild mushrooms, but first we must inspect a "local lore" museum. While an in-house guide drones on interminably about one stuffed animal after another (only truly interesting one is a badgerlike creature, the glutton, which we are advised can eat a whole elk and then turn around and eat another), Ellie and I once again strike off on our own and for the first time since we've arrived in this country see likenesses of Josef Stalin—in newspapers dating back to 1941. Some of the exhibits in this section are quite timely: the December 16, 1986, English-language edition of *Pravda*, for one (we don't get to see this export version of the paper over here), with the headline "M.S. Gorbachev Meets With Senator G. Hart."

The pièce de résistance at lunch is Siberian beefsteak pie—mushrooms, beef, peppers, herbs, onions, eggs, sour cream, and wine. This is the last meal we'll share with Gerry and Eleanor, who are heading for Moscow and home. Irina writes something in the restaurant's guest book and translates it for me: "A group of American students [does she really think that's what we are or is she teasing us about our age?] thanks the restaurant for good Siberian cuisine and service."

Ellie checks out a supermarket and says it offers mostly pickled tomatoes, rice, tea, apple juice, canned fish, dishes, and utensils.

21 September

One last visit to Akademgorodok before we fly down to Tashkent. Our principal targets today are Novosibirsk State University and an appendant preparatory school, two-thirds of whose graduates move along to the university. The school concentrates on physics, chemistry, and mathematics; and competitions for admission to it are so intense they're called Olympiads. The university has thirty-seven hundred students, about half of them female. (Half, too, are children of intelligentsia, we are told by one professor. Thirty percent hail from workers' homes and twenty from farmers'.) Novosibirsk State opened its doors in 1959—not literally, because the earliest matriculants lived and studied in tents and built classrooms between classes. "We were young and had to work hard," says another prof, who was introduced to this academic township as a freshman twenty-eight years ago. "That influenced our character. It was that hard kind of work that makes Akademgorodok special." Many of the four thousand scientists currently affiliated with the place are alumni of Novosibirsk State, which has twelve thousand graduates. Its curriculum—normally a five-year one—is heavily tipped in favor of the physical sciences, but there are courses in English literature, and I was happy to learn that among the American writers on the required reading lists—Faulkner and Hemingway predictably there—is my longtime friend the late Irwin Shaw. I wonder if Irwin ever heard of Akademgorodok.

For the last couple of years, the prep school has had an exchange program with Phillips Andover, an academy I know well. Terry, Joey, and Tony all went there, and I've spent so much time on its campus that I sometimes almost feel as if I were an old P.A. boy myself. This fall, for five weeks, ten Russians traveled to Massachusetts, and nine Americans, all Russian-speaking, to Siberia. "I took calculus at P.A.," one Andover girl says, "but I feel lost in math class here. I love the people, though. They're warm and caring. At Andover, there are fakes. Here, for one thing, they don't care about clothes. It's not how you look [she looked neat enough] but who you are. They never talk about sex, by the way. And you know what? The boys here pay for everything for me in the cafeteria. I'm not used to that sort of thing back home."

A male P.A. emigré says he likes everything about the exchange program except his inability to keep on top of American sports results. "Russians think both that all Americans are rich and that there are millions of homeless and jobless," he goes on. "Some think that in America today there are toilets just for blacks and just for whites. And they ask, 'Can your mother vote?' 'Don't you have to have money to vote?' 'Can blacks vote?' 'Can Indians?' My roommate, who keeps quoting Lenin to me, is absolutely convinced that capitalism will turn into socialism and socialism into communism. Do you happen to know what's with the Red Sox?" I'd been planning to ask him.

Another Andover girl cuts in. "It doesn't seem to me that the Soviet Union wants to take over the world," she says, "but I wish I knew where America is heading nowadays."

It is two hours and forty-five minutes by Aeroflot to Tashkent. En route, I look over two more airport-lounge handouts. One of them, "Jews in the USA Through the Eyes of Americans," has a catchy red, white, and blue cover. "This booklet attempts to depict by drawing upon views and opinions expressed by Americans themselves. . . . the variety of negative phenomena which plague the American Jewish ethnic group," it says, and it continues, in the "you're another" tone that characterizes the entire publication, to mention "the factors which force American Jews to live in an atmosphere of perpetual fear and disillusionment with American reality." The second, less colorful, features a set of questions addressed to Valentin Pavlov, chairman of the USSR Committee for Prices. Asked "How to correlate the Soviet worker's wages and the price for imported jeans?" he responds forthrightly that "not everything can be compensated for by lowering the rate of labour remuneration. It is impossible to demand higher labour productivity and, simultaneously, to cut wages. This would be absurd. So, we have to substantially increase prices of non-foods. And, quite naturally, in this category status-symbol imported things still come first." So there!

We land at Tashkent at 7:05 (8:05 Novosibirsk time), and Irina informs us, before disappearing into some bureaucrat's hideaway, that we'll have to depart for Tbilisi at 6:20. But that's absurd, some of us mutter after her; we'll have not quite twenty-four hours here. No, another Intourist representative interjects. We leave at 6:20 in the *morning*. Ellie storms off to track down Irina and do battle. Will I ever see my beloved wife again? If she is locked up, should I offer to join her, or can I be more helpful staying outside and getting Amnesty International to intervene? I wrote a glowing "Profile" of Amnesty when it was still in its infancy; maybe it owes me one. But Irina has an out. The instructions we received before we set forth on our expedition clearly said that Intourist reserved the right to alter our itinerary as it saw fit. Ellie returns, unbloodied and unbowed, and in a manner quite uncharacteristic of her describes what is going on as a royal fuckup.

Well, here we are, however fleetingly, in Tashkent, a city of two million, fourth largest in the USSR, two thousand years old, just north of the Afghanistan border, haven for two hundred thousand Soviet orphans after the Second World War. We have time en route to the Hotel Uzbekistan to visit a monument astride the epicenter of the 1966 earthquake that leveled 40 percent of the city. We get to the hotel at eight-forty-five, late for dinner, and are told that our bags will be picked up at four. Defiantly, we go to a bar in the basement and stay there until we are jolly well prepared to eat.

22 September

A knock on our door, porter for our luggage, at 3:30. No problem. We haven't unpacked and slept with our clothes on. There was one puzzlement during the night, if I can call those few hours that. At 3:00 A.M., I distinctly heard a tower clock strike four times. There is a sign in the lobby saying that Intourist can arrange for visitors (those of course who have the time to spare) to take in an authentic local wedding. "During the wedding," I read, wondering how the bride and bridegroom feel about this, "you can buy handicraft wares."

Now we head farther south, to Georgia and Tbilisi, formerly Tiflis. We're in the Caucasus now, where a lot of tea is grown, where there are eighteen special schools for training midwives, where jaywalkers are humiliated by having their pictures published in the newspapers, and where—this makes our senior-citizen ears prick up—there are fifty-one centenarians per thousand people. The trick is to drink yogurt every morning. This is also Stalin country. A park at the summit of a funicular still bears his name, but the pedestal on which his statue used to stand is bare. His visage can still be seen, though, in bas-relief on the wall of the Institute of Marxism and Leninism.

After lunch, we're supposed to visit the State History Museum, but only five of the ten of us—Dave and Jeanne Schwarz, Fag Goodhue, Ellie, and I—feel up to it after last night's turmoil. Once again, it's pre-Communist relics offered for our view: venerable gold and silver objects steeped in aristocracy and hard to reconcile with the sight of the old woman on her knees scrubbing the floor outside our hotel elevator door in the middle of the night.

The rest of the gang recovers in time to make it to dinner at a restaurant that Corinne Abel has the impression is a quaint out-of-the-way establishment, but it turns out to be the place to which all Intourist's sheep are induced to flock. At the Mukhrantubani, we are herded into a semiprivate dining room, with only one other table occupied. But we have got used to this special treatment. Never at an airport, where we have seats in spacious waiting rooms, have we mixed with the huddled masses in the main preboarding areas. I can't help suspecting that we are kept so relatively isolated in large measure also to keep us unaware of the hardships attendant to everyday life over here.

23 September

More ancient history—this time an excursion, along the Georgian Military Highway, to a sixth-century church, the Dzhvari. Like many of the other shrines on our agenda, this one was constructed by slaves, with a life expectancy, it seems not unreasonable to surmise, of considerably less than a hundred. At the foot of the hill, with two grazing sheep nearby for photo opportunities, sits an organ-grinder, who epitomizes one difference between the Soviet system and our own: he won't accept a tip if you try to put it in his hand but does not protest if you stick it in his pocket.

Another antiquarian museum this afternoon. In a vestibule, just before we depart, a man arrives with sets of souvenir postcards and gray felt Georgian hats, but they are not for us, our guide explains—only for VIPs. According to a guest book in that chamber, Margaret Thatcher was here on April first (presumably she got a hat), and she wrote (or could this be an April Fool's joke?), "Thank you for a wonderful tour of this treasure chest of Georgia."

Corinne and I decide to walk part of the way back to our hotel. A bookstore we enter has nothing to be seen in English. In a sporting-goods store where they've never heard of an American Express card—now we're surely off the Intourist beat!—I buy, for rubles, a Ukrainian tennis racquet and she a set of dominoes. After a while we get on a bus that stops at our hotel (fare five kopeks, roughly one American penny), and—indeed we are far from home!—a man arises and offers Corinne his seat.

24 September

Archer Trench, who has prudently refrained until now from letting us in on his secret, passes around a critique of our Novosibirsk hotel in the 1987 edition of Fodor's *Soviet Union*: the "Tsentralnaya is terrible—avoid at all costs! When last we stayed there it needed replumbing and general renovation—or demolition." The Hotel Adjara here may need some replumbing in our wake. Fag leaned a bit too heavily on his bathroom sink and it came loose from the wall.

Coincidence: Ellie and I will be in Frankfurt three days hence. Today, when she buys a book at the Adjara's *Beriozka*, she pays with a twenty-dollar bill and receives her change in deutsche marks issued by a Frankfurt bank.

As we are about to go to lunch, we are met by the First Deputy Chairman of the Press Ministry of Georgia. Our status as tourists has evidently been upgraded overnight, and he has come to present to each of us a packet of postcards and a gray felt hat.

When we enplane for Leningrad this afternoon, there are no security checks at the Tbilisi airport. Maybe the reason for not inspecting our carry-on luggage or putting us through a metal detector is that the USSR believes it has nothing to fear from the terrorists who are plaguing so much of the rest of the world. Can it be—one hesitates even to harbor the horrid thought—that if certain parties are not actually in cahoots with certain others, they are at least not unsympathetic to their activities and are accordingly let alone?

At Leningrad, we are booked into Block 2 of a giant modern hotel, the Pulkovskaya, on the outskirts of town, right alongside the memorial to the city's 900-day wartime siege. Ellie has brought along, appropriately, Harrison Salisbury's *The 900 Days*. Built in 1975, the grandiose monument boasts 900 always-flickering torches. Dede ascertains that Mario Cuomo is registered in Block 1. Out of our window, I watch a minor courtyard drama. A man has got out of a bus and has fallen down, apparently injured. He lies on the ground for a while, with a friend hovering over him, and then a police car arrives. The casualty is helped to his feet but refuses to get into the police car. Instead, he staggers into the hotel. I go down to the lobby, out of curiosity. He wasn't injured, it turns out; he's simply plastered. I take him to be Finnish. I wonder how, in view of Gorbachev's stern dicta against drinking, the cops would have dealt with him if he hadn't been a foreigner.

25 September

We remembered before going to bed last night to get some bottled water, for toothbrushing. We've been told that Tchaikovsky died of cholera from drinking Leningrad water.

Dede has made a date for Mario Cuomo to join us, for drinks in Rusty's room, at six. Corinne saw him on TV last night but couldn't hear what he said, because there was a voice-over in Russian.

An urban sight-seeing tour this morning, some of the ground familiar to me—look! there's the Hotel Europa, where Jinny and I stayed in 1958!— but all new to Ellie and to most of the rest of us. A rural afternoon, going out to the Summer Palace at Petrodvorets. Along with the majestic array of fountains there, Catherine the Great had some hidden ones installed, so she could amuse herself by having unwary courtiers drenched. When I was here in 1958, our Intourist guide amused herself by having some members of our tour thus unexpectedly sprayed. Today it is raining so hard that the game would hardly be worth playing.

We get back to our hotel in time to receive Cuomo. Rusty has laid on sixty-five rubles' worth of olives and cheese. The governor, who unlike G. Hart hasn't seen Gorbachev and doesn't expect to, has met with Andrei Sakharov and thinks that the Russians are using refuseniks as bargaining chips. "I'm keeping a diary and it's going to be published," Cuomo says. That's what a lot of diarists innocently believe. He says we must all remember to put the Soviet Union in perspective; that the Russians did after all lose 20 million people during the war—and where better than Leningrad for us to reflect on that sobering statistic?—and he concludes, before rushing off to some banquet, in a lighter vein: When his wife and he were at Petrodvorets today (yes, it was their convoy with its police escorts that almost pushed us off the road) and were told of Catherine's once treating her friend and adviser Potemkin to a palace, "Matilda said to me, 'too bad she wasn't *your* patron saint.' "

26 September

Today's highlight—the highlight for ten thousand people every twenty-four hours—is a pilgrimage to the Hermitage and its cornucopia of art treasures, among them an ornate peacock clock that Potemkin, no mere recipient, once gave to Catherine. The French impressionists on the upper level are as impressive as ever.

In the evening, some of us go to the circus. It's disappointing. For one thing, it's being put on in a large arena about the size of Madison Square Garden. The music is canned, and so is much of the applause. The children in the audience appear to be enjoying themselves the most in the entr'acte, when they scamper down into the main ring and perform an impromptu dance.

After the circus, Rusty Crawford's bar, like the nation's nightclubs, is closed for the evening, so those of us who are still up and about adjourn to Archer's room for a nightcap and small talk, no doubt inspired by Mario Cuomo's emergence on our scene, about the political situation way back home. Somebody says it's remarkable, considering how long it's been since we were college kids, how well we've held up on what, all things considered, has been a rather arduous expedition. "You know," Archer is moved to observe, to no one in particular, "if you bought a dog today, it would probably outlive you."

27 September

We are to go our separate ways today—all but the Abels and the Kahns, heading for Frankfurt. It's amazing—and heartening—that in the sixteen days we've all been together there have been no spats, no cliques, none of the petty differences that you might expect when a dozen (in the end, ten) people who were acquaintances more than good friends are thrown together in unrelieved intimacy. Whether the credit should go to our comparative maturity, our good sense, or conceivably even to our Harvard bond, I hesitate to guess. But we have become so close that at breakfast, when we exchange farewells, Corinne insists, although it is Ellie who has the sore throat, that I take a vitamin tablet. And we all make a date, after ascertaining that the Abels will be in New York then because Brent has a board meeting to attend, to reconvene for dinner on December ninth.

The USSR, like South Africa, doesn't stamp visas into your passport. Rather, it issues a separate document, in duplicate, and when you leave the country takes back both copies. So there is nothing in your main travel credential to show you have ever been there. Smaller countries apparently care more about being remembered. The visa emphatically stamped upon my passport by the government of Mali bestrides two pages.

I have now observed that there are certain similarities between some Soviet customs officials and some African ones. As we are being processed out of Leningrad, a man in line ahead of us—Slavic in appearance—opens his handbag at the request of the functionary in charge. The customs agent espies a carton of cigarettes, takes out one package, puts it in his pocket, closes the bag, and waves the traveler ahead. It may have been his awareness of this sort of goings on that made President Reagan dub the USSR an evil empire.

There's a German-language newspaper on our plane, dated as recently as

September twenty-third, but it's a letdown to perceive, at second glance, *"Herausgegeben von der 'Prawda'."* Aeroflot does serve lunch on this flight, with even a gob of caviar, but although it's well past 2:00 P.M., no drinks. Happily, though, before we all parted Rusty distributed CARE packages of our leftover vodka.

The Abels are greeted at the Frankfurt airport by Klaus Herbig, an executive of a correction-fluid company called Tipp-Ex, who joined the German navy at seventeen and, when Brent sank the U-boat, was its second-in-command. Herr Herbig escorts us all to our hotel in the tidy Frankfurt suburb of Höchst, only a couple of hundred yards from a riverboat restaurant where a reunion dinner will be held the day after tomorrow. Herbig expects twenty-nine of his countrymen. Seven of them were, like him, on the U-boat when it went under. Vinzenz Nosch, the Austrian policeman whom I talked to briefly at Fall River, will not, I'm sorry to hear, be among them. He apparently expended most of his available funds and energy on that trip abroad. Herbig's lapel sports a button that he identifies for us as an insigne of an international submariners' brotherhood. He takes pains to inform us that most navy officers of his era weren't especially pro-Nazi. Most members of his own family, he says, were in Estonia when the Russians took it over and committed suicide.

Back in our hotel, the Höchster Hof, I borrow an IBM electric typewriter from the desk, so I can type out, for telexing to Sheila in New York, a "Talk" piece about Cuomo that I scribbled on the plane. Corinne admires my bravado. She says Brent's secretary had to go to school for a month to learn how to master just such a machine. If I can get my copy to New York fast enough, maybe Gottlieb will throw it into the issue before the governor either declares his candidacy, which he disavowed in Leningrad, or unequivocally declares his unavailability. We have no idea so far how the press at home has been handling his Soviet visit.

But we do get the weekend edition of the *International Herald Tribune* at Höchst. Gorbachev's recent disappearance from public view may have been occasioned by Mrs. Gorbachev's having appendicitis, it says. The United States has captured an Iranian warship somewhere. Joseph Biden is out of the presidential race (can that mean that Bork has been confirmed for the Supreme Court?), and the Mets are in trouble. The Yankees (good!) are dead, the Red Sox deader.

28 September

At seven o'clock (nine by yesterday's time) I am up and doing the *Tribune*'s weekend puzzle. A hunger greedily assuaged. I am relieved that I still know how to solve one.

In the dining room, we find Brent's crewmate Joe Aucoin, the retired automobile repairman, already at a table with his wife Louise. The Abels and Ellie and I are going to be driving to Corinne's brother's grave today, and we all get to talking about cars. When I mention that the air conditioner in my 1978 Chevy is on the blink, Joe says he is not surprised; these things were not designed to last forever. Brent wants to know whether I've driven much in Germany. I sense that, Californian though he may be, he is not altogether happy about coping with autobahns, where 130 kilometers per hour (that's 80 MPH) is *recommended*. I say I'll be happy to take up the challenge.

There's a more serious problem. France, far less blasé about terrorism than Russia, has begun demanding visas at its borders. The Saint-Avold cemetery may be close to Germany, but still it's on French soil. We talk to a chap at the American Consulate in Frankfurt who says there are interminable delays in picking up visas here (we are far from downtown anyway), and—off-the-record—why don't we just take a chance? So we do, and when we reach the border (I have been pushing a hired Mercedes to 150 KPH and cars have been zooming past me), Brent hops out to talk to the French sentry on duty. We can see the man shake his head. Ellie, whose French, unlike Brent's, is fluent, hops out next, and after she has explained the thrust of our mission—to pay respects to a hero in the Franco-American war against the Nazis—he capitulates. He tells us to go ahead, but not until he has hidden his face in his hands so nobody can accuse him of having witnessed our trespass.

At Saint-Avold, we check in at the cemetery office. An affable French caretaker invites us aboard an oversize go-cart and drives us, past row upon row of symmetrical white crosses, to David Waybur's resting place. We seem to be today's only visitors. Because Corinne's brother was one of merely three men out of the more than ten thousand buried here who won the Medal of Honor, his cross is inscribed in gold letters. He died on March 28, 1945—a familiar date because it's Ellie's birthday. She was a schoolgirl then and can't remember, understandably, where she was or what she did that fateful day.

29 September

I guess I should call today *Der Tag*. Robert Bell, the missionary son who thanks to the U-boat spent twenty days on a raft, arrives at dawn. He has to get back to his school on Long Island and can only stay for twenty-four hours, but this is an event he would not dream of missing. He, too, is wearing a submariners' pin.

Brent has just heard on the radio that the San Francisco Giants have clinched their division title and thus will have a shot at the World Series. His law firm represents the team, and he has had twenty of its baseball caps shipped here to distribute as souvenirs to the U-boat people. He was bemused to be advised yesterday that he had to pay one hundred and four marks' duty (about sixty dollars) on the caps.

The international edition of *USA Today* is available at our hotel desk. It is printed, thanks to satellite transmission, right here in Frankfurt. When the paper first came out at home, hardly anyone ever glanced at it, save at airports, where it was distributed free. Today's issue arrives at the Höchster Hof much appreciated and ahead of the *Tribune*, and it mentions Gorbachev's not having met with Cuomo. *The New Yorker*, assuming my copy got through all right, already knows that. The *Tribune*—I am glad to see that John Hay Whitney's name, in memoriam, is still on its masthead—is of course considerably older than its upstart competition and indeed is celebrating its hundredth birthday this year. Today it reprints an item it carried fifty years ago. I was a working adult then, but that's hard to believe when I read what sounds like incredibly ancient history:

BERLIN—Peace speeches were made by Premier Benito Mussolini and Chancellor Adolf Hitler on Berlin's Mayfield this evening (Sept. 28) before 650,000 spectators. But the peace that Fascist dictators offered the world was a Roman peace. . . . Declaring that the Rome-Berlin axis would stand firm despite intrigues from outside to break it up, Mussolini and Hitler made it clear that the object of their entente cordiale was the definitive liquidation of the French Revolution. Democracy and the League of Nations were ridiculed as bitterly as Bolshevism. The Führer and Il Duce served a notice on London and Paris that it was no use hoping to divide the two dictators by playing one against the other.

The desk clerk informs me that there seems to be some difficulty at the receiving end, not here, with my telexed story. I phone Sheila. It turns out that the telex number I have been careful always to carry with me is no longer operative. She gives me a new one. So now my little piece may get to Gottlieb too late—depending on what the New York press has to say about Cuomo's trip when he comes home—for the magazine to make any fruitful use of it. As they used to say during the French Revolution, and *après*, too, "*C'est la guerre.*"

Ellie and I take a walk around Höchst. We stroll past shop after shop brimful of every conceivable kind of consumer goods. The contrast between this opulence and what we saw in Russia is as sharp as it was when we crossed the vast socioeconomic gulf between Canton and Hong Kong.

We have a drink with the Abels while waiting to board the *Schiffshotel* for the reunion dinner. Brent, in a logically reminiscent mood, tells of the time his destroyer escort carried a physician responsible for a half a dozen such ships. They would transfer him back and forth, when necessary, by breeches buoy. He was a surgeon by training and to keep in practice persuaded a number of Brent's shipmates that circumcision greatly enhanced the pleasure of sex. The ship pulled into a liberty port not long afterward, and, Brent recalls sorrowfully, a couple of his men tried to test the doctor's theory before they were fully healed.

The reunion dinner, which I'll obviously be writing about at length for *The New Yorker*, is in a sense anticlimactic after so much expectation. There are speeches galore. Brent, who before the evening is out has a submarine insigne on his lapel, delivers his prepared remarks in both English and (*"Mein vater ist in Mannheim gebornen"*) German. *"Sehr gut!"* calls out a woman down the table, which is decorated with miniature flags of both countries. Klaus Herbig pays homage to the "first reunion of former soldiers [his word] who fought against each other in the terrible war of World War Two." Brent and Joe Aucoin and their shipmate Bob Burg, the only other American who makes it to the gathering, are presented with souvenir plates inscribed with the dates of their encounters on the high seas and tonight and, in English, "Enemies become friends." When it's Corinne's turn, she proposes a toast to her brother—killed by a German sniper, she says, at the same instant he killed the German. I am emboldened to say a few words myself; I feel somehow that it's important for the guests to know —Brent is treating all hands—that the twenty-eight-year-old American naval officer who was both their destroyer and their savior has had a distinguished peacetime career wholly apart from his derring-do nearly half a century ago. One of the Germans has brought along an accordion, and as the beer begins to flow so does the singing. When Ellie and I withdraw, leaving the now in some instances exuberantly friendly former enemies to themselves, a few of them, wearing Giants' baseball caps, are immersed, in what sounds like an impromptu blend of two languages, in "My Bonnie Lies Over the Ocean."

30 September

At 4:00 A.M., no more able to sleep than I am, as we both brood on this strange postwar alliance, Ellie tells me that Herbig said to her during dinner that when he went to school he and his classmates were taught that Jews took all the Germans' money and all their girls; and that he and his contemporaries knew nothing about any concentration camps. Ellie had noticed earlier, taking a walk while I was struggling with the electric typewriter, that one glaring exception to the notable tidiness of this suburb was a little square, full of pigeon droppings and other litter, a place that, according to a plaque on a wall, had once been the site of the local synagogue.

The definition for 13-across in today's *Tribune* crossword is "Lusitania's undoing" and the answer—I should be surprised?—is "U-boat."

We all board a bus to visit Herbig's factory, where we are treated to champagne and cookies. Each of us also receives a Tipp-Ex umbrella and a sample bottle of correction fluid. The executive who hands me mine seems overjoyed to hear that I still use an old-fashioned non-self-correcting typewriter; I do not disillusion him by confessing that instead of tidying up errors with fluid I simply "x" them out and sail ahead.

In the course of the morning, one of the Germans presents Herr Abel with a submarine-service necktie. Brent, who is tieless at the moment, says he'll later give his newly made friend a Harvard '37 cravat in exchange. I happen to have one on and offer it up to facilitate an on-the-spot swap, but Brent says no, he will handle this himself, as he does when, in a chat with Herbig, he is heard to say, "To err is human, to correct is Tipp-Ex."

At a fast-food stand outside Frankfurt on the grounds of the Saalberg Castle, a restoration of an old fort built by Romans long before anybody from their neck of the woods thought that their enemies who lived in what is now Germany would ever become their friends, frankfurters are known as hot dogs.

1 October

An annual ritual: I tear up my old American Express card. I baptize the new one in checking out of the hotel.

Our Northwest nonstop flight to Boston departs four hours late. Something to do with a delay at Shannon. Meanwhile, the Abels, flying over the Pole to California, are probably halfway to San Francisco. Before we separate, Brent, who is not given to strong public displays of emotion, says he was very touched by the whole German episode.

Today's *Tribune* has a story about a *New Yorker* piece by Herbert Mitgang, on the FBI's having kept dossiers on dozens of allegedly left-wing writers. I wonder if I made the list. It might be embarrassing, at a time when that branch of the federal government was preoccupied with such shenanigans, to have been ignored. Let's see—how could I qualify? I did belong for a while to something called the Book and Magazine Guild, of unimpeachably sinistral bent. I did incur the wrath of various right-wing journalists by defending Larry Adler and Paul Draper against their attackers. And then there was the business of Westbrook Pegler all but calling Frank Sinatra and me a two-man rat pack. How in the light of all that could I be overlooked?

When we are finally airborne, I settle back with the October fifth issue of *The New Yorker*, which offers Shaplen on the Philippines and a joint-byline piece about Scottie dogs by a couple named Stern, who I think I've heard of as Elvis Presley's biographers. A Knopf book, probably in the works when Gottlieb still reigned there. The article has got to be an assignment of his; I can't conceive of Shawn's having authorized it, let alone having run it. There's also a review by Terrence Rafferty, another new name, of the last Truman Capote book, in which he refers to "third-person reportage of unsurpassable formal perfection"—an assertion that, considering that Capote and his admirers contend that he never took a note during an interview, strikes me as ludicrous.

By the time we've retrieved the car we parked at Logan (what we had to pay to buy it back is too painful for me to relate) and battled the traffic back to Truro it's 8:15 (1:15 A.M. in Frankfurt). I phone Joey, who says grandson Jaime has broken his right wrist in a skateboard accident. I phone Palmer, who says our court has been almost entirely unplayable in our absence. (Wellfleet, after a fairly arid summer, had five inches of rain one single day.) How quickly one readjusts to being home!

2 October

I arise at 6:00 A.M. (11:00 A.M. Frankfurt time; I should be ashamed of myself), unpack, and arrive at the post office at 8:30. Boy, are they glad to see me! It takes most of the morning just to sort out and open the accumulation of mail: letters (form ones) from Senators Moynihan and D'Amato, both assuring me that they are against a new tax law limiting authors' deductions for expenses; invitation from Don and Ginger Reiman to Bud Benjamin's seventieth birthday party tomorrow (Don has drawn a caricature of Bud in a tennis shirt, jumping over a net, which I never saw him do in real life—but no matter, we tend to exaggerate our prowess in all fields as we get older); more stuff about women and the Century; an invitation to become a Special Backgammon Member of the Cavendish Club for half dues (I will have the right to sponsor new members and attend chouette parties); some clippings I asked Archer Trench to send me about the reception he got in Tokyo from the shipwrecked Japanese whose lives his destroyer escort saved during the war; a letter from Joe Wapner, wondering if we can dine together in Boston or New York when he comes east to promote his book; and a request to *The New Yorker* from a Yale professor who wants permission—he absolutely must have it by October 1 — to duplicate my Wapner "Profile" and use it as a teaching tool in a writing class. Too bad the office didn't just say okay instead of forwarding it.

I collect Hopi. The kennel people say they'd love to keep her permanently, though as a rule they deem huskies the most despicable of breeds next to rottweilers. But of course any true husky fancier could tell you at a glance that Hopi, with her telltale brown eyes instead of the standard blue, isn't a purebred. She seems delighted enough to see me, but then a lack of discrimination—she would wag her tail at a veterinary surgeon poised to strike—is one of her more pronounced, presumably inbred, traits.

Publishers Weekly has a review of Phil Hamburger's forthcoming book and a Dick Harris obit stating that he was working at his death, as rumor has long had it, on a book about *The New Yorker*. The "the" in our title isn't capitalized. This seems unsporting on the part of *PW*; we have always honored its wish to delete the logical apostrophe from *its* name. *Publishers Weekly*—see?—is also kind enough to mention that my ten-year-old *About The New Yorker and Me* is finally coming out in paperback. Ellie and I confer in the middle of the night whether I should expunge a couple of passages to which, when that book was originally published, people we know took exception. We also discuss, now that we are wide awake, a copy of the piece that my Castle Hill student has sent along—an effusive panegyric about the two of us as a married working couple, flawed mainly by her description of Ellie as an "authoress." Not as bad as an intended synonym for "writing" I ran across a while back: "authorizing"—but, as I must try to remember to instruct my pupil, avoidable, if indeed not impermissible.

3 October

Up, refreshed, at 2:30 A.M. I let the dog out, go back to bed, arise again at 7:00. This ought to be my last day of jet lag.

The *Times* says that at a meeting at the Century last night so crowded that members were standing on the stairs, the majority voted, "with humor and resignation," to admit women if a city law against gender discrimination is held constitutional. Sidney Simon, who's against letting women in and is forever being quoted in accounts of our presumptive change of life-style is wondering this time around how a building with landmark status can be subjected to the alterations that would be required to install separate-but-equal ladies' rooms.

Joan Fox tenders us a welcome-home dinner. Palmer W. is the only one present who nods knowingly when we mention our stay in Novosibirsk. When Barbara and he were aboard the Trans-Siberian, the train stopped there, but they never got beyond the station.

4 October

Last night, while we were out, one of those overnight delivery services, called Sureway, left a package containing galleys of my Ku Klux Klan piece on our porch. Precisely how it got to Truro I don't know; but the "HYA" on the parcel would suggest that it traveled to Hyannis by air. Reading one's own prose is an agreeable, narcissistic way to begin a day. And how much better one's words look when they have been magically transformed into nontypewriter type! It is, like childbirth, a recurring miracle.

This is Sunday, and the first page of the *Times*'s book-review section boasts the start of a long piece by Brendan Gill—part of an introduction to a forthcoming reissue of *his* book about *The New Yorker*. Brendan, with whom I am back on speaking terms after a protracted hiatus following the first-time-around publication of both our books, says he has been at the magazine for more than fifty years. I must find out how far behind I lag. Brendan says he wouldn't mind if he were asked by the magazine's new owners to leave; but inasmuch as he is one of the few of us believed to know the Newhouses socially, I think he is safe. I hope I am, too, because I would mind. Brendan does refer, accurately, to some editorial deadwood that might advantageously be pruned but refrains from even hinting at any individuals. He is getting to be positively Edwardian in style; he reads as though he were writing in carpet slippers. But I shouldn't harbor such mean thoughts. After all, we have made up, and we even appeared chattily together a couple of years ago at a forum conducted by Garson Kanin and the Authors League, another lost-apostrophe outfit. I remember the occasion well because whoever provided Garson with biographical data on the participants he had to introduce had clearly done no research on me beyond 1950.

Lexy phones. He is working in a Santa Fe bookstore. Some copies of Ellie's *On Glory Roads* just came in, and there is one *The Problem Solvers* in the business section. Maybe when no one's looking he can switch us both to a best-selling-non-fiction perch.

Palmer stops by for backgammon. Why I persist masochistically in trying to compete against someone who can throw three successive double-fives *on command* is beyond me.

Fierce winds today, and cold. The time of year seems to have arrived for me to move my work area from my unheated outbuilding study to a corner of the kitchen.

Ellie, still a mite jet-lagged, stays home while I go to Judy's and Tony's for dinner. I fulfill Matthew's one request for a souvenir from our trip: a lacquered bowl and spoon like the ones his big brother got from my 1980 trip to Russia. For a welcome change, I involve myself in a game where chance is not a factor, and Ian proceeds to wipe me off the chessboard. I would like to be able to pretend that I let my grandson win.

5 October

I finish typing up the notes I took on our journey—about fifteen thousand words' worth—and start to answer the backlog of mail, including one fund-raising letter on behalf of an acquaintance of mine who will be seventy in October, "and, at a time when most people are cutting back . . . ." If that's what they want to think, more power to them.

Archer Trench has sent me a Xerox of a December 1962 *Times* account

—Gay Talese wrote it when he was still a reporter there—about his having been decorated with the 4th Class Order of the Rising Sun for rescuing forty-five Japanese from a sinking junk seventeen years earlier. "Then Trench flipped to the map of Korea and looked for the tiny speck that would mark Cheju Island off southern Korea," Gay wrote. "He could not find it." I could have helped them. In 1951, when I was a war correspondent in Korea, I left the mainland peninsula one day to fly over to Cheju-do in the retinue of the Chief of Staff of the South Korean army. As he traveled around the island—a singular one, where women of almost Amazonian size and reputation then dominated their menfolk—a fleet of vehicles followed in his august wake. I was in a jeep, toward the end of the high-flying procession, and my driver, trying too hard to keep up, flipped over. I escaped death (not for the only time during that peculiar war) only because I landed in a ditch too narrow to accommodate the jeep when it came to earth on top of me. Eventually somebody dragged off the vehicle and I climbed out, unscathed. I forget what happened to the driver. He may have run away to hide behind some local woman's skirts. Nothing stays the same. Cheju-do, I read somewhere, is now a favorite South Korean honeymoon resort.

6 October

For breakfast-table reading, I have a food-and-beverage report submitted to all us members of the Harvard Club's Board of Management. It recounts in awesome detail how female agents of some restaurant-checking organization have been visiting the premises, unheralded, and concentrating on such minutiae as the counting of servings of butter pats.

Calvin Trillin has apparently not submitted his passport for a Soviet visa. In a *Nation* piece of his—humorous, of course, in his normal vein—about the West German Mathias Rust who flew into the middle of Moscow, Bud avers that "in his defense I might say that there was no immigration officer available in Red Square that morning to stamp his passport."

Edwin McDowell calls. He is doing yet another of those Shawn-to-Gottlieb transitional pieces for the *Times*. I can't give him much new intelligence (surely he wouldn't be concerned about our switch in telex numbers), but he gives me some; he has heard that the Newhouses were glad to jettison much of Shawn's bank of articles, because their riddance was good for tax purposes. I ask McDowell if Mitgang got into any trouble for giving *The New Yorker* first dibs on his piece about the FBI's dossiers on writers, in view of Herb's being, after all, on the staff of the *Times*, and thus sort of scooping his own paper. Well, says McDowell, he got off with a mild reprimand, more like a chiding, really, though the management did feel constrained to issue a general memorandum suggesting that this was not to be considered an acceptable precedent.

McDowell now wonders why Dick Harris got a longer obit in *The New Yorker* than did Howard Moss. So do I. Maybe there was nobody around our shop who knew our poetry editor well enough to devote additional prose to him. Our obit does state that Howard once calculated he had spent three months of his life in *New Yorker* elevators. But if he actually said that it was surely in jest—a statistic otherwise no more meaningful than were I to argue whether I have spent more hours of my life brushing my teeth than my wife has looking for her eyeglasses.

Ellie is getting a taste of the troubles she may inherit as the new president of Castle Hill. The roof of the structure serving as its office leaks, and after a recent storm the Xerox machine was awash. Apparently the previous administrations had gone in heavily for deferred maintenance.

We drive to Hyannisport, for drinks with the Trenches at the big house that Hope's grandmother built on the site of *her* mother's house, not far from where the comparatively parvenu Kennedys established their compound. Archer already has his USSR photos—one of them an à deux portrait of Lenin and me—neatly pinioned in a scrapbook; we dropped off Ellie's films to be developed only earlier today. But then he is retired.

8 October

With Joan Fox and Robin, Ellie and I go to South Wellfleet to see "Fatal Attraction." Five dollars a ticket, but I get in for three as a senior citizen. A baffling credit: "Screenplay by James Dearden from his original screenplay." This memoir is by me from my original memory.

9 October

I have been reading Joe Wapner's book in bed these last couple of predawn days, while waiting for Hopi officially to rouse me. A warm and gentle and thoughtful memoir. This is turning out to be memoir year. Ellie has been putting the finishing touches to hers, Annie Dillard's is in the stores and selling briskly, and Joan Colebrook stopped by just the other day with an advance copy of hers—an engaging account of life in the Australian outback that deserves to fare equally well.

When I pick up the mail, what do I find in this week's *New Yorker* but my Cuomo "Talk" piece! I hadn't even been aware that Gottlieb had received it. I am pleased in more ways than one. As a journalist, I always feel guilty, if not downright irresponsible (and this goes beyond questions of the deductibility of expenses), if I travel somewhere and don't have something published about the experience. Now I can scratch that particular item from the list of worries I maintain to brood about on sleepless nights.

Brent Abel phones. He is sending me a copy of a tape Corinne and he made at one Frankfurt gathering Ellie and I missed. It will give me a chance to hear the familiar German-American chorus in a never-before-heard rendering of "On the Banks of the Sacramento."

We dine at the Blacksmith Shop with the John Wilsons and the Dick Waterses. Dick seems unusually calm and cheerful, considering that the Dow-Jones went down ninety-one points the other day and hasn't yet recovered its ground. Maybe he's been selling short. I wish I were shrewder about the market.

10 October

Palmer and Barbara are heading back for New York. She brings so many beautiful cut flowers from her about-to-be-abandoned gardens that our dining-room table looks as though it was set for a gangster's funeral. P. W. has calculated that—only because I lucked out extraordinarily yesterday afternoon—I ended up the backgammon season a C-note ahead. In the light of the number of hours we have devoted to this enterprise, my proceeds have got to average out to far less than the minimum wage may be in the most remote nonunionized rural areas of Burundi or Rwanda.

At exactly 3:05 this afternoon, a PBA airplane (né Provincetown-Boston Airlines) flies over our court at an altitude of not much more than a hundred feet. As soon as we finish playing, Ellie is on the phone to both the Provincetown and Hyannis airports, trying vainly to find somebody to complain to. Naturally, this being the age of air transportation, she gets nowhere.

The October twelfth *Nation* has more or less the same piece, by another writer, about the FBI that Mitgang had in *The New Yorker*. The race behind the scenes to get to press, to which I am not privy, must have been something. (Let Bob Gottlieb cover it in his own history of the era, which he once jocularly told me could be titled "Transition—Exclamation Point.") This one does have an exclusive set of facts—something about Shawn's having declined to designate Kay Boyle as a *New Yorker* correspondent to somewhere back in 1952. News to me. But it would perhaps have been inappropriate for Mitgang to have gone into this (Gus Lobrano is somehow also implicated) in our family magazine.

11 October

A diagramless-puzzle Sunday in the *Times*, also a gray and wet day. I suspect the tennis court will never dry out enough to be playable again this year. Anyhow, I have some urgent typing to do; I want to get a piece off to Gottlieb that I am pretty sure he doesn't want. How do you spell masochism?

The last post-office Sunday mail pickup is at 11:00 A.M. As Hopi and I arrive at 11:01, there to my horror is a mail truck with its backup lights on. But it cannot get under way after I've skidded in behind it. I rush, envelope in hand, around to what I think is the driver's side, forgetting that many of American postal vehicles, to facilitate access to rural mail boxes, sensibly are right-hand-drive ones. I have never heard anybody else mention this ingenious solution to a widespread national problem.

On the way to the IGA to buy enough hamburger to tide me over while Ellie's in Cleveland visiting her mother, I run into Cindy Worthington, who has resigned from the Truro Board of Appeals. Why? She's hoping to get instead on the Finance Committee, she explains, because that's a better springboard from which to run—again—for Selectman. Last time out, she lost by only fourteen votes. I must talk to an accountant or somebody knowledgeable about switching official domiciles; it might make more sense for Ellie and me to become formal Truroites, and it might make our ballots, about which Ed Koch couldn't care any more than I care about him, represent something useful or even crucial.

In Lloyd Shearer's "Intelligence Report" in today's *Parade* section of the *Globe*, I am informed that every tenth driver on West Germany's autobahns travels at 110 miles per hour and that as a result the country anticipates ten thousand fatal automobile accidents a year. I have rarely read anything anywhere that surprised me less.

12 October

Ellie has Castle Hill business: to go with Kirk Wilkinson and architect Carmi Bee to the abandoned North Truro Air Force Base, on the long shot that it might conceivably be a usable site in the event that the school decides to move. I feel sort of like Margaret Thatcher's husband in these deliberations, but Ellie asks me to tag along, and anyway I'm curious to see the installation—for the first time in the more than thirty years I've been so relatively close to it. What a place it turns out to be! Huge commissary building and a baseball diamond with lights. If only Castle Hill could get the land, or even part of it, for free! Can the federal government take a tax deduction for a gift to a nonprofit institution?

Back home, the phone rings. "Mr. Kahn?" Yes. "Hold for Richard Clurman." There is no approach that makes me want more to hang up. But Dick is an old friend. He says that after Clare Luce's funeral, he was riding in a car with Henry L.'s son Hank, who disclosed that he had a batch of Luce *père*'s correspondence, and did Dick think I might be interested in making this the basis of a new biography of the *Time* man? The letters were apparently unavailable to W. A. Swanberg, whose life of Luce I recall reading with pleasure and admiration when it came out in 1972. For a variety of reasons, I beg off, and Clurman sounds relieved. I sense that he is passing along a message to which he hopes I won't respond affirmatively. Dick says we must have lunch in December, when I return to New York and before he takes off on one of his cruises with Bill Buckley. After we hang up, I remember that I forgot to ask Dick how *his* book is coming; if I had a secretary, I'd have her call him back and invite him to hold until I can get there to pop the question.

Cindy and John Worthington are among our dinner guests. John, who has become a Truro resident again after a long hiatus, says it's been thirty years since he crossed my threshold. I have some oysters to serve on the half shell and while passing them around take occasion to inform John how it was his father, John, Sr.—probably more than thirty years ago—who taught me, then a simple city boy unaccustomed to unshucked shellfish, that the proper way to open oysters was with a knife and not, as in my innocence I had been trying to do, with a hammer. John, Jr., discourses authoritatively about how, back in 1942 when he was sixteen, some Germans, presumably off a submarine, came ashore at our own Ballston Beach and were spirited off by the FBI and the Coast Guard. Five of the intruders were shot along our very own Pamet River, he goes on, and nary a word about it was ever made public. I am very U-boat-conscious these days, obviously, and I urge him to get the whole story on paper. Maybe I should try to write it up myself, but one U-boat piece at a time seems enough.

13 October

Ellie has to get up at seven-thirty to leave for Cleveland, and we don't seem to have a functioning alarm clock, so after I awake at five-fifteen I don't dare go back to sleep. And since we are taking Hopi along—I have to stop off at the vet's to get her a shot—I am obliged to walk her on a leash this morning. Otherwise she might elect to take a four- or five-hour stroll. So it goes.

But what a gift from my wife! After I went to bed last night, I discover, she cleaned up all the dinner mess, two dishwasher loads' worth. Some people know how to go straight to a man's heart.

I had a big dinner planned for Tony, Judy, and the boys, but Judy phones, they'd forgotten Ian had a soccer game in Orleans. So I cart my hamburgers and mushrooms and strawberries to Wellfleet, and then we proceed en masse, in the chill of a late-fall evening, to the scene of action. Wellfleet loses, 1–0. There are very few parents (or grandparents) present, even though—how different from the old Little-League days!—girls as well as boys are on the field. The missing old folks are probably home, cozy and warm, watching

228

the big-league playoffs on TV. I must try hard to suppress whatever feelings of envy are stirring inside.

14 October

There was a piece in the *Times* yesterday about a chap who teaches CEOs and others how to remember. He himself once purportedly remembered the names of all 644 people in a room (sounds more like a convention hall), and he can memorize *Time* or *Newsweek* in an hour. I would like to get hold of him, for a lesson or two, but the paper got thrown out and I can't remember his name. (At a party years ago, I was terribly impressed and flattered by a stranger who, as soon as we were introduced, began quoting to me astonishingly large chunks of my own prose; and it wasn't until some time after I decided that we should become buddies that I learned he was an actual, documented idiot savant.)

Coincidence: I picked up a copy of *Sports Illustrated* at 6:00 A.M. and found in it one of those advertorials written by Walter Bingham. And at 11:00, who should turn up at the post office but Bing himself, here to close his house for the winter. Word has got out that I am leading a bachelor's life, and Bing somehow knows that Cindy Worthington is planning to bring me some kale soup for my supper.

15 October

I wonder what the U-66 survivors who got the San Francisco Giants' hats from Abel are thinking this morning. Or do they know (or care) that the Cards licked their team in the seventh game of the National League playoffs last night? I suppose I may be partly responsible for San Francisco's downfall. I watched the game, capless (gave mine to grandson Jaime), and with the Giants behind 5–0 in the sixth inning, I conceded and went to bed. Might they have rallied had I had the guts to stick with them to the end?

Natasha phones from the office. United Parcel has delivered a package to me there, from Michigan, and do I want it forwarded? But I haven't ordered anything to be sent to *The New Yorker* from anywhere. I propose that she open the package, but she says it's so beautifully wrapped I should have the pleasure myself, so she'll mail it. The substance of our conversation is trifling. How wonderful, though, when one is living alone, to have the phone ring and a familiar voice to chat with! How horrible must it be to be a relatively friendless shut-in!

New Yorker covers, in the Gottlieb era, are getting to be splashier.

The current one, by Barbara Westman, depicts in vivid color a man and a woman coming out of a video store with a package. Someone who believes I am an insider at the magazine asked me yesterday whether the contents of the package were X-rated. I should have replied that I don't have X-ray vision, but, alas, these killing ripostes always seem to come to mind too late.

16 October

Hopi rouses me at 3:30. She would never dare take such advantage of me if Ellie were around. By 3:40, I am reading Annie Dillard's forthcoming *An American Childhood*. Joey, who is recovering better than I'd expected from the Giants' debacle, said on the phone yesterday that Annie hadn't been in the Canadian Rockies at all, that her alleged trip there was just a pretext for her to get away from home. Nonsense; I am looking at a photo of Annie and Ellie on horseback. Annie was born in 1945—only four years ahead of Joey. In the book, she speaks of her father frequenting Jimmy Ryan's on Fifty-second Street, in the good old prewar days, and listening to Eddie Condon and Pee Wee Russell and their gifted musical peers. Inasmuch as I was covering nightclubs for a couple of years then, I was probably an even more frequent frequenter than he was. Maybe we sat at adjoining tables every so often.

I take time off from trying to write about the Harvard Law School's eminent alumnus attorney Abel and some of his postgraduate exploits to leaf through today's *Cape Codder*. I am arrested by a photo of an attractive teenager with a tiara and a trophy, captioned—I wonder if Tony wrote it— "Victoria Rae Grinder, 13-year-old daughter of Ken and Ann Grinder of Tennessee, formerly of East Harwich, was crowned 'Little Miss America' in Gallatin, Tennessee, September 26. Victoria wants to continue to compete in pageants but her main goal is to become an attorney. She plans to attend Harvard Law School." She sounds uncommonly confident, and perhaps with good reason. It may sound sexist, but I'll bet the chances of a Miss America (or near-Miss) getting admitted to any male-dominated institution are bright. Look at Princeton and Brooke Shields.

17 October

Hammacher Schlemmer writes to advise me that it has received the items I returned and is crediting me. What items? I don't recall any. And the handsomely wrapped package Natasha forwarded is also a surprise. It's a mantel clock, from Horace Mann, thanks for my having spoken at the school last spring. A practical, but not too costly, method of softening up potential contributors. Harvard doles out smaller clocks and coffee mugs. To each his own.

Publishers Weekly reports that Hollywood has picked up Budd Hopkins's UFO book, which *PW* categorizes as nonfiction. Bah, humbug! There are some things that we professional authentic nonfiction writers should band together to take a stand against.

The World Series begins tonight. With the Twins and the Cards the participants, I somehow doubt that there's much sustained interest in the games beyond Missouri and Minnesota. I glance at the lineups when they're flashed on the TV screen and there isn't a familiar name in the lot. One of the starters—and not a pitcher, either—is credited with a batting average of .080. Hell, grandson Ian—who tied for fourth in a chess tournament this morning—could do as well as that.

18 October

E. is due back from N.Y.C., where she stopped off to take in, with the Patrick Smiths, Peter Brook's nine-hour opera *The Mahabharata*; and, with Martha Lear, *Cry Freedom*, the new film about Steve Biko and Donald Woods. (Ellie has a much higher opinion of the opera than does Mimi Kramer, *The New Yorker*'s sharp-tongued new drama critic.) I'm eager to see the South African film myself, because although I never met Biko—few whites did before he died so young—I got to know Donald Woods when I passed through East London in 1966 and again in England's London after he had fled South Africa. I wonder if by any wild chance the movie producers included a feat of Donald's that I described in *The Separated People*—". . . is in demand at parties for his knack of simultaneously playing Afrikaner nationalist songs on the piano with his right hand and African nationalist ones with his left." But he was more carefree back then than I imagine he would like to be depicted today.

The big news Ellie brings back is that David and Anath have decided to get married next fall and to have the ceremony take place here at Truro, which is nice. Judy and Tony are working a wedding somewhere today themselves, and while they're making music money their kids are in my custody. Ian is so grown up that I can leave Matthew and him alone while I go to fetch Ellie at Hyannis.

19 October

I have spent the entire day writing about the Second World War, and it's not till I turn on the evening news that I'm made aware that like Pearl Harbor this day—with the bottom falling out of the stock market—is one that will be long remembered. (I spent most of December 7, 1941, writing a *New Yorker* piece in a Fayetteville, North Carolina, hotel room; and it wasn't until I returned to Fort Bragg at dusk that I became aware we were at war.) The Dow-Jones has dropped more than five hundred points, and much as I respect David Rockefeller I wish I could be entirely reassured by a statement of David's in the papers this morning that what has been happening on Wall Street—a total minus score of something like two hundred and fifty *last* week—may be a cause for concern, but not for alarm.

A day of double losses. Our beloved dog seems to have vanished. She took off about noon, which isn't unusual, but when we are ready to turn in tonight she hasn't returned. Ellie says neighbor Ding Watson believes that Hopi has gone wild and is killing and living off deer—and with the deer-hunting season coming up she is likely to get her comeuppance from some trigger-happy gun-toter. Will I never learn to keep reminding myself one should never let one's self become overly attached to a pet?

20 October

At 2:30 A.M., by instinct or hunch or whatever, I check out the screened porch. There is Hopi, wagging her tail, unapologetic. She has clearly not been stuffing herself with fresh venison, for she makes straight for the breakfast I served up in her bowl nineteen hours earlier and bolts it down. Then she curls up and goes to sleep and doesn't budge until I arise at 7:30.

After letting her in, I went back to bed. Lying there, I recalled a conversation I had with my broker several months ago. "Bernie," I said, "I don't like the look of the market. If and when the Dow hits twenty-six hundred, sell everything." I admired my prescience for quite a while. Then I woke up. I wonder if my stockbroker uncle had any such dream, the last crash around, before he committed suicide.

Are small-town lawyers really as good and shrewd as they're sometimes cracked up to be? When I bought the Truro house, the one I engaged to handle the transfer of title stopped by after several months. I assumed he had everything wrapped up, but it turned out he had only one request: he wanted to know how to spell my name. I am reminded of that today when Ellie, who has been working with a local attorney for weeks on some philanthropic matters, gets a letter from him, neatly typed, addressed to "Mrs. Eleanor Kuhn Munroe."

Jim Grant, whom we got to know when he was writing his biography of Bernard Baruch, is on the evening news, holding forth about bear markets and how they grow. It's nice to have him recognized as an expert. I'm sorry that when I was helping him with his Baruch research I hadn't heard a yarn that's been more latterly circulating around the Harvard Club: that B.B.

was turned down for membership because he tried to bribe the Admissions Committee with South Carolina quail.

21 October

Last night's evening news reported that Dizzy Gillespie is seventy. This is *news*? Who isn't?

What I suppose is legitimate news is a story in today's *Times* about a sixty-nine-dollar computer device, called Spelling Ace, to accommodate cross-word-puzzle solvers. It was bad enough when computers intruded into backgammon and chess, but this is going too far. Apparently if you are trying to figure out the name of a newspaper and have got no further than Ti—es, the computer, with a vocabulary of eighty thousand words, will come to your rescue. Stanley Newman, of the Crossword Federation of America, is reported in the account as being unimpressed. Me, too.

I finish up—except for the tedious business of copying—the first draft of my Brent Abel piece. It may not be the final draft; Bob Gottlieb has proved himself to be no pushover. After I call Brent to check a few facts, I get to musing about people I've written about. In my line of work, casual acquaintances—nay, total strangers—can while you're dealing with them reportorially become close, if not intimate, friends. And then they fall away, sometimes becoming estranged, more often merely distant. If I should phone Brent ten years hence would his secretary, assuming she is still around (and assuming of course that Brent and I are, too), know who I am, or care? Of course, the situation is even worse when you spend a lot of time on a piece and then, for one reason or another (a switch in editors of *The New Yorker*, say) it never runs. I doubt, for instance, that I'll have many more Sunday breakfasts with my other Jim Grant—James Pineo G., of UNICEF.

22 October

The market went down only seventy-seven points today. Yesterday it was up two hundred and eighty-odd. This is getting to be silly.

23 October

Jack Kelley calls at 8:45 A.M. There are three express packages at the post office—all for Ellie. At times, despite what should be one's better judgment, one cannot easily curb one's feelings of jealousy and envy.

Terry phones. Granddaughter Jacquelene's birthday is going to be celebrated tomorrow. I am not prepared, though naturally I know that she is
always fêted on an off date, because her real birthday is the twenty-sixth
of December. At that she's better off than her paternal grandmother; Jinny
was born on Christmas Day and never had a birthday party in her life until
her three kids and I gave her one.

Robert J. Lurtsema announces that he's not going to be on WGBH tomorrow, if I hear him aright, breaking a record of sixteen years of seven-
days-a-week radio appearances. Now there's a man with stamina! In response
to one of his station's fund-raising entreaties a few years back, I enclosed
with my check a letter to him explaining that I would give more to keep
him off the air than on it, because my wife was in love with him and I saw
no reason to help prolong her infatuation. Lurtsema, in response, sent Ellie
a Valentine in the form of a hand-drawn self-portrait.

24 October

Yesterday and today both devoted chiefly to galleys of Ellie's forthcoming
memoir. I am supposed to be going over them as a copy-reader, or proofreader, or editor-at-large, but I am reading with the eyes of a husband and
lover who is learning more about her past in eighteen hours than in the
preceding eighteen years. I had forgotten, incidentally, if I ever knew it,
that her father and his parents moved long ago to Manhattan's Upper West
Side, and specifically to Claremont Avenue, in 1916. That was the year that
I was born, at home, at 25 Claremont.

To Tony's to watch, à deux, the sixth game of the World Series. (The
Twins win and even the score to date.) Tony shows me a piece by brother
Joey in the *San José Mercury News*, on how he missed a 1962 Subway Series
game between the Yankees and the Giants (yes, grandchildren, there was
a Giants team in New York way back when) because he was in bed with
the flu. I'd taken Tony instead, and the TV set on which poor Joe was
obliged to watch—had color TV yet come on the market?; was my children's
rearing deprivational?—was black and white.

25 October

Daylight saving ended early this morning. The afternoons will be oppres-
sively short from here on in, though of course more protracted than the
time Ellie and I flew to the North Slope of Alaska one winter, when daylight
was a fleeting commodity and you could, if you so desired, walk on the
Arctic Ocean, for even saltwater froze in the prevailing temperatures. My

lowest ever, for the record, is minus fifty-six Fahrenheit, at Fairbanks, on another Alaskan jaunt, when somebody jostled my elbow while I was holding a cardboard container of coffee and the liquid turned solid before it landed on the hood of an automobile.

I manage to set the kitchen clock back an hour—with the aid of our new mail-order tool kit, and without having to remove the clock from the wall. In my circle, this has got to be considered a breakthrough comparable, in other milieus, to the invention of the automatic transmission and the zipper.

I go through a pile of mail. The N. Y. Public Library, which has been on a fund-raising jag ever since Vartan Gregorian took over, is sponsoring another dine-with-celebrities drive. The Mike Stones used Ellie and me as their literary come-ons a couple of years ago. This time, it's $250 a head for the paying guests. I certainly will not even consider paying $500 so the two of us can break bread with—I might pay something, out of loyalty to his onetime target Bill Shawn, to throw bread at—Tom Wolfe.

Today's Sunday *Times* book-review section has full-page ads for four lucky authors I know: Annie Dillard, J. K. Galbraith, Bud Trillin, and Joe Wapner. There's a core group I'd be happy to try to build a dinner party around! I must try to remember to tell Gregorian next time I run into him.

Ellie and I are still wrestling with her book proofs. Two "f's" and one "b" in "Krafft-Ebing"? Better look it up. And does "Dewar's" have an apostrophe? It does—how fortuitous to have it at one's beck—in a *New Yorker* ad. I have those two knotty problems unraveled before she returns from a lecture up at Dennis, though her outing started off inauspiciously when the vial in which she was carrying her nerve-steeling champagne spilled all over the car floor before she'd had even a sip of it.

To dinner at Ding Watson's. I go home early, to catch the seventh game of the Series on TV (Twins win). I retire before the champagne starts getting dumped on the clubhouse floor. I must inquire some time about the disposition of the champagne presumably on ice in the locker room of the team that's fated to lose.

26 October

I have to look up something in my own 1979 memoir, and I'm glad I do, because I perceive at some point in travels of mine in the Deep South that Ellie's maternal grandfather's store in Gadsden, Alabama, was built in 1903. But why does this give me pause? Because, I now remember, in Ellie's forthcoming book the date is 1910. I must be right; Lexy and I saw the year carved in stone on the building itself. So from my bygone tome I am able to bestow a correction on her as yet unpublished one. She is grateful, as she should be. I hope Lexy and I actually saw what I wrote we saw.

Here's a new term of address, and a heady one, I must concede: The International Backgammon Association (which turns out, anticlimactically, to be based at Fort Lauderdale) sends me a postcard addressed to "Monsieur E. J. Kahn." In a box of correspondence that Nancy Webb has transported from our New York apartment, which her daughter Sophie has been occupying temporarily for four months, there's also a printed solicitation from the Scott Meredith Literary Agency. Evidently he wants me to join Judith Krantz and Mailer in his stable of clients. "I am sending you another copy of our folder," goes the Meredith missive, "to remind you of our continued interest in working with you." Another? Continued? I didn't know he'd ever even heard of Monsieur Me. I wonder what mailing list he has latched onto. Authors Guild? PEN? Is one version or another of my names for sale to anybody?

Joey phones. He can't remember, either, how I came into the World Series tickets he couldn't use. Maybe from Bing Bingham, he suggests, from his *Sports Illustrated* allotment. After all, Joey adds, it was Bing, wasn't it, who got us all into the Yankees' clubhouse the year before? I am too proud to confess I don't remember *that*.

I do vividly remember, though, the next name Joe brings up—that of an Andover buddy of his who called on us at the Cape one day and, although his belongings seemed to consist only of a baseball glove, stayed the remainder of the summer. Baseball freaks are a weird lot. Bob Shaplen, who has sometimes seemed to believe he is the reincarnation of Jumpin' Joe Dugan, once came to stay with Jinny and me at Truro. While he was out, she undertook—we had probably not long before been visiting the Charlie Engelhards', where unpacking for houseguests was routine— to open his suitcase and put his things away. She reported afterward that although she hadn't made a complete inventory his luggage seemed to consist almost entirely of, along with his fielder's glove, a pair of shorts and a jockstrap.

27 October

The stock market took another dive yesterday, and a poor guy in Florida, before committing suicide, shot to death a Merrill, Lynch man who he apparently thought was responsible for his misfortune. I have decided to stop worrying, at least in daytime.

While trying to get to sleep last night, I forced myself to change the subject of my thoughts and concentrate on how Dale Maple—the Second-World-War American soldier I once wrote about who was sentenced to death for unduly fraternizing with German prisoners of war—might have reacted had he heard about Brent Abel's reunion with the U-boat men in Frankfurt.

Bruce Cagwin comes by to shut off our outside water. Just in time; it turned cold last night. Bruce apologizes for not having done the job sooner. He got my note asking him to, all right, but it was on a *New Yorker* letterhead, and he looked at it too hastily, at first glance, and went and turned off Gene Kinkead's water down the road. Ah, small-town life! I'm glad that our redoubtable plumber (also chairman of the school committee) does not, like me, throw most of his mail away once he's under the impression he has attended to it.

Peter Ahrens phones. He is arranging a table for Bruce Bliven at the Century's annual new-members' dinner, and can I make it? I can't, alas, and when I phone Bruce to say I'm sorry I learn, to my further regret, that Naomi B., book critic par excellence, broke her arm tripping over a box of review copies. And it was her right arm, what's worse, the one she reviews with.

28 October

According to the evening news, Harold Stassen, eighty, is running for President again. Of course! I've been backing Jimmy Carter all along, as the only man whose brains and experience qualify him for the job, but maybe we need a fresh approach.

I take some children's books to Judy. It is 5:00 P.M., and she is trying to persuade Matthew to eat some of his lunch. I am concerned about his seeming lack of weight, but am equally concerned about the risks of grandparental interference.

29 October

Ellie says she dreamt about Shawn last night—something about him and *The New Yorker*'s handling one of her books. I assure her that that needn't trouble her any more. I hope she doesn't start dreaming such dreams about Gottlieb.

Gottlieb phones. For real. He wants me to put more resonance in my Abel piece. I promise that I will. Now all I have to do is try to figure out what that means.

The Williamses are back on the Cape—mainly, it seems, to go to the dentist. Palmer is the first big-city toff I've talked to since the crash (though Ellie did have a phone conversation with George Apelion at Lazard Frères, who advocated sitting tight). He says Barbara saved some whacking amount by switching to money markets or whatever in the nick. Then the lucky son of a bitch proceeds to add to his already swollen assets by relieving me, who didn't switch to anything, of four dollars at backgammon.

30 October

I can dream, too. Last night I suddenly couldn't remember to which fire station the engine I was driving in Manhattan had to be returned; and I was glad there was no urgency because I couldn't figure out how to activate the siren. Instead of bothering to garage the vehicle, eventually I left it on the street and, with Bruce Bliven and somebody else, went to a theater with a live porn show. Hopi woke me, unfortunately, before I got to see hardly any of it.

A Halloween Eve ghost story? The phone rings, and Ellie tells me, with an odd look on her face, that Ed O'Connor is on the phone for me. But he has, alas, been long since gone. We are both relieved when my caller turns out to be Etta Connor. She has a question: did I know Harold Ross? Yes, indeed. Well, is it true—as she has it on what she has long believed to be good authority—that to no matter whose authorship the book *Old Mr. Flood* may be attributed, Ross actually wrote it? I tell her that she now has it on even better authority—mine—that Joseph Mitchell wrote it single-handed.

Thinking about Halloween inspires me to drop everything else and get carving the pumpkin that we naturally have to have ready when Ian and Matthew, whose costumes I must try to pretend I have not seen before, come by tomorrow to astonish us.

31 October

Ellie doesn't think I got the eyes right on my pumpkin, but otherwise this year it passes muster. I thought I had given them just the right blend of idiosyncracy and insouciance.

A doctor who complained to me earlier about some medical fact in my mountain-climbing piece now sends me a whole sheaf of correspondence re the idem with various people at the magazine. It's interesting that at one point Bob Gottlieb wrote to him personally, and spiritedly, defending his writer against the nagging critic. Hey, I like that.

Barbara and Palmer take us to dinner at Napi's, very crowded this holiday night, and then we all move on to the P'town Art Museum, where Judy and Tony are providing the music for a costume dance. Tony, interestingly, has chosen a tassel-and-mortarboard getup, though he never yet had occasion to wear a graduation robe in real life. I'm glad he has come to grips with all that. Palmer says he had lunch with Don Hewitt in New York, and when Don wondered why "60 Minutes" was slipping in the ratings (although it's still, where so many other shows would give anything to be, in the top ten), Palmer told him it was because Mike Wallace wasn't being his old tough self and was beginning to baby people like Jesse Jackson.

1 November

Ellie was sore last night because we didn't stay at the dance after eleven. But it is eight-fifteen Sunday morning and she is still asleep, and the dog and I have been up and about for a couple of hours.

Department of Nasty Shocks: I pick up the *Times* magazine and there on the cover is the face of a black woman and "The Woman Who Beat the Klan, by Jesse Kornbluth." But this is *my* Ku Klux Klan piece, and why did nobody in Alabama let me know there was going to be this kind of competition? (Why? Possibly because a piece in the *Times* means more to my sources than one in *The New Yorker*.) Is my article dead, or stillborn? There are differences in the two pieces, I perceive when I can bring myself to look further at this one. But the similarities loom large. *The New Yorker* and the *Nation* both ran stories about the FBI's snooping around writers. Is that a useful precedent to cite if I have to argue for my article's survival or resuscitation? It is a tribute to my sheer guts, if you ask me, that instead of hurling the *Times* mag into a fall hearth fire I plunge on through it to the puzzle page.

And why is "Jesse Kornbluth" so familiar a name? I've never laid eyes on him. But wait! Yes, of course, he was the stranger (still is) who phoned and asked if I'd interview, for *Interview*, his girlfriend about her book on soldiers' letters, and when I talked to her, and wrote it, she claimed it never arrived, and I didn't have a carbon so I rewrote it more or less from memory, and weeks later I got a call from a woman at *Interview* wondering if I'd been paid, and no, I hadn't, and well, they needed more words, but I had written the six hundred I'd been told at the outset was the maximum, and I said I'd done all I was going to in the matter, and now I don't know if the interview ever got published, and when I stop to think of it, I do know that they never paid me a cent.

This Kornbluth, whoever he is, really has it in for me.

The *Times* Book Review has a letter from an archivist at Bryn Mawr, where Katharine White's papers are, saying that what Brendan Gill said about her in the excerpt from the preface to his new edition was ass backward. I wonder if the edition has already been printed up, or will Brendan have a chance to straighten things out?

Sister Joan reports that Frank Sinatra is giving a concert in New Jersey on my birthday. She thinks he ought to invite me, and she is going to write him and tell him so. You can't say Joan doesn't have spunk.

2 November

The next worse thing to having to go through an income-tax audit is to get a substantial bill from your tax accountant in November for work he did last April that you'd long since forgotten you hadn't yet paid for.

Reagan's second Supreme Court nominee, Douglas Ginsburg, may be in trouble, too. For one thing, it seems his physician wife used to perform abortions, which is a no-no. Eventually, the White House may have to come around to Joe Wapner. I'll bet he could get confirmed.

There's a TV commercial from Kellogg's on the air, for a new cereal from Germany, called Müeslix, with the slogan "What breakfast was meant to be." Are we to infer therefrom that they mean they're sorry about all the kinds of breakfast foods they've been so vigorously touting up to now? I can be dispassionate about this, since I am a noncereal man. I generally choose between a boiled egg and sausages. I suspect that to many Germans sausages have long been what breakfast was meant to be.

3 November

Until the last few days, when the frost hit, we've had some stunning leaf colors hereabouts. Now nearly all our breathtaking reds and yellows have turned to brown, and if some neighbor wanted accurately to describe the state of our foliage, he or she would only have to grab a paint brush and on the South Pamet Road sign off Route 6 insert a comma between "Dead" and "End."

Tonight, we watch a TV documentary on the Panama Canal Zone. I took Ellie down there with me, when I was reporting on the place shortly before we gave the canal to the Republic of Panama, and I was able to give her a chance literally to bestride it, with less than a foot of open water between her feet. Nothing is too good for my wife. For me, that trip was in a nature of a homecoming. I spent nearly a year down in the zone during the Second World War, having accompanied my General Harding to his command there as I had traveled with him from New Guinea to Australia and back to the States. I shared, with his aides-de-camp, the general's quarters, a spacious house on the edge of a golf course, with maid service.

Let me add hastily that living conditions in New Guinea were incomparably different.

4 November

A mail-order wristwatch I sent for arrives. Joey and Jaime are due this weekend, and they'll be all the more welcome, because I have a hunch my grandson will be able to decipher the complicated instructions and get the consarned object ticking. They must teach kids *something* useful at school these days.

It's a bit early to be worrying hard about Christmas, but our gift problems may be solved. The Limited Editions Club catalog has also arrived, and the last two items listed are portfolios of Robert Motherwell lithographs, with special prepublication prices—one at $26,000 and the other a bargain at only $22,000. The question is, which people on our Xmas list get which, and would it offend a $22,000 donee to learn that a friend, or worse yet a relative, has got the other? No rush to decide, and when the Nieman-Marcus catalog comes along, there may be something even better.

Ellie has decided we should cut back on magazine subscriptions, inasmuch as there isn't time to read all the ones we get. I propose that we observe what I believe to be an accounting acronym, LIFO—last in, first out. By that criterion, we can give up *Chronicles*, the most recent issue of which calls members of Congress who had the presumption to confront Supreme Court nominee Bork "reptile-faced politicians putting insolent questions to a distinguished jurist."

So farewell, Anthony Harrigan, a name I find it hard to part company with, for this very conservative *Chronicles* writer, originally Anthony Hart Harrigan, is a living commemoration if ever there was one of my biographees Edward Harrigan and Anthony Hart.

Having made our decision not to be seduced by prospectuses of new magazines, we can airily dismiss three that are offered today: something titled *Righting Words*, whose very name eliminates it from consideration; one *Bits & Pieces* that seems to consist largely of aphorisms attributed to John D. Rockefeller, Sr.; and another called simply Z, which because of name alone would go to the bottom of most lists.

5 November

CBS is having trouble with a Cronkite documentary on South Africa. It seems Walter went in on a tourist visa (Could I try that? and for God's sake, didn't they recognize *him*?) and interviewed a bunch of young indigenes, white and black; and his producer (not Bud Benjamin this time) contrived to tape daughters of both P. W. Botha and Winnie Mandela. That strikes a mnemonic chord. When I was allowed over there during the John Vorster regime, through some university students I arranged a blind dinner date with *that* prime minister's daughter, and she sounded very cordial on the phone. But a few hours before our rendezvous, there was another phone call—this from a man with that distinctive Afrikaner accent we know so well—informing me brusquely that Miss Vorster would not be keeping our appointment.

There's a picture in the *Times* of a psychiatrist we know socially. He has been called in by the American Civil Liberties Union for an opinion, on the basis of what would appear to be sketchy knowledge, of the condition of a sad homeless woman whom Mayor Koch has had plucked off the sidewalk, where she lived, and where she also relieved herself. The shrink declares that she is not psychotic and should be allowed to reside—though her own sisters have said she's ill—wherever she chooses, indoors or out. I wonder whether our doctor friend and his fastidious wife would like to have her park herself outside their front door. Or, as *pro bono* therapy, would he invite her to share his waiting room with his tidier patients? Or would he prefer house calls, squatting alongside her at a subway grating and hoping not to be trampled by passersby? I don't mean anything personal, but why is it that you can always find a psychiatrist somewhere who will testify on almost any side of every question?

Full moon tonight. We betake ourselves, cum dog, to Ballston Beach. It's my first visit this year, and there's nary another soul in sight. The ocean's so calm it could accurately be described as gently lapping at the shore. True, there are a few other footprints, and dog prints, on the sand, but whoever made them has decamped, and we have the whole place, so swarming in July and August, to ourselves. Seems almost like a private moon, too. Ellie is inspired by it all to wonder if we shouldn't plan to stay through December. She's committed to giving a couple of talks off-Cape early next month, but she could always leave and come back. And of course we can once again do much of our Christmas shopping by phone and credit card and hope for the best. But what if Sinatra should want us all to sup together after his December fourth recital in Jersey?

6 November

Early this morning, after letting the dog out and returning to bed just for a minute or two, I may have drifted off, because I found myself staging Irving Berlin's forthcoming 100th birthday party. (It was presumptuous of me, I concede; why, I didn't even first ask George Abbott, who turned 100 himself recently, if he'd like the job.) Anyway, I decided on Madison Square

Garden. Could have accommodated a bigger crowd at the stadium, of course, but didn't want to take a chance on the weather. I can't decide which of two big scenes to use as a finale: (1) Ronald Reagan, live on TV, starts singing "Happy Birthday" at the White House, is joined there by Nancy and the Secret Service, then at the Garden by Sinatra and the rest of the professional singers on stage (yes, they are all here, who would dare not be?), and then by the whole audience; (2) the disembodied voice of Kate Smith, in total darkness, launches softly into "God Bless America," and then as her volume increases the lights gradually go up as Berlin is ushered on stage by an escort of soldiers, sailors, airmen, and marines; and the whole audience rises and joins in, and an announcer calls out to the TV audience across the country (bigger than the Super Bowl's, the ratings later reveal), "On your feet, America!" and damned if the entire nation doesn't stand up and sing along.

I sometimes wonder why I ever listen to the evening news. Today it's MacNeil-Lehrer, often a cut above the rest of the pack, and Charlayne Hunter-Gault, once a player on Shawn's team, is talking to a spokesman for the Sandinistas, and with reference to the Contras he is telling her that "technical operational modality" is not to be confused with "political bargaining." I hope Bill Safire is also watching, so he can tell us someday what all this means.

Gottlieb was hoping to keep pieces shorter than of yore, but here is a new *New Yorker* with the first of three longish parts on the Federal Reserve, by yet another writer unfamiliar to me—William Greider. Bob was lucky to have it around, of course, after the market crash, ready to throw into the magazine with an updated lead, and it's probably important for us to run these excerpts from a book (I assume that's what it is) at a time like this. Yet I wonder how many people—including me—will get all the way through all three installments.

Maybe Shawn and Gottlieb aren't too different. In a rare fifteen-minute talk I had with Bill a couple of years ago, he said that he almost dreaded looking at unsolicited manuscripts, because there might be among them something he wasn't interested in and didn't imagine many people would ever read but that he would purchase and publish notwithstanding because it was important and *because he had to.*

We stop at the post office this afternoon on our way to the bayside to watch a glorious sunset, and while I am driving away Ellie says I have an envelope, hand-addressed, from *The New Yorker.* I take my eye off the road and say—correctly, it turns out—that it's from Gottlieb. It's interesting that I recognize a script with which I am really not all that well acquainted. When we stop, I learn that Bob, too, was distressed to see that Sunday *Times* article about the Klan, and he hopes we'll be able to figure out a way of salvaging my piece. "I suppose this kind of thing happens in journalism," he writes, "but I'm not experienced enough to be fatalistic." I suppose after half a century *I* ought to be experienced enough, but I'm not, either.

7 November

Joey and Jaime (who gets my new watch ticking with no apparent effort, though I guess, come to think of it, modern-day watches don't tick) arrive, and we are joined for a cookout dinner by Tony and Judy, Ian and Matthew, and Judy's sister Tina, she bringing along a young man who seems a decent sort and, apparently, unconcerned that he has lost one earring. In view of Tina's having spent a school year in the Philippines, I ask her what she thinks of the situation there right now, and when she replies that one of the families she lived with has decided to move to Australia, that may be saying a lot. Joey, like any tourist fresh from Washington, has brought back souvenirs: two clippings from the *Post*. One is about Annie Dillard, who's quoted as saying that our annual Fourth of July beach picnic at Truro (it's not Ellie's and mine at all, really; it's a communal affair) is the kickoff of the Outer-Cape summer social season. The second story harks back to Brendan Gill and Katharine White and features an ad hominem attack on Brendan by her son Roger Angell. According to the *Post*, "Angell perceived the essay as another in a series of attempts by Gill to promote himself at the expense of the magazine and the people who work, or worked, there. . . . 'Gill's loyalties and affections are reserved for people with power and great wealth,' said Angell." The current issue of *The New Yorker* contains a "Sky Line" department by Brendan, with Jacqueline Onassis among the cast of characters. Bob Gottlieb has told me that thinking about *The New Yorker* keeps him awake at night; this public flare-up between two elder statesmen in his domain is hardly likely to mitigate that insomnia.

It's Sunday, and diagramless-puzzle day, but I have too much work and too much family to tackle either of the offerings. I construe it to be nobody's business but mine that I elect to skip them.

A lot of tennis—Tony and Judy, Ray and Lee Elman, et al. I don't believe our clay court has ever before been playable this late in the year. Tony says that may not be a good omen; he has heard that this winter's weather may be worse than last year's, which was memorably bad.

9 November

The *Times*'s indefatigable McDowell is at it again. "Gottlieb Reign Alters The New Yorker," is the headline he's given this time around. Still, I probably ought to be grateful for some enlightening news he conveys; that

Chip McGrath, for instance, now has the formal title of Deputy Editor. And—this is a real eye-opener—that Gottlieb is putting some writers on salary. I was in that category once, for the first six months I was on staff. Twenty-five dollars a week. I imagine people begin at a somewhat higher level now, what with inflation and everything, maybe as much as fifty per.

The *Globe*, for its part, has a big feature today on Brian Urquhart, whose book about his days at the UN is out. When Brian retired as an Undersecretary General he must have been the organization's most senior official. He was there when I met him in 1945. (The Sunday *Times*'s recent long review of his book, curiously, omitted one consequential biographical fact: that he miraculously survived a bone-breaking parachute jump when his chute failed to open. Brian was telling his *Globe* interviewer about techniques his compatriots had for easing out people they couldn't manage—one of which was to give them a box at Ascot. But the reporter was evidently unacquainted with the British horse-racing scene, and what we read today is "award them the Order of the Garter, cover them with gifts, give them a private box of ascots."

Nature note: Steve Williams drops by. He wonders if we remember the turtle that our dog captured and that Steve's father rescued. Yes. Well, Palmer gave it to him, and when Steve was about to release it he noticed that it was injured. Also, it wouldn't eat the hamburger he tried to feed it, so he took it to the Audubon Society, where he learned he should have proffered earthworms. When it was pronounced fit and he picked it up, planning to let it loose somewhere in the Wellfleet woods, he was instructed that turtles like to stick to their own turf and if set down in alien territory will devote the rest of their lives, like a dog or cat in a newspaper tearjerker, trying to get home. So, says Steve, every single turtle he has plucked from the middle of a road it was crossing over these many years, to save it from being run over, and has considerately put to earth far from the danger spot, is now presumably searching restlessly for its homeland, and no thanks to him for his meddling interference. Steve has deposited Hopi's tortoise, accordingly, in our very own woods, hoping that's where Hopi found it in the first place.

I start scrubbing the grill I cooked on for my grandchildren the night before last. My mother's father used to play host at cookouts for his grandchildren, too, at his Westchester place, but they were somewhat different. His cook, Emily, who wore white tennis socks indoors and out, would carry everything from her kitchen to a tree-shaded picnic spot a few hundred feet away, and she would attend to all the culinary chores. I can't remember Grandpa, who had a hearty appetite, ever doing anything at these Sunday meals beside eating. I suppose Emily must have scrubbed the grills later on, while he was attending to his afternoon nap.

10 November

At the post office, a giveaway copy of a preview edition of a new journal, *Cape Cod Seniors*. The headline for the lead story is "Grandparents Have Legal Visitation Rights." I should jolly well hope so, unless the kids have a thing against gifts. That's the least of my worries. Matthew came by to see me today, and on Thursday I'm supposed to watch Ian in a play—if the show goes on. It seems that a piano stool collapsed beneath the music teacher who's directing the performance. In the professional theater, "Break a leg" is a good-luck phrase; amateurs aren't as richly endowed with understudies.

This elders' paper, a monthly, is going to cost five dollars a year, but I can get the first three issues free if I fill out a questionnaire, and I can also earn twenty-five dollars for "profiles"—the general public long ago usurped *The New Yorker*'s once jealously guarded private word for short biographies—of senior citizens up to a thousand words long. I must keep that in mind if things go sour on West Forty-third Street. The back page is full of ads for dentists, featuring dentures. I must keep *them* in mind if my own falsies keep falling out.

The CBS evening news echoes my own dark fears that knowledge of geography is rapidly and inexcusably eroding. Thirty-nine percent of Boston high-school students couldn't name all the New England states. A not inconsiderable proportion of them, given a blank map of the earth, couldn't fill in the United States. One kid said this sort of ignorance was irrelevant and on being asked why, answered, "Because I am here." Shades of prewar isolationism! As for the schools remiss in geographic instruction, their excuse seems to be that they're too busy giving courses in sex and the like.

11 November

Today is Veterans Day, and yesterday the President announced he was going to give the head of the V.A. cabinet status. Whether Reagan's doing this to keep vets from complaining when Gorbachev comes to call or to get them to support his Supreme Court nominees is uncertain. I don't need a Cabinet member to look out for my special interests, and aside from sick or wounded veterans I'm not sure there should be any such interests. I get on fine with professional veterans when I have to. When I went out to Franklin, Ohio, for General Harding's funeral, most of the other chief mourners connected with the armed forces were American Legionnaires in full regalia, but none of them even raised an eyebrow at my unadorned mufti.

I am not much on war memorials, either, but when Ellie and I, during our last trip to Washington, walked from the National Gallery to the Vietnam Memorial, on arrival we were both surprisingly and profoundly moved.

This used to be called Armistice Day, and it's my gloomy hunch that more than 39 per cent of all high-school students anywhere, asked "Armistice of what?," would look as blank as the young black woman on TV the other evening who had seemingly never heard of Ethiopia. I would hesitate to guess, indeed, how many contemporary high-school students could readily distinguish between V-E Day, V-J Day, and V.D.

It-Never-Rains-But-It-Pours Department: Just as Ellie and I are wondering what to do about the collapsing ceiling in our downstairs Truro parlor, the phone rings, and it's Sophie, in the New York apartment, saying that it rained hard yesterday and the ceiling is crumbling in our bedroom there.

12 November

Snow on the ground, and the Lower Cape may get four inches or more. Upper Cape already has six. Practically nobody, naturally, has got around yet to having snow tires put on. The only living creature unfazed by the sudden turn of events is Hopi, who has got what she's clearly long been yearning for.

People are forever griping—I loudly among them—about the grievous diminution of interpersonal relationships in this computer-driven age. So it is probably only fair for me to note that when our electric bill came in yesterday there was appended to it the message—printed and unsigned, to be sure, and no doubt computer-generated, but it's the sentiment that counts—"Dear Customer, Our records show you have an excellent credit rating and we want you to know we appreciate your prompt payments. It's a pleasure to serve you. Thank you."

I wondered to Ellie if we should contribute something to the New York civic organization that's putting up the annual Christmas-tree lights in the middle of Park Avenue. Turns out she's already sent along a check, with a praiseworthy note to the effect that it might have been bigger if the display were somehow extended beyond the invisible Ninety-sixth Street barrier that separates Us from Them almost as effectively as barbed wire.

13 November

My hopes of salvaging the Ku Klux Klan piece received a tiny boost when I read this morning of the capture in Mexico of Louis Ray Beam, Jr., a militant right-winger who figures in my article but not, happily, in that opus in the *Times* magazine. The more such post-Kornbluth developments there are, the better my prospects would appear to be.

Hopi and one of her disreputable four-footed friends deposited a still-breathing chicken on our driveway. (What do you expect? Today is Friday the thirteenth.) Ellie wrapped it in a towel, and after several calls to neighbor Mooneys' workplaces was directed to a chicken coop down the road, behind their barn. The coop was a shambles—wire ripped and flattened, not a bird in sight. We had never credited our pet with such power. E. finally gets Mrs. Mooney on the phone and contritely (omitting to mention their cattle on our tennis court) offers full restitution for all their damages. The lady says that shouldn't come to too much; there were probably not more than a dozen fowl in the pen altogether. But then George M. gets home from work and calls back. The ravaged coop E. had seen was being dismantled, and the chickens in the new coop are all accounted for, and the one Hopi brought home, which we figured at the least had a broken wing, is going to be OK. Maybe George means it is going to taste OK.

Tom Kane and Judy Gibbon drop in for drinks, and then they and we and the Waterses adjourn for dinner to the Blacksmith Shop. Much talk of old houses and their residents, and I wish I could remember the name of the elderly lady who came by last summer and asked if she could look inside ours because, around the turn of the century, she'd been born in our borning room. She must have preceded Ian's in-house birth by a good seventy-five years.

14 November

Drew Middleton, in a *Times* review of *The Korean War*, by the Englishman Max Hastings, writes, "Some may criticize Mr. Hastings for devoting considerable space to the exploits of the Commonwealth Division, particularly its long, vain, brave fight on the Imjin River. But he is British and Americans can be justly charged with paying scant attention to the British role in Korea or, in fact, to the part Britain played in World War II." This American pleads emphatically not guilty to any such charge. I wrote a whole *New Yorker* piece from Korea about that Imjin River business, and was rewarded by a letter warmly thanking me for it from Buckingham Palace.

Newsweek has a story on the Andover exchange students who were at the Novosibirsk Secondary Special Boarding School of Physics and Mathematics but nowhere mentions that it's located at Akademgorodok. It's nice to be privy to esoteric information like that. *Newsweek* also, in a piece about Senator Dole and his Presidential candidacy, has a photo of him on Dwayne Andreas turf—the Sea View complex at Bal Harbour, Florida, where Robert Strauss also hangs out, and where, the story says, "Andreas and Strauss talked about world leaders they knew." Dwayne once had made up for me a list of these, and although a few of the names were misspelled, it was a powerful lot.

The dog took off at six-thirty this morning, and when she hadn't returned nine hours later, I got worried and went out searching for her. No luck.

15 November

Ellie and I are supposed to go to the Ray Elmans' for a gourmet breakfast, but I can't eat. Hopi has been missing for more than twenty-four hours, her longest absence ever. She can't be lost; she knows the area too well by now. Enough is enough. I've put as much of my emotional potential into dogs, over all these years, as I have a mind to. I don't want to have to go through this again. No more dogs, *ever*. I will try to lavish some of the affection I would normally have reserved for them on people.

Ellie suggests that the family who own a black-and-white dog that Hopi sometimes consorts with might have a clue. Nobody home there, not even the dog. We run into Bill Miller on South Pamet Road, walking his dogs. He has two; we have none. This is democracy? Bill suggests we try Collins Road, but that's not one of Hopi's preferred thoroughfares. Still, what do we have to lose? The unutterable part of this, as we head there, is: am I searching for a live dog, or, at the edge of the road, a dead one? Am I looking where I'm going? On a dog search, one's rearview and side mirrors are as crucial as the stretch ahead. We have barely turned into Collins when my peripheral vision spots her. She is in a yard, frolicking with another dog, within plain sight of our house, unabashed, at 10:32 A.M.—more than twenty-eight hours after abandoning us without a by-your-leave.

The truth comes out. Ellie takes a walk and at the Ormsbys' is told that when a troop of Boy Scouts marched by yesterday en route to a Saturday overnight at Jack Kelley's camp up the hill, Hopi—whom all our neighbors know by now—was prancing at the head of the pack. That may be where she spent the night, and if she did I daresay she ate better—hamburgers, hot dogs, potato chips, marshmallows—than she would have at home. Wouldn't you think, though, that she might be a tiny bit apologetic, or at least embarrassed?

I am beginning to feel more and more peculiar as the day goes on, and it has nothing to do with dogs.

16 November

It's the flu, I guess. Temperature: 103. Worst is the chills. Not as bad as those with malaria or babesiosis, not the bone-breaking kind, yet, but no fun, either, and I can't hold a thermometer in my mouth for long lest my chattering teeth break it in two.

17 November

Was it last night at 3:00 A.M. I had to talk E. out of calling an ambulance to take me to the hospital? At least she doesn't drag me into a cold shower, as she did once before to save my life. She refrains from that drastic emergency measure, as a rule, until I get up to 106.

18 November

I seem to be alive. It always comes as a welcome surprise.

Thomas Winship, who since his retirement as editor of the *Globe* has become president of the Center for Foreign Journalists, based in Virginia, was a participant in the April conference I attended about the South African press, where he said, "I beg everyone here to think long and hard about the central question—how can we help the desperately struggling press of South Africa to survive and go in this twisted country?" Winship has an op-ed piece in today's *Globe*. South Africa gave *him* a visa, it seems, so he could attend a conference about the press. He urges American businesses to help support the struggling and largely black alternative newspapers over there by buying advertising in them. (I've done my small part by subscribing to the weekly *New Nation*, whose editor is in detention.) Tom also compares the government functionary who deals with the foreign press to Senator Joseph McCarthy, which makes me wonder what the reaction will be the next time a Winship visa application passes across that personage's desk.

Women are smarter than men, as has been suggested to me more than once. Now hear this! (I am trying to put more resonance into my Brent Abel piece and thus am in a nautical mood.) We've been laying living-room fires these recent chilly evenings, and it's not been easy, because the andirons keep coming apart, as they have for several years, and sometimes collapsing. Kevin Shenk stops by today to tidy up and she wonders why we don't swap them for a sturdy pair down in my study, where I haven't lit a fire in ages. So we make the switch. Never would have occurred to me unassisted, nor probably to any other male, to come up with so brilliant a proposition.

Our first Christmas card arrives, from our old acquaintance Ma Haide, Mao Tse-tung's legendary doctor friend, who's now chairman of the China Leprosy Association/Foundation. The card contains a poem by another patriarch we met over there in 1973, Rewi Alley—*Out With Leprosy*. Well, the Chinese wiped out venereal diseases, and according to Dr. Ma's card they've already treated somewhere between twenty thousand and a hundred thousand lepers; and I wouldn't put it past them, if push came to shove, to declare and win a war against AIDS.

I wonder what, if anything, Dr. Ma has done about smoking. When we were there—way back when United States passports were imprinted "Not valid for travel into mainland China"—practically everybody, including doctors in hospitals, smoked incessantly; and at every hotel we stayed at the management favored us with a plate full of free cigarettes and replenishments as we used them up. When Herb Schwartz, the doctor in our group, remarked to a professional colleague one day that it was widely believed in the United States that cigarettes were detrimental to health, the Chinese physician snapped back, "Propaganda!"

Town meeting tonight, and Moderator Malcolm Preston leads his troops unflinchingly through a warrant of thirty-two articles. As nonvoters, Ellie and I are supposed to take side seats, but we arrive at the school late and see empty places only in the center section, so we slip in there, and when there's action to be taken we conscientiously keep mouths closed and hands at sides. We end up—talk about coincidences!—sitting alongside legitimate voters Herb and Roz Schwartz.

The meeting begins at seven-thirty, and at eight-fifteen—this is a small town at its lovable best—Malcolm says, "Does anyone in the hall know if the Boy Scouts have provided us with some refreshments this evening?" There is no response. Ellie and I dare not exchange glances, for we are harboring the same awful thought: maybe Hopi ate them all up. Herb wants to know between articles what I'm working on, and when I say "Rewriting," E. chimes in with an allusion to Robert the Bruce: "Seven times the spider threw the silk against the opposite wall of the tent." The arachnoid analogy may be apposite enough, but that "seven" seems going a bit far; I wish she cared more about sports, in which case she could have likened me to a pole vaulter poised for his third effort to clear the bar.

19 November

An Indian-summer day like today should be invigorating enough without further inputs, but—another pleasant footnote to the story of small-town life—it is tonic at the post office to have a police car pull up and the officer who emerges say with a smile (I am embarrassed to have to admit I do not know his name), "How are you, Mr. Kahn?"

Postmaster Jack Kelley confirms that Hopi spent the night with Boy Scouts. But not with his; rather, a detachment from Falmouth that came down to use the Truro camping facilities. Hopi's behavior, Jack has heard, was without demerit. She slept in the scoutmaster's tent.

With the 1988 Presidential elections looming closer all the time, the Democrats have decided to put up a fight to keep me out of the enemy's camp. Here in the mail is a letter from Paul G. Kirk, Jr., chairman of the Democratic National Committee, informing me that I am a Contributing Member and enclosing a membership card. He wants money in return for it, to be sure, but nowhere in his communication does it say that if I don't come across I have to send it back.

Sports Illustrated has a jocular piece about Presidential candidates, the conclusion of which is that Bill Bradley should be elected, which of course isn't a bad idea at all. Twenty years or so ago, manifestly in jest, I used to "explain" the political scene every so often for *New Yorker* "Notes and Comment" readers. But we rarely engage in that kind of sport any more in those columns and perhaps never will again. The heavy hand of Jonathan Schell still rests upon us.

20 November

At Bill Miller's suggestion, I drive with him to Hyannis. The former chief editorial writer of *Life* and the *Herald Tribune* wants us to have lunch with Bill Breisky, the editor of the *Cape Cod Times*. I am surprised to hear that the paper has sixty employees on the editorial side alone. "There's a lot of space to fill between the Sunday ads," Breisky explains. We get to talking about the Cape Cod Hospital, and he singles out two men as the very best doctors there. By happy chance, they were the very two who, unknown to me beforehand, attended to me when I was wheeled in there a decade ago burning up with fever. But most of the conversation is about journalists one or two or all of us have known—up to and including Abe Rosenthal, who since he left the editorship of the *Times*, we concur, is in grave danger of becoming as obsolete as Gerald Ford or Jimmy Carter. We dwell, commendingly, moreover, on Mal Hobbs, who in forty-some hardworking years has built the *Cape Codder*, where son Tony is now gratifyingly installed as Feature Editor, from a $25,000-a-year business to a $2 million one.

Bill M. happens to bring up a minor-league Truro tradition—an annual Thanksgiving-Day soccer game in which all Kahns on the scene (and whatever ringers they can lure to their ranks) play against whoever else materializes. (This year, the Jerome Alan Cohen clan is slated to be the nucleus of the enemy forces.) Breisky, before we part, asks for my phone number, and I've barely returned home when there's a call from his reporter Karen Jeffrey, wondering if it'd be all right for her to come down and cover the game for the *Times*. They must *really* be hard up for copy to fill those interstices.

To dinner, with Joan Colebrook, at the Paul Grabbes. There is much talk about Russia and the old days there. Paul, who is eighty-five, has no wish to go back. He doesn't think, incidentally, that Gorbachev will stay-in power long. In the course of the evening, he corrects one misapprehension I have long harbored. Our longtime late Outer-Cape friend Nina Chavchavadze was not, Paul says, a niece of the last czar but merely a cousin.

21 November

Ellie is up early and off to attend a Castle Hill theater benefit in New York. I watch the Harvard-Yale game, alone, on television. (H 14–Y 10.) It is bitter cold in New Haven, and I am glad to be rooting my team home in my own living room, with a warm fire crackling above my firmly emplaced andirons.

Tony treats me to a ride in his new blue pickup truck. Then we switch vehicles and ride up-Cape to watch Judy perform at a Dennis church that is doubling as a coffeehouse. The buffet is overwhelmingly vegetarian.

22 November

Triple date day: the anniversary of Kennedy's assassination and of, sixty years apart, both my mother's birth and death. It's something of a shock to reflect that I've already lived a whole decade longer than she did.

I'm awakened at seven by a neighbor, searching for a child's sneaker that Hopi apparently borrowed for a toy. He saw her take it, and could have retrieved it, but he was unaware of the friendliness of her disposition, and she does after all resemble a wolf. Is it possible to buy a single sneaker? We will probably have to stand for the conventional pair.

The top of the front page of today's *Times* has a three-column photograph of a rooter at yesterday's H-Y game, fellow in a coonskin coat with a little bow tie holding up a Harvard banner. My God, it's Killiam! Yes, Paul Killiam, my classmate and friend, producer of and collaborator with me on reunion shows for a quarter of a century. What a moment of glory for him and reflected glory, in a sense, for all of us of '37! I check the caption for corroboration: "Paul Killiamer, Harvard '37 . . . ." Oh, no! I can hear him responding to the *Times*'s request for identification: "My name is Paul Killiam—K-i-l-l-i-a-m—er—class of 1937."

The *Globe* has a friendly feature story about neighbor Tommy Kane and the newspaper column he's been turning out for forty-two years. They get the name right. An accompanying photograph shows him at his typewriter—a venerable Royal standard just like the one I have as a complement to my two no less antique Underwoods. I must ask Tom some day if at this stage of his creative life he is encountering any ribbon-reversal problems.

23 November

A note from Gottlieb, in response to one of mine: Bob wonders if a visit to a factory in Hibbing, Minnesota, that produces chopsticks for export to Japan, could result in anything beyond a long "Talk" piece; and in that event, would it be worth going way out there? Maybe I can persuade him when we next chat that it might make a short long piece.

When I drop off some stuff to be typed at Etta Connor's, her son David is there. He brings up my Dwayne Andreas "Profile" and expresses his belief that eventually the world may be saved from starvation by soybeans.

24 November

Just before noon, the phone rings. "Mr. Andreas is calling." The familiar voice is that of Claudia, Dwayne's chief of staff in Decatur. When he comes on, he never mentions that nine months have passed, with no word from him or anybody close to him, since the "Profile" appeared. It seems a publisher has been after Andreas for a book about himself and his views on feeding the world. Do I think there's merit in it, and would I be interested? Yes, and yes conditionally; I would not want to be a ghostwriter and do not consider myself an "as-told-to" person. But I say I'll talk to the publisher, and later today I do. What if anything at all this may lead to is highly speculative. I never expected to have occasion to return to Decatur, Illinois, but now, who knows?

25 November

The eve of Thanksgiving. This one should be relatively quiet, with only Terry, Rose, and their three arriving during the day and David not due until tonight. But with fourteen guests expected for dinner tomorrow (including Annie Dillard and her new friend Bob Richardson), there's an enormous amount of shopping to be done. I elect to collect the turkey we've reserved in Wellfleet, and Ellie takes off for Orleans to pick up everything else.

Whatever happens, it won't be as frenetic as the day before Thanksgiving seventeen years ago, when for the first and only time Ellie and I collaborated on a piece of writing. We'd been in Japan earlier that year and had had a memorable lunch—arranged by our friend Bernie Krisher, then *Newsweek*'s

Tokyo correspondent—with Yukio Mishima. Just the four of us—at a restaurant near Mt. Fuji, where the Japanese writer's private army had its training quarters. Mishima arranged the seating at our table, so that he was framed in a large picture window with directly behind him—it was an uncommonly clear day—the fabled mountain in all its majesty. The day before that bygone Thanksgiving we learned of Mishima's having committed hara-kiri. Ellie and I had both taken copious notes at our lunch, and then if ever was the time to make use of them. So, for "Notes and Comment," she wrote some paragraphs, and I did, too. Next, I rewrote her and she rewrote me, and eventually we agreed on a text and wired our only joint effort up to then (also up to now) to Shawn. That not only consumed most of our energy but also most of the time on the eve of Thanksgiving. So today's preparations are a comparative breeze.

26 November

For dinner—family: Terry, Rose, Ely, Jacquelene, Curtis, Tony, Judy, Ian, Matthew, David, and Joey; friends Annie and Bob. But first, the annual soccer game. It had been raining earlier, but by midmorning the weather, if not ideal, was tolerable. Karen Jeffrey, camera in hand, arrived to cover the fray. I guess there must have been about thirty players involved, though not necessarily all on the field at the same time, and when the score got to be 2–2, the Cohens and the Kahns, who were nominally competing (along with various Elmans, Friedmans, Traums, Webbs, and unidentifiable strays), decided to call it quits. Perhaps the best part of the game was that no one got seriously hurt.

At dinner, Annie says she is building a library in her Middletown basement to house Bob's seven thousand books. Why is there never room, no matter how many new shelves one constructs, for all one's books? Why is it so difficult, especially for writers, to throw a book away? Can a lawyer not bring himself to part with a brief or a CEO with an annual report?

I forget how we latch onto this subject, but Annie reminds me of a time when I was in Seattle—or was it Portland—and I was going to meet a stranger in my hotel lobby, and he said I'd have no trouble recognizing him because he'd be wearing a blue raincoat, and he was indeed easy to spot, though it might have been easier, in that all-white environment, if he had said he was black.

Then until sleepiness triumphs we break out this year's vintage of beach-plum brandy and play Dictionary, that stimulating parlor game in which one gets points either for guessing the real definition for an obscure word or for conning others into voting for his made-up one. Everybody's reminiscing this evening. Terry reminds me, flatteringly, of his all-time favorite, my very own invention for "lavolta": " 'In ancient Thebes, in molten dreams, Lavolta's legions lust'—Henry IV, Part II." Neither of us can remember what "lavolta" actually means, but who cares?

27 November

I wonder if the *Cape Cod Times* has ever won a Pulitzer Prize. I am tempted to nominate Karen Jeffrey for one, because what does her paper have this heady morning but a front-page story about our soccer game with two large photos of the participants!

Terry started pulling up the tennis-court tapes yesterday, and we wrap up the tedious chore today. Could have been worse, could have been snowing, as has been the case a couple of times. This perennial ritual might make a nice feature for the *Cape Cod Times* one of these Thanksgivings. Ray Elman is already talking about commissioning Ms. Jeffrey to do a feature on our Thanksgiving soccer game for his *Provincetown Arts*.

Meanwhile, this afternoon, Terry takes me and a tape recorder into a back room to carry out an assignment Ray has given *him* for that publication: E. J. K. III to interview E. J. K., Jr. Terry says that when John Cheever was once interviewed by Susie, he told his daughter what questions to ask him, and would I consider following suit? No thanks. I am not trying to be ornery. I just don't have the foggiest notion of what I'd be interested to have him learn about me that he doesn't already know.

28 November

Up betimes . . . that's got to be a no-no word in Gottlieb's lexicon, and I might as well start conforming right now. Up early, then, with the grandchildren. Ellie has meetings all day with Castle Hill people, so I just sort of hang around until it's time to go to the Cohens' for drinks. There's talk of Dick Neustadt's impending marriage to Shirley Williams, also about how a memo that Jerry C. and Jim Thomson sent to Kissinger right after Nixon's election in 1968 paved the way for opening up United States relations with China. Jerry's just attended two interesting conferences—one, in Virginia, of old Nixon hands, including Haldeman and Ehrlichman; and the other in Beijing, a conference on international law. Ed Meese was there, and Jerry says the Attorney General made quite a good impression on the crowd and on him, too.

Then Peter C. shows some slides of their recent trip to Tibet, just before that country turned cool toward foreigners. The Cohens say the altitude makes you feel uncomfortable and that outside of Lhasa the hotels leave much to be desired. I can think of other places I'd rather go to first.

These Orientalists are more sensitive about symbols than some of the rest of us. Jerry points out something about the *Cape Cod Times* coverage of the alleged captains of our soccer teams that I hadn't noticed; the paper made a thing about me being the guy in the white hat and Jerry being the one in (Ms. Jeffrey stopped short of "black") the dark hat.

Back home, Ellie and I discuss *their* forthcoming wedding with David and Anath. We calculate that just the immediate family—aunts, uncles, nephews, nieces, stepsiblings and their mates—will come to fifty or so bodies, and that's before we get around to inviting a single friend.

29 November

We're going back to New York tomorrow, much earlier than usual, because Ellie is committed to a couple of off-Cape speeches early in December. So today is devoted to packing, except for a trip to Brewster for lunch with Anath's parents. Dan Golomb reminisces about a German he knew while both were scientists working, postwar, for the U. S. Air Force in the North African desert—a fellow countryman whose mother a few years earlier had made him close the shutters of their home whenever Dan and other concentration-camp inmates were marched by in their stripes on their early-morning way to forced labor.

30 November

When you're pressed for time, and need every possible day to do all you have to do, why is it that that's when you run into a month that has only thirty days in it?

Not that I suppose it matters much today—pack-up-and-drive-and-unpack day. We have room way in the back of the station wagon, for a change, for the dog, but after three hours or so I take pity on her and invite her up to the middle of the front seat. Ellie has brought along, on cassette, Beryl Markham's fascinating account of her life as a bush pilot in East Africa. When she speaks of flying low over the Serengeti Plain, we remember doing that ourselves in 1971—with thousands of animals scurrying beneath us—in a plane that cannot have been too much larger than hers, with barely enough room for, aside from the pilot, two adult passengers holding two goggle-eyed small boys in their laps.

We get to the New York apartment in time to watch Mikhail Gorbachev give Tom Brokaw some tips on how to handle an American TV audience.

1 December

I did make one high-priority phone call last night—to our early-morning dog walker. Ruth has new hours, won't be picking up Hopi this year till seven-forty-five. I guess I should be grateful for the extra half hour's sleep, but how am I supposed to condition myself to get out of the habit of waking up, willy-nilly, at six-thirty? Worse still, how do you get a dog to reset her own trustworthy inner alarm clock?

I check in at the magazine. Alison Rose has a small red-and-white flag on her eighteenth-floor reception desk. Garrison Keillor has an office here now, she explains, and as I surely know he also has a Danish wife. If the Munro clan has a flag along with a tartan I suppose I could bring one in and demand equal space, but if everybody followed suit Alison's desk might begin to resemble an Olympic Village, with no room for messages.

Various memos on *my* desk: we have a new printing plant and a new going-to-press day. Nobody is going to be able to accuse *The New Yorker* of capitulating to the advances of high-speed technology. The change means that the whole magazine has to be put to bed earlier than it used to be. A new telephone system is imminent, what's more. We will have direct-dial numbers of our own. I guess this can be construed to be a step forward.

My office typewriter needs a new ribbon. I get one from the messengers' room, fuss with it for half an hour, and give up, hands probably inked for life. This calls for someone with enhanced skills. I throw myself on the mercy of Bruce Diones, eminently qualified to take over. In twenty more minutes, all the head of our messenger department achieves is the sacrifice of another good pair of hands. He suggests we go to the summit of in-house expertise. Assistant office manager Ben Narvaez finds time for us. Twenty of his precious minutes produce nothing more than an emergency phone call to an outside professional typewriter-ribbon changer. One duly materializes with a tool kit the size of a suitcase. It could probably fix an elevator. I forget to clock his struggles. When he gives up, he says he will send somebody around tomorrow to remove my machine to a typewriter hospital, or wherever what has to be done to it is carried out.

I wonder how long it would take me to get the hang of a word processor. Or do they come with ribbons, too?

2 December

I had already decided to stay at home and tackle the mail there when I woke up this morning and discovered I couldn't talk. Laryngitis is annoying, but not so bad—Ellie has to spend much of the day in Connecticut, where she's talking to Peggy Knapp's library group—if you have an answering machine to take telephone messages.

3 December

I am more or less obliged to go to the office, though not until after lunch, because I've signed up for a lesson today in operating our new phones there. I can talk enough to say "Hello" and "Who?" and "Good-bye." There are eleven of us in the class, and the instructor requests and then addresses us by our first names—all but Paul Brodeur, who arrives late and, unaware of the system, replies reasonably enough, when asked for identification, "Brodeur." So that is what she calls *him*. Mark Singer and I share one newfangled instrument, which has more buttons than I know I could ever learn to master. I congratulate Mark on his recent "Profile" on an antiques dealer, who I thought had been neatly skewered, if not drawn and quartered. Mark says that, on the contrary, the subject was so enamored of it he is trying to buy two thousand extra copies of the magazine. There is no accounting for tastes.

Our new phone is called a Rapport, and our company, one I never heard of before, is Northern Telecom. The kind of service we're going to enjoy is called DID. We editorial people have not, however, been tied into something called Corporate Speed Call. We are each given a batch of postcards that we can, if we so desire, send out to people we want to have our private number. On the cards is a reproduction of a 1981 Warren Miller cartoon about telephones. Warren is the first person I encounter on returning from the tutorial session, and when I congratulate him on having his work given such further special recognition, he is surprised. He hasn't gone to class yet, and nobody has told him he was going to be thus involved.

4 December

My birthday. Hardly worth getting excited about. After all, "seventy-one" is one of those ridiculous numbers that can't be divided by any other whole number, isn't it? Ellie gives me a brand-new typewriter table, to use at home, and so I pull out from under the dining-room settee the ancient Underwood I bought from the office last spring, and dust it off, and once I drag in the standing lamp from the living room, why, I practically have a new office.

At my other, downtown, office, I run into Bob Shaplen, fresh from China, and across the street at the Harvard Club into Chuck Barber, my onetime Scarborough neighbor, who rose high in the corporate ranks and became the CEO of ASARCO, which in the days when company titles were comprehensible stood for, if I recall aright, American Smelting and Refining. Chuck, whom I've long thought of as the epitome of conservatism, says he's into venture gold mining these days; I get an inkling into what kinds of perks the business world dispenses when he says that even though he's retired ASARCO still gives him an office.

It's not the new phones around here that are causing trouble, it's the people involved with them. My new instrument rings mutedly (Jim Lardner down the hall thought its initial peal a bit shrill and asked me to turn it down), and a male voice asks for "Eve." It is Andrew Porter, and he is trying to reach one Eve Kahn. But who on earth is that? She is a new checker, that's who, and Martin Baron seems to have hired her without warning me of the possible consequences. It was bad enough in the old days, when Emily Hahn and Ed Koren and I had nobody to be confused with but the mere three of us. I guess we can always make room for another swimmer in our nomenclatural whirlpool.

5 December

How do you explain to a dog that this is a Saturday and that her walker only walks five days a week?

The Sinatra concert that Joan hoped Frank would give us VIP seats for was canceled fifteen minutes before it was supposed to start because the sheet music hadn't arrived. Liza Minelli was apparently prepared to go on anyway, but not Himself. But Good Lord, couldn't they have winged it with just a piano player? They could have made musical history.

Ellie's *On Glory Roads* made the Sunday *Times*'s list of 225 "notable" books of 1987, praise be. Annie Dillard and Eileen Simpson are there, also the big architectural book by Robert A. M. Stern et al. that has so much in it about my father.

6 December

On the way to Betty and Patrick's for dinner, I stop off to call on my stepmother. Now that Lilo is eighty-two, she is thinking of slowing down. Patrick is worried about getting to his Washington flat when he goes down there tomorrow morning, because with Gorbachev in town all sorts of areas may be blocked off for security reasons, and Patrick has no proof that he lives where he does while he's at work in the District.

When Betty was in Washington the other day, she went to the National Gallery and stopped to look at the David Smith that they sold some time back and whose worth may by now well be astronomical. She was interested to note that the dent is still there—one created not by the sculptor but, rather, by a friend of Betty's son Matthew, who in a wrestling match with him years ago knocked it over. Well, as they say—or should say—in the art world, caveat emptor.

7 December

Pearl Harbor day, also Gorbachev arrival day. I wonder who selected the date.

The *Times* illustrates a story about the reopening of the Rainbow Room with a picture, though he doesn't seem especially involved in the proceedings, of Paul Draper. The caption says that he is, improbably, seventy-eight. One memorable night a couple of years ago down at the Ballroom, when Larry Adler was on the bill, Paul—then I guess, a youthful seventy-six or thereabouts—was in the audience, and Larry invited him up on stage, and the two of them did an impromptu nostalgic reprise of the act they put on so glitteringly more than thirty years ago.

Joan Fox is in from Cincinnati, to sign a book contract for a romance novel she's been writing with Robin Howard, under a nom de plume they haven't yet chosen. The story is laid in Truro, and its protagonists meet while sea-clamming. Ellie and I will be watching this one carefully for intimations of invasion of privacy. Joan says that heavy-breathing sex scenes are not tolerated in this particular genre of love story and that indeed one of their original scenes—Robin's contribution, her collaborator hastily adds—had to be toned down because it was too steamy.

Joan and Robin are both going to the Jerry Traums' for dinner and poker. I tag along, because Ellie has a meeting tonight of one of her feminist groups (I forget which of two rival factions is on this evening's docket), but only for food. Poker is not and never has been my dish. The Traums are living in what they call a welfare hotel until the municipal landmarks people let them remodel a brownstone they've bought. There's a long, half-kidding argument between Jerry and his son Teddy. It seems Jerry inadvertently twice paid a doctor's bill for the boy. A refund check duly came back for eighty-five dollars, and inasmuch as it was made out to "Edward Traum," Teddy claims it is his and won't relinquish it. Jerry finally agrees to give him five dollars for it. I'd have sent him to bed.

Leon Friedman told me the other day that I ought to watch, at least once, the Channel 9 television show of Morton Downey, Jr., who attracts a noisy, right-wing studio audience, and where the atmosphere gets so wrought up that everyone approaching the arena is put through a metal detector. So I switch on the program when I get back home—Downey and a sheriff and a Guardian Angel are arguing about crime prevention—and am just beginning to settle in with it when the phone rings. "Ely Kahn?" I know this won't be personal, because the only friend who calls me "Ely" is Bob Wolf, and this is not his voice. "I represent Senator Daniel Patrick Moynihan and he . . . ."

Given the right circumstances, I can be just as testy as anyone participating in or watching the Morton Downey, Jr., show. "I know Pat Moynihan," I interrupt, "and he wouldn't call me at this hour."

8 December

I work at home all morning. At noon, walking through Grand Central on my way to the office, I am hailed by a person who looks vaguely—closer up, very—familiar. It is Douglas Leigh, the man responsible for lighting up Times Square and the towers of much of the rest of Manhattan. A "Profile" I wrote about him ran in June 1941, just before I was drafted. Now Doug says he has turned eighty. But he is still at it. His next big project, he says, is the illumination of Cincinnati, which is about to celebrate its 200th birthday. (I make a mental note to tell Joan Fox about this when I get home; when not sidestepping sex scenes, she writes features for *Cincinnati* magazine.) But before that, Doug says, he must attend a tower-lighting ceremony a fortnight hence, down at Two Park Avenue, and, come to think of it, didn't my father design that building? He did indeed, I say, and what's more, he had his offices there from the time it was finished, in 1927, till his retirement some forty years afterward. In that case, Doug says, he'll see to it that when his lights go on I'm invited to the scene. I make a mental note to inform Ely's widow and his daughters. He was always called "Ely," which was a sensible reason for me not to be.

It must be interesting to be famous, like Garrison Keillor. Bob Arnold, the manager of the Harvard Club, read in the *Times* that he has an office at *The New Yorker* and urges me to bring him around for lunch. I say that might be difficult because I don't believe Keillor wears a necktie to work. Mr. Arnold, who is ordinarily, as he must be, a stickler for proper attire, says not to worry; he'll furnish a tie himself.

At the office, Jim Lardner wonders if I know what the term is for long, one-piece men's underwear that ends in "suit." I venture "union suit," and he concurs, and then we both speculate about its origin. Jim surmises that it had to do with labor unions, but my hunch is that the garments were issued to Northern troops during the Civil War. The fanciest undergarments I ever possessed were two sets made of pure cashmere, which on my way to the Korean War in the winter of 1951 I purchased from Abercrombie & Fitch at some hideously expensive cost to *The New Yorker*. (Does sixty dollars a pair sound right? That was real money then.) But how could Ross and Shawn, after all, expect to get any usable copy from a half-frozen correspondent? The cashmere made the venture tolerable—or considerably less uncomfortable than it might otherwise have been—but soon after I got home, a laundress who perceived that my clothes were in sore need of cleansing made the innocent mistake of putting all the underthings into a washing machine.

It is *glasnost*-and-*perestroika* week, and in dutiful observance thereof Ellie and Joan F. and I go to the CUNY graduate center on Forty-second Street for a PEN poetry reading by two visiting Russians—Yunna Petrovna Morits and Aleksandr Semyonovich Kushner. Susan Sontag presides and introduces all concerned, with one curious omission—a quintessential interpreter.

9 December

I had a dream last night in which a houseguest, Henry Kissinger, was going over a book of mine about foreign affairs practically line by line. When he was finished, I walked over and thanked him profusely for taking such pains, but his only response, while walking out toward a waiting limousine, was to call back over his shoulder, "This book is an abomination." Last time he'll be invited to stay with *us*, you can be sure.

Dwayne Andreas and David Rockefeller were not at the poetry reading. I realize why, when I read the guest list for Reagan's dinner with the Gorbachevs. They were both invited, along with Chris Evert, Mary Lou Retton, Joe DiMaggio, and Kissinger.

It's double-reunion day. First our annual Harvard '37 lunch, with thirteen of us in attendance, including Paul Killiamer or whatever his name is. (Gerry Piel has to leave early, for a meeting in Washington with Gorbachev, but he'll fly back this evening in time for a get-together of the members of our Soviet trip.) There is going to be a fifty-fifth reunion in Cambridge for the entire class, in 1992, at the Hyatt Regency, which someone at the table points out unkindly is near both the Yard and the Mt. Auburn Cemetery. We each put up fifteen dollars for three guesses—winnings to be distributed at next year's lunch: (1) Who will be the Democratic candidate for President, (2) How many points will Harvard score in the Harvard-Yale game, (3) Where will the Dow-Jones stand one year hence. My entries are Cuomo, seventeen, and 2,100.

Back at the office, a call from my older sister. She has heard from a Sinatra woman who says she might have been able to get us into the New Jersey concert (which apparently went on after one postponement) if she had only got Joan's letter on time.

I look up my Doug Leigh "Profile" in the library. He said yesterday he was eighty, but in 1941 I had him born on May 24, 1910. Seventy-seven. Why would anybody add on to his age, if that is what he's doing? (Maybe the answer to that question is that when you get to be oldish you're proud that you're still productive when so many of your contemporaries are either retired or—perish is certainly the thought—gone.) I am still pondering this when the phone rings—mutedly, Lardner can probably not hear it. Sona Olson is on the line, works for the people who now own Two Park Avenue, and as my father's son would I say a few words at the lighting ceremony on the seventeenth? Sure. Maybe Brendan Gill, whose Frank Lloyd Wright biography is reviewed in this morning's *Times*, will write me up in his next "Sky Line" department.

With Corinne and Brent Abel, who are staying at the Harvard Club, I head toward a restaurant, the Kalinka, which the Piels have picked for our Russian group's reunion dinner. They've also invited the Nobel laureate Wassily Leontiev to be a special guest. What they evidently didn't know was that their restaurant is only a wine-and-beer establishment. Fortunately, Fag Goodhue and I both discover, when we set off separately in an endeavor to make the festivities suitably festive, that there's a package store only a few blocks away. Leontiev's news of the day, which I haven't yet heard attributed to Gorbachev or any of his entourage (although of course the General Secretary may have told the President about this *in camera*) is that Russians are now allotted six eggs a week apiece instead of five.

10 December

Ellie has a weird letter from a woman who's adopted an East Indian name and says she's a therapist who tithes and accordingly sends each month, to somebody who's given her spiritual guidance, a check. Here's one made out to Ellie for $100. It would seem insulting merely to send it back, so E. decides to endorse it to an organization she knows that supports women artists.

Linda Asher says at the office that she was out at Jackson, Wyoming, in August the day my mountain-climbing piece came out and that it was the talk of that town. News to me, but welcome, naturally.

I meet Ellie on Third Avenue to see *The Last Emperor*, which whatever its flaws has some marvelous shots of the Forbidden City and other Beijing locations. When we were in what was then Peking, in 1973, what impressed us as much as anything else was how many peasants and workers were wandering around the once off-limits courtyards of the Forbidden City, gazing at the glittering relics of a national past so antithetical to the austerity that then prevailed. We couldn't help wondering what the indigenous sightseers thought about all the time and trouble that must have been expended to drag one huge slab of marble to the scene; it was hauled there in the wintertime, when the roads were slick with ice, by a team of a thousand horses. In one treasure room filled with works of art in gold, silver, and jade, a resident guide essayed a small joke for us Americans, at the end of a narrative about a certain Empress who, displeased when one of her emperor's concubines refused to jump into a well, had her pushed. "You see, contradictions among the ruling class," the guide told us.

It was my sixth journey across the Pacific, but the first to China, though on an earlier trip I had got close enough, on the offshore island of Macao, to gaze wistfully across at it. We were American Friendly Personages traveling as guests of the Chinese People's Association for Friendly Relations with Foreign Countries. The Soviet Union was then not a Chinese Friend (I dug up a symbolic shovelful of earth to help some Red Guards who were building an anti-Moscow bomb shelter); and in Hong Kong, en route, Ellie and I stayed up late one night scrubbing Smirnoff labels off a couple of vodka bottles, discovering too late that the alien word was also etched into the glass.

By coincidence, we were both engaged in research about China. Ellie, whose exposure to Chinese art and history dates back to her childhood, was gathering material about the American missionary movement there; I, for a book eventually titled *The China Hands*, about the American Foreign Service Officers, a few of them missionary sons, who had worked in China just before the Communist takeover in 1949 and who, in the days when McCarthyism was in vogue, had been pilloried for "losing China." I was especially eager to get up to Yenan, where Mao and his confreres had functioned from their caves; and I was terribly frustrated when a plane at the Sian airport, waiting to take us there, never left the ground because of weather.

Maoism was rampant. One of our guides had a six-year-old daughter who, the mother said, was beginning to learn English. And what was her vocabulary so far? Oh, very small—"She knows 'eye,' 'ear,' 'nose,' 'mouth,' 'bed,' and 'Long live Chairman Mao.' " The Chairman's likeness was displayed in every schoolroom we visited. One math class we were taken to had a quotation from one of his works on the blackboard; I never did get a translation, but an escort confided that it was supposed to inspire the students more easily to analyze the dimensions of a cube.

In an English class, where I could more or less follow the proceedings, forty-odd students were reading aloud, in unison, from "The Cock Crows at Midnight," a fable about a cruel landlord who's outfoxed by a twelve-year-old boy. I can read English faster than four dozen orchestrated young Chinese, so while the landlord was getting his lumps I copied down Lesson One, which was in verse:

The army cherishes the people,
The people support the army.
They are inseparable,
Like fish and water,
One heart and one will,
A Great Wall of Steel;

The army and the people
Form a united whole.
Chairman Mao's teachings
We always keep in mind.
With guns in our hands
We defend our motherland.

Seeing *The Last Emperor* reminds me of some semantic troubles our hosts were having with "imperialism." Mao was forever carrying on about it, as in "by relying on the people we can definitely defeat imperialism and its lackeys and achieve world peace."

Well and good. When we were driven to our hotel in Shanghai, though, there was a trade mission in residence from Ethiopia, at the moment the only empire in the world. And how did the Chinese handle that? In English, at least, rather clumsily. For according to a daily news bulletin, at a Chinese government reception for that particular group of African Friendly Personages, "Minister Fang Yi asked the distinguished guests to convey the highest respect to His Imperial Majesty Haile Selassie I and the profound sentiments of the Chinese government and people to the Ethiopian government and people. He said: 'Let us support each other in the struggle against imperialism . . . .' "

11 December

A Friday—good day not to bother to go to work downtown and also to leaf through a newish biography of Dorothy Parker. The author (Marion Meade) has spliced a quote of mine from an interview and a phrase of mine from *About* The New Yorker *and Me* into a single sentence but with no harm done to meaning or to me. So many familiar faces' names leap out at me!

To the Century, for a pre-Xmas concert by the Yale Russian Chorus and the reading of a Russian fairy tale. The place is mobbed. Women haven't yet been admitted, but the old customs are crumbling fast. I step into the sacrosanct Members' Bar, and there is a female ordering a drink without a by-your-leave and next to her a child who can barely see over the top of the bar and who says to Paddy, "You remember *me*."

12 December

Tony and Judy are having their kitchen floor redone, so they move into our Truro house, and naturally this would be the one time when our oil tank runs dry.

To Max Lerner's eighty-fifth birthday party at the Townsends'. When I met Max half a century ago he was teaching at Sarah Lawrence, to the widespread delight of its then all-girl student body and to his I imagine as well. He looks happy, and ageless. Among those who've come to pay respects are Jill Krementz and Kurt Vonnegut, Cecille and Wallace Shawn, and the Daniel Patrick Moynihans. Jill says the best photo she ever took of Kurt was when she and her future husband called on Ellie and me at West Cornwall a dozen years ago. Cecille says that Bill has been deluged with manuscripts ever since he teamed up with Farrar, Straus. Liz Moynihan reminds me of an evening at their house in Cambridge, when I was working on my *Harvard* book and Pat was still teaching; Lillian Hellman was there, too, Liz recalls, and fell asleep. Mary Ellin Barrett—no disrespect to Max meant—talks about Irving Berlin's forthcoming *100th* birthday. She says her father never leaves his house.

On to dinner at the Irwin Rosses'. Bud and Aline Benjamin are there, preparing to go on a Scandinavian cruise to celebrate their forty-fifth wedding anniversary. Another guest, who lives on Beekman Place, says she sometimes sees Irving Berlin out for a walk in the neighborhood. You never know whom to believe any more.

13 December

The *Times* says that in the newly refurbished Rainbow Room, tonight, there will be a $1,000-a-plate Municipal-Art-Society black-tie dinner dance, "at which Jacqueline Onassis and Brendan Gill will honor William Shawn and *The New Yorker* magazine." Funny that Cecille, who knows me well enough to have asked me yesterday to zip up the back of her dress, never mentioned it. Funnier still that as far as I know nobody at the office has been made privy to the tribute. If Bill is to be thus exalted, it does seem odd that his underlings weren't at least offered the opportunity— though at that price tag presumably few would have seized it—of taking part.

Marjorie Iseman has E. and me to lunch at the Lotos Club, along with painter John Hubbard, over from England for two simultaneous shows of his work. Many artists we know would give at least one eyetooth for a single exhibit. Despite his authentic British accent, John is an American; turns out to have gone to Harvard with Michael Arlen and while on some college publication there to have been John Updike's editor. I am beginning to get tired reminding myself that this is indeed a small world.

Marjorie is active in the Municipal Art Society, and she remembers being apprised of a fund-raising function at the Rainbow Room, but she does not recall that the invitation mentioned either Shawn or *The New Yorker*. We eat in the club's basement grill room, the walls of which swarm with rather explicit portraits of nudes. Marjorie says she's surprised, now that this once all-male precinct has been desegregated, that feminist members haven't complained about the paintings.

14 December

At lunch at the Harvard Club, I stop to chat with Jim Greenfield and Annette Grant. Now that he has taken over, at the *Times*, the Sunday magazine, Jim is expending most of his energy on that; and like Gottlieb at *The New Yorker*, one of the first things he did was to jettison most of its accumulated inventory of purchased articles. I refrain from expressing my regret that he didn't kill the Kornbluth opus on the Klan case. When I happen to mention yesterday's little item about the Rainbow Room gala for the Municipal Art Society, Ms. Grant says she remembers a press agent's telling her a couple of weeks ago that Shawn would definitely be there in person. I offer to bet that he wasn't. Considering Bill's well-known feelings about elevators, how would he have *got* there? By helicopter? Parachute? How much would she care to wager? Prudently, she holds back. A couple of hours later she phones. No, Shawn didn't make the party, but he received some kind of award, and Brendan read thanks that Bill had composed for the occasion. That puts Brendan two up on the rest of us—his first such coup, of course, having been when he somehow chivied Shawn into writing a memoir of Harold Ross as an epilogue to Gill's *New Yorker* book.

Ellie phones. She just talked to Dwayne Andreas, who wonders if we can join him for dinner tonight. We can't; it's my last black-tie Board of Management dinner at the Harvard Club before my term expires, and I've brought my tux to the office to change and I want to be there. Ellie says Dwayne told her it had taken him a long time to get over the shock of my "Profile"; apparently he'd had no inkling that—as is true of most such pieces—I'd be going into such considerable detail. He also told her that he'd been to all the Gorbachev functions in Washington, which was no shock to me; I'd have been surprised if he hadn't.

Alongside the coffee machine on the twentieth floor, Edith Agar emerges from her accounting realm and introduces me to one of my newer colleagues, Terrence Rafferty. Then Edith asks if she isn't correct in thinking I once wrote a "Comment" item about the taste of coffee. I don't believe so, but I parry—could I be showing off for a newcomer?—with the observation that if I did I'm sure I never got paid for it, so if she'd be kind enough to. . . . Later, Helen Stark tells me that Edith called the library to ascertain the truth, and Helen went through all the "Comments" I'd written for some time back and couldn't find any such thing. What would I have said if I had? That some coffees taste better than others? That I drink espresso for breakfast? That my all-time favorite coffee cup is the blue-and-white one given me once by one of my sons and inscribed "God could not be everywhere so he created Fathers"? A bit mawkish, perhaps, but what father would not be proud to chug-a-lug from it?

These fancy club dinners! Tonight's pièce de résistance is roast saddle of venison; and because it's so close to Christmas, the pastry chef has built gingerbread houses for each of us to take home. Broward Craig is stepping down as president; he gets (and deserves) a Tiffany clock to boot.

In this cockeyed world, one occasionally still comes upon some sense of proportions. We are informed at the dinner that among recent guest appearances at the Club, the Iran-Contra interrogating lawyer Arthur Liman—and not because he is also on our Board—outdrew Dr. Ruth.

15 December

Working at home all day, I take an afternoon respite and turn on the television. There is Gary Hart, saying something about his wife and children supporting him. Wondering why anybody would be rerunning some seven-month-old film clips, I switch to another channel. It is several hours later before I realize that I was tuned into him live and that for better or worse (for the Republicans' better, is my initial reaction) he has reentered the race.

Ellie and I go to the Brooklyn Academy of Music to see the new opera *Nixon in China*. There are more blacks in the cast than there may be in China, but what the hell; in our ill-fated *Harrigan 'n Hart* musical, a black woman was cast as Mrs. Annie Yeamans, as Irish a character as ever trod the boards. The opera seems to have—like so many other shows that run out of wind—second-act trouble, especially when the Henry Kissinger character becomes the personification of the evils of capitalism (I think that's what was meant), and is portrayed in a manner that seems to have overtones of anti-Semitism. And John Adams's music sounds to our ears in many instances like warmed-over Philip Glass.

We hire a car to take us to Brooklyn and back. The opera ends at eleven and we are home at eleven-twenty. A basic rule of mine could, I suppose, apply to all Manhattanites spending an evening in Brooklyn; if you're ahead at backgammon, get a limousine; subways are for losers.

With the mail, we get a free copy of the *New York Observer*, a fledgling daily owned by Arthur Carter, whose stable now also includes the *Nation*. The *Observer* is printed on salmon-colored paper, like the *Financial News*, and it carries, praiseworthily, a British-type crossword. Our freebie has an interesting piece by Francine Gray on the Russians over here as guests of PEN. The woman poet whose reading we went to the other night has some complaints about American hotels vis-à-vis Russian ones: no samovars on every floor, for round-the-clock tea, and inadequate lights for those poets whose muse materializes after dark. Yunna Petrovna Morits, fortunately for her, does not undertake to compare the elevator or bath-towel services in Soviet hotels to ours. Some of Gorbachev's retinue in Washington, probably the elite of it, are staying at the Madison, the favorite hostelry there of, among others, Dwayne Andreas and me; the papers say that they empty out their minibars every night. Anyway, my dear Yunna Petrovna, in many American hotels we can make do without the samovars, not alone because of minibars but also because we have a thing you may well never have heard of called room service.

Oh, how fortunate to be an author whose new book includes a "Profile" of Vartan Gregorian! Phil Hamburger is the guest of honor this evening at a delightful publication party in the Trustees' Room of the public library. So many familiar faces, including those of memorable *New Yorker* alumni like Harriet and Bill Walden. Gottlieb makes a brief appearance. Shawn once again—though there are no elevator problems here—sends Cecille and Wallace as his emissaries. Martin Baron promises he'll introduce me to his checker Eve Kahn, who he says is a Harvard Phi Beta Kappa and summa— or, he interrupts himself, in his best head checker's fashion, was it just a magna? I have a pleasant chat with my long-ago schoolmate Katharine Scherman, who it turns out has also had dealings, or nondealings, with my friend at Little, Brown. Once he didn't read a manuscript she sent him for six months, which seems an idiotic way for anybody in the book-publishing game to have treated the daughter of the founder of the Book-of-the-Month Club. In presenting the guest of honor to the assemblage (most of whom know him well), Gregorian (who is co-host with Barbara Tuchman and Andrew Heiskell) says that when Phil was interviewing him for the "Profile", he took no notes. One should never be jealous of another writer's success, but I sure do envy Phil his gift of recall.

17 December

The son—grandson, too—of a longtime friend told me last summer that he was thinking of applying to Harvard, and I said I'd write a letter of rec-ommendation if he decided to. I hear from him today. In asking me to proceed, he says—damned if I can figure out whether he's serious or not— that Harvard has ended up as his first choice in part because of "its extraor-dinary feature of unlimited ice cream for everyone in the 'House' system." I have made a decision on my own: not to allude to his priorities in any correspondence with Admissions.

Dwayne Andreas has made *The New Yorker* again—this time in Elizabeth Drew's interminable piece about Republican candidates, in which she men-tions such of his Bal Harbour, Florida, buddies as Bob Strauss, Tip O'Neill, David Brinkley, Howard Baker, and, especially, the Bob Doles. Drew doesn't bring in Tom Dewey, that especially special Andreas friend who died down there—while occupying, I suspect, the very apartment I stayed in during my visit to the high-class enclave.

It's lights-on day at Two Park Avenue. I look up my father in *New York 1930*, that splendid architectural history by Stern, Gilmartin, and Mellins, and find a 1927 Lewis Mumford quote I'll be glad to use in my remarks: that the building "strikes the boldest and clearest note among all our recent achievements in skyscraper architecture." It's not really all that skyscraping—only twenty-seven stories. Ely's office, where I spent most of the summer of 1934 helping him write his book *Design in Art and Industry*, was on the twenty-fourth. Doug Leigh and I are introduced to the audience—mostly real-estate and financial people, I gather—by Bernard Mendik, its owner and the host for a champagne-and-cheese reception in the lobby. Then we all march across Park Avenue to gaze up at Leigh's luminous handiwork.

On to Daphne Shih's for dinner with the Shaplens and Jayjia's daughter Lisa. Daphne is going to Sri Lanka again despite all the recent troubles there. Troubles? "Butcheries" would probably be more accurate. But Daphne, who plays her harp serenely in subway stations and other out-of-the-way auditoria, is hardly to be fazed by mere mayhem.

18 December

Irene Coletsos, one of our summer tenants on Park Avenue, stops by to pick up some of the things she left behind. She has found a place on West 112th Street and runs in Riverside Park but only, in answer to my question, by daylight. For her master's thesis at the Columbia School of Journalism, she's writing about the gentrification of downtown Manhattan and is also doing a piece on Judith Malina. It's hard to imagine what would or could offend Judith, but Irene says her subject keeps accusing her of asking impertinent questions.

I agree to meet Ellie this afternoon at the Deutsches Haus, on Washington Mews, for a levee at Jocelyn Carlson's New York Institute for the Humanities. (Daphne has lugged her harp down here, too.) Though born and raised in New York, I don't think I've ever before set foot in the Mews, now owned by New York University. It's a big city. I am not the only trailblazer who has made it almost all the way down to Washington Square. Brian Urquhart is another. Now that he has finished his own memoir, he's working on a biography of Ralph Bunche, whose life, Brian says to my surprise, nobody else has yet written. Jeremy Bernstein, who's just had a piece on Tibet in *The New Yorker*, makes it, too. He says in his experience Gottlieb is a tough, hands-on editor and that that may very well be the last piece

Jeremy ever does for the magazine. But you mustn't believe everything these nuclear scientists tell you; Jeremy swore to me at least three years ago, when Shawn still reigned unchallenged, that he would never—I forget why— write for *The New Yorker* again. I myself have permanently severed relations with the magazine many times, over the years, but never in public and rarely beyond the dawn of the day following the troubled night of my firm unalterable decision to call it quits.

We wend our way uptown and take in John Huston's *The Dead*. It's a Friday night, but the house isn't even full. Too soon, maybe, for the rave reviews to have had an effect. But then we are living in an age where James Joyce could hardly expect to compete for favor with Eddie Murphy.

19 December

Mary Cheever's Christmas card invites me to write—"for my new book"— a pithy paragraph about life in Scarborough in the fifties. She mentions two of the many activities in which her John and I were both involved: the volunteer fire department and backgammon. I'll try to oblige and will, of course, include others of our mutual interests in those halcyon days: ice-skating and Labrador retrievers. In *About* The New Yorker *& Me*, I mentioned that John and I used to keep track of our backgammon rivalry on a flyleaf of *A Bell for Adano*. When later that year I wrote to Cheever to congratulate him on one of his many deserved prizes, he replied, "The only reason I won the Pulitzer is because I continue to write my backgammon losses in the backs of novels. If the world knew about my vast insolvency I wouldn't win anything."

I try to explain to Hopi the difference between weekdays and weekends by using different-colored leashes for dog-walker days and me-walker days, but this may be too subtle a distinction even for a pet as smart as ours to grasp. John, the apartment handyman, says that his kids want a dog for Christmas; would I object to telling him how much a fine dog like Hopi costs? When I inform him that she was a gift, more or less a throwaway, he looks surprised; it is not in the 1095 Park Avenue scheme of things, I sense he believes, for anything of any value to come free.

We go to a Hanukkah party at the Roiphes'. Anne and Herman have a daughter whom I take for a teenager but who turns out, to my consternation, to be a pregnant psychiatrist. Not wishing to make a complete fool of myself twice, I ask the doctor if the mature-looking sister standing next to her could be as old as thirty. Seventeen. I back off as politely as I can, only to be confronted by a vaguely familiar woman who asks right off if I have forgiven her. I have no idea what for. There could certainly have been no ruptured romance with the likes of this one. I am suffused with holiday spirit, however, and say sure, she's forgiven. A few minutes late I remember: it was she who at a party a couple of years ago turned on me, although we were barely acquainted, and delivered as blistering a personal attack as ever I've been subjected to. I reeled from that inexplicable abuse for several hours. (I always got along affably enough with her late husband, whom I knew much better.) Now that I realize who she is I'm not sure I want to have forgiven her. But I already have.

I don't believe I've ever been to a Hanukkah ceremony before, and I certainly am not familiar, unlike many of the rest of those present, with the Hebrew song they knowledgeably break into at, if I remember correctly, the lighting of the sixth candle.

In the babble that ensues, I hear somebody utter the word "Novosibirsk." Now that's familiar. I track down the voice to Lionel Tiger, who doesn't seem to have been there but has heard about the place. He is one of the few male authors on hand (the female roster includes, along with the hostess, Martha Lear, Phyllis Rose, Vicki Goldberg, Patty Bosworth, Betty Rollins, and Francine Klagsbrun) and one of the few men who isn't, like Herman, a psychiatrist. Lionel and I talk, guardedly, about Dan Wakefield's vehemently antipsychoanalysis piece in tomorrow's *Times* magazine.

I gave up on psychotherapy not long after my first direct encounter with it. This was shortly after Ellie and I were married, and I undertook to share her two sons' upbringing. There were tensions, inevitably, and it seemed advisable for me to seek professional help to ease mine. After a few one-on-one sessions with Dr. S., in which I felt he was making more progress than I was, he proposed that he meet with all four of us at once. A date was set, on a day when I had to go on some mission in the family car, and I said I'd meet Ellie and the boys at the doctor's office. I couldn't find a place to park, and by the time I arrived our hour—sorry, fifty minutes—was all but over. We abandoned psychotherapy thereupon and have lived happily ever after, I think.

You really feel old when you are at your conversationally most dazzling with the prettiest young thing in the room, who has even taken your phone number on some business pretext (though she neglected to give you hers), and halfway through one of your most enthralling reminiscences she leaves you abruptly for a total stranger who happens to have some cigarettes.

20 December

Ann Garrity stops by with son Colin, who's home for the holidays from Scotland's University of St. Andrew's, over where golf began. To facilitate his being allowed to hold a job in Europe if he decides to work there after graduation, Colin has an Irish passport along with his American one. He got his alternate by being able to prove he had a grandfather who was born in Ireland, which wasn't easy, because the aval birth certificate, when he was finally able to track it down, had the name (the grandfather was illiterate) spelled "Geraughty."

While Ellie goes to a holiday-music recital at the Metropolitan Museum with her nephew Douglass Smith, Lexy and I head for the art gallery Ethan Cohen's now running in Soho. Ethan, after some trial and error, has reverted to monochromatic hair. Many of the other guests seem to be junior affiliates of Jerry Cohen's law firm, but Ethan's father assures me there was no coercion, that they all turned up in the depths of Soho on a Sunday night because they wanted to. I am touched. One of them, who is Chinese, runs the Chinese part of the Paul, Weiss computer program, which he assures me is a big step up from his previous job—waiting on tables in a Chinese restaurant.

The Korean elections are over, and the Olympics may have survived; the president-designate was head of the organizing committee in Seoul.

Gary Hart is interviewed by Ed Bradley on "60 Minutes." Hart looks relaxed, and there is no talk about his private life. There is also nothing he says that would make me want to vote for him. Hell of a spot for a Democrat like me to find himself in.

21 December

Lunch at the Knick with Dwayne Andreas. He never mentions the "Profile" (nor, when I stop by his apartment on the way to the club, does Inez), but it is a cordial enough reunion, and for all either of us yet knows, a book of some sort may evolve from it. We both like one of his pet phrases—"My dog eats better than I do"—for a title, but I probably won't use it if push ever comes to shove. A lot of interesting things have happened to Dwayne and his business since we last talked, nearly a year ago. The catfish industry has grown so big down south, for instance, that one of his Archer-Daniels-Midland plants is now churning out a thousand tons of soybean meal a day solely as feed for fish farms. When Mother Teresa (who has a place in Havana and is soon, Andreas says, to have one in Moscow) wanted to get some food for Ethiopia, she came to him, and together they went to see Cardinal O'Connor, and then on to the White House, and got the President to release some $30 million worth of supplies to her. Then Dwayne asked Gorbachev to get Ethiopian dissidents to lay off interfering with the deliveries of relief food. Raisa told him in Washington she got on fine with Nancy. He is contemplating a joint venture with the Soviet Union that might ultimately involve five giant soy-processing plants, producing milk and protein and meal for bread. He sees Bob Strauss as a possible Democratic candidate, though Paul Simon, like all the other contenders, is a close friend. Inez and he are dining tonight with Happy Rockefeller and Malcolm Forbes. He is an interesting man, and it could be an interesting book.

22 December

We have a message that our Video Room membership—which entitles us to delivery and pickup of rented cassettes—will expire if we don't renew it instanter. Ellie suspects that the urgency may relate to October's market crash (A-D-M stock went from twenty-six to eighteen in October, but Andreas said it is coming back) and people's subsequent cutting down on what they deem to be nonessentials. She cites as putative evidence thereof a colloquy she had yesterday at the dry cleaner's. There were far fewer clothes hanging on racks than normal. When she asked why, the answer, in one grim word, was "Yuppies." It seems that before October nineteenth, every time a male yuppie wore a suit he would have it dry-cleaned and pressed; now two or three wearings is closer to the pattern.

The current *New Yorker* has a centerfold ad that plays a tune when the magazine is spread open. It's an ad for a vodka. The *Post* says the campaign's costing its sponsor a cool million, but for the moment I can't remember what brand is involved, and what good is any amount of advertising if it makes you remember a gimmick and forget the name of the product?

A Christmas card arrives from one of the U-boat men we dined with abroad. I must have given him my business card, for his envelope not only bears my name and address but also my phone number. I am under the impression that son David is supposed to have some proficiency in German before he gets his Ph.D., so I beseech a translation. When he starts off by pronouncing "Ich" "Ick," though, I decide not to commandeer any more of his precious time.

I rush out on an emergency mission—to buy my Christmas-wrapping wife some Scotch tape—and am overjoyed that on my way back home, in the dark, without my glasses on, I can recognize my eye doctor, as Dr. Weisberg's path and mine converge.

Shaplen says he had a spirited conversation with Gottlieb, who evidently hasn't been clued in on *New Yorker* writers' territorial rights. Bob S. blew his stack on learning Bob G. had authorized some alien reporter to go to Indonesia, which Shaplen has long claimed to be his domain. (He has never yet quite forgiven me for once trespassing, according to his lights, in Thailand.) I can no longer legitimately claim South Africa as mine, I suppose, being denied admittance to it; but I wonder if Micronesia still belongs to me, and perhaps I should restake my claim when next talking to Gottlieb. Shaplen adds that our editor apologized and then asked if Bob S. knew of any available younger writers who might fit into *The New Yorker* picture. I think I'll propose my son Joey, who's recently gone back to free-lancing and can write rings around a number of men and women down the hall from Shaplen and me. With so much nomenclatural confusion already on the premises, one more Kahn couldn't hurt.

23 December

The office Christmas party has been moved from its traditional eighteenth-floor site to a much more commodious nineteenth-floor location, right outside Gottlieb's own roost. Among the guests are a slew of young women I don't believe I've ever laid eyes on before; maybe they are the owners of some of the mysterious names that have cropped up of late as contributors to "Talk." I finally get introduced to Eve Kahn, who near as I can make out from her reaction believes she has just as much right to our name as I do.

I've had both breakfast and lunch by the time I get to the party, but Gottlieb tells me, almost in the manner of an old German nurse, to be sure to eat to keep my strength up. Sheila, our latter-day incarnation of guide and protectress, poses Bruce Bliven and me flanking the corridor portrait of Harold Ross. I don't feel especially festive, however. I don't know why, exactly, but I leave the party to do some shopping and don't return.

To cocktails at the Patrick Smiths'. I discuss my father's work with architect Francis Booth, who is striking out on his own and is launching this phase of his career by designing and building a house in western Connecticut. He will let me have it, unfurnished, for only $650,000, if present estimates hold up.

24 December

Last-minute shopping, but all in the neighborhood to avoid that hysterical downtown crush. Then our annual Christmas-Eve do, though we've back-slid from a sit-down dinner to a buffet. The usual extended family is on hand, including Ruth and Lizzie and Adam Schwarz, along with assorted friends who drift in and out. Sister Joan, who presumably gets her information straight from the Shawns' mouth, says that Jonathan Schell's new magazine is actually going to appear. Well, the more the merrier, I guess.

Lilo wonders before any presents get opened whether I could arrange for her to get Xeroxes of the pages about Ely in that big architectural book, unaware that a bulky package with her name on it under the tree contains the book in toto.

25 December

Merry Christmas from me to me. Hopi's Xmas present to me—only one *she* got last evening was from Joan, who has no use for dogs or any other pets but regards herself as a human cornucopia—is to let me stay abed till eight-thirty. My first present to Ellie is to clean up the kitchen before anyone else in the household arises.

Phone calls to Cohasset, where Terry is playing host to his generation of the family and their offspring. Most of our mail-order gifts have arrived, I learn, but a 100-percent record would be too much to hope for. During the opening of gifts in New York, it develops that the ensemble I bought for E. is made of acrylic, which ladies don't wear. Why does nobody ever share these arcana with me?

Then it's off to the Smiths' for, among other memorable goodies, Betty's fig pudding. I agree to have a glass of port with Patrick, even though it may bring on the gout. But how do you expect to get anywhere in this world if you don't take chances? Patrick says that Alton Peters is going to serve on the Century's admission committee. His reasoning is that that should be an interesting function to perform over the next three years, when women members may well become a reality. I admire Alton's astuteness; as a member of the committee, he will be ineligible to nominate candidates and will thus have a marvelous excuse when importuned by females to propose them.

26 December

Today is Jacquelene's birthday, but I don't phone my only granddaughter because it was celebrated in October and I'm not sure she's reminded of it when it actually comes around.

Ellie and Anath take off this morning with what if I weren't in a mellow mood I might describe as indecent haste to exchange acrylic goods and other no-nos. They return and put on a kind of fashion show—Anath in a party dress with cascades of ruffles, Ellie in a bright silk tunic that of course I would have bought myself, had I chanced to espy it, instead of what my ignorance compelled her to take back.

To the Pragers' for Lucy's annual birthday party. The Rod Perkinses are there, and Joan is interested to hear that we were in Russia with their old friends the Goodhues. (We had a holiday card this morning from Dede and Fag, enclosing a couple of photos from last June's class reunion. There's something peculiar about a shot of me with Ellie and the Piels, and to my dismay I finally perceive it; I am holding a drink in each hand.) Joan broke a knee in Moscow and is not the least impressed with the state of Soviet medicine. Rod, who as president of the Harvard Club of New York was the key figure in getting women admitted, is less certain about them and the Century. Over the years he has also served as president of the Harvard Alumni Association, and now he urges me to write its history. I am flattered, but not swayed.

I am further flattered when our host introduces me to another guest, Federal District Judge Whitman Knapp, as an expert on communism. His Honor confides to me that he, like our mutual judge friend Morris Lasker, is generally considered to be a nonhanging jurist. Meanwhile, a woman asks our hostess for an introduction to Max Lerner. But Max isn't here. The woman means me. It has happened before, and Max reminded me of it at *his* birthday party. Abby Friedman, for her part, wants to know if I've seen the Provincetown movie made by our other alleged look-alike, Norman Mailer, who bought the Friedmans' house there when Bob and she moved upscale to Long Island. I haven't. Abby says the film is so colossal a failure that it will shortly be available at video rental stores. I'm glad Ellie's renewed our membership.

Ellie and Anath and David and Lexy go downtown to a Living Theatre party, but I hang back at home. Most New York taxis will take only four passengers to begin with, and my dereliction enables me to watch "57th Street" on television and thereby to be introduced to a bunch of phonies— they call themselves "chanellers" and profess to be part of the "New Age"—who make a lot of money by pretending to speak with voices from outer space.

27 December

Anath volunteers to walk the dog, without my even hinting. I don't know whether to construe the gesture as a Christmas or New Year's present, but it is something rare and special. She is going to make a hell of a daughter-in-law.

At sister Olivia's annual post-Christmas party, Cecille Shawn says that *New Yorker* people—no names bandied—are phoning Bill all the time to complain about the present state of the magazine. News to me.

An unfamiliar face: Barbara Perlmutter, the local representative of a Frankfurt book publisher. When I mention our having been there not long ago, and why, she expresses surprise that the local press didn't cover the enemies-become-friends happening. I was sort of surprised myself but saw no reason to urge Herr Herbig or any of his shipmates to summon potentially competing journalists to the scene. Mrs. Perlmutter wants me to let her know when my piece comes out; she thinks she might be able to sell the German rights.

Sister Joan produces a Christmas drawing made by her grandnephew Matthew, whom she acclaims as a genius. There's no doubt in my mind that Matthew, and my other five grandchildren, are all geniuses, but how Joan can determine that from a single drawing by a five-year-old is beyond me.

28 December

The first person I run into at the office is Bob Gottlieb, who wonders why I was in over the weekend. Obviously *he* was, and he must have scrutinized the sign-in list down in the lobby. Nothing to be ashamed of had I come to the office, but I suggest to him that the guilty party was probably his new checker Kahn. I knew there'd be continuing confusion. Bob is proud, he says, once we have that straightened out, to have two new Harvard checkers, one a Phi Beta and one a summa. I'd thought Eve K. was both. I hope one of them reads German, because Brent Abel has sent me copies of letters he's received from several of his *Schiffshotel* dinner guests.

It's nice to have two television sets. In the living room downstairs, this evening, I watch a documentary about the Olympics and politics, which takes us back to Berlin in 1936 and eventually—I remember all these well— to the Mexico City riots and the black-power salutes of 1968; the 1972 murders of Israelis at Munich; the 1976 African boycott at Montreal; and the tit-for-tat abstentions of the United States in 1980 and the Soviet Union in 1984. There's not much in the program, curiously, about the forthcoming Games in Korea, but it's beginning to look as though, for the first time in sixteen years, nobody with the possible exception of Cuba will, for reasons not connected with sport, sit them out.

Then I go upstairs and join Ellie and the kids in front of *The Thin Man*. It must have been considered a racy film when it was first released; why, here is Myrna Loy brazenly referring, vis-à-vis her procreation, to a gleam in her father's eye! All the male characters wear hats, and everybody smokes, and to my amazement I am the only person in our bedroom familiar with the name Asta, the all-time best-in-show dog to crossword-puzzle makers.

29 December

First snow of the year's on the ground when we arise. Hopi, predictably, is ecstatic. A predicted full-scale blizzard failed to materialize, but I'm glad I decided in advance not to go to the office. When I lived in Westchester, I was often envied (if not despised) by neighbors with office jobs who had to commute, or try to, no matter how bad the weather was. If I didn't like the look of it, I'd just stay home. Mind you, I may have spent more time than they did plowing and shoveling. I wonder if I should go into any of this when I send Mary Cheever (John kept his own hours, too) the paragraph she wants about life there in the fifties. When I spoke to her about her project yesterday, she said it's a history she's putting together for a library. When I ask her how soon she needs my bit, she says she's still back in the 1930s, so there's no rush.

Writers are strange. Ellie has had no appetite for several days. Then a woman who E. was hoping would come through with a blurb for her forthcoming book phones one in, and it's a beaut. Dagwood might have blinked at the lunch Ellie proceeds to pack away. As for me, I never let the status of my work affect my disposition, except, on more occasions than I care to think about, for my eating, drinking, sleeping, and attitude toward children and dogs.

It's party night at the Liftons', with the usual mob. Leon Friedman comes straight from a Morton Downey show about whether or not criminals should be allowed to profit from books about their crimes. I forget which side Leon said he was on, but he seems chiefly pleased that he escaped alive. Roger Straus says Shawn has found a café near the Farrar, Straus offices that serves the kinds of oranges he likes for lunch.

I have a long talk with Aileen Ward about how deplorable it is that nobody seems to care any more about teaching proper English usage. When I was a prof at Columbia—and these were graduate students aspiring to be professional writers—the level of spelling and punctuation was in some instances so low that I couldn't help wondering how some of the class had ever become Bachelors of Arts. Aileen and I agree, perhaps a trifle smugly, that the trend toward illiteracy may be irreversible; but she is still teaching and so has a chance to do some good if she can get anyone to listen to her. I forget to ask her if she's seen that recent abomination of a TV ad for Shearson Lehman Brothers featuring the phrase, "Whichever of these investments are right for you?"

30 December

It's bitter cold. Hopi is just about the only dog in her walking group who isn't wearing an overcoat. Yet there seems to be only a handful of vagrants in Grand Central when I pass through. Were they all hauled off to shelters in the middle of the night?

On West Forty-fifth Street, a dramatic holiday confrontation. A Traffic Department tow truck has an illegally parked car all trussed up and ready to drag away when its owner rushes up, followed by a woman and a small child. He says he'll move the car at once. No, he won't, he is told, politely but firmly. He will have to retrieve it at the municipal pound for stray vehicles, Twelfth Avenue and Thirty-eighth Street. "But I'm *here*," the man expostulates. His captors shrug. I have to move on to an appointment before the denouement, but I imagine these Traffic men have their quotas and are not in the habit of throwing back fish once they've been hooked. I hope the woman and child don't get pneumonia before the family reclaims its vehicle.

Tobacco advertisers really have their backs to the wall. Here is the Benson and Hedges answer to people who contend that cigarette smoke can harm nonsmokers: pretty young female thing with her hand on the shoulder of much older, Daddy-Warbucks-type man, and in that hand a lit cigarette, smoke bound to curl straight up into his nostrils; and he is beaming, perhaps not quite yet orgasmic, but the very incarnation of boundless bliss.

31 December

The final 1987 issue of *The New Yorker* emphatically bears the Gottlieb stamp: Adam Gopnik on art, Mimi Kramer on theater, Terrence Rafferty on books, and the principal long-fact piece by Raymond Bonner.

Kristin Kunhardt has come to spend a few days with us. She's just been to a screening of *Lifeboat*. She wonders if I remember that as it starts flotsam and jetsam are shown drifting on the sea, and one of the identifiable objects that float by is *The New Yorker*. The producers of that ancient film can hardly have anticipated the events of 1987. But why did Kristin have to notice this just now? Whether it means we're in trouble or have a unique capacity to survive abrupt change the next year is likely to reveal.

We celebrate New Year's Eve by going to the theater with the Cohens and the Liftons. (*Breaking the Code*—super performance by Derek Jacobi, but a little heavy on the homosexual stuff.) Because taxis are often hard to hail this night, we've hired a limousine. When we come out of the theater, though, our cross-steet has been blocked off—has to do with trying to maintain order in and around Times Square—so in all our finery we ride the Eighth Avenue bus (among us, we assemble just enough coins) up to the Lee Falks' party.

En route to the theater, Ellie and I picked up the Cohens at a friend's flat—50 East Eighty-third Street. But that is my family homestead! Or was—my father's parents' brownstone, its stoop now gone and its interior carved up into apartments. Jerry and Joan were visiting the third floor, where, if I recall, the Turkish Room had been installed. I suppose the dumbwaiter from the kitchen up to the dining room has long since vanished, too.

At the Falks', Herman Badillo draws me aside. He may be a delegate to the Democratic Convention, and do I think he should be for Dukakis or Simon? He says Cuomo will positively not be a candidate. Jerry Robinson draws me aside to wonder if I am aware (he has recently been to Russia, too) that Soviet newspapers are soon going to be carrying political cartoons.

While Ellie is on the phone trying to reestablish contact with our limousine driver, I learn that all our scrambling for coins was unnecessary; on New Year's Eve, all New York City public transportation is free. I hope somebody'll remind me of that one year hence, when I fear I may be compelled to agree with Sheila McGrath, who has been insisting for rather some time that my hair, which I continue to perceive fondly as brown, has turned unarguably gray. I don't even want to think about the shade after that.

Index